"I

Lo   at
hap   e it
for

"Let's see who can find the North Star and the Little Dipper first."

Logan joined her on the blanket with a laugh. "I grew up stargazing, and I have ten years on you. I'll give you a head start."

"You may be ten years older, but I doubt you spent as many nights as I did wishing on the stars. Look"—she pointed—"a shooting star. There's another one." Jenna closed her eyes and squinched up her nose.

"What did you wish for?" he asked.

"That your mom's okay, and that you are too."

"You shouldn't have wasted your wish on me," he said.

"It was better than wasting it on me. I don't know what I want anymore."

Logan cupped the side of her face as he leaned in to touch his lips to her cheek, but she turned her head and his mouth settled on hers instead. He went to draw back, but she said, "Don't stop. I want you to kiss me."

PRAISE FOR DEBBIE MASON'S
HARMONY HARBOR SERIES

Driftwood Cove

"Mason rolls out the excitement in the fifth book in the Harmony Harbor series."
—RTBookReviews.com

"I love second-chance romances and Debbie Mason has written another good one in her Harmony Harbor series with some pretty significant obstacles between our hero and heroine and their happy ending. Mason has a talent for creating depth in her characters that brings out a multitude of emotions in this reader."
—TheRomanceDish.com

Sugarplum Way

"4 Stars! Harlequin Junkie Recommends! An amazing addition to this sweet and sassy series."
—HarlequinJunkie.com

"I really enjoyed this story...It had a lot of elements that put together made for a Christmas where dreams really do come true."
—RomancingTheBook.com

Primrose Lane

"4 Stars! This is a book worth savoring as it has all the elements of a fantastic read."
—*RT Book Reviews*

"Wow, do these books bring the feels. Deep emotion, heart-tugging romance, and a touch of suspense make them hard to put down, while the humor sprinkled throughout keeps the emotional intensity balanced with comic relief."
—TheRomanceDish.com

Starlight Bridge

"4 Stars! Mason gives Ava and Griffin a second chance at love. There's a mystery surrounding the sale of the estate...that adds a special appeal to the book."
—*RT Book Reviews*

"I loved this book. Debbie Mason writes romance like none other."
—FreshFiction.com

Mistletoe Cottage

"Top Pick! 4½ Stars! Mason has a knockout with the first book in her Harmony Harbor series."
—*RT Book Reviews*

"*Mistletoe Cottage* is anything but typical. It's a fast-paced story with colorful characters, lots of banter, and even more twists and turns."
—*Fort Worth Star-Telegram*

Sandpiper Shore

ALSO BY DEBBIE MASON

The Harmony Harbor series

Mistletoe Cottage

"Christmas with an Angel" (short story)

Starlight Bridge

Primrose Lane

Sugarplum Way

Driftwood Cove

The Christmas, Colorado series

The Trouble with Christmas

Christmas in July

It Happened at Christmas

Wedding Bells in Christmas

Snowbound at Christmas

Kiss Me at Christmas

Happy Ever After in Christmas

"Marry Me at Christmas" (short story)

"Miracle at Christmas" (short story)

Sandpiper Shore

DEBBIE
MASON

FOREVER
New York   Boston

Copyright © 2018 by Debbie Mazzuca
Excerpt from *Driftwood Cove* © 2018 by Debbie Mazzuca

Cover illustration by Tom Hallman. Cover design by Elizabeth Turner Stokes. Cover copyright © 2018 by Hachette Book Group, Inc.

Forever
Hachette Book Group
1290 Avenue of the Americas, New York, NY 10104
forever-romance.com
twitter.com/foreverromance

First Edition: June 2018

Forever is an imprint of Grand Central Publishing. The Forever name and logo are trademarks of Hachette Book Group, Inc.

The publisher is not responsible for websites (or their content) that are not owned by the publisher.

The Hachette Speakers Bureau provides a wide range of authors for speaking events. To find out more, go to www.hachettespeakersbureau.com or call (866) 376-6591.

ISBNs: 978-1-5387-4422-2 (mass market); 978-1-5387-4421-5 (ebook)

Printed in the United States of America

OPM

10 9 8 7 6 5 4 3 2 1

This book is dedicated to my amazing readers who love happily-ever-afters as much as I do. I'm truly grateful for all the love and support you've shown to me and my books. And an extra special thank-you to reader Mary Manella, who gave Pippa her name. xo

Sandpiper Shore

Chapter One

♥

Jenna Bell made a living helping women find their Prince Charming. At twenty-nine, she still believed in the fairy tale—in one true loves and happily-ever-afters. And while her success rate as a matchmaker was well publicized, she hadn't found her own true love until six months ago. Admittedly, the past several months hadn't been all hearts and flowers. Through no fault of her fiancé, of course.

Lorenzo had proposed to Jenna three days after her stepfather died. Some people might think his timing was off. Her stepsisters, Arianna and Serena, certainly did. And yes, maybe even Jenna had too. But his heart had been in the right place. He'd wanted to give her something to look forward to, something to take her mind off the loss of the only father she had ever known—the man who'd made her believe in fairy tales and happily-ever-afters.

Richard Bell had lifted her and her mother from a life of poverty to a life of luxury in a matter of weeks. More important, he'd loved them heroically.

He'd treated her mother like a queen and Jenna like a princess.

Thinking about her stepfather brought tears to her eyes, and she tried to blink them away. When that didn't work, she frantically fanned her hands in front of her face. "Don't cry. You're not allowed to cry," she murmured to herself while standing in the changing room at her stepsisters' bridal shop in Harmony Harbor.

She was terrified a mascara-tinged tear might fall on her wedding gown. She'd just had her final fitting of the dress her stepsisters had slaved over for months. It was an Arianna Bell original, designed specifically with Jenna in mind. The dress was beyond gorgeous. She felt like a princess in the breathtaking, strapless tulle gown with intricate floral detailing from the bodice to just below the warm white satin bow at her waist.

Arianna had decided the color suited Jenna's auburn hair and green eyes better than winter white. She'd been right of course, which wasn't a surprise. When it came to fashion and style, no one could hold a candle to Arianna. Her ability to turn Jenna into a fairy-tale princess was a perfect example since Jenna wasn't exactly fairy-tale princess material. Her stepsisters were though.

And sometimes, more so when they were younger, they treated her as abysmally as the stepsisters in a fairy tale. Which was why Jenna couldn't afford to have anything go wrong. They'd had an amazing day together. It was everything she'd ever dreamed of as a little girl. The laughter, the good-natured teasing, the . . .

Her thoughts were interrupted by the steady chime of the door opening and closing and the sound of

Lorenzo's smooth voice, with its exaggerated, lyrical accent, greeting the customers and her sisters. Jenna reached back to unzip her wedding gown. She wasn't comfortable leaving her fiancé alone without her to intercede if things went sideways like they so often did.

All she needed was for Arianna and Lorenzo to get into a knock-down, drag-out fight before the wedding. They were both volatile and stubborn and mixed as well as oil and water. But the only sound she heard was Pachelbel's Canon in D coming through the speakers. She was just about to chide herself for worrying over nothing when she heard it…a feminine sob.

If Lorenzo had made Arianna cry, they would have words. She bowed her head. If Jenna had words with her fiancé, he'd probably cry too. He was a sensitive soul. She wouldn't admit it to anyone else, but sometimes she found his proclivity to melodrama annoying. Then again, she'd much rather Lorenzo be a kind and sensitive—albeit dramatic—man than a brooding alpha.

In all her years in the matchmaking business, Jenna had met her fair share of alpha males. Like bad boys, they weren't for her. She found them too masculine, domineering, and full of themselves. Admittedly, she was in the minority. Ninety percent of the women she matched wanted an alpha or a bad boy. At least she'd saved herself the heartache and found Lorenzo, who was somewhere between a beta and a metrosexual.

As Jenna steeled herself to pull back the changing room curtain and discover the identity of the crying person, there was the muffled *ping* of an incoming text. She found her iPhone buried beneath her clothes on the chair, releasing a relieved breath when she read the text from Serena. Her stepsister identified the crying woman as a bride who'd just been unceremoniously dumped ten days before her upcoming wedding. Her sisters were both busy, and Serena asked Jenna to provide a little TLC to the jilted bride until one of them could take over.

No problem, she texted back, happy for the opportunity to help out.

Jenna returned her phone to the pile of clothes and then pushed back the curtain. She spotted the woman right away. Half-buried beneath a garment bag, she sat slumped on a velvet slipper chair on the other side in the fitting area. Her veil was askew on her gorgeous updo, congealed streaks of black mascara and blush on her cheeks. She must have been having a trial run of her hair and makeup for the big day. Despite her heart breaking for the poor woman, Jenna pasted a warm, professional smile on her face.

"Here, why don't you let me hang this up for you?" Without waiting for a response, she gently removed the garment bag from the woman's arms. "I'm Jenna Bell, Arianna and Serena's sister. Would you like a coffee or tea…? How about a glass of prosecco?" Jenna asked as she returned from hanging up the gown in a fitting room.

"A *bottle* of prosecco would be good," the woman said, her attempt at putting on a brave face failing when she burst into tears.

Jenna gathered up a champagne flute, the bottle of bubbly, and a box of tissues. She nudged a small table and chair closer to the woman and sat down. "Do you want to talk about it?" she asked as she poured a glass of prosecco.

The jilted bride hiccupped a sob while reaching for a tissue. "I don't know what happened. I was just leaving the salon, and he called and said h-he couldn't go through with the wedding. H-he blamed me. He said he never wanted to get married. He said I push…pushed him into it."

Jenna put down the bottle to comfort her. "Is there anyone I can call for you?"

The woman lifted her head from Jenna's shoulder to accept the tissues Jenna gently pressed into her hand. She blew her nose. "Sorry for crying all over your beautiful gown. My name's Kimberly, and I'm not usually a crier, but…"

"Please, don't apologize. I just wish there were something I could say that would make you feel better." Jenna handed her more tissues. "I don't know if this is helpful or not, but I own a matchmaking company in Charleston, and so many of my clients have been exactly where you are right now and they've gone on to find true love. I know it doesn't feel like it right now, Kimberly, but trust me, this might be the best thing to happen to you."

"I can't see how. He's the love of my life." Sniffing, she pulled out her phone to show Jenna pictures of her with her fiancé.

Jenna studied the couple in the photo. Her matchmaking company had a 90.9 percent success rate for a reason. And it didn't have anything to do with her stepmother's super-secret computer program like Gwyneth liked to tell people.

Jenna had a gift.

She knew within moments of a couple sitting across from her if they were meant to be or not. A pretty pink light would dance between the couple, and Jenna would get a warm, fuzzy feeling deep down inside and be overcome by a sense of joy and well-being. Sometimes the feelings were so powerful she was sure the inner glow must show on her face. No one had ever said that it did though. And maybe because she didn't have tangible proof, the few people who knew about her gift pooh-poohed it. Including her stepmother. At least when it suited her. Which was why Southern Belle didn't have a hundred percent success rate. Because when it came to true love and happily-ever-afters, Jenna was always, always right.

In this case the couple weren't sitting across from her so she couldn't be one hundred percent positive, but she felt eighty percent confident. "Kimberly, I've been doing this a long time, and trust me, he's not your one and only. Give yourself a couple months to get in a better place and then give me a call, and I'll help you find a man who is."

"Really? You don't think we were meant to be?"

"No. If you were, he wouldn't have called off the wedding. A couple months from now, you might want to thank him. I know it's hard to see this now, but what he did took courage, Kimberly."

"Oh, *bella*, what you say, it is the truth. I am so glad you understand. I knew you would."

Jenna glanced over her shoulder. She should probably be alarmed that her fiancé had just seen her in her wedding dress, but she didn't think her wedding could be cursed twice. Lorenzo had already seen her in the dress when he'd walked in on her during the fitting for his tux.

"I don't know what you mean, Lorenzo. Understand what?"

The beatific expression on his too-handsome face dimmed, and his sensuous mouth turned down. "What you just told your friend. I must have the courage for the both of us."

Jenna came slowly to her feet. "Are you...? Are you breaking up with me?"

"*Sì.* I have found my true love, and now I must set you free to find yours."

This couldn't be happening. She reached for the back of the chair in case her suddenly weak knees gave out. In the distance, she heard Arianna say something to Serena and then the click of high heels coming their way. Jenna knew she should continue the conversation someplace private, but there seemed to be a disconnect between her brain and her mouth. "Y-you told me *I'm* your true love."

"I was mistaken. My heart, it belongs to Gwyneth."

She practically fell off her heels and tightened her grip on the back of the chair. "Gwyneth? You're in love with my stepmother?" Her heart was pounding so hard she could hear her pulse in her ears and wasn't sure if she'd yelled or whispered the words. At the sound of high heels hitting the tiles at the rate of machine-gun fire, she went with the former.

"Ah, you knew, then. You should have told me, *bella*. It was not fair you kept me from my love for so long."

"And I thought I was having a bad day." Kimberly leaned over to hand Jenna the bottle of prosecco. "Either drink it or hit him with the bottle. Personally, I'd hit him. And no offense, but if you didn't know he wasn't your one, how am I supposed to trust you to know who's mine?"

Emotion swelled in Jenna's throat, making it impossible to respond. She'd never had the true-love feeling with any of her boyfriends, Lorenzo included. Psychics were the same. Their gift was for other people, not themselves.

But Jenna couldn't find the energy to defend her abilities. Gwyneth had stolen everything from her now. The woman she'd spent the last decade trying to mollify and please had just sunk a sixteen-inch serrated knife into Jenna's chest and torn out her heart. And here she stood with the blood draining from her body and her knees about to give out, and the man she thought loved her, her very own Prince Charming, was watching her with a perturbed expression on his face because she'd kept him from her forty-five-year-old stepmother.

She glanced at the bottle in her hand. The temptation to hit him over the head and replace his aggravation with shock and pain was hard to resist. Arianna wouldn't hesitate, and neither would Serena. But Jenna couldn't bring herself to do it and handed the bottle back to Kimberly. "I can't drink and drive." She forced the words past her quivering lips and rapidly blinked her eyes. She had to get out of there before she broke down. All she had left was her dignity.

"I'll be right back. I need to put more money in the parking meter." She lifted her skirts and ran past a confused-looking Lorenzo and her wide-eyed sisters. She ran to the front of the shop and out the door. It wasn't until she was about to run across the street to her car that she realized she was still in her wedding gown and didn't have her keys. A deep voice cut through the fog of her grief.

"Hey, Cinderella, you lost your shoe."

She registered her lopsided gait and the warm pavement beneath her foot and stopped. She turned. And there, bathed in June's golden light, stood a tall, dark-haired man with her glass shoe resting on the palm of his hand.

Chapter Two

♥

Logan Gallagher had seen some interesting things in his twelve-year career as a Secret Service agent, but this was a first for him. He glanced from the dainty glass shoe he balanced on the palm of his hand to the shop, Tie the Knot, behind him and wondered if he'd gotten it wrong. Maybe the woman wasn't playing princess after all. Maybe she was a runaway bride.

She stopped, turning to stare at him through luminous, pale green eyes. She kept staring. He wondered if he knew her, but he had a good memory for faces and couldn't recall hers. He smiled and held up her shoe. "I think this is yours."

Her red-bowed lips parted, and then her big, long-lashed eyes darted past him. A tall, dark-haired man in a powder-blue tuxedo burst through the doors of Tie the Knot. Cinderella gave a panicked yelp before whirling around to run across Main Street. Logan caught a glimpse of a red Camaro heading directly for her and took off at a run.

He reached her seconds before the car did and

scooped her into his arms. The driver of the Camaro braked hard, the smell of burning rubber filling the air. The car's grille brushed the side of Logan's leg, and he felt the heat through his jeans. Acknowledging the clearly shaken driver with a grateful chin lift, he jogged to the sidewalk across from Tie the Knot and Tuxedo Guy.

Logan glanced at the woman in his arms. "You okay under there?" he asked, doing his best to keep the amusement from his voice. Given the day she appeared to be having, Cinderella probably wouldn't find it funny that her dress had blown up over her head. There were enough layers of fabric that she wasn't flashing anything other than a shapely pair of legs.

She batted at the gauzy white material and her big eyes appeared over the mound of fabric. "Thank you. I can't believe I did—" He picked up on a touch of the South in her voice before Tuxedo Guy interrupted her, shouting to make himself heard over the honking horns as he wove his way through the oncoming traffic to reach them.

He gesticulated wildly, pointing at his head. "*Stupido*, running away like that! *Madonna mia*, what were you thinking? My dress, you could've ruined it, *si*?"

Logan shot the guy a look while carefully lowering his charge to the sidewalk. "Back off and give her a minute." He didn't say *jerk*, but he wanted to. The woman was obviously distraught, and the guy was calling her stupid. She was also as dainty as her shoe, and he could feel her tremble in his arms, which was probably the reason Logan felt like punching the guy.

Instead, he placed a hand on her shoulder to steady her. "You okay?" he asked.

Beneath his fingers her skin was warm and satiny smooth. She had pretty shoulders and a delicate collarbone. The flush deepened on her cheeks, and he lowered his hand, turning his attention to the two women headed their way.

He recognized the blue-eyed, blond sisters, Arianna and Serena Bell. Arianna had dated his brother Connor. If Logan remembered correctly, it had ended badly for the pair. But it would've been more of a surprise if it had ended well. His brother didn't exactly have the best track record with women, even back then.

"What were you thinking, Jenna? You nearly got yourself killed over…over that idiot." Arianna flung out her hand in Tuxedo Guy's direction.

"You see, her sister, she agrees with me. What Jenna did was *stupido*."

Logan looked down at the woman beside him, surprised. He couldn't recall hearing that Arianna and Serena had a sister. There wasn't much of a family resemblance.

He looked up and caught Tuxedo Guy's eyes on him, realizing then that the man had been addressing his remark to him. Obviously, he'd read Logan's earlier *what a jerk* expression. He wondered if he should point out to Tuxedo Guy that Arianna had just called him an idiot, but it looked like she was about to handle that herself.

Arianna got in the guy's face, stabbing him in the chest with a white-tipped fingernail. "Believing one word out of your mouth was stupid. Saying yes when you asked her to marry you was stupid. And we were stupid for letting her do it. But even more stupid was her taking off and nearly getting herself killed because you dumped her for our stepmother. She should've—"

A small, embarrassed groan pulled Logan's attention back to the woman beside him. She looked like she wished the sidewalk would open up and swallow her whole. "You might want to take this somewhere else," Logan suggested to Arianna, lifting a hand to indicate the growing crowd.

"Thanks for trying," Jenna murmured when her sister ignored him and continued to tell Tuxedo Guy what should've been done to him. She was creative and kind of scary, and Logan thought his brother had gotten off lucky.

Serena stepped around Arianna to poke the guy's shoulder. "We knew you were just a sleazy Casanova, Lorenzo. The only reason you were with Jenna was because of her company and a green card, and it's on us that we didn't step in before you broke her heart and stole Southern Belle out from under her. Because don't think we haven't figured out that you're in this up to your big ears with Gwyneth."

"You wanna get out of here?" Logan asked Jenna.

"You no-good, lying, cheating scum bucket! Taking advantage of a nice girl like her, and cheating on her with her stepmother!" a woman wearing a veil shrieked, brandishing a bottle of prosecco at Lorenzo.

"Do it! Hit him with it!" a bloodthirsty woman in the crowd shouted.

Jenna gave Logan a desperate nod. "Please, let's leave."

He took in the escalating situation, torn between wanting to get her out of there and keeping the peace. In the distance, he heard a siren and went down on one knee. "Okay. Just let me take care of this first."

He lifted the now-dirty hem of her wedding dress and gently wrapped his fingers around her ankle, raising her foot to his knee. Her foot was as pretty and as soft and smooth as her shoulders. Her toenails were painted sky blue with a stripe of gold on each center.

"Look, it's right out of a fairy tale. Cinderella and Prince Charming!" a woman yelled. *Ooh*s and *aah*s were followed by the sound of pictures being taken on cell phones.

"If it doesn't fit her, you can try it on me, gorgeous," a woman yelled.

"No way. I saw him first. I should get to go before you," her redheaded friend said.

"You have feet the size of flippers. Don't waste his time—"

At the sound of a fight breaking out between the women, Logan bent his head and groaned. To think he'd come downtown to grab a beer with his brother in hopes of figuring out what was up with their mother.

He heard a strangled sound and looked up, worried that Jenna had reached the breaking point—he wouldn't blame her if she had. Instead, she appeared to be holding back laughter and not tears. Her eyes were shiny, her full, red lips pressed tightly together.

He grinned at her. Any woman who could laugh moments after being thrown over for her stepmother was the woman for him. The thought took him aback.

So much so that he felt the need to remind himself he didn't do relationships. Not anymore. Or at least for a good long while. He liked his life simple and entanglement free. It allowed him to stay focused on his career.

The laughter in her eyes faded. His discomfort must've shown on his face. He slid the shoe onto her foot and smiled as he came to his feet, offering his hand. "All set?"

She hesitated and then gave him a small smile and shook her head. "It's all right. I've taken up enough of your time. Thanks again for saving me from becoming roadkill." She took his hand to shake it. "I think that makes me your slave for life, doesn't it? So if there's ever anything I can do to repay you, please let me know. I'm Jenna Bell, by the way."

Whatever was making the citizens of Harmony Harbor crazy today must be contagious, because Logan suddenly had all kinds of dirty and creative thoughts about Jenna being his slave. He gave her hand a light squeeze as the sexy images burned into his brain. "Logan Gallagher. I keep people safe for a living, so don't give it another thought."

She glanced at her sisters, the woman in the veil, and the two wannabe Cinderellas who'd all backed Lorenzo against a storefront window. "You're obviously very good at your job. I find people their one true love for a living." She sighed, acknowledging the irony by raising a shoulder.

His eyes followed the movement. He didn't know what was wrong with him. He was a leg man, not a shoulder man. "Don't be so hard on yourself. We all make mistakes. None of us can be on our game a hundred percent of the time."

"I can be with everyone else, just not myself. I probably should save him from my sisters."

He glanced at Lorenzo, who covered his face and shrieked like a girl. "Why would you want to do that?"

Her eyebrows drew together. "It feels like the right thing to do."

His attraction began to make sense. He didn't only protect people for a living; it's who he was. Jenna brought out his protective instincts. She was obviously sweet and tenderhearted. She needed a keeper. He had to remind himself he wasn't up for the job and nor did he want it. But just this once, he could save her from herself.

He put his hands on her shoulders and ducked to look into her green eyes. This close, he saw flecks of gold in her irises. Tiger eyes, only she was a kitten. "I'm calling my debt. Let your sisters take care of Lorenzo. And if you have joint property with the guy, hire a lawyer. My brother's one. I'll call him. He can advise you on your next steps."

A patrol car pulled up to the sidewalk and an officer got out. "Ladies, let the man go." He came around the hood of the car and walked to where the women had Lorenzo cornered. They didn't move until the officer reached past them to grab the other man's arm.

Lorenzo straightened his tux. "*Grazie*, Officer. I am in your debt." His eyes narrowed on Logan and Jenna, and he headed their way.

Letting his hands fall from Jenna's shoulders, Logan

straightened. "Keep moving, buddy. The lady has no interest in talking to you."

"Talk, it is not necessary. All I want is my dress and ring."

Logan frowned, thinking he must've misunderstood. "You want her dress?"

"*Sì*, and my ring. It is a family heirloom to be worn only by my countess. I'm a count, you see." He made an odd rolling motion with his right hand.

"Right, Count Dracula out to suck our family dry," Serena quipped, pushing her hair from her face, looking a little worse for wear.

Logan felt guilty he hadn't intervened earlier, even though Jenna had needed him more than her sisters. He'd seen Arianna and Serena in action at a beach party years before. They could take care of themselves. Which Arianna appeared ready to prove.

"You want your precious ring, you tell Stepmommy Dearest to give Jenna back her company. And as far as that dress goes, you'll get it over my dead body. I made that dress for my sister, and I'll be damned if Gwyneth wears an Arianna Bell original."

Anger came alive in the man's dark eyes, and Logan moved to stand in front of Jenna, which only seemed to further infuriate the guy. Then, with the skill of a consummate performer, Lorenzo replaced his anger with a conciliatory expression. Leaning to the side so he could see Jenna, he said, "I am sorry that, like Richard, I have hurt you, *bella*. But it is not Gwyneth's fault that she makes men weak with desire. Your father's last wish was that she live the life she has become accustomed to.

Don't let your sisters blacken your heart with their petty jealousy. Now be a good girl and give me my family's ring."

Logan wondered if Jenna was taken in by the guy and glanced over his shoulder. With her head bent, her shoulder-length hair hid her face as she tugged at the ring on her finger. His gut twisted in response to seeing a tear splash onto her thumb.

As though realizing what her sister meant to do, Arianna elbowed Lorenzo and then Logan out of the way. If he hadn't wanted to move, she wouldn't have been able to budge him. But there was part of Logan that didn't want Jenna to give in to the guy and hoped Arianna could reason with her. He just wished she weren't planning to do it on Main Street. Then again, what more damage could they do? They'd already aired their dirty laundry for all the town to hear. Poor Jenna; they'd be feasting on this for the next month at least.

"If you give the ring back to him, I'll never speak to you again. Neither will Serena," Arianna threatened her sister.

Jenna lifted her gaze. Logan briefly closed his eyes at the stark pain etched on her face before he intervened. "Come on, Arianna. Don't you think your sister's been through enough?"

"Evil witch, you will not encourage her to rob me," Lorenzo said as he pushed past Arianna to grab Jenna's hand.

Arianna stumbled, releasing a shocked cry. Between that and Jenna's pained gasp, the cop, who'd been talking to Serena, finally looked their way. Logan righted

Arianna and then lunged for Lorenzo. Wrapping his fingers around the other man's wrist, Logan squeezed.

Lorenzo cried out, dropping Jenna's hand to clutch his own. "Officer, arrest this man. My wrist, he broke it."

"I'll break more than your wrist," Arianna said, and launched herself past Logan to take a swing at Lorenzo, who raised a fist. Logan put up his hand, stopping Lorenzo before he followed through. Like an enraged bull, the man bared his teeth and took a wild swing at Logan. At the last second, Logan decided it was probably best if the guy got in one punch. Lorenzo's fist glanced off Logan's jaw.

Satisfied that others had seen Lorenzo's fist connect even if the cop hadn't, Logan threw a left uppercut that landed with a satisfying *crack*. The guy would feel that for a day or more. Thinking he deserved at least a week of pain and suffering for what he'd done to Jenna, Logan drew back his arm to land another blow. Only Lorenzo surprised him. The other man's eyes rolled back in his head. Before Logan could grab him, he crumpled in slow motion to the ground.

The lady in the veil, who'd been leaning against a lamppost drinking, zigzagged her way over. She looked down at Lorenzo and then up at Logan. "You're a hero. The hero of jilted women everywhere. If I give you my ex-fiancé's name, will you beat him up for me like you beat up Lorenzo for Jenna?"

The cop, who'd joined them to call an ambulance, looked up from where he'd crouched beside Lorenzo. His eyes narrowed. "Were you contracted to do this?"

"You've got to be kidding me. You were standing here the entire time. Flirting with Serena, I might add, instead of helping defuse the situation." Noting the man's wedding band, Logan shoved his fingers irritably through his hair. A married man wouldn't appreciate being accused of flirting in public.

"Don't use that tone with me, Gallagher. Oh yeah, I know who you are. Your daddy used to be the governor, and you boys thought you were all that. Now you're a big deal with the Secret Service." He made a *whoopee* gesture with his finger. "Too bad it's not going to get you out of this."

Logan tensed. As an agent, he couldn't afford to be arrested. "What do you mean *this*?"

Jenna, who'd been looking down at Lorenzo in shock, glanced from Logan to the cop. Without saying a word, she bent down to half-drag her now groaning ex to the garbage can. She propped him against it, slowly straightening as if hoping to avoid notice, and then she slunk off down the sidewalk. Three stores over, she broke into a run.

The cop was too busy trying to remove his cuffs from his belt to notice she was gone. "You know exactly what I mean. You're going down for this. Who knows? It might end up being murder one."

"Am I dead? I'm not dead, am I?" Lorenzo asked from where he slumped against the garbage can cupping his bloody nose.

No one paid him any attention. They were focused on the cop. Logan was trying to figure out if the guy was actually serious and, if he was, who in the Gallagher family had done him wrong. Because there was something more going on here.

"Ryan, don't be ridiculous. If you arrest him, you have to arrest all of us," Serena said.

"Who said I'm not planning to?" The cop angled his head and said into the radio clipped to his shoulder, "Immediate backup required at 295 Main Street."

Chapter Three

♥

Clutching fistfuls of tulle in both hands, Jenna hiked up her wedding gown and took off at a run down the sidewalk. People stopped to turn and stare as she raced past them on her way to the corner of Main Street and South Shore Road.

Jenna glanced back to check on her sisters and found her attention captured by a man's intent gaze. Ryan might not have noticed that she'd left the scene of the crime, but someone else had. Logan would though, wouldn't he? Unlike Ryan, Logan was really, really good at what he did for a living.

The man was a true hero and not just because he'd rescued her from becoming a tulle-wrapped pancake. Only months before, while he'd been off duty, he'd foiled the kidnapping of a princess from a small European country on the border of France and Spain. He was a Secret Service agent and had been stationed in Europe for several years. And now, because of Jenna, his job might very well be on the line.

Determined to ensure that didn't happen, she refocused her attention on her destination instead of on the handsome man being put in handcuffs by Ryan. She wasn't about to let Logan be charged for assault just because he'd been trying to protect her from becoming roadkill and Arianna from getting punched in the nose.

She prayed Logan's brother, Michael, was holding court at the Salty Dog like he did most Saturdays. A former assistant district attorney, Michael had gone back to practicing law in Harmony Harbor after he left the FBI four months before. It was a standing joke in town that he did so to keep his fiancée— and Jenna's childhood best friend—Shay Angel out of trouble. Jenna prayed he could keep his brother out of trouble too.

A droplet of sweat splashed onto her lashes. Without thinking, she let go of her dress to lift her hand to her eye, rubbing it to stop the stinging. Midrub, she realized her mistake. It was too late. Her glass shoe got caught in the tulle, and she barely got her hands out in front of her to stop herself from landing face-first on the sidewalk. Her palms and chest broke her fall, knocking the wind out of her.

She was lying on the sidewalk gasping for air when she heard the sound of a siren. No, sirens. There was definitely more than one police car headed this way. As she struggled to her feet, two older gentlemen reached out to help her.

She forced her pained grimace into a smile. "Thanks so much," she said, and then fisted her hands in her dress once again, this time hiking it to her knees.

Within two steps, she realized sprinting on what felt

like a sprained ankle was out of the question and hob-
bled the rest of the way to the redbrick building on the
corner of Main Street and South Shore Road.

"Thank you, sweet baby..." she began when she
reached the door. *Jesus* didn't make it out of her mouth,
and she didn't make it through the front door. A tall
man mowed her down as he came flying out of the Salty
Dog. Lucky for Jenna, he had good reflexes and saved
her from landing on her behind. It was Michael Gallagher.

"Sorry, Jenna. Are you okay?" he asked, giving her
a cursory glance while carefully setting her out of his
way.

"Yes, thank you. I'm fine, but—"

"I've gotta go. Tell Shay your drink's on me." He
patted her shoulder and then went to hurry away.

"No, you don't understand, Michael. Logan needs
your help. He's—"

Walking backward, he held up his phone. "I know.
He texted me." As two patrol cars turned onto Main
Street with their sirens blaring and lights flashing,
Michael rushed off.

Jenna was about to hobble after him when a hand
closed around her bicep. "Oh, no you don't, Cinderella.
I've got orders to keep you out of the fray and to check
your ankle. Come on."

Jenna sent one last anxious glance over her shoulder before doing her best friend's bidding. Shay Angel wasn't someone you argued with. She kicked
butts and took no names. Jenna wished she were more
like Shay. The woman was fearless, a real-life super-

hero, just like Logan. The thought brought Jenna up short.

Leaning against the door to the pub, she held it open. "I know my sisters are just trying to protect me from Lorenzo, Shay. But I have to go back and say something in Logan's defense or Ryan is going to railroad him. He has something against the Gallaghers." She'd overheard him complaining to her sister one day about Aidan Gallagher, who was a detective with the HHPD. It had sounded like his hostility went deeper than professional rivalry. But at the time, Jenna had been swamped with worry over Serena's involvement with the man and hadn't paid much attention to his rant. Now she wished she had.

Shay turned, her long, dark ponytail swishing across the back of her black T-shirt. "What are you talking about? It wasn't Serena or Arianna who told me to keep you away. It was Logan. Now get inside. You're letting in the hot air."

"Logan?" Jenna pressed a hand to her stomach in hopes of keeping a warm, fuzzy feeling at bay. Lord knew she shouldn't be having the warm fuzzies about another man less than twenty minutes after being dumped by her fiancé. Admittedly, it was kind of Logan to be concerned about her welfare when she was the reason his career might be on the line. And it did feel kind of nice to be looked out for again. When she was younger, her stepfather had looked out for her. At least until Gwyneth had come into his life. The only person Lorenzo ever looked out for was himself.

Now, where had that thought come from? she

wondered. Arianna, of course, said it all the time, but not Jenna. She'd never had a truly negative thought about Lorenzo the Louse. Looked like she just did, and it actually felt good to say something derogatory about him. Even if it was just in her head.

"Yeah, it was Logan who texted me." Shay's eyes flicked over Jenna, and then she put an arm around her shoulders, guiding her into the pub, which smelled like their famous warm pretzels and craft beer. "Look, I get that you can't see it right now, but this is the best thing that could've happened to you, Jenna. The guy is a loser. He was bound to break your heart one day. If you ask me, it's better now when there's no kids involved."

Less than an hour earlier, Jenna had said more or less the same thing to Kimberly. Although hopefully with a little more sensitivity than Shay. Which wouldn't be difficult because Jenna had more tact in her baby finger than her best friend had in her entire body. Of course, Jenna couldn't take credit for her social graces. The exclusive Swiss boarding school she'd been sent to at fourteen—at Gwyneth's behest—was not only famed for their stringent academics, but their graduates were taught the social graces necessary to converse with world leaders, kings, and queens as well as every upper-class cultural ritual known to mankind. Still, she thought it was a wonder Kimberly hadn't hit *her* over the head with the bottle of prosecco when she'd told the hours-old jilted bride that her fiancé had done her a favor.

Jenna rolled her eyes at herself and then at Shay. "Bless your heart. It might have been nice if you'd shared with me how you really felt about Lorenzo before today. Seeing as you're my best friend and all."

"Uh-oh. What's got our Southern belle's dander up?" asked Cherry, the assistant manager at the Salty Dog. Since Cherry was also Shay's best friend, Jenna had adopted her as her own BFF. Cherry was a little wild, brash, and outspoken, but also really sweet and kind. And right now Jenna could use some of Cherry's brand of sympathy rather than Shay's.

"Lorenzo just dumped me for my stepmother," she said, her voice catching on a sob. She stood there, head bent, hands at her sides, waiting to be enfolded in Cherry's sympathetic embrace. Cherry was the one person Jenna could count on for a little compassion. She hadn't gotten any from her sisters or Shay, and she really could use some right now. The reality of what had happened had finally hit her.

"Thank God. You don't know how many times I wanted to rip those rose-colored glasses off your face, but Shay wouldn't let me. She said you'd figure it out before it was too late. If you didn't come to your senses before next Saturday, I was going to kidnap you. I had a couple guys on board to help me out. At least Gwyneth will be saddled with the loser and not you."

Jenna swallowed the lump in her throat while sniffing back tears. "As far as best friends go, you two suck," she said before limping toward the one unoccupied barstool. "And just FYI, I don't wear glasses or contacts."

Six feet from the barstool, Jenna was enveloped in a cotton-candy-scented hug from behind. "I'm sorry,"

Cherry said. "I've been hanging around Shay too long, and I was just so glad I didn't have to kidnap you. The FBI frowns on that sort of thing, you know."

Cherry was dating Michael's former FBI partner. As far as Jenna could tell, the couple was a perfect match, just like Shay and Michael were. Everyone was a perfect match except Kimberly and her fiancé...and Jenna and Lorenzo.

Behind her, she sensed Cherry staring at Shay while nodding at Jenna. "Shaybae."

"No. I'm not doing a group hug, Cherry. We're in the middle of a crowded bar. Jenna doesn't want—" Jenna glanced back at Shay, who then pressed her lips together and walked over. "Fine." She moved in front of Jenna, wrapping her arms around both her and Cherry. "I'm sorry, okay? I should've said something about Lorenzo, but you supposedly have this gift so I thought I must be wrong. And for your sake, I wish I had been wrong about him. I'm sorry he hurt you, Jenna. I really am. I'd go beat him up for you, but it sounds like Logan took care of him."

"Boys, it looks like the girls are about to put on a show," said one of the older men at the bar. His friends swiveled on their barstools to face them.

"Great. Are you two happy now?" Shay said, clearly annoyed as she stepped back.

Obviously, it was a rhetorical question that spoke more to Shay's embarrassment than to Jenna's mental state. Because while she did feel a little better after the shared hug, she couldn't find much to be happy about. Other than Logan punching out Lorenzo's lights. And that reminded her why she was even standing in the middle of the pub. "Can you text Michael and see if he needs me to go to the station and—"

"Wait a sec. Logan Gallagher, our very own Secret Service man, beat up Lorenzo?" Cherry interrupted her.

Jenna gave her a quick nod, hoping against hope to avoid the outrageous comments Cherry was famous for when it came to handsome men.

An intrigued smile turned up the other woman's burgundy-glossed lips. "This is good. Very, very good. You gotta get back in the saddle right away so those feelings of inadequacy can't take hold, Jenna. And who better to make you feel like a desirable woman than Tall, Dark, and Deliciously Ripped? He's perfect, isn't he, Shay? He's not dating anyone at—"

Until Cherry mentioned it, Jenna hadn't felt inadequate. No doubt she would have, once she'd had time to process everything. How could she not feel like she was lacking when Lorenzo dumped her for her much older stepmother, a statuesque, blond bombshell? As though Shay could tell Cherry's offhand comment had hit its mark, she took Jenna by the arm and shot the other woman a *zip it* look. "Let's get you settled at a table and check out your ankle."

"What? She needs a rebound guy. And if you ask me, there's no one better than Logan for the job. He's not only drop-dead gorgeous, he's strong, kind, and considerate. And have you gotten a look at the size of his hands and feet? Well, I have, and let me tell you, they are *big*. You know what they say—"

"Would you stop? I don't want to be thinking about

how big Logan's...hands and feet are, thank you very much." Shay pulled out a barrel at one of the tables, directing Jenna to sit.

Shay's uncle Charlie had decorated the pub to resemble a pirate ship. The floors and walls were cedar and gave off a warm, fragrant scent. There was a raised stage at the far end of the room, a dance floor, and at least twenty tables with barrels serving as chairs. The cedar walls were decorated with muskatoons, ropes, and swords, one of which was reputed to have belonged to William Gallagher, Michael's and Logan's great-grandfather many times over, who was rumored to have been a pirate. It was purportedly where the family's wealth had come from.

Where there wasn't a weapon, there were framed photos of Charlie and his staff dressed as famous pirates. The waitresses wore serving wench costumes in green and burgundy, like the one Cherry had on. Only Cherry's revealed more leg and chest than anyone else's. On purpose, of course. Unlike Shay, who refused to go along with her uncle's pirate fantasy and wore her uniform of black T-shirt, jeans, and high-heeled, butt-kicking boots.

Shay helped out at the bar on weekends to give Charlie a break. During the week, she split her time between counseling women who'd served time in prison and their children and doing investigative work for several high-powered attorneys.

"Cherry, why don't you get Jenna a mimosa float and some of those grilled veggie pretzel crisps?"

"No prob. You want anything else, Jellybean?"

"Maybe just the mimosa float. I don't think I could eat anything, thanks," Jenna said, her stomach turning when Shay removed her glass shoe and Jenna's foot began to throb. Obviously, the pressure of the shoe had kept the pain at bay.

"Grab an ice pack while you're at it, Cherry," Shay called after the woman while propping Jenna's foot on a barrel and then joining her at the table. "I don't have to tell you to ignore sixty percent of what Cherry says, do I? Because having a one-night stand with any man, least of all Logan, is a really bad idea."

"Don't worry. I'm not planning to hit on Logan. He'd never be interested in someone like me anyway." Even though it was true, she knew it was the wrong thing to say to Shay, whose gray eyes narrowed. "I'm just being honest. I know exactly where I fit in the scheme of things, and it's not with a man who is a ten. Look where that got me with Lorenzo."

"You know what your problem is? You still see yourself as that twelve-year-old kid who didn't fit in," Shay said.

"You didn't fit in either."

"But it didn't bother me like it did you."

"Probably because you were gorgeous even back then, and I was far from it," Jenna said.

"You don't have to look at me like that. It's hard enough to be dumped a week before your wedding, but to be dumped for your stepmother..."

She fought back the tears welling in her eyes and cleared them from her throat. "Whether you believe me or not, I'm a confident person, and I'm generally happy with who I am. I don't put a lot of stock in looks. But this, well, it would shake most women. At least average women like me. I'll get through it though. With a little help from my mimosa float," she said when Cherry returned to the table with her drink and an ice pack.

"I went a little lighter on the vanilla ice cream and white chocolate sprinkles and heavier on the champagne," Cherry said.

Jenna gave her a thumbs-up. "Good call."

"You're needed at the bar, Shaybae," Cherry said, shooing her away. Once Shay headed somewhat reluctantly to the bar, Cherry leaned across the table. "Okay, whatever she said, ignore it. She hasn't got a clue what she's talking about. How could she, right? The woman is a twelve without makeup. You and me though, we're a six on a good day. And let me tell you, Jellybean, there is nothing wrong with being a six if you know how to work it. And Auntie Cherry is going to teach you how to work it. Because trust me, the only way to get over a man is to find another one."

She cupped her chin in her hand and looked around the bar. "Pickings are a little slim right now, but the day is young and the night is long." She glanced at Jenna with a look in her eyes that made her nervous. Jenna drained the mimosa float because of it and then nearly choked on a chocolate sprinkle when Cherry said, "I've never given you a striptease lesson before, have I?"

Cherry had worked as an exotic dancer in Las Vegas before moving to Harmony Harbor. "No, and I don't think today would be a good day to learn." Jenna nodded at her foot on the barrel.

Cherry bent over to lift the ice pack. "Doesn't look bad at all. A couple more mimosas, another hour or so of rest, ice, compression, and elevation, and you'll be as good as new. Trust me, Auntie Cherry knows all."

Jenna might love Cherry as a best friend, but she absolutely did not trust the woman when it came to her idea of how to mend a broken heart, and she made a mental note to limit herself to one mimosa float. It was a well-known fact that Jenna was a lightweight when it came to holding her own against fancy, sweet drinks. And after the day she'd had, Jenna just might be susceptible to Cherry's more outrageous healing-a-broken-heart ideas.

"Where is my stepsister?"

Jenna looked up at the sound of Arianna's sharply pitched voice. Or, as Jenna thought of it, her murderous voice. She slunk down on the chair, but Serena spotted her. Serena nudged Arianna, who whipped around and immediately marched toward their table. Jenna got a squeamish feeling in the pit of her stomach. She'd had plenty of experience reading her oldest stepsister's moods, and the way her eyes and lips were narrowed suggested Jenna was about to receive a piece of her mind, which was as sharp as Arianna's tongue. At the moment, Jenna's mind obviously wasn't because she couldn't figure out why Arianna was mad at her.

Cherry rested her elbow on the table, placing a hand over her eyes. She shook her head. "Here we go. She's got her bi-at-ch face on. I'm telling you, that woman needs to get laid."

"Please don't share that with her. It's better just to

let her rant, okay?" Jenna said, preparing herself for the mental pummeling she had no doubt was about to come when the two women reached the table.

Arianna crossed her arms, Serena following suit. They stared down at her, faces pinched. "I'm sorry you got dragged into it," Jenna felt compelled to say, even though her stepsisters had managed to make the situation so much worse. If not for Arianna, Logan wouldn't have punched Lorenzo.

"Sorry isn't going to cut it, Jenna. Our reputations are now at risk thanks to you and that…that Italian gigolo."

Cherry twisted on the barrel to look at Jenna's stepsisters. "Maybe I missed something, but the gigolo didn't break up with one of you a week before your wedding, did he? He didn't cheat on you with your stepmother or destroy the dream wedding you've been planning since you were ten, did he?"

"I'm really not in the mood to listen to you defend my stepsister, Cherry. Serena and I were photographed in handcuffs and have just come back from being grilled at the police station and slapped with a restraining order, while Jenna's sitting at the bar drinking. I can't afford to lose business because of this." Her sister's eyes went wide, and she slowly lowered herself onto the barrel whispering, "The deposits."

"Cherry, would you mind getting drinks for me and my sisters?" Jenna asked. Arianna looked as if she were suddenly carrying the weight of the world on her shoulders.

The other woman nodded and got to her feet, mouthing, *Holler if you need me.*

"Are you okay?" Serena asked, putting a hand on her sister's shoulder.

Arianna buried her face in her hands. "We handled all the deposits for Jenna's wedding. It's too late to get the money back." Her voice was muffled, but Jenna had made out the gist of it.

"You don't have to worry about the deposits, Arianna. I'll take care of them, and I'll"—Jenna looked down at the wedding gown her stepsister had spent weeks creating and carefully shuffled the chair closer to the table so Arianna wouldn't see the blood spatter from Lorenzo's nose or the bedraggled hem—"pay for the dress, of course."

Arianna lifted her head from her hands. "And how exactly do you plan to do that, Jenna? You can't access the money Daddy set aside for your wedding."

"I know, but I didn't plan on letting him pay for everything. I have money put away." She'd set up a special savings account for her wedding the day she'd gotten her first babysitting job. Since she was very young, she'd known exactly how she wanted her wedding and hadn't wanted to compromise on the vision or ask her stepfather for the money to make her dreams come true. She'd wanted to do it on her own.

"Oh, I see. Well, that's a relief at least." Arianna stood up. "Come on, Serena. We'll see if we can convince the Hartes to lose the photos of us. I'm sure they've got better ones of Logan in handcuffs and one

of Lorenzo crying over his bloody nose." The Hartes
owned the *Harmony Harbor Gazette.*

"Logan didn't get charged, did he?" Jenna asked,
crossing her fingers.

"What do you think? Lorenzo was yelling that Logan
ruined his beautiful face and... You better add covering
the cost of his tux to your list of expenses. We'll never
get the blood out."

Jenna opened her mouth to tell Arianna to bill
Lorenzo, but she knew that would be like trying to get
water from a brick. "Of course. So they charged Logan
with assault?"

"He'll be lucky if that's all they charge him with.
Ryan and Lorenzo were going for attempted murder."

"That's ridiculous!" Jenna was about to jump to her
feet when she remembered the state of both her dress
and her ankle.

"Relax, Jenna," Serena said. "Michael and Aidan
were there to defend Logan. Not that he needed them
to, really. Arianna and I shared our version of the event
too. I'm sure, once Kimberly sobers up, she'll corrobo-
rate our story. Although she's being charged with drunk
and disorderly." She looked from Jenna's empty glass
to her face. "Once you've finished commiserating with
your friends, you should go to the station and give your
side of the story. After all, Logan did save you from being hit by the car."

"I would've gone right away, but Logan asked that
I stay here while Michael handles things at the station.
I'll go as soon as I get changed. Promise."

Arianna frowned, as though just noticing Jenna still

wore her wedding gown. "Why didn't you change when you ran back to Tie the Knot?"

"I haven't been back to the shop. I came here—"

"Oh my God, Jenna! We thought you'd at least think to lock up while we were being hauled off to jail!"

"If we've been robbed because of you—" A red-faced Arianna broke off when Serena grabbed her hand, dragging her away.

Cherry, who was carrying a tray of mimosa floats to the table, turned to watch Jenna's stepsisters race out of the pub. "I guess we don't need two of these, do we?"

Jenna gestured for the drinks. "Yes, yes, I do. And keep them coming."

Chapter Four

♥

Three hours after he'd been cuffed and hauled to the station, Logan returned to the scene of the crime.

"Looks like it's hopping downtown tonight," Michael said as he parked his Range Rover on Main Street. "At least we know Jenna's still at the pub, so you don't have to chase her down. Though, from what Shay said, you might have to sober her up."

The last thing Logan wanted to do was drag Jenna into this, but it had become patently clear that Ryan Wilson had an ax to grind against the Gallaghers and he was going to use Logan to sharpen the blade. He frowned as what his brother said sank in. "Jenna's drunk?"

After the day she'd had, he didn't know why it surprised him that she'd drown her sorrows at the bar, but it kind of did. Probably because of her big, innocent eyes and sweet girl-next-door vibe.

"Yeah. Shay says Arianna and Serena headed straight to the pub after they were released and tore into her. They assumed she'd lock up the shop. Guess she didn't."

Looking across the street at Tie the Knot as he got out of the SUV, Logan slammed the car door in frustration. "Because she went to find you for me, and I texted Shay to keep her at the pub." And she'd hurt herself on account of him too. He'd kept an eye on her while Wilson arrested him and saw her fall and limp her way down the street. "You'd better come up with another way to get me out of this. I'm not using Jenna."

"What do you mean, using her? All you're doing is asking her to call Lorenzo and get him to drop the charges against you."

"You were at the station, right? Do you honestly believe he'll drop the charges if all Jenna does is ask?" He caught the grimace his brother tried to hide. "Yeah, that's what I thought. He'll want the ring and her wedding gown. To give to her stepmother." Logan cracked his knuckles. "I should've punched him harder. It might've turned him into a decent human being."

"Okay, that's good."

Logan stopped on the sidewalk. "You want me to punch him again?"

"No, of course I don't. But if we end up in court, I'll use the fact that your fists are lethal weapons and you could've killed the guy had you wanted to. Which proves you were defending the women, not acting as Jenna's hired thug, as Wilson and Lorenzo claimed."

Logan dragged a weary hand down his face. "I'll have to call my supervisor. I'll probably be put on administrative leave until this is settled."

"Don't call him yet. You have an exemplary record. You don't want this on there. Hold off for a couple days. It's the weekend, and Aidan figures he can buy you some time. And, bro, as much as you don't want to hear this, Jenna is your best bet for making this go away."

"No, it's on me. I hit him. I'll pay him off."

"Don't even think about going there. You'll be handing Wilson the evidence he needs to bury you."

"You're right. You're right. What's the guy got against the Gallaghers anyway?"

"Aidan's going to dig deeper, but he thinks it has something to do with GG."

Knowing GG, their cousin Aidan was probably right. Colleen Gallagher, their great-grandmother, better known as GG, had been a shit disturber of epic proportions when she was alive. She'd also been one of Logan's favorite people. Some of his best memories were from the summers and holidays he'd spent at Greystone Manor, the family's estate. Built to resemble a medieval castle, the manor was situated on five thousand acres of woodland and oceanfront property west of Harmony Harbor. It now served as a hotel.

If Colleen had had her way, every single member of the extended Gallagher family would be living in Harmony Harbor. Nineteen months ago, she'd died at the age of a hundred and four, leaving everything to Logan, his brothers, and his cousins. There was a catch though. They all had to agree to keep the estate in the family or sell. So far, his four cousins and his baby brother were on the Save Greystone Team. Logan didn't have a strong opinion either way, but he highly doubted they'd get all the cousins on board, especially his uncle Daniel's girls. They'd rarely spent time at the manor.

Then again, Logan had learned never to underestimate his great-grandmother. Even from the grave she seemed to be controlling them...and the town. Her memoir, *The Secret Keeper of Harmony Harbor*, had been missing since the day she died. As the title indicated, GG had spent decades poking her nose in everyone's business. Which meant she'd no doubt ticked off a fair number of people. He couldn't help but wonder if that included members of Ryan Wilson's family.

"Aidan should hunt down GG's memoirs. He'd probably find what he's looking for there," Logan suggested.

"No doubt. Word of advice though. Don't mention GG's memoirs to anyone in town. It's calmed down some, but those first few months after she died, people were tearing apart the manor to find the book." Michael looked around and lowered his voice as a young couple walked past. "Between you and me, I think her memoirs have been found."

"It makes sense Jasper would know where the book is. He and GG were thick as thieves." The seventy-something man had worked for the Gallagher family for as long as any of them could remember. A strict disciplinarian with stiff upper-crust manners, he'd managed both the manor and the Gallagher great-grandchildren. Yet while he was tough and not overly demonstrative, they'd never doubted he loved them and had their backs.

"Yeah, and speaking of thick as thieves, Mom and

the Widows Club have picked the manor's Bachelor of the Month."

"And this is important how?"

"Because it's you." Michael lifted his phone and swiped his finger across the screen, turning it to Logan. "Hello, Mr. June."

It was a picture of Logan from a few years back at Kismet Cove. He'd been rising from the surf when the photo was taken. He scowled at his brother, who laughed and said, "Looks like a cover shot for *Men's Health*. Women must like the wet and half-naked look. Supposedly you've got more hits than me, and I crashed the manor's website more than once."

"So you didn't think my day was bad enough; you had to share this too? Just tell me they're not auctioning me off like they did you?" He glanced at his conspicuously silent brother and bowed his head. "I talked about this to Mom. I'm too busy with work to think about dating. I shouldn't even be here this weekend."

"Yeah, well, dating isn't her main objective—or Grams's and the Widows Club's for that matter. They want you married by the end of this summer."

"You can't be serious." Sadly, he knew that Michael was, and so were the older women. "You gave them a false sense of success, baby brother. I'm not interested in dating right now."

"They don't care. They have an agenda and…" Michael stopped by the wooden sailboat mast attached to the redbrick wall of the Salty Dog. His voice had lost its teasing tone, his expression now serious. "It's starting to feel like Mom's on a deadline. Like she won't rest until she sees the three of us happily married before the year is out. I'm worried she might be dying."

Maura, their mother, was the reason Logan had come home for the weekend. They'd known something was up in February but hadn't been able to figure out exactly what. She'd left their dad, her husband of forty years, with the excuse that she'd been derelict in her duties as a mother and it was time to devote her life to ensuring her three sons were settled and happily married. To the women of her choosing, of course.

Michael had been the subject of Maura's matchmaking attention for the past few months. Recently, when it began looking like Logan was next in line, he'd decided it was time to get to the bottom of what was driving her. Not in a million years had he expected to discover she was sick. "Why do you think she's dying?" Logan clipped out.

"You don't have to take off my head. I'm as upset about it as you are."

"Sorry. Have you talked to her or Dad about your suspicions?"

"No, but I was hoping we could do that this weekend. Connor's coming to the manor tomorrow for Sunday brunch."

Connor was the middle son, a high-powered Boston attorney with a passion for all things expensive, including fast cars and even faster women. In some ways, he was most like their father and mother. The three of them liked the good life. They were addicted to power and control. Although their dad had mellowed over the past few years and had recently retired. Logan had assumed his retirement was the real reason their mother had left him, focusing all her energy on them to fill the void. Now he wasn't so sure.

"This weekend just keeps getting better and better," Logan said.

"I know, and I don't want to put any more pressure on you. I really don't. But if Mom is sick, she doesn't need to be worrying about you losing your job. You know how proud she is of you, especially now that you're working the president's security detail. So do us all a favor, yourself included, and talk to Jenna. If you're uncomfortable asking her to call Lorenzo, I'll do it or Shay will."

As much as he hated to admit it, Michael was right. The news would upset their mother whether she was sick or not. "I'll talk to Jenna."

Michael opened the door to the pub. Shay was behind the bar, looking unhappy as she stared across the room to where the music played a loud, sexy beat. A wooden wall blocked their view of the stage.

His brother raised his voice to be heard over the rowdy cheers coming from the other end of the pub. "Good. I'm sure Jenna will be more than happy to make the call, Logan. Knowing her like I've come to, she'd probably be more upset if she found out she could've helped and you didn't ask her."

"Just don't expect me to ask if she's crying in her beer. I'm more comfortable handling an assassination attempt than I am a woman in tears," he yelled back.

Michael stopped halfway to the bar and did a double take. "I don't think that will be a problem."

Logan followed the direction of his brother's gaze, and his eyes went wide. Jenna stood on the raised stage twirling the bottom of her wedding gown over her head. The top part of her dress remained, and a very short crinoline thing acted as the skirt, revealing long, shapely legs in her glass shoes. To the delight of the crowd gathered around her, she tossed them the bottom part of her gown.

"Okay, so it looks like Lorenzo won't be getting the dress. Maybe he…" Logan trailed off when Jenna took a sexy stroll to the pole in the center of the stage. Sending an exaggerated wink over her shoulder to the cheering crowd, she tossed her hair and then walked straight into the pole, bouncing off of it.

"I'm okay. I'm okay." She waved off the audience's concern while holding her nose.

"Cherry, get her off the stage now," Shay called out in a voice that even Logan wouldn't have argued with.

Michael stuck his hands in the pockets of his khaki shorts, grinning like a fool at his fiancée. "God, you're hot."

Shay rolled her eyes at him, but Logan caught the small uptick at the corner of her mouth. Well, it had been tipped up until she realized Cherry had no intention of removing Jenna from the stage. At that moment, she was boosting the younger woman up the pole.

"This isn't going to end well," Logan murmured as he set off to rescue Cinderella from herself.

By the time he made his way to the front of the stage, she'd managed to turn herself upside down, those sexy legs of hers wrapped tightly around the pole. Cherry clapped like a proud mother, and the audience cheered.

Jenna responded to the applause with a grin, a little like the one his brother had given to Shay. Only Jenna didn't look like a fool. She looked adorably cute. Then, as though to give the audience their money's worth, she tightened her arms around the pole, taking what looked like a deep breath before jutting out one leg.

"Woo-hoo!" she yelled, obviously pleased she hadn't fallen on her head. She kicked her foot and her glass shoe went flying. Logan stretched out a hand, catching it before it hit the redhead in front of him.

"Thanks," the woman said over her shoulder and then blinked up at him. "It's you. Hey, look everybody, it's Prince Charming. Wilson arrested him for protecting Jellilicious this afternoon."

At the news, he received offers of free drinks and several shoulder pats. Jellilicious was clearly a fan favorite.

"Logan, you're here!" Jenna yelled, and in her excitement, she lost her grip on the pole.

Logan jumped onto the stage, reaching her just in time to save her from breaking her neck.

"My hero," she said, the words slightly slurred as she smiled up at him.

He would've returned her smile, but he got a look at her ankle. Scooping her into his arms, he straightened. "You should've been resting your foot, not dancing on it."

She wiggled her bare toes. "No pain. It feels wonderful, and so do you." She wrapped her arms around his neck with that adorable smile still on her face.

"We'll see how you feel in the morning once the alcohol wears off."

"You're a buzzkill."

"Yeah?" He laughed as he carried her off the stage. "In your case, I think that's a good thing. Your buzz needs to be killed. How about some coffee?"

"I'd rather have more sex on the beach." Clearly, his surprise was evident on his face because her smile widened, showing off a dimple in her cheek. "It's a drink, silly. And it's so good, I bet it's better than actual sex on the beach. At least sex on the beach with Lorenzo. You know, Italian men are supposed to be passionate, but he wasn't. At least with me he wasn't. He's probably passionate with Gwyneth, my stepmother." She drew her arms from around his neck to flap her hands in front of her face. "Eww, eww, eww. I never thought about that. What if he was having sex with both of us? You don't think he'd—"

"Probably best if you don't think about it." At least while she was in his arms. His search for an empty table was taking longer than it should. With her running commentary about sex, he was having a hard time thinking straight. It didn't help that he hadn't had sex in a while and she had her tight little body wrapped around him. She smelled as sweet as she looked, like oranges and white chocolate.

"You're right, but I can't seem to help it. You know what Cherry would say?"

He'd spent some time with Shay and her best friend, so he had a fairly good idea how Cherry's mind worked, which was why he kept quiet and settled Jenna onto a barrel. "You stay put." He pulled another barrel over. "I'll grab you a cup of coffee and an ice pack. Get you something to eat too."

As he placed her foot gently on the barrel, she reached over and fisted her hand in the front of his T-shirt, tugging him so they were almost nose-to-nose. "You're supposed to ask, what would Cherry say, Jelli-licious? That's my stripper name. You know what? I'm going to call myself *Jellilicious* all the time. It's sexy, don't you think? Way better than Jenna. Jenna sounds like the plain Jane next door who worked at the library and was the nerdy girl in high school." She sighed. "I was all three, so my mom must've known something when she named me. Or maybe I was just trying to live up to the name. What do you think?"

As he carefully removed one finger at a time from his T-shirt, relieved that she seemed to have forgotten her initial question, he said, "Your mom knew exactly what she was doing. Jenna's a pretty name for a pretty lady. Now, I'll just be a few min—"

Once again, her fingers closed around the fabric of his T-shirt, and she pulled him closer. For a little thing, she was surprisingly strong and tenacious. "You can't go until you ask me what Cherry would say."

"How about I ask Cherry once she's finished with her lessons?" He lifted his chin to where the woman in question was instructing a couple of ladies and one man on the art of pole dancing.

Jenna chewed on her bottom lip and then leaned forward, bringing her mouth to his ear. "Cherry would say the best way to get the image of Lorenzo and Gwyneth having sex out of my head is to have it with you. What do you think?"

"No. That's not a good idea. Not a good idea at all. It's actually a really, really bad idea, Jenna. You've had too much to drink, and you've had a shock."

She lifted a shoulder. "It's okay. I knew you wouldn't want to have sex with me. You're beautiful, and beautiful men aren't interested in women like me. I mean, look at Lorenzo. He's beautiful, and he dumped me for my stepmother. She's gorgeous, you know. Her boobs..." She put her hands on either side of her head, nodding. "Yep, they're about the size of my head. Daddy bought them for her on their tenth wedding anniversary. She thought I should get mine done too, but"—she cupped her breasts—"I'm too petite to have ginormous boobs. Now, Cherry, she suits hers, don't you think?"

"You're killing me here, Jenna."

She angled her head to the side and smiled. "I like you, Logan Gallagher. You're a very nice man, and you're my hero. Thank you for rescuing me twice."

"I think I might have just rescued you a third time, Jenna Bell." From himself.

Chapter Five

♥

After consuming her fourth cup of coffee and her third cheese-stuffed pretzel, Jenna began to feel the throb in her ankle and the heat of embarrassment washing over her cheeks. It was too bad her now-sobering brain couldn't delete her drunken propositioning of Logan. From under her lashes, she glanced at the man sitting across from her at the table in the darkened corner of the Salty Dog.

He was more ruggedly handsome than beautiful, she thought, blaming her earlier perception on her fancy-drink goggles, acknowledging that Cherry might have a point and they had a pink hue. Although Jenna was color-blind, so she really didn't know if the hue was pink, green, or somewhere in between. What she did know from intently studying the man sitting across from her for the past hour was that Logan's features were strong and masculine. His dark-as-night hair was cut military short, a five-o'clock shadow darkening his chiseled jaw. The only thing the least bit soft or feminine about him was his long, dark lashes that framed his extraordinary eyes.

He glanced at her, and she decided she was wrong. His eyes were beautiful, as beautiful as his deep, smoky voice, which caused her nerve endings to sizzle and the muscles low in her stomach to contract when he spoke to his brother, Michael, who sat beside him.

Okay, so maybe she wasn't completely sober. But tipsy or not, she could see that Michael wanted Logan to ask her something, which he apparently refused to do. She'd always assumed her ability to read people better than most was another benefit of her gift. Or maybe it was the chicken-and-the-egg thing and her gift had developed from her ability to read people so well.

She gave a scornful snort. She hadn't done a very good job of reading Lorenzo or her stepmother, now, had she? Maybe everyone was right and Jenna's gift didn't amount to a hill of beans. She'd been fooling herself all these years, pretending to be someone she wasn't. Pretending to be special when she was just plain old Jenna Bell.

"I said no. Go give Shay a hand." Logan pointed his beer bottle at the crowded bar and then brought it to his lips.

Lips that definitely belonged on her beautiful list. He was three-for-two now. Nope, she thought, suddenly transfixed by the way his Adam's apple moved in his powerful throat and the way his world-class biceps flexed; rugged and masculine totally won out. The man was swoon-worthy.

Michael pushed back the barrel he'd been sitting on,

drawing Jenna's attention to the look of frustration on his face. As though he sensed her watching him, he glanced at her and then at his brother, who gave him a *don't even think about it* look that Jenna would've listened to if she were Michael. He didn't.

"Jenna, I need you to do my brother a big favor."

"Don't listen to him. He doesn't—"

"Of course, anything." She cut off Logan. She meant it too. Whatever he needed, she'd do. And not just because Logan Gallagher was the type of man any women would sell their soul for just to earn a smile, or because he'd saved her twice in one day. There was nothing Jenna liked better than to lend a helping hand. Some people—Arianna for one, Gwyneth for the other—had remarked that it was because Jenna needed to feel needed. They seemed to think that was a bad thing. Jenna didn't. Until Michael told her what he wanted her to do.

"It'd be a big help if you could get Lorenzo to drop the charges against Logan."

She might've missed the fact Lorenzo was gaga for Gwyneth, but it didn't mean Jenna didn't know the man. There was only one way she could get Lorenzo to drop the charges against Logan. She'd have to give him back his ring. Of course, she wanted to give it back. She wasn't a vengeful person, and it was a family heirloom, after all. Truth be told, the thing weighed a ton and was a little ostentatious for her, but Arianna was right. The ring was Jenna's only leverage.

Lorenzo was more terrified of his traditional, close-knit family than he was of pleasing Gwyneth, and his uncle and cousins were flying in from Italy for the wedding. Which meant Lorenzo would be highly motivated to do as Jenna asked. And if anyone could convince Gwyneth to relinquish her rights to Southern Belle (stolen though they may be) to Jenna, it was Lorenzo. Still, Jenna reminded herself, she owed Logan her life.

She nodded her agreement to Michael's request.

From the expressions on both men's faces, it had been more of a reluctant nod than a convincing one, so she added a smile and said, "Of course. Absolutely. I'll call him right now." She looked around for her phone. "I don't know where..." She grimaced. "I left it in the changing room at Tie the Knot."

Which reminded her why she'd been drinking like a frat boy at his fraternity initiation. Her stepsisters hated her again. If possible, they'd hate her even more when they learned she'd returned Lorenzo's ring. They wouldn't care that a good man's career was on the line because of her. They no doubt saw the ring as their leverage too. They wanted Gwyneth's version of their father's will overturned as much as Jenna did.

"No worries. You can use mine."

She blinked at the smartphone Michael proffered. Her vision was blurry. She blamed the alcohol for the tears filling her eyes and forced a smile. "Great. Thanks." Just as she reached for the phone, it disappeared from view.

"It's fine, Jenna. I appreciate the offer though." Logan tossed the phone at his brother. "I said no. I meant it."

"Yeah, well, excuse me if I'm trying to keep you off

administrative leave. And what about Mom? I thought we agreed—" This time the look Logan gave his brother worked. Michael instantly clamped his mouth shut.

Jenna didn't blame him. Logan's expression was aggressive, all authoritative male. That look right there was one of the reasons she'd never dated an alpha and never would. It made her shiver just a little, and Logan's attention left his brother to focus on her. Almost immediately Logan's gaze went from impatient to warm. "Go talk to Shay, baby bro. Get her to turn down the air."

There was a hint of an apology in his deep, smooth voice. And attentiveness in his request to have the air turned down. Evidence that, despite being an alpha, he was clearly as good a man as she thought him to be. A good man who didn't deserve to be put on administrative leave for defending her and her sister.

Jenna didn't want to cause any more problems between the two men and waited until Michael headed for the bar to say, "May I have your phone, please?"

Logan's mouth kicked up at the corner, and he put down his beer bottle. "No, you may not." He folded his arms on the table, leaning toward her to trap her in his intent gaze. "I know you want to help, and I appreciate it. But you and I both know there's only one way you'll get Lorenzo to withdraw the charges, and I'm not letting you give him back the ring. I heard enough today to know it might be your only chance to get your company back."

"We're hiring a lawyer. It might take time, but eventually I'll get Southern Belle back." If Gwyneth didn't manage to bankrupt the company before then. "I need to do this for you, Logan. I won't be able to live with myself if you lose your job because you got sucked into my drama."

"I appreciate that. But I'm the one who hit the guy, not you. And if I had to do it all over again, things would've gone down exactly the same way. Don't sweat it, Jenna. Honestly, I'm good. Everything will work out."

"You don't know my stepmother. Once she finds out what happened to Lorenzo, she'll get involved. And Gwyneth makes Arianna look like a saint."

"Bring it. She'll find out what she's up against pretty quick. Someone takes on one of us, they end up fighting us all. We'll let her know the same applies to you."

"Thank you. That's very sweet of you." She studied him with a half smile, thinking back to the days she'd sat in her bedroom window staring up at Greystone Manor.

At the age of four, Jenna had become addicted to happily-ever-afters and lay partial blame for her obsession at the door of Greystone Manor, the fairy-tale castle that stood sentry over her small, coastal hometown. Granted, the blame lay not so much on the manor as on the handsome Gallagher princes, who'd made it their holiday home. Somewhere around the age of ten, the heroes in Jenna's favorite fairy tales began to take on an uncanny resemblance to the dark-haired and blue-eyed Gallagher boys.

"You're like handsome knights in shining armor coming to the rescue of damsels in distress."

"Most of our armor is pretty tarnished. And Michael was rescued by his damsel, not the other way around." He laughed and lifted his beer to his mouth.

"Shay's my shero. If I were more like her, I wouldn't have lost my company and Lorenzo to Gwyneth."

"Don't know about the business, but I'm a pretty good judge of character and, honey, I'd say take the win, because that idiot breaking up with you was definitely a win."

She lifted a shoulder, wishing she had seen what everyone else did. Then again, if she had, she wouldn't be sitting in the Salty Dog with Logan Gallagher, one of her childhood fantasy crushes, and he wouldn't have just called her *honey*. Back in the day, each and every one of the Gallagher great-grandsons had played, at one time or another, a leading role in her daydreams. Actually, Logan and his cousin Griffin less so because they were older than her by ten years.

"Sorry, that's probably not what you needed to hear right now."

"It probably is." Especially the *honey* part said in a voice that felt like a tender caress. She gave her head a slight shake, pushing the thought away. It was hard enough sitting across from him without hearing Cherry's voice in her head. And right now Jenna had other things to think about, really important things, like how to save Logan's job.

She lifted the cup of coffee to her mouth, trying to come up with a way to make him see reason. Obviously, the man was a protector, a defender of the weak and helpless, a... That's it. She had to show him she was far from helpless and weak and that by doing this for him, she was taking back her power.

Taking back her power...She liked that. It felt good and gave her a sense of control that she'd been missing since her stepfather died. The ostentatious pink diamond winked at her in the light from the brass lantern hanging overhead. She put down her cup of coffee and looked Logan in the eye. "You have to let me call Lorenzo and barter for your freedom with the ring."

"We've already had this conversation and—"

"No, we didn't have a conversation. You talked and I listened, but I need you to hear me out. If the circumstances were different and I was engaged to anyone other than Lorenzo, the first thing I would've done was give the ring back. But I'm keeping it for revenge, and that's not healthy. I need to get into a positive place, and being angry and vengeful isn't going to get me there. It'll just make it harder for me to heal."

"I don't know much about you and your business, Jenna. But from what your sisters said, you worked hard to get your company off the ground, and now that you've started to reap the benefits, your stepmother stole it out from under you. You're not being vengeful keeping the ring; you're being strategic. Lawyers cost money. Why waste it if you can get what you want by using what Lorenzo wants as leverage?"

"That makes sense if I wanted my company back, but the more I think about it, I'm not sure that I do. Want it back, that is. Gwyneth was always looking for ways to generate more income from the business, and some of her ideas bordered on illegal—like selling our clients' information. Now that I'm not there to rein her in, and haven't been for the past two and a half months, she's probably implemented them."

"You'll figure out how to turn things around. You can't let her—"

"Win? She kind of already did. But you know, it's not just that." She looked down at her coffee. "I didn't see what was right in front of me. What I had with Lorenzo was a lie. What Kimberly had with...I don't know what her fiancé's name is, but their relationship was a lie too. So many of my clients had been cheated on before they came to me, cheated and lied to." She lifted her gaze to his. "I don't think I believe in happily-ever-after anymore, Logan. How can I sell something I don't believe in? It's why I was successful, you know. I believed in the fairy tale." She looked away, blinking back the tears that once again gathered in her eyes.

It felt like a part of her had died. But it was about time she lost her innocence, the rosy pink hue she saw life through. She was twenty-nine, after all. And it wasn't as if her life had been easy. Maybe she had to stop pretending it was or that there was something heroic about suffering or that someday her prince would come.

A big hand closed over hers, warm and strong. "I'm sorry. I wish I'd knocked out his teeth and broken his nose. Give yourself some time, Jenna. Don't make any major life decisions just yet."

She stared at the thumb that stroked her hand, wondering how his simple, comforting touch could cause erotic thoughts and butterflies to take flight in her head and her stomach. She blamed Cherry and her racy comments earlier. Afraid Logan would pick up on her inappropriate reaction, Jenna turned her hand over to give his fingers a quick, light squeeze. Then she slipped her hand out from under his to bring her coffee cup to her lips.

She took a sip before putting the cup down. "I understand what you're saying, Logan. But the thing is, some people believe I have a special talent, a gift, and that I can tell if they were meant to be together or not." He looked like he was having difficulty understanding what she meant. "Like I knew the minute I sat across from them if he was her one true love, her one and only."

He laughed.

She sighed. She should be used to that reaction by now. "Let me guess. You don't believe in soul mates or psychics."

"Good guess." He looked at her more closely. "But you do." She thought she heard him say under his breath, "Why am I surprised?"

"I did. Now I'm not sure that I do, but more important, no one else will believe I have the true-love gift. Not after I was dumped by a man I thought was mine. Which means, whether I like it or not, I'm done in the happily-ever-after business. Washed up at twenty-nine."

"Look, I'm not going to say what you should or shouldn't do. You know what's best for you."

"Thank you, I do. Now I just have to figure out what that is." She looked over at her best friend, who was coming their way. "Maybe I'll become a counselor like Shay. You do a lot of counseling in the matchmaking business, you know." She nodded, liking the idea the more she thought about it. "I'll go back to school and get my masters in social work." And do her thesis on the perils of believing in fairy tales. "My wedding account will fund my education."

"Sounds like a better use for the money, if you ask me."

She wasn't surprised Logan felt that way. Ninety percent of the alpha men she'd met over the years hadn't been a fan of weddings, especially big weddings. Lorenzo had been. He was the reason their budget had ballooned out of control, not her. She was just beginning to wonder if they were all right about Lorenzo and she'd gotten off lucky when Shay arrived at their table with a Tie the Knot bag in her hand.

She rested it on the table. "Sorry. I got busy and forgot to bring you this. Serena dropped it off a while ago."

"A while as in two hours ago?" Jenna prayed it wasn't during her stripper routine and glanced at Shay, who tried to hide a wince. Jenna groaned, looking up at the wood-beamed ceiling as she did. "What did I do to deserve this? I always look for the best in people. I'm kind to everyone. I go out of my way to help people."

"And that right there is your problem," Logan said.

"It's not a problem. Courage and kindness will see you through all the trials life has to offer."

"Yeah, who told you that?" Shay asked.

"Cinderella," Jenna said without thinking, and then sighed when both Logan and Shay began to laugh. She leaned over to grab the gigantic ball of tulle from the chair beside her and then stood to take the bag from Shay, swallowing a pained gasp. She'd forgotten about her ankle. "I guess I better go home and face the music."

Logan stood too, reaching in the back pocket of his jeans to take out his wallet.

Shay waved him off. "As if. Thanks for taking care of Jenna earlier. Appreciate it."

"You make it sound like I need a keeper," she grumbled.

"You do," Shay and Logan said at almost the same time. He came around the table, took the bag and wedding gown from Jenna's hands, and then slid his arm around her waist. "Okay, Cinderella. Lean on me, and I'll get you back safely to your evil stepsisters."

"They're not evil, just mean. Well, Arianna is, and not all the time. She's actually been very kind to me these past few months."

And it had been wonderful and oh so welcome. Jenna didn't know how she would've made it through the past several months without her sisters' support. She hated that she'd disappointed them and wished she had a way to make it up to them. She fingered her engagement ring. Giving it back to Lorenzo certainly wouldn't win them over.

She glanced at the profile of the tall, powerfully built man carefully steering her through the bar. He'd made it clear he didn't need or want her to step in on his behalf. Obviously, he was perfectly capable of looking out for himself. As he further pointed out, the Gallagher clan was fiercely protective of their own and had the financial means to ensure a favorable outcome for Logan.

Still, she felt responsible for the position he was in, and not doing anything to help didn't sit well with her. But for the past nineteen years, all she'd ever wanted was for her stepsisters to love her, so instead of taking her cell phone out of the Tie the Knot bag and calling Lorenzo, she rested her weight against Logan, doing her best to ignore Cherry's obscene gestures and chortling cheers as Logan guided Jenna to the door.

Chapter Six

♥

Logan cast an amused glance at the woman leaning heavily against him. Head turned, face pressed into his side, Jenna waved a *knock it off* hand in Cherry's direction at the other end of the bar. "What's she trying to get you to do?"

"Trust me, you don't want to know," Jenna muttered, her breath warming the skin beneath his T-shirt.

He glanced at Cherry, who was now gyrating on the stage, and quickly figured it out. He didn't think it was necessary to share with Jenna that they were absolutely not doing *that*. He was trying to work out a way to politely share that when his sister-in-law-to-be yelled, "Cherry, knock it off. You've got customers waiting."

Jenna lifted her head, her fingers tightening at his waist as she looked around his arm at Shay. "Thanks. You're the only one she listens to."

"Don't give me too much credit. I have a feeling she got a look at Logan's face. Anyway, are you sure you feel like putting up with Arianna's crap tonight? You can stay with me and Michael."

"I appreciate the offer, but I have to face them sometime. I might as well do it now. The slight buzz I've got going on should deaden the pain of their barbs."

Shay pressed her lips together, clearly not liking the idea of Jenna having to deal with Arianna tonight. Logan didn't like it much either. He wasn't sure about the dynamics of the sisters' relationship, but there'd been signs they weren't BFFs. Shay's reaction seemed to validate his suspicions, as did Jenna's wry quip.

"Don't worry, Shay. I'll hang around for a while. Make sure Jenna's okay before I leave."

"Good. Thanks," Shay said at about the same time Jenna said, "That's very kind of you, but you don't have to stay. I can handle Arianna."

Logan fought back a grin, wondering if Jenna knew how easy her face was to read. "Don't play poker," he advised as he lifted his chin at his brother, who was behind the bar mixing a drink.

Michael's gaze moved pointedly from Logan to Jenna and back again. "Don't forget, brunch with Mom tomorrow at eleven."

"I'll be there." The serious nature of the brunch was clearly evident in his voice.

Jenna glanced up at him. "Are you okay?"

"Yeah, I'm good." Removing his arm from around her waist, he transferred the bag and the ball of fabric to the other hand before reaching for the door. He held it open, placing his hand at the small of Jenna's back. "Let's get you off that foot," he said, and caught his brother's eye. As if unsure Logan got the gist of his earlier pointed stare, Michael raised his eyebrows at Jenna and nodded.

His baby brother hadn't changed. He'd never been one to give up on anything. Something else Logan knew about his brother was that he was a hell of a lawyer. So if Michael was still pushing for him to get Jenna to call Lorenzo, it meant he was worried about Logan's chances of beating the charge. The odds of keeping the news from his mother seemed about as good.

Releasing a resigned breath, he gave his brother a clipped nod. Logan wasn't thrilled to ask the favor of Jenna, though she'd made it easier by confessing that she was ready to give up her claim to the business anyway. To his mind, no matter what she decided to do, she should leave Charleston. It was a fair-size city but not big enough to avoid her stepmother and her ex. At least here she had family and good friends. If her sisters, namely Arianna, got their heads out of their asses, he didn't see why Jenna couldn't work at Tie the Knot. They were all in the wedding business, after all.

He thought of Jenna telling him about her special talent and hoped he hadn't offended her by laughing. Seriously though, there's no way she could tell if someone had found *their one*. Then again, he didn't believe in psychics or soul mates. If he did, Noreen probably had been his, and he'd lost her years before.

Like it always did when he thought about his former fiancée, his chest got tight. Jenna reminded him of Noreen. They were both impossibly sweet and naive. Noreen had no business being a cop, but nothing he'd done or said had dissuaded her from her career of choice. She'd died six months after joining the force. Two weeks after he'd proposed to her. Three weeks before she was to meet his family. Weeks after he'd lost her, he made a vow to never again get involved with a woman like Noreen.

Or like Jenna.

He frowned, wondering where the thought had come from. He didn't need the reminder. Beyond today, it was doubtful he'd see her again. Other than in town when he came to visit the family, he supposed. Or in court... He couldn't put it off any longer.

"Logan, are you sure you're okay?" Jenna repeated as he followed her onto the sidewalk.

"Yeah, I'm good, Jenna. It's just that, as much as I don't want to ask you to call Lorenzo on my behalf, I don't have much of a choice according to my brother. If you don't mind doing it, I'd really appreciate it."

"Oh, I...Of course, of course I'll call him." She pointed at the Tie the Knot bag. "I'll just need my phone."

He didn't miss the slight hesitation in her voice or the way her shoulders bowed like she'd lost an important battle. "Jenna." He waited until she looked up at him. "It's okay. I understand if you don't want to."

"No. I want to do whatever I can to help. It's just Arianna and Serena—" She leaned past him to dig in the bag, and pulled out a cell phone with a pink, jewel-encrusted case. "But I'm sure they'll understand. Eventually." She frowned, her head half in the bag now. "That's weird. I can't find my keys... or my wallet. My bra isn't in here…" She trailed off as she removed her head and hands from the bag.

In the light from the old-fashioned lamppost, he could see her cheeks were flushed. "They're probably under the chair," she murmured, focusing on her phone. She caught her bottom lip between her teeth, glancing up at him from under her long lashes before quickly returning her gaze to the phone.

"Bad news?" he asked when she swallowed hard.

"No, everything's good." She glanced around. "You know, it's so beautiful out. I think I'll sleep on the beach tonight."

"All right, tell me what happened."

"Nothing happened. Honest." She held up her phone. "I'm calling Lorenzo right now."

He covered her hand and the phone with his. "Not until you tell me what's going on."

"Nothing new. Arianna's just being Arianna." She shrugged when he cocked an eyebrow, silently demanding more. "Serena saw me doing my Jellilicious routine. They weren't impressed. I can't say I blame them. They worked really hard on my wedding and the dress. And then there was the whole me-forgetting-to-lock-up-the-shop. Don't worry though. They'll get over it." She made a face and then gestured down the street to Tie the Knot. "But the lights are off in the apartment, and there's no way I'm waking them up on top of everything else."

"You're not sleeping on the beach. You can stay at the manor. I'll get you a room."

"Please don't take this the wrong way. I know you're

just being nice, but all everyone has done today is tell me how I should feel and what to do, so I'd like to do what I want to. And what I want to do is listen to the waves roll onto shore, watch the fireflies dance in the sea grass, and maybe make a wish upon a falling star."

He held back a smile at the last. As much as Jenna professed to be done with happily-ever-afters, he wasn't buying it. Not that he'd share that with her. "Sounds good to me. Let's do it."

"Do what?"

"Spend the night at the beach. I haven't done that since I was in my teens. It's a great idea. And you're right, it's the perfect night. I'll just grab us a blanket and my jacket in case it cools down." He crouched down. "Hop on."

"I, ah, don't think that's a good idea. People might get the wrong idea, and I'm—"

He laughed. "No, they won't."

"Of course. You're right. What was I thinking? You're Logan Gallagher, after all. Secret Service man extraordinaire, and I'm just plain-Jane Jenna Bella." She held up a hand at the look he gave her. "Excuse me. You're right. I'm Jellilicious, stripper extraordinaire." She wiggled her butt, making him smile, and then awkwardly climbed on his back. "Here's the deal. You can sit with me for a while, but then you have to leave."

There wasn't a chance in hell he was leaving Jenna on her own tonight. It wasn't like Harmony Harbor was a hotbed of crime and corruption. It was a picturesque coastal town on the North Shore. A town where people looked out for their own. Still, bad things happened everywhere, even in peaceful small towns. Especially to cute women who didn't have a clue how to protect themselves. Cute women with big, innocent eyes who trusted that most people were as good as they were. They couldn't see past a man's handsome face and charming ways to the snake that lay within, waiting to strike. Jenna hadn't seen it, and neither had Noreen.

Now he had to find a way to get Jenna to let him stay. "What if I told you I need a night at the beach as much as you? Would you let me stay then?" She wrapped her arms around his neck, her warm body pressed tight against him, her silky hair brushing his cheek, and he kinda hoped she'd come up with a good argument for him to leave her alone. He'd sit several yards away where she couldn't see him watching over her.

"I'm sorry. Of course you can stay. In the end, your day might end up being far worse than mine." She went quiet as he walked along the nearly empty sidewalk, passed the storefronts housed in sea-green and ocean-blue clapboards, her body tensing when he crossed to the other side of the road.

"I parked my truck just up from Tie the Knot."

"Oh, okay." She relaxed against him once more. "Michael mentioned you're having brunch with your mother tomorrow. She'll be upset about this, won't she? Worried that you'll lose your job. I mean, any mother would be upset if their son lost his job, but yours isn't just a *job* job. You're a Secret Service agent."

"It's not just that. My mother hasn't been acting like herself. She left my dad a few months back for no apparent reason. Now it seems like she's consumed with marrying the three of us off. The quicker the better. We think she might be sick. My brother actually thinks she's dying."

"Oh no. I'm so sorry, Logan. I hope he's wrong, but don't you worry. I'm going to take care of this right now," she said as she sat up, clinging to his shoulder with one hand while retrieving her cell phone from her pocket. She cleared her throat. "Lorenzo, it's Jenna. If you want your ring back before your family arrives from Italy and you have to explain why I have your priceless family heirloom, tell Officer Wilson and everyone else at the Harmony Harbor Police Department that Logan Gallagher didn't lay so much as a finger on you. You tripped over your big... What?" she asked when Logan made a grab for the phone, holding it away from him.

"Jenna, I laid more than a finger on him, and there were witnesses who testified to that. Officer Wilson for one."

She sighed, disconnected, waited a second, and then pressed a key. "It's me again. I know I don't have to remind you how important this ring is to your family, so if you want it back, you tell everyone at HHPD the truth. You went to punch my sister, a poor defenseless woman"—Logan snorted, and she nudged him with her knee—"and Logan stopped you the only way a man like you would listen to, with a fist to the face. And since you have an incredibly low pain threshold, you fainted and smashed your nose. And, Lorenzo, I know you're a God-fearing man, so if you do this and withdraw your complaint against Logan,

I'll forgive you for being a lying, cheating, scum-sucking, stepmother-loving piece of—"

Logan reached back and took the phone from her. He disconnected and shoved it in the front pocket of his jeans. "Feel better now?"

She returned to her earlier position with her warm body plastered to his back, her arms around his neck. "No. I'm madder than a wet hen."

Laughter rumbled in Logan's chest and a second later escaped out his mouth.

"It's not funny. Some of what Lorenzo said this afternoon is finally beginning to sink in. Can you believe he actually wanted to give Gwyneth my wedding gown? Maybe it's a good thing he bled all over it. Too bad he bled all over his tux though. Arianna's going to charge me for it."

"Doesn't seem fair to me. He should be the one paying, not you. But seriously, that tux was so ugly he did them a favor bleeding all over it. No self-respecting man I know would be caught dead in a powder-blue suit."

"What are you talking about? His tux wasn't powder blue. It was navy."

He stopped beside his pickup, turning his head to look at her as he opened the passenger door. "Trust me, the tux was powder blue."

"I can't believe he lied to me." She went to slide off him.

He reached back, thought better of putting his arm under her ass to keep her there, and instead said, "Stay put. I'm just grabbing a blanket and my jean jacket.

But I think I'm missing something. How exactly could Lorenzo lie to you about the color of his tux?" He stuffed the blanket and his jacket in the Tie the Knot bag and then tossed the bottom half of Jenna's wedding dress in the back of the cab.

"I'm color-blind. I guess I shouldn't be surprised he went ahead and ordered a baby-blue tux when I told him I wanted him to wear navy. You'd think he'd been the one planning his fairy-tale wedding since he was ten and not me. Almost from day one, it was all about him. Even my dress. Although that was a toss-up between him and Arianna. At least my sister has taste."

He shut and beeped the lock on the door. "I thought only men were color-blind."

"No. One in two hundred women are color-blind, so it's obviously not as common as in men. For them it's one in twelve. And if that's not special enough, I have the most uncommon variety—tritanopia. I see the world in greenish pink tones. Do not laugh and say *why am I not surprised*."

"Why would you think I'd laugh and say something like that?"

"You said so yourself. You're not a man who believes in happily-ever-afters and knights in shining armor and true love. I told you that I did, and now you know I see the world in rosy pink hues. Honestly, I wouldn't be offended if you laughed. Shay used to laugh at me all the time. Other than my mom and stepfather, she's the only one I ever told. And now you know too."

"Why wouldn't you tell anyone else? Your sisters

must've figured it out." As he waited for her to answer, he Googled *tritanopia* on his phone. He wanted to see what her world looked like, how different it was from his.

It was very different, and to his mind, not in a good way. His heart broke a little for her when images of sunsets, rainbows, and summer gardens filled the split screen, one side with how he and most people saw the images and the other side with how Jenna did. The way she saw the world was weird, like something out of a Tim Burton movie.

"I never fit in. I don't know why. I just didn't. So when I realized there was something wrong with me, that I didn't see things the way the other kids did, I learned to hide it. I became really good at pretending I saw things the way everyone else did, pretending I was normal. And Arianna and Serena made it pretty obvious when we were first introduced that they thought I was weird, and there was nothing I wanted more than for them to like me. I wasn't about to prove them right by telling them I wasn't."

"You're not weird, Jenna. But I imagine life is more difficult for you than me."

"Why? I can see, and I don't know any different. This is how my world has always looked. It's just as beautiful to me as yours is to you."

"On one hand, you have a great attitude, while on the other... You shouldn't keep this a secret. You make it harder on yourself than it has to be."

"Says the man who was no doubt Mr. Popular all through school and voted Most Likely to Succeed.

You have no idea what it's like to be the kid everyone picked on."

"You're not that kid anymore, Jenna. You're a successful woman who's made a great life for herself. You have friends who love you, and I think you gained a whole lot more after your performance tonight, Jellilicious."

She groaned into the nape of his neck, her lips tickling his skin, her breath warming it. And suddenly Logan was aroused and thinking about Jenna's earlier proposal. Sex was sounding pretty good right now. Probably because for the past few months he'd been too busy settling back into the States and in his new job to meet anyone he wanted to have sex with. And the more time he spent with Jenna, the more he liked her.

She was his type, a type he'd spent years trying to avoid. The type of woman who needed to be looked out for, a woman who was soft and sweet. Innocent. Vulnerable. The opposite of the women he purposely gravitated toward now—confident, strong, ball-busters. A woman no man could take advantage of or fool.

"Thanks for the reminder. Although I should probably be happy I've gained some friends since I lost a fiancé today. And my business."

Way to go, Gallagher, he muttered in his head. The last thing he'd meant to do was remind her of how crappy her day had been—or the last few months from the sound of it. He wanted to give her a few hours to forget about everything. He could use the same. And as he'd discovered throughout the years, there was nothing better than some time at the beach to cure whatever ails you.

"Hang on tight, Jellilicious," he warned as he took off down the sidewalk at a run, cutting through yards and back alleys to get to the ocean.

Jenna bounced around on his back, shrieking with laughter, slapping his ass to hurry him up when he slowed to a jog.

"Quiet. You'll get us arrested," he warned, relieved when he spotted the path to the beach.

She returned to her previous position, wrapping her arms around his neck. "They can't arrest you twice in one day. It's called double jeopardy."

"No. Double jeopardy means that if you're tried and acquitted of the charges, you can't be tried again for the same crime."

"Oh, like when they find you innocent of assaulting Lorenzo, they can't charge you again?"

"Right. Only I'm hoping we don't make it to court."

"You won't. I'm going to do everything in my power to ensure that Lorenzo does the right thing. You're my entire focus for the next few days. I'm going to make sure you don't lose your job and that you stay out of jail."

"Appreciate it, but how about we forget everything else for now and just enjoy the rest of the night?" He tossed the bag onto the sand, reaching back to help her down. He steadied her when her feet sank into the sand. "Hang on."

After helping her out of her shoes, he breathed deeply of the salty sea air.

Jenna did the same. "I've been home at least six times since February, and I never made it to the beach. I don't know why. There's nothing more peaceful than the sound of the waves rolling onto shore." She tipped her head back. "Look at that sky. I forgot how beautiful it is here at night." Her voice fell to a whisper. "Silently, one by one, in the infinite meadows of heaven, blossomed the lovely stars, the forget-me-nots of the angels."

He smiled. "*Evangeline*. Longfellow was one of my great-grandmother's favorites."

"Mrs. Gallagher introduced my mother to him. She lent her books from the library at the manor. My mother worked for your family in the dining room. I used to come for high tea. Your great-grandmother was very kind to me."

"GG was a feisty, outspoken old girl. She got worse as she got older and wasn't shy to let anyone know how she felt about them. She must've liked you." He smiled, thinking about his great-grandmother while at the same time wondering why he didn't remember either Jenna or her mother.

Then again, he'd never lived in Harmony Harbor full-time. When they were young, summers and the occasional holiday were spent at the manor. Back then, if he and his brothers had their way, they would've lived there year-round, but his mother had hated the manor and his grandmother and great-grandmother. And now Maura was living at Greystone and was best buds with his grandmother and the Widows Club. If that wasn't telling, he didn't know what was.

"It's such a gorgeous night, I'm surprised no one else is here," she said as he pulled the blanket from the bag.

He spread it out. "That's what happens when you live in a place too long. You take it for granted, get caught up in the minutiae of everyday life and don't take advantage of what's in your own backyard. The grass always looks greener on the other side."

"I wouldn't know." She grinned, hobbling to the blanket. He reached out to help her down. She immediately stretched out on top of it, patting the spot beside her.

Logan straightened, shoving his hands in his pockets as he watched the way the light from the full moon turned the waves into rolling spools of silver. He needed a minute to remind himself why he was here before he took his place beside Jenna, who lay there waiting for him. With her inviting smile, feminine curves, and sexy legs on display, she didn't look like a woman who'd just had her heart broken. She looked like a woman ready to take advantage of the starlit night and secluded beach.

Until she said, "Come on, my trusty steed. Let's see who can find the North Star and the Little Dipper first."

Logan relaxed and joined her on the blanket with a laugh. "I grew up stargazing, and I have ten years on you. I'll give you a head start."

"You may be ten years older, but I doubt you spent as many nights as I did wishing on the stars. I'm the one who should be giving you a head start."

No doubt she was right. Most of the time, he went stargazing with a date. They didn't spend much time looking at the night sky.

"Look"—she pointed—"a shooting star. There's another one." She closed her eyes and squinched up her nose.

"What did you wish for?" he asked.

"That your mom's okay, and that you are too."

"You shouldn't have wasted your wish on me."

"It was better than wasting it on me. I don't know what I want anymore. I don't feel like me."

He cupped the side of her face as he leaned in to touch his lips to her cheek, but she turned her head and his mouth settled on hers instead. He went to draw back, but she covered his hand with hers. "Don't stop. I want you to kiss me."

He stroked her cheek with his thumb, looking into her pretty eyes, which reflected the light from the moon. "Trust me, you think it'll make you feel better, but it won't. You've had a crappy day. You've had a lot to drink. It's not a good idea."

"I'm not stone-cold sober, but I'm not drunk. I know exactly what I'm doing and what I want. And what I want is to have sex, with you. Cherry's right. I need—"

"Don't listen to Cherry, Jenna. Rebound sex is not what you need right now."

"I don't think you have a magical penis and everything will be better because we have sex, Logan. I just want to feel something other than this tightness in my chest and this heavy weight in the pit of my stomach."

He was torn between laughing at her magic penis remark, wanting to kiss the hurt from her face, and easing his own worries about his mother and his job by losing himself inside of her. Just when he thought the laughter would win out, she rolled into him. "Please," she whispered before pressing her lips to his.

And Logan, who'd never been able to deny a woman what she wanted—and he reluctantly admitted to wanting it too—gave in despite the feeling that he was making one of the biggest mistakes of his life.

Chapter Seven

♥

Jenna had sex on the beach, and she wasn't talking about the drink. Worse, she had a feeling she was no longer alone on said beach, and she was definitely not alone on the blanket. Logan was sprawled beside her, bare-chested, bare-footed, but thankfully jeans-clad, even if said jeans were unbuttoned and revealing a tantalizing...

Any further thought about Logan's happy trail slammed to a halt when a cool morning breeze flirted with her upper thighs and inched its way higher. Praying she was wrong and she wasn't as naked as the day she was born, Jenna lifted the jean jacket that covered her. Nope, she was not wrong, not wrong at all.

At the sound of young male voices just beyond the sand dunes, she swallowed a panicked whimper and pushed up on an elbow to look for her missing clothes. Unless they were buried in the sand, her panties, crinoline, and the top of her dress were gone. Wondering if the laughter she heard in those young male voices had anything to do with her missing clothes, she pushed herself higher to peek through the tall grass swaying in the breeze on the adjacent dune. She clutched Logan's jean jacket to her chest, thinking she was lucky he was a big man because she wasn't as indecently exposed as she might've otherwise been.

"Jesus." A gruff, sleep-laden voice came from behind her, and she glanced over her shoulder, unable to swallow an *oh crap* cry when she realized her front might be covered but her behind was exposed. And she realized this because Logan's eyes had gone wide.

Somewhere in the far recesses of her mind she was wondering what was with the shocked expression on his handsome face. She knew for a fact the man wasn't a prude. Besides that, it wasn't as if her clothes had magically come off on their own. He'd gotten her naked, with some help from her, of course. Okay, so a lot of help. She'd helped him get naked too. She blamed what might be characterized as her overly enthusiastic helpfulness on the full moon and an almost fervent need to erase Lorenzo and Gwyneth from her mind.

Logan had proved incredibly adroit at erasing them off the face of the planet. She frowned at the shadowy memory swimming its way to the surface. She could tell by the way her stomach jittered and jived that whatever she'd forgotten about last night she didn't want to remember right now. Yesterday's debacle had been more than enough to deal with, thank you very much. Today was all about regrouping and finding a way to move on, which meant she'd need some help from the man who now had an *oh crap* look on his face.

"Sorry, I—" She was two words into apologizing for

mooning him when he shot to his feet with the corners of the blanket clutched in his hands. Doing the walk of shame down Main Street half-naked would've been better than this, Jenna decided. He obviously regretted last night big-time.

Hoping to ease the morning-after awkwardness, she said, "So, I gu—" The *ess* came out on a squawk as Logan whipped the blanket out from under her, rolling her face-first into the sand. She blinked her eyes in shock and then lifted her head to spit out the grains that filled her mouth. What had happened to her incredibly hot, protective, and considerate one-night stand? Barely had the question formed in her head than her stomach did a nosedive to her toes, taking that shadowy memory from late last night along with it. Jenna had a feeling once she remembered what her mind was clearly trying to protect her from, she'd want to dive into the deep end of the ocean.

"I didn't moon you on purpose, you know. And I get that you obviously have somewhere else you'd rather be, but you didn't have to practically drown me in the sand." She looked up as the blanket floated over her and then covered her, leaving her in the dark.

"Be quiet," he muttered, and sat on the blanket, his hip tucked into her side. "Don't move. Poppy Harte's at the other end of the beach, and she has a long-range lens on her camera."

Along with owning the *Harmony Harbor Gazette* with her brother, Poppy did wedding photography on the side, which was how Jenna had met the woman last month. Arianna had hired her for Jenna's big day, which meant Poppy was one more person she had to call and cancel, and one more deposit to cover. She groaned into the arms she'd crossed beneath her face to avoid inhaling any more sand.

"I'm serious, Jenna. Not another word or sound and stay perfectly still. She's headed this way," he whispered, and it sounded like he was doing it out of the side of his mouth.

Okay, so it wouldn't look good if they were caught. Especially for Jenna, who was half-naked, and who, up until approximately sixteen hours ago, had been a happy, albeit clueless, bride-to-be. But she and Logan were consenting adults and the *Gazette* was a small-town paper, not the *National Enquirer*. It wasn't like they'd want half-naked pictures on the front page of the paper, even if the shirtless and shoeless man beside her looked like he'd stepped off *People*'s issue of the Sexiest Man Alive. So maybe they'd want Logan's photo on the front page after all, but Jenna had liked Poppy and didn't think the woman would take advantage of the situation for professional gain. Unless...

"You haven't slept with Poppy too, have you?" she whispered, her cheeks warming a bit as she asked. It wasn't her business, but it was a legitimate question given their current situation. If the answer was yes, he had indeed had sex with the attractive blonde, then Poppy might not be willing to keep this on the downlow.

"No, I haven't had sex with Poppy. Why would you even ask? Don't answer. I'm not joking around, Jenna.

If Wilson finds out about this, it gives credence to his theory , so not another word."

Jenna angled her head under the blanket, thinking about what he said. As she did, it hit her that they'd have far bigger worries to contend with than Officer Ryan Wilson if word got out about Jenna and Logan's night at the beach. Because while Lorenzo might've cheated on her, with her stepmother no less, the idea that Jenna would jump under the blanket with another man mere hours after Lorenzo dumped her... Yeah, his Italian-male pride wouldn't be able to handle the hit. He'd lash out. And Logan would be his target as much as her.

She shivered, and a heavy hand came to rest on her lower back mere inches from her behind, which sent another shiver down her spine. Only this one was heated and quickly spread throughout her body to settle low and heavy in the pit of her stomach. It wasn't a sexy, sultry heat; it was more. A feeling she'd experienced before. For other people, not herself. She certainly didn't want to feel it now, with him. She quickly shoved a niggling memory from the night before back in the protective vault.

"Hey, Poppy. How's it going?"

Jenna tensed under the blanket, wondering how Logan could sound so calm and cool. A silly thought given what he did for a living, she supposed. His strong fingers gently kneaded her lower back. She had a feeling he meant his touch to be comforting, but comforting wasn't the word she'd use. *Arousing, suggestive, erotic* were just some of the words that instantly came to mind.

She wished she could say the same of the feelings she'd had only seconds before. They'd be easier to explain if all they spoke to was desire.

"Good. How's it going with you?" Jenna heard Poppy ask, picking up an undertone in the woman's voice she couldn't read.

"I've been better."

Well, that didn't say much for their night together, Jenna thought, and then silently berated herself. How did she expect the man to feel knowing he could lose his job and his mother might very well be dying? He'd opened up last night and shared his worries with Jenna. Having lost a mother to cancer herself, she could commiserate.

"I'm not surprised. We ran the story on the front page." Okay, so that explained the hesitation Jenna had heard in Poppy's voice. "Don't worry. You came off a hero. Ryan and Lorenzo are no doubt getting hate e-mails as we speak. I'm sorry, Jenna. The guy's an idiot. You deserve better."

She felt Logan twist at the waist, like he was looking around. "Jenna? I don't know—"

"Long-range lens, Logan. I saw her. You can come out now, Jenna."

Now what was she supposed to do? As she tried to come up with a story to protect Logan, Jenna rolled over and sat up, clutching both the blanket and jean jacket to her chest. "Hi, Poppy," she said sheepishly, speaking in a depressed monotone. "Please don't tell anyone about this. I'm so ashamed. I don't know what came over me. The thought of losing my business and

Lorenzo to my stepmother was just too much for me to bear." She placed a hand on Logan's muscular forearm. "He really is a hero. I'd be dead if he hadn't come along and saved me."

Logan bowed his head and his broad, golden-brown shoulders rose on a deep inward breath.

Poppy looked from him to Jenna. "Are you saying you tried to...kill yourself?"

"It's so hard to hear you say it out loud. And I'm deeply ashamed to admit my weakness, but yes, I tried to drown myself. I heard it was a peaceful way to go. That's what happens when you drink too much and you're in a really bad place."

Logan lifted his head to stare at her. "Jenna."

She squeezed his forearm and refocused on Poppy. "Please don't mention this to anyone. I'd die if word of this got out, especially to my sisters. And Lorenzo."

"You can count on me. Mum's the word."

"Thank you. I'm so embarrassed you saw me like this. Logan gave me his jean jacket and T-shirt to wear, and now I can't find my clothes. You wouldn't have seen them, would you?"

Poppy shook her head and then turned to scan the beach. As she did, Logan leaned over and grabbed his T-shirt from the sand, holding Jenna's gaze as he shook it out and then tossed it to her, obviously not pleased.

She lifted a shoulder. What did he expect her to say? He should be thanking her for throwing herself under the bus on his behalf.

His lips remained flat and he gave his head an annoyed shake as he removed the blanket from her hands,

creating a tent for her to make herself decent in privacy.
Or as decent as you could be wearing an oversize
T-shirt without a bra and panties.

She put on the jean jacket too, looking up when Logan asked, "What were you doing down here anyway?"

She peeked over the edge of the blanket to see that
he was speaking to Poppy, not her.

"Someone found a nest of peepers last week, and I
wanted to take some photos." She lifted her camera, her
eyes narrowing at the distant sound of boys laughing.
She brought her camera to her eye, twisting the lens.
Seconds later, she said, "I think I've found your missing
clothes."

Logan stood, shielding his eyes to look down the
beach. She was thinking how incredible he looked
while at the same time wondering how much effort it
must take to keep his body in the shape it was in when
she caught his lips twitching. She sighed. "They're
wearing them, aren't they?"

"Nope, using them as flags."

Jenna was all for letting them keep her clothes—
the thought of retrieving her underwear from the
boys was embarrassing—but Arianna would kill her
if she didn't come home with her wedding gown. She
thought of the tattered, bloodstained layers of tulle
sitting in Logan's truck and considered driving back
to Charleston instead. Both options were equally un-
appealing. Maybe she'd start over someplace new,
like Timbuktu.

She started off at a determined walk when her ankle
reminded her that it was sprained, shooting a jarring

pain down her foot. It was all she could do to keep from crying out.

"Are you okay?" Poppy asked.

"I'm good, thanks."

Logan took her by the arm, turning her back to the blanket. "Sit. I'll get your clothes."

"Bossy man. Annoying too," she said as he headed off down the beach, glancing under her lashes at Poppy to see if her cranky tone of voice had fooled the woman. Jenna had to play the role of devastated jilted bride. And devastated jilted brides wouldn't be drooling over another man. The thought gave her pause. Why did she have to playact? She *was* a devastated jilted bride, wasn't she? Her lack of emotion didn't validate the description of herself, at least the devastated part, and that gave her cause to pause again. Maybe she was in shock.

"Don't forget off-the-charts gorgeous. Look at how ripped he is. The man's back forms a perfect V," Poppy said, joining Jenna on the blanket.

She was relieved when the woman brought her camera to her eye, hoping it meant she'd stop talking. Jenna already knew Logan was exceptional in pretty much every way and didn't need Poppy to validate her opinion. Okay, so that probably wasn't a good sign. She was having more of an emotional reaction to her one-night stand than to her ex-fiancé dumping her.

"Oh my gosh, I never thought I'd capture anything like this. It's amazing."

"I don't want to sound judgy or anything, but I'm not sure it's appropriate for you to be objectifying Logan that way. I understand it's hard to look at him and not—"

"What are you talking about?" Poppy said as she pushed to her feet. "I found the nest and a baby peep."

"Really?" She'd lived in Harmony Harbor for twelve years before moving to Charleston and had never seen a baby sandpiper, or a *peep*, as the locals called them. Jenna carefully rose to her feet to follow.

"Here, lean on me." Poppy offered her arm. "How did you hurt your ankle?"

"When it looked like Lorenzo and Ryan were going to make trouble for Logan, I ran to get Michael at the Salty Dog and tripped over my wedding gown."

"Ah, so that's where you were going." At Jenna's quizzical frown, Poppy said, "I must've taken the photo of you before you tripped. We entitled it *Runaway Bride*. You're on the front page."

Jenna stopped halfway up the sand dune. "So, basically, you've put every moment of one of the worst days of my life on the front page of the *Gazette*."

"Second and third pages too. These two are my favorites though." She turned the screen to Jenna.

The first was a photo of Logan striding across the road with her in his arms. "I didn't see you there."

Poppy tapped the lens. "Long range."

"Oh, right. I..." She trailed off as the second photo came into view. Logan was down on one knee, carefully fitting Jenna's foot into the glass shoe. Poppy had captured the one instant when Logan's and Jenna's eyes had met. And in that moment, Jenna knew what she'd been avoiding, the feeling she'd been pretending not to feel. She saw it now with her very own eyes. Logan Gallagher was her one and only.

If it were anyone other than herself, she'd be saying how this proved she was never meant to be with Lorenzo. And whether she wanted to admit it or not, he'd done her a favor calling off the wedding. They never would've been happy together.

"I thought I told you to stay put."

She turned to see Logan making his way toward them, fabric balled in his fist. It looked like her crinoline and top. She kept her eyes there. She didn't want to meet his gaze, afraid of what he'd see. What she'd see. She had to be wrong. This kind of thing didn't happen to her.

"Jenna, are you okay?"

She nodded to where they were headed. "Poppy spotted a nest and a peep."

When Logan reached them, Poppy transferred Jenna's hand from her arm to his. "I'm just going to take a quick peek. I'll come back when the tide's out and get a few shots of them leaving the nest."

Feeling self-conscious after what the photo revealed, Jenna removed her hand from Logan's arm. "I can take them. Thanks," she said, reaching for her clothes.

"It's okay. I've got them. Not all of them though. Your, ah, underwear is missing."

She was thankful that Logan hadn't retrieved it from the boys and wasn't carrying it around. It was a good thing it was missing. Or so Jenna thought until Poppy called out from where she crouched in the tall grass.

"I think I found your underwear." She stood up, looking pained.

Which meant Jenna was feeling pained. Could she

not catch a break? And then Poppy cleared up her mis-conception. Poppy's pained expression had nothing to do with Jenna's underwear. "I'm afraid the peep is dead. Can you check, Logan?"

"Sure."

Jenna limped after Logan, holding down the bottom of the T-shirt as she went to kneel at his side. The nest was nothing more than an indentation in the earth—her underwear mere inches away. Gingerly, she picked up her panties and pocketed them, eyeing the unmoving baby sandpiper as she did. It was a tiny ball of fluff, its legs twiglike, its beak long. Jenna looked around for some sign of its family. "He's all alone. Why would they abandon him?"

"Peeps leave the nest the day they hatch." Logan gently stroked the bird with his forefinger. "Maybe he's sick or hurt." Logan went to stand up.

"We can't just leave him."

"The boys probably stepped on him when they took off with your clothes, Jenna. He's too little to recover from that," Poppy said.

Jenna brought her face within an inch of the bird. She heard a tiny *peep*, and then the bird lifted its head, its eyes meeting hers. "It's okay. I won't leave you. Come here, baby," she said, carefully scooping him into her hand. She brought him close to her chest.

"Should've known," Logan murmured as he reached down to help her to her feet. "My brother uses a vet in town. I'll give him a call and get the name for you."

His cell rang, and he pulled the phone from the front pocket of his jeans. "Hey, I was just going to call you."

He paused, frowning. "What are you talking about? You said ten thirty. Okay, relax. I'm on my way. Don't worry about it. Jenna took care of it. She left Lorenzo a message last night. Told him she'd give the ring back if he dropped all charges."

"You're giving the ring back?" Poppy made a face when Jenna nodded. "Arianna is going to be ticked."

"I know, but it's a family—" Her gaze went to her ring finger, her naked ring finger, and she cried out, "It's gone! My ring is gone."

Chapter Eight

♥

Colleen Gallagher predicted that the guests dining on the patio at Greystone Manor would have their peaceful Sunday brunch ruined within the next fifteen minutes. Colleen's great-grandsons had staged an intervention for this morning. Knowing their mother, Maura, for as long as she had, Colleen gave the intervention a million-to-one odds of going as the boys had planned and one-to-one odds of Maura throwing a tantrum and making a scene.

Now, if it had been the boys alone who were approaching their mother with their concerns, the odds would've been in their favor. But they'd made the critical error of including their father, Colleen's grandson Sean. Back in February, Maura had left her husband of forty years without an explanation. Colleen didn't need one to know what was going on.

Sean, who years before had been governor of Massachusetts, showed no interest in another political career and had recently retired as partner at the high-powered law firm where he'd worked for more than a decade. A state of affairs that wouldn't have gone over well with her social-climbing granddaughter-in-law and was the reason Colleen believed Maura had really left Sean.

But, she conceded, there had been signs these past few months that the boys' concern over their mother's health was warranted. Namely, that Maura had lasted this long at the manor without eviscerating the staff, guests, members of the family, and the people of Harmony Harbor while in a temper. It was as though she was putting her best foot forward, making up for past transgressions to ensure Saint Peter opened the pearly gates instead of slamming them shut, leaving her to waste away in purgatory. Colleen could empathize.

She'd died nineteen months before, on All Saints Day, and her worries had been similar to Maura's, she imagined. Luckily, she'd missed her ride to heaven and had been using her time living betwixt and between to right her wrongs. Over the years, she'd had a tendency to meddle in everyone's affairs. But what could she say? If you lived to be a hundred and four like she had, not only did you think you knew better than everyone else, you most likely did.

Only she'd made the mistake of writing down everyone's secrets, including her own, in her book, *The Secret Keeper of Harmony Harbor*, without considering the consequences should it fall in the wrong hands. Last Christmas, her daughter-in-law Kitty had found Colleen's book and shared it with Jasper, Colleen's former right-hand man and confidant, and they'd been getting up to no good.

Now, if you asked the pair of them, they'd tell you they were simply righting Colleen's wrongs. There was some truth to that to be sure, but they often made a hash of it before things eventually worked out as Colleen had planned. Because not only was she trying to make up for the hurts she'd caused in the past, she was trying to ensure her great-grandchildren's happily-ever-afters. And unlike half the town, who apparently had matchmaker-itis, Colleen knew exactly what she was doing. She had a gift, you see. So far, she'd successfully matched five of her great-grandsons with their one true loves. Next up was Logan, who was admittedly causing her some concern.

She'd known who was his perfect match for years. Only wouldn't you know it, the woman was getting married at the manor next Saturday. It was an outdoor wedding or Colleen might've been able to come up with a way to scare off the groom. But she was tethered to the manor and couldn't put so much as a toe outside.

A shame, because it wouldn't take much to scare off the groom. Of that she was certain. She'd listened in on their wedding planning session at the manor and was disappointed to think the girl could be fooled by a pretty face. She'd expected more of Jenna. She'd seen so much potential in the child growing up.

Oh well. It looked like it was back to the drawing board for Colleen. She'd take a peek at Maura and Kitty's list of matrimonial candidates for Logan. Just as a jumping off point, of course.

There they were now. Kitty was walking with Maura down the stairs into the dining room, chummy as all get-out. They were both outfitted in lovely, and no doubt expensive, spring floral dresses. Maura's nut-brown locks were cut in a chic style, as was Kitty's white hair, and their makeup was impeccable. Their current relationship bore no resemblance to the backstabbing in-laws they'd been in the past. Colleen supposed it was best this way. Maura would need an ally once her husband and sons began their intervention.

Colleen shook her head at the idea that they'd taken four months to get to this point. "I would've gotten to the bottom of the matter a week after she'd arrived, Simon," Colleen told the black cat who sat at her feet. If she was a witch, he'd be her familiar. But she wasn't a witch; she was a ghost. A ghost of her former self sounded better to her than the idea of being an actual ghost, which always brought to mind the television show her great-grandchildren used to watch—Casper something or other.

Colleen looked down at herself. She had on the black shoes, dress, and pearls they'd buried her in. She shuddered at the thought and corrected herself—the outfit they'd buried her *body* in. She looked up to see Kitty and Maura headed across the dining room. Set in one of the manor's towers, the room was an octagon and decorated in a rich, nautical theme.

The smell of bacon and eggs coming from the kitchen mingled with the strong scent of lilacs wafting through the open French doors that led onto the patio. It was a warm day with plenty of sunshine. Colleen wished for rain. She didn't know how else to keep the two women inside. It wouldn't be easy for her to pick up the gist of their conversation lollygagging around the French doors.

Besides, people would be walking through her left and right if she was hanging about there. With all the time that had gone by, she should be used to people walking through her body, but she wasn't. It gave her a bone-deep chill and caused her stomach to turn each and every time they did. Oh well. Like the younger generation said these days, she'd have to suck it up.

Kitty and Maura had stepped onto the patio, greeting the guests at the surrounding tables in a friendly manner. All Colleen could think while watching Maura with a genial smile on her attractive face was the woman must be sicker than she'd thought.

And it looked like they were about to find out because Maura's husband had arrived. Classically handsome with his distinguished silver hair brushed back from his face, Sean wore a blue short-sleeved shirt that matched his eyes and a pair of navy pants. He looked polished and prosperous and slightly perturbed as he stood surveying the room. His expression lightened when Connor, his middle son, joined him.

A high-powered attorney, Connor was as polished and prosperous-looking as his father. Only his hair was jet-black, his shirt white, and his pants black. They greeted each other warmly. Sean had a close relationship with his sons despite his problems with his wife. He might be a stranger at the manor these days but not in their lives.

They were chatting at the top of the stairs leading

into the dining room, so Colleen made her way back to them, hoping to get the inside scoop.

"It wasn't my idea, Dad. It was Michael's."

Sean nodded as he slid his hands into his pockets, looking toward the patio. "It won't work, you know. She has no interest in coming home, no interest in me or our marriage."

No matter that he tried to hide it, Colleen heard the hurt along with the anger in his voice. Sean was a proud man, and Maura leaving him for no apparent reason had undoubtedly wounded his pride. He was stubborn to boot, which only made matters worse. Instead of coming after his wife, trying to get her to talk, he'd stayed in Boston and gone on with his life. There was a reason they said pride goeth before a fall.

Connor rubbed the back of his neck while looking around the manor's lobby. There was a bar in the corner, empty save for the bartender taking inventory, and a massive stone fireplace in the center of the room, beside which an elderly man in the brown leather wingback chair read the weekend edition of the *Harmony Harbor Gazette*. Across from where Connor and Sean stood was the grand staircase. Connor's brothers were nowhere to be seen. She assumed that was who he was looking for. The lad didn't like conflict unless it was in the courtroom and did his best to avoid turmoil and messy emotions.

He was searching for naught. His brothers had yet to arrive. Colleen had checked Logan's room earlier, and he wasn't around. It had struck her as odd at the time until she remembered his penchant for running. The lad ran for miles no matter the weather.

With a resigned look on his handsome face, Connor said, "Dad, this isn't about you and Mom splitting up. Neither of you seem interested in reconciling so, mostly, we've given up."

Colleen saw a hint of disappointment in Sean's eyes before he blinked the emotion away. "Then I don't understand what I'm doing here, son."

"Michael and Logan should be here by now. I'll give them a call." He pulled his cell phone from his pocket.

Sean's hand closed over Connor's. "What aren't you telling me?"

Connor pulled in a deep, noisy breath, briefly averting his gaze from his father's before admitting, "We're not sure, but we think Mom's sick, Dad. Michael finally got Gloria to talk. The afternoon before Mom ended up at the manor, she'd gone to her doctor. She was upset when Gloria talked to her later. She said something about tests the doctor ordered, but that she didn't need tests to tell her what she already knew."

Sean looked like he'd been sucker punched. "Why didn't she tell me? Why would she want to go through this alone?" He briefly closed his eyes. "Her mother," he said, and then strode down the stairs to the dining room.

"Hold up a sec, Dad," Connor called after Sean, groaning when his father ignored him and walked determinedly in the direction of the patio. "Of course, I'd be the one left holding the bag and dealing with the fallout," he muttered to himself as he took off after his father.

Too busy riffling through her memories, searching

for a clue as to why Sean had mentioned Maura's
mother, Colleen didn't follow the two men weaving
their way through the tables and waitstaff. She knew
the answer was there. Somewhere in the recesses of
her mind lay the answer to everything. The reason behind Sean and Maura's breakup, the reason for her
granddaughter-in-law's silence.

There was more to their story, things Colleen had
long forgotten. They'd be in her book though. She'd
need Jasper's help. He couldn't see or hear her, but he
knew she was about. He'd sensed her presence mere
weeks after she'd passed. Simon was her tell. Jasper
knew wherever the cat was, Colleen wasn't far behind.
For the most part that was true.

She looked around for Simon and caught sight of him
through the French doors. He was perched in a tree. "A
fine time you chose to go gadding about." She grimaced
at the expression on Maura's face. She'd spotted her es-
tranged husband coming her way.

As Colleen started toward the French doors, she
spied her great-grandsons, Michael and Logan, making
their way across the lobby, or great room, as she still
thought of it. She quickly backtracked. They seemed to
be having a disagreement of sorts.

"We can talk later. Right now I've gotta grab a
shower. I won't be more than ten minutes," Logan said,
heading for the grand staircase. He was staying in the
tower room, Colleen's old suite.

She'd like to tell him to grab a shirt while he was at
it. Unlike his brother, who was neatly turned out in a
golf shirt and navy pants, Logan had on jeans and a jean

jacket and not much else. And he looked like he'd been rolling around in the sand.

Michael grabbed the back of his brother's jacket. "We can't talk later. Look." As Logan turned, Michael pointed across the room. "Dad's already here, and Mom looks like she's close to losing it."

Logan took in the situation. "She'll be fine. Grams and Connor are with her. They'll calm her down. So will you, once you stop wasting time lecturing me."

Colleen didn't necessarily agree with Logan. Maura loved all three of her sons equally, but Logan had a way with his mother. His quiet strength and calm manner steadied her.

"Lecturing you? I'm not lecturing you. I'm trying to protect you."

"I know, and I appreciate it. But until Jenna hears back from Lorenzo, there's nothing more that either of us can do."

Colleen frowned. What did Jenna and her fiancé have to do with Logan? And what exactly was Michael protecting his brother from?

"Other than making sure Mom doesn't happen to get a glimpse of the front page of the *Harmony Harbor Gazette*? I have no idea," Michael said.

Logan looked past his brother. "Connor and Grams could use a hand."

"You better make that five minutes, big brother," Michael said before rushing off toward the dining room stairs.

Frustrated with her inability to get the information she needed, Colleen felt like her head was about to explode. This was the problem with being unable to communicate and to step foot outside the manor. If she were able to get out and about, she'd know exactly what was going on. And there was definitely something going on if it was on the front page of the *Harmony Harbor Gazette*.

She was sure she'd seen the newspaper somewhere. All she had to do was remember... There, by the fireplace. She hurried across the great room to the older gentleman perusing the *Gazette* in a leisurely manner. She crouched down to look up at the front page, a smile slowly spreading across her face as she read the story.

She'd been worrying for nothing. Jenna's fiancé had conveniently taken care of matters on his own. The girl had gotten off lucky in Colleen's opinion. She hoped Jenna realized that sooner rather than later. She had plans for her after all—plans to marry her off to Logan.

And while Colleen would rather have had Logan leave the Secret Service of his own accord with his exemplary record intact, she highly doubted the lad would've left before retirement. His job was his life, his passion. And no doubt the reason why he was still single. Which worked to Colleen's advantage because he was still single but also to her disadvantage because he obviously intended to remain so.

She had enough on her plate with Maura and Sean, so she'd look only at the advantage. Logan would remain in town to fight the charges against him, and Jenna, from what the boys said, was doing her best to help, which gave Colleen time to work her matchmaking magic on the pair.

Her plate felt a little lighter, and she rose to her feet with a smile still on her face, thanking the good Lord for giving her a break. She had a feeling she'd need all her mental acuity to deal with whatever lay ahead for Maura and Sean. She cocked her head at the sound of upraised voices coming from the dining room and looked at the anchor-and-chain clock above the bar. Exactly fifteen minutes, just like she'd predicted. She was good.

But her prideful moment was cut short not only by concern for the guests who were having their leisurely brunch disturbed, but by the hulking man who pushed open the manor's dark medieval door and stood there taking everything in like he was king of the castle.

"Aye, it's good to be home, it is," he said in a thick Irish brogue with a roguish grin Colleen would recognize anywhere. And if she hadn't recognized the slash of white teeth in his ruggedly handsome face, she'd have recognized his twinkling Gallagher blue eyes. Daniel had come home to Harmony Harbor. The last time they'd seen him at the manor was ten years before, at his father's funeral.

If her heart were still beating, it would've given a nervous hitch. Wherever Daniel went, trouble was sure to follow. Women too. He'd been a lady's man from the moment he'd come out of Kitty's womb. Colleen had adored the wee charmer, but she'd had her grandson's number. She always could tell when he was up to no good. And right then, she could practically see a plan forming in his canny brain.

"What is it, my boy? What's brought you home at

long last?" At almost the same time as she asked the question, the fragment of a memory crossed her mind and a puzzle piece fit neatly into place. She'd been right. There'd be no peace at the manor. Daniel was the missing piece in the Maura-and-Sean puzzle. "Lord help us."

* * *

Logan bowed his head as another frantic text came in from his brother. He'd received texts from his father, his mother, his grandmother, and Michael seconds after stepping out of the shower.

This was Connor's third text. Logan didn't respond as he closed the tower room door and headed for the spiral staircase to the floor below. It always struck him as odd that Connor, one of the top defense attorneys in Boston, couldn't deal with his own parents. Then again, Logan supposed he shouldn't be surprised. It'd always fallen on him to act as intermediary in family disputes. Maybe because he was oldest.

He glanced at his phone when he reached the third floor, wondering if he'd missed a call from Jenna when he was in shower. Jenna, the woman he'd made love to last night on a public beach. He gave his head an irritated shake. Who was he to be critical of his brother? Logan protected people for a living, and he'd broken every rule in an agent's handbook. He hadn't done either himself or Jenna any favors. His attempt to lose himself inside her, forget about his worries, help her forget about hers, had just opened a big can of whoopass. And his ass deserved to be whooped. He'd seen the way she looked at him this morning, and it was a look he recognized all too well.

She probably thought she had feelings for him now. The female brain was wired differently than a man's. When women had sex, they bonded, formed an attachment. It was just the way their neurochemicals worked. He knew it was a generalization, but it fit with what he'd learned about Jenna. A woman who believed in knights in shining armor and happily-ever-after. For her sake, he hoped Lorenzo had cured her of the beliefs. Healthier for her if he had. But whether it was healthier or not, Logan would much rather it be her ex and not him who'd cured her of her happily-ever-after fantasy.

He sighed. It seemed Jenna wasn't the only one who'd formed an attachment. It wasn't a big deal, he told himself at the tension tightening his shoulders. She was sweet, funny, and surprisingly sexy...and unsurprisingly giving, even in bed. And he'd left her cradling a half-dead bird in one hand while digging in the sand with the other, trying to find the ring that had been meant to buy his freedom. He wanted to stay, but she insisted he leave, apparently as concerned about his mother as he was. No, not just apparently. One thing he knew for certain about Jenna was she was kind and compassionate. Her concern had been genuine.

As genuine as her attempt to protect him this morning with her crazy cover story about why she was half-naked on the beach. Another strike against him; he should've gotten them out of there before the sun came up. His mother's voice reached him then, just as he hit the second floor. He glanced over the wooden railing, noting shadows in the atrium just off the lobby. When he'd suggested they get her someplace private, he was thinking along the lines of the library or study. The outer wall of the atrium was frosted glass cubes, and its wall of windows faced onto Kismet Cove. Far less privacy than his mother on a tear warranted.

He glanced at his phone, scrolling through recent calls and messages. The last thing his mother needed was to hear about his arrest on top of everything else, but if she did, he wanted to be able to give her something to alleviate her worries. His too, he supposed. And his brother's.

There was nothing from Jenna. Which meant she hadn't found the ring or heard from Lorenzo. No matter what Michael said, Logan couldn't put it off any longer. He had to reach out to his superior. But as he walked down the grand staircase, his finger hovering over the key, his mother ran crying from the atrium.

He shoved his phone in his pocket and rushed down the stairs. "Mom," he called out to her, but she waved him off. She hurried into the sitting room near the bank of elevators, slamming the door shut. His father and another man nearly knocked him over as they raced after her, arguing.

"Where the hell do you get off? She's my wife, not yours, Daniel."

"She would've been mine had you not stolen her from me all those years ago," the other man said with a thick Irish accent. "But I'm here for her now. And it's a good thing I am. Leaving her to fight the cancer on her own." The man *tsk*ed. "Makes me ashamed to call you brother."

Logan reached them in time to catch his father's fist before it landed in his brother's face.

"Thanks, laddie. You've got a good grip on you. A fine punch too. I saw the damage you did to that Italian lad's nose in the paper. You got that from me, you know." His uncle shuffled his feet and did a two-punch jab. "I did a bit of boxing in my day. Shame about him charging you though. You want, I can talk to him. I've got a way with words. Something of a charmer, I am."

The door opened, and his mother appeared, a tissue pressed to her nose.

"Aw, there's my girl. Come here. Let Danny Boy give you a hug."

His mother ignored the man, her focus instead on Logan. "What is he talking about, darling?"

Logan moved to his mother, recognizing his mistake a second too late. His father took the opportunity and punched his brother in the face.

Chapter Nine

♥

Jenna sat in the passenger seat of Poppy's Accord. The other woman glanced at her as she pulled in front of a white Colonial on Main Street. "Don't get too attached to her, Jenna. The vet didn't hold out much hope of her surviving."

"Don't listen to her, Pippa. You're going to be just fine," Jenna murmured to the baby bird, who the vet had informed them was a girl and who, he'd surmised, had been accidently stepped on as the boys raced by. Which only served to make Jenna feel a certain kinship toward the wounded peep, twice as guilty, and permanently attached.

After a few minutes of digging in the sand failed to turn up Lorenzo's ring, Poppy had offered to take Jenna to the vet. They'd stopped off at the other woman's house first so Jenna could clean up and change into a pair of Poppy's shorts and a T-shirt. The last thing Jenna had wanted was to go home looking like she did without the ring on her finger.

"Yes, because the best way to stay unattached is

to name the bird," Poppy said, her voice laced with sarcasm.

"You sound like Arianna," Jenna said, stroking the top of the bird's fuzzy head where she lay tucked in brightly colored silk. Poppy had given her a scarf, and Jenna had tied it around her neck, fashioning a sling-type carrier for Pippa.

Poppy laughed, but the amusement didn't quite reach her eyes. "Bitter and cold?"

"No, of course not." She tilted her head to the side. "Do you really think my sister's bitter and cold?" It would almost be a relief if Poppy did. Jenna had seen Arianna with her customers and had been out with her socially. She was lovely, far kinder to other people than she'd been to Jenna throughout the years. But maybe Jenna had missed something and Arianna could be as sarcastic and cutting with others as she'd been to her in the past.

"I shouldn't have said that. It just popped out."

"No, I don't think it did."

"I guess you're right. I heard her with you yesterday. You shouldn't let her get away with speaking to you like that, Jenna. Especially ... " She twisted in the driver's seat to face her. "Promise me, if you ever feel anything close to what you did last night, you'll call me."

She'd hardly known Poppy when she told her the lie this morning, but after spending so much time with her today...

"Don't be mad at me, but I lied to you this morning. I wasn't so distraught after Lorenzo dumped me that I tried to drown myself."

Poppy reared back. "Shut up. You had sex on the beach with Logan Gallagher?"

"Okay, I know it's pretty unbelievable. But you could've faked that it wasn't entirely inconceivable that a man like Logan could be attracted to me."

She frowned. "What are you talking about? I'm not surprised Logan would be attracted to you. Why would I be? What surprised me is that *you* had sex with him on a public beach just hours after your fiancé dumped you. I don't know. I guess I took you for a goody-goody."

"You're right. I'm a ho."

"Trust me, no woman in her right mind would give up the chance to have sex with Logan Gallagher. Ho or no ho." She undid her seat belt and opened the driver-side door. "Was he as good as I'm imagining he was?"

"Better," she said without thinking, and then realized what she'd done. Even though it was the truth... "This is off-the-record, Poppy. You can't tell anyone. Ever. Ryan and Lorenzo would use it against Logan."

"I never thought about that, but you're probably right. Ryan definitely has it in for the Gallaghers, and if Lorenzo didn't have it in for Logan, he would if he found this out."

"I know, right?" she said as she closed the passenger-side door and joined Poppy on the sidewalk.

"Yeah, men. You can't live with them, and you can't live without them." Poppy sounded a little bitter and cold just then.

"Yes, you can... live without them, I mean. And that's exactly what I plan to do. I'm thinking about starting a self-help group for women who were brought up on fairy tales and believe in true love and Prince Charming." Okay, so she sounded a little bitter now too.

"Sign me up."

"Really?"

"Yeah. For sure. Julia might even let us use Books and Beans for our meetings."

"Um, Julia has a weekly story hour for the kids and dresses up as characters from fairy tales. I can't see her wanting anti-fairy-tale women holding their meetings at her bookstore, Poppy."

"You're right. She'd probably stage an intervention. I bet Shay would let us hold our meetings at the Salty Dog."

"She's marrying a Gallagher prince, remember?"

Poppy opened the door to the newspaper, walked in, and turned on the light. "We can hold our meetings here. I have a feeling we won't have all that many members." She turned, frowning at Jenna. "Wait a minute. Does this mean you're staying in town?"

She nodded. Logan had suggested it last night when they were lying in the afterglow, looking up at the night sky to find the North Star. "At least until the will gets settled." Her cell phone buzzed with an incoming message. Being careful not to jar Pippa in the sling, Jenna pulled her phone from her pocket. "It's Arianna again. I better get going."

"Just go. I honestly don't want your money."

Poppy hadn't cashed Arianna's deposit check, but it was important to Jenna that her stepsister saw that she'd taken care of it. She'd return the check to Arianna, along with the paid-in-full deposit invoice. "Everyone else is getting paid their deposit, Poppy. I want you to take it. You could've booked another wedding."

"Fine. But I'm only taking a hundred bucks." She nodded at Jenna's cell phone. "Did you ask her where they moved your car?"

"I'll do that now." Jenna had noticed her car wasn't where she'd left it when she and Poppy had driven by. Her keys hadn't been in the Tie the Knot bag, so she assumed Arianna or Serena had them.

Poppy walked to the desk across the room, pushing papers aside to locate the cash register underneath. "My brother's a slob," she said as she punched in the charge. "I'm running my photography business through the newspaper, so it'll show up as the *Gazette* on your statement."

"Great." When she didn't receive a response about the car from Arianna, she walked over and held her iPhone over the cash machine. "You're set up with Apple Pay, aren't you?"

"Yeah." Poppy reached over and cleared the machine when an insufficient funds message appeared on the screen. "Try again."

She did and got the same message. She was positive she'd used her wedding savings account, which had more than sufficient funds. Though it was possible she'd used her checking account, which could be running low. "I'm sure I used the right account. Would you mind trying again?"

"No problem," Poppy said, but she eyed the machine nervously.

INSUFFICIENT FUNDS flashed once again on the screen. "I don't understand."

"Jenna, you said your car keys and your wallet weren't in the bag Serena left at the bar. Is it possible someone at the Salty Dog stole them or that someone stole them from Tie the Knot? It was unlocked for—"

"Oh no, don't say that. Arianna will never let me live it down if that's what happened. It couldn't have happened at the Salty Dog though. Shay had the bag behind the bar with her, and no one messes with Shay." She wished she were more like her best friend.

"Same could be said for Arianna, you know. And everyone knows Ryan is interested in Serena, so I don't think they'd mess with her either. Unless…Jenna, is there any chance Lorenzo stole your car and the money from your account?"

"No. Logan said Lorenzo wasn't charged with anything and left right after giving his statement. They interviewed him first so he could go to the hospital."

"Okay. Give me a minute. I'm going to check on a couple things." Poppy pulled out a chair and had Jenna sit while she went to the neat and uncluttered desk in the corner of the room.

While she waited, Arianna responded. *How would I move your car? I don't have your keys. Not to mention, why would I?*

Which most likely meant she didn't have her wallet either. She was about to share the information with Poppy, but she was on the phone with North Shore General. She disconnected and met Jenna's gaze. "Lorenzo never showed up at the hospital last night. In Bloom is across from where you parked. They have a security camera." She was back on the phone before Jenna could tell her not to bother.

As much as she didn't want to admit it, she could see Lorenzo striking out at her like this. He was probably holding her car and bank account hostage until she gave him back his ring. A ring she didn't hold out much hope of finding. She called him. It went straight to voice mail again. This time she didn't leave him a message; instead she called her bank. She'd have them freeze her account. Within seconds of giving her banking information and punching in her security password to prove her identity, she learned she had nothing to freeze.

"They got him on camera stealing your car, Jenna. He had your keys, so that probably means he has your wallet too. You should call your bank."

She stared at her phone, her vision blurred. "I did. He cleaned me out."

"Don't panic. We'll call the police. You weren't married yet, so it's not like he can claim communal property, right? You know what? You should call Logan. Get him to put you in touch with his brother Connor."

Jenna bowed her head and squeezed her eyes tight. Tears still managed to leak out the corners. How had she not seen who he was?

She felt a hand on her knee. Poppy was crouched beside her. Jenna cleared her throat. "A couple days ago, he suggested we have a joint account. Supposedly his family gives cash as a wedding gift, and he said the bank was giving him a hard time setting up an account because he only had a visitor's visa. I didn't check out his story. I just did as he asked. But I didn't think he'd have access to my savings account. It was only supposed to be the checking account. I feel like such an idiot."

"The guy stole your car and your money. Don't let him steal anything else. You need a lawyer, Jenna. Call Logan. He'll—" She broke off when a tall man with blond hair rushed into the office. "What are you doing here? I thought you were having brunch at the manor."

"I was until all hell broke loose. Hey. Jenna, right? I'm Byron. Poppy's brother." He smiled and came around the desk. Pulling out his chair, he plunked himself down, pushed up his sleeves, and wiggled his fingers.

"You get a big story or something?"

"You got it," he responded to Poppy. Then he glanced at Jenna and grimaced "But I just realized it's not going to play in Logan's favor, and he's a good guy."

"What happened?" both she and his sister asked at almost the same time.

"Things got out of hand, and he was trying to break up a fight between his father and his uncle." Byron took out his phone and held it up. "As you can see, it looks bad for him. I think he was trying to block his uncle's punch and elbowed his father in the nose while he was at it. Someone must've called the cops, and Wilson arrived on the scene. He started shooting off his mouth about Logan having an uncontrollable temper and thanked him for strengthening their case against him. Then Logan's father and uncle came to his defense. Wilson didn't take kindly to their threats and arrested them."

Poppy reached across the desk and took his phone, deleting the photo. "You're not writing the story. I've got a better one."

"It better be, because I guarantee there are several versions of that photo already online along with the story, Pop-Tart. It won't look good that the local newspaper isn't covering the story and everyone else is. In fact, some people might say we're in bed with the Gallaghers."

Jenna hoped no one was saying that about her. Although right now, she'd love to rub it in Lorenzo's face that she'd slept with Logan last night and that he was a far better lover than Lorenzo could ever dream of being. After the total humiliation of knowing that she'd been taken in by him, of knowing that he'd stolen her car and the money she been saving since she was a little girl, she wanted him to suffer. No, she needed him to, so she poured out her anger and humiliation into a text.

As Poppy and Byron discussed a replacement story, Jenna scanned what she'd typed, imagining Lorenzo's shock when he opened it, his fear that she really would hire a lawyer who'd go after him with the sole purpose of not only getting back her car and her money but sending him back to Italy without his precious ring. Her finger hovered over Delete All as she vowed to get rid of not only her text but him for good.

"Did you not hear anything I just said?" Poppy asked, taking the phone from her, no doubt as a means of getting her attention. It got her attention all right. She heard the familiar *whoosh* of a text being sent. Poppy must've read the panic in her expression because she looked from Jenna to the phone's screen and said, "Oh crap."

"What's going on?" Byron reached across the desk to take Jenna's phone from his sister before she could stop him. As he scanned the text, an eyebrow shot up. "Are you sure you want to write a story about how Lorenzo conned Jenna? Because I'm thinking our female audience would love to hear just how amazing Logan Gallagher really—"

Poppy grabbed the phone from him. "No one thinks you're funny. That was privileged information, and Jenna will sue if she finds out you've breathed a word of it."

"We're partners, sister dearest. If she sues me, it means she's suing you too."

"Byron," Poppy muttered.

"Relax. I'm sorry, Jenna. I shouldn't have teased you. We'll do the story on Lorenzo. If there's dirt on the guy, we'll find it. And while we're at it, we'll look into Wilson. Find out why he's got it in for the Gallaghers. There, am I back in your good graces, little sister?"

"If you get enough evidence on Lorenzo to get him kicked out of the country, maybe."

He leaned back in his chair to study his sister. "I should've known. It reminds you of what happened with—" He lifted his hand. "Off-limits. Understood. We all have a right to our secrets. Except Lorenzo and Wilson, of course."

And Jenna, because obviously she'd just agreed to have the story of how badly Lorenzo used her, how big a fool she really was, splashed across the front page of the *Gazette* for everyone in Harmony Harbor to see, including her stepsisters.

"You know, I think we'll have enough of a story to serialize it. Maybe run it for three to four weeks," Byron said to his sister.

Jenna got unsteadily to her feet. "I should get going. Pippa's probably hungry, and the tide will be going out soon." And maybe she'd spend another night at the beach, this time alone, because the last thing she wanted to do was go home and prove to Arianna and Serena that they'd been right about her all along.

But thirty minutes later, when she'd finally limped her way onto the beach, she discovered she wasn't alone after all. Logan was there, moving a metal detector over the spot she'd searched that morning. He looked lost in thought and not happy. Knowing what she did, she couldn't say she blamed him.

As though sensing someone's presence, he looked over, his smile more subdued than the one she'd seen yesterday. "Hey. I wasn't expecting to see you. How's the ankle?"

"It's okay. The compression bandage helps." Along with the T-shirt and denim shorts, Poppy had loaned the bandage.

"Did you walk over from Main Street?" At her nod, he gestured to a mound of sand. "Sit down and give your ankle a rest. I've gone over that spot a couple of times already."

She looked at the white-capped waves rolling onto shore; she had some time before the tide went out. He took her arm and guided her to the spot. "I can manage myself, you know," she said with a smile.

"I know." He smiled back, and this time it was more like the one she remembered. She realized why when he nodded at the scarf. "I see you haven't given up on him."

"It's a *she*, not a *he*, and her name is Pippa," she said as Logan helped her awkwardly lower herself to the mound of sand.

He stroked the top of the bird's head. "Cute."

His gaze held hers, and she grew flustered, more from the way her body was responding to the look in his eyes than the intensity in his gaze. Which was probably why she blurted, "How's your mom? Michael wasn't right, was he?"

"Yeah, he was."

"Oh, Logan, I'm so sorry. I shouldn't have said anything."

"No, it's fine." Obviously it wasn't because he backed away, putting some distance between them. Picking up the metal detector, he returned to sweeping it over the sand.

She didn't know what else to say and considered leaving him on his own. But she didn't want to. He'd stayed with her on one of the worst days of her life. She didn't want to think what it would've been like without him there to lean on. "Are you okay? Is there anything I can do?"

"I'm just trying to process it all. Figure out how to

get my mom to go to the doctor, have the tests, deal with it instead of burying her head in the sand." He glanced at the metal detector, giving his head a slight shake at his choice of words, she presumed.

"Does she not want to have treatment?" After a year and a half of chemo and radiation, her mother had refused to have any more.

"She doesn't even have a definitive diagnosis. The doctor wanted to do more tests. She never went back. She got into her car and came here. Her mother, my maternal grandmother, had ovarian cancer. Today was the first time my brothers and I heard about it. The first time we heard about a lot of things, actually. Anyway, as soon as the doctor brought up the possibility she had ovarian cancer, she shut down. She was in her late teens when her mom was fighting the disease. I guess it left a pretty big impression on her."

Jenna nodded, knowing a little something about that herself. "It would. But now that it's out in the open, she has her family to lean on. You can talk about her options and figure out next steps."

"She doesn't want to talk about it, at least to us. We're hoping my grandmother can get her to open up."

"Give her time."

"That's the thing, Jenna. She might not have time."

"You probably don't want to hear this, but in the end, it's her decision. You just have to find a way to support her."

"Easy for you to say. You're not the one who has to stand by and watch your..." He bowed his head and then raised his gaze to hers. "I'm sorry. That was a crappy thing for me to say. I forgot you lost your mom to cancer."

"It's okay. I do understand how you feel, Logan. You're dealing with a lot today."

He gave a dry laugh and came to sit beside her. "You have no idea."

"I might. I was at the *Gazette* when Byron came back from the manor."

"You're kidding me. He was there?"

"Yes, but don't worry. He's not printing the story." She stopped short of telling him about the story Byron *was* publishing. As hard as it would be to tell her stepsisters how badly Lorenzo had used and abused her, it would be far worse having to share with Logan. She had no doubt he'd be kinder and more compassionate than Arianna upon hearing the news, but Jenna didn't want him to know just how big a sucker she'd been. And that was something else she didn't want to delve too deeply into—her feelings for the man sitting beside her.

"At this point, it doesn't really matter if he does or not. Wilson didn't appreciate my uncle and my father threatening him and took it upon himself to call my supervisor. Until further notice, I'm on administrative leave." He looked out to sea as he slowly moved the metal detector back and forth over the sand between his bent knees.

"I'm so sorry. This is all my—"

He placed a finger gently on her lips. "No, it's not. Maybe it's for the best. I can take some time to spend with my mother."

Her lips tingled, her body aglow from just that simple, innocent touch. If Poppy knew how Jenna felt right now, she'd kick her out of the anti–Prince Charming club before it even got started. A metallic *ping*ing drew her attention. It was the metal detector. Logan leaned over and began digging in the sand. Seconds later, he grinned and held up the ring. Rubbing it clean on his jeans, he took her hand and slipped it on her finger. "At least one thing went right today."

She didn't have the heart to ruin the moment. She couldn't tell him just how bad things had gotten.

Chapter Ten

♥

It took a concerted effort for Logan to place the pink diamond on Jenna's finger. It had nothing to do with size. The ring slid easily onto her narrow finger. The problem was he didn't want to see another man's ring on her hand. The thought brought him up short. Clearly, Logan had too much going on right now and wasn't thinking straight. Thinking straight? He was having a hard time breathing right.

Despite his brothers' earlier worries, and his own for that matter, it was still a shock to discover his mom had cancer. Then, as if it couldn't get worse, she more or less told them she had no interest in fighting. Not fighting was anathema to him. How could she just give up like that? It felt like she was giving up on them. He didn't know if he could stand by and watch her die. He wasn't made that way.

And maybe that's why, while he was sliding an engagement ring on Jenna's finger with a smile that he wasn't close to feeling on his face, he said to her, "How? How am I supposed to support her if she won't fight?"

Jenna made a soft sound of sympathy and leaned forward. Placing her hands on his shoulders, she touched her forehead to his. "I promise, when the time comes, you'll know how to support her. You've had a terrible shock on top of a crappy twenty-four hours. Give yourself a break."

"A few of those hours weren't crappy." Neither of them had said a word to each other about last night. At the time, he'd thought it was the best way to play it. No embarrassing morning-after rehash. Granted, Poppy's arrival was hardly conducive to intimate conversation. But he didn't want Jenna to think he was blowing her off, that she was just a booty call. She was more than that.

And as he sat with his forehead touching hers, his hands resting on her bare thighs, asking a question he couldn't bring himself to ask of anyone else, he realized their time together meant more to him than he'd expected it to. More than it should.

"No, they weren't. They were lovely. Thank you," she said.

"Lovely, huh. I must not have brought my A game last night."

"Trust me, you did," she mumbled, her cheeks flushing a pretty pink. She ducked her head to peek in the scarf. "Oh, look, somebody's waking up." Her relief at the distraction was obvious.

He glanced over his shoulder at the beach, thinking she had the right idea. It was best to drop both subjects. "Good timing. Tide's out. I'll give you a hand getting her some grub."

"It's okay. I have lots of time to kill, and I'm sure you're busy. You already wasted part of your day finding my ring." She rubbed her forehead as though rubbing his touch away. "I didn't even say thank you. Sorry, I don't know where my head is at today. That was sweet of you to come and look for it when you have so much more important stuff going on."

"I didn't mind, Jenna. To be honest, I'd much rather be here than at the manor."

"Well, you know what they say. Everything's better at the beach." She bent to unwrap the bandage from her ankle, glancing at him. "I get the impression that you don't want to talk about your mom anymore. But if you ever do, you can call me, Logan. Anytime, day or night."

"Appreciate it. Thanks, Jenna."

"No problem."

He stood up and offered her his hand, carefully pulling her to her feet.

"Thanks." She smiled. "And this is the last I'll say about it unless you bring it up, but talk to your mom, Logan. Find out why she doesn't want treatment. It'll help you understand what she's dealing with. Let her know how you feel. Why it's so important to you and your family that she has the testing done, and then the treatment if she needs or wants it."

"Your mother chose not to have the treatment, didn't she?"

"She fought hard for more than a year, but yes, in the end, she chose not to continue with the treatment. She didn't want to spend the last few months of her life fighting. She wanted to spend them living and enjoying what time she had left."

He gave her hand a gentle squeeze. "That would be a choice I could accept and support. Your mom sounds like she was a smart lady. I'm sorry you lost her so young. It must've been tough."

"I couldn't have wished for a better mother. Which made it even harder to lose her, I guess. But I had my dad. He was amazing too. It was almost harder to lose him than it was my mother. She'd suffered and fought so hard, but one minute my dad and I were making plans to meet for lunch, and less than an hour later he was dead."

From the expression on her face, the wound was still fresh and painful. And then, as if losing her father wasn't difficult enough, her stepmother had stolen her business and her fiancé. He hoped there was a special place in hell reserved for Gwyneth Bell and Lorenzo Romano. Logan should've done more than give the guy a bloody nose. "I take it you haven't heard from your ex."

She gave him a startled look. "No. Why?"

He frowned. "What's going on? You look like—"

"Nothing. Nothing's going on." She gave him a forced smile and let go of his hand to fuss with her scarf, clearly avoiding contact of any kind.

Which meant something had happened, and if it involved Lorenzo, that something wasn't good. Now to figure out a way to get the information from her. "Okay. You seemed upset. Not surprising though, right? It hasn't been that long."

"Long enough for him to ruin my life," she murmured, and then grimaced. "Yours too. But now that we have the ring, I can use it to get Lorenzo to back off. And if I can't get through to him, I know someone who can. His uncle. Lorenzo looks up to him. Even better, I think he's afraid of him."

To Logan's mind, the less she had to do with Lorenzo and his family the better. "You do what you want with the ring, Jenna. After what went down at the manor this morning, it won't make much of a difference whether Lorenzo drops the charges or not. Here's an idea. Give the ring to Arianna. See if she can use it to get your company back."

She barely managed a nod and a weak smile. It looked like she was carrying an albatross around her neck and not a baby sandpiper that weighed less than a couple ounces.

That did it for him. He had to get to the bottom of this. She was worse off than she had been last night. Lorenzo must've contacted her. Logan waited until they reached the mud flats and she'd gently removed the bird from the scarf to tenderly place her on the wet sand. It looked like a cotton ball sitting there. All it would take was a strong wind to blow the peep away. Jenna must've come to the same conclusion and crouched to block the light wind. Finally giving in to the obvious pain the position caused, she moved from a crouch to a kneel. And that's when he put his plan into action.

He took his phone from his pocket, moving it around as though he couldn't get a connection. "Jenna, you mind if I borrow your phone? I wanna check in with Michael. See how my mom's doing."

"Yes, of course." She pulled her phone from her back pocket and naively typed in the passcode before handing it over.

"Thanks." He walked a short distance away and then turned his back as though protecting his privacy while he invaded hers. He pulled up her texts, hit Lorenzo's, and scrolled down until he reached the last one. It was from Jenna to Lorenzo and was about the length of a small book.

Okay, so apparently he had brought his A game last night. He covered a laugh with a cough at the way Jenna emasculated Lorenzo by using Logan's sexual prowess as a knife. However, the further along he read, the less he felt like laughing or smiling or high-fiving her. Nor could he pretend he didn't know that Lorenzo had basically bankrupted her.

Pulling out his own phone, Logan called his brother. Connor picked up on the second ring. "I have a case for you."

"Wish I could help you out, but I can't, big brother. My caseload just doubled, and I'm down two assistants."

"That wasn't a request. I'm calling in my marker."

"No way. You've already got Dad and Michael on your case. And, I might add, Uncle Daniel, who isn't a lawyer but has the BS down. So you'll be fine."

He heard the amusement in his brother's voice when he referred to their uncle. Logan found it interesting that they seemed to have bonded in such a short time, especially after learning that his uncle and mother had apparently been involved when they were younger and his uncle seemed anxious to take up where they'd left off. Logan didn't trust the older man.

"It's not for me. I have a friend who needs your help," he said as he walked toward Jenna. She looked up from trying to feed the baby bird. He handed her back her cell phone.

As she wiped her fingers to take it, she caught sight of her text to Lorenzo on the screen and her eyes shot to Logan.

He held her gaze and continued. "Her fiancé broke their engagement a week before their wedding. He's involved with her stepmother. It sounds like her stepmother may have forged Jenna's stepfather's will, taken her company from her, and her fiancé stole her car and cleaned out her savings account."

"She needs a cop or a hit man, not a lawyer. Who is she?"

"Jenna Bell."

"Is she related to Arianna Bell? She was Arianna Summers for a while, owns a bridal shop on Main Street."

He found it interesting that his brother seemed to know exactly what his ex-girlfriend had been up to all these years and filed the fact away for another conversation. "I know who Arianna is, Connor. Jenna's her stepsister."

"All right. I have to be back in Boston by four. Any chance I can talk to Jenna between now and then? I can meet her at Tie the Knot if that'd be easier."

He almost laughed at how easily his brother had acquiesced, but instead said to Jenna, "My brother Connor's going to take your case. He wants to meet with you. How does Tie the Knot in an hour work for you?"

Her eyes went big, and she shook her head.

"Jenna, I'm not taking *no* for an answer. Trust me, you need Connor. You couldn't ask for a better lawyer to—"

"I know. It's just—" She lowered her voice to a whisper. "Arianna doesn't..." She made a pained face before finally admitting, "She hates him. I think he broke her heart. But Serena says he's a shark, and Gwyneth and Lorenzo are piranhas, so I need him. But it's Sunday, and your family has had a difficult morning. If it's okay with Connor, I'll call his office tomorrow and set up an appointment."

"I heard," his brother said, and he didn't sound happy about it, which led Logan to believe Connor heard more than he was meant to. "Tell Jenna to call in the morning. I'm out of the office all afternoon."

"Golf game?"

"Yeah, with one of the top oncologists in the city, smartass."

He smiled. "You shouldn't try so hard to make people believe you're a douche, bro. You might have an easier time keeping your assistants."

"They don't leave me because I'm an asshat, buddy. They leave me because they fall in love with me."

"Hanging up now." They'd had this conversation before.

Logan pocketed his phone and crouched beside Jenna. She wouldn't look at him. She had a streak of mud on her cheek. He gently grasped her chin with one hand while raising the other to rub away the mud. "Why didn't you tell me he stole your car and money, Jenna?"

"Why wouldn't I want you to know that not only was he having an affair with my stepmother under my nose, but he also stole my keys and wallet because I left my sister's business unlocked while I was pole dancing at the Salty Dog? I don't know, Logan. Maybe—" She glared at him when he couldn't hold back a laugh. "It's not funny."

"Trust me, I wasn't laughing about Lorenzo. It's just that I wouldn't call what you were doing at the Salty Dog pole dancing. It was cute, but definitely not—"

She made a *blech* face. "Cute. Just what every woman wants to be called by the man they had…" She bowed her head, her hair falling forward.

He tucked it behind her ear, taking note of the red and gold streaks. "You have pretty hair."

She tried to hold back a smile but failed. "Yours is lovely too."

He laughed. "Thanks, I think." He gestured to the bird. "How's she doing?"

"Great. She nibbled on a fly and drank a little water. At least I think she did. It's hard to tell." She looked up at him. "You don't think she did, do you?"

"Like you say, it's hard to tell. I wouldn't get too attached, honey." The last thing she needed was to lose something else. After what she'd lost in the last twenty-four hours, he honestly didn't know how she was still standing, not to mention trying to take care of him and a baby bird. He had a feeling he'd misjudged Jenna Bell and the woman was a lot stronger than she looked.

"I'll give you a ride back to your sister's place once you think Pippa's had her fill."

"You go ahead. I'm good, thanks."

"You haven't been home yet, have you?"

She shook her head. "Poppy lent me some clothes. After we finished up at the vet's, we went to the *Gazette*. That's how I found out I had no money. I went to pay Poppy for the deposit. I would've found out at the vet's, but they don't have Apple Pay. I signed an IOU."

He made a note to drop by the veterinarian hospital and pay her bill. Connor could tell her he was taking her case pro bono as a favor to him. Still… "Don't get offended, Jenna. But I can loan you some money until everything gets settled."

"That's very kind of you, but I'll be fine. I'm pretty sure Arianna will let me stay with her…" She flexed her fingers and looked at the ring. "Maybe I can pawn this."

"No. Keep it. The ring obviously has value in Lorenzo's eyes. It might work to your advantage." He surreptitiously nudged the baby bird. As far as he could tell, she hadn't moved. The peep lifted its head and fixed her eyes on him. Well, that settled that question. She was clearly still alive. He scooped her up. "Let's bring her closer to the water's edge. See if she'll stand."

They didn't get her to stand, but she seemed to have some life in her at least, and she definitely took some water and poked at a dead minnow. Jury was out if she ate any of it. And he'd gotten Jenna to agree to let him take her home, which to him felt like a win. She might be afraid to face her sisters, but she needed them. "Have you given any thought to setting up your matchmaking business at Tie the Knot?" he asked as he gently splashed water at the bird with his finger.

"If I'd suggested it a few days ago, Arianna might've gone for it. Not now though."

"It must be a busy time for them. Maybe they can hire you."

"I need a job if I'm going to pay room and board and cover the deposits for the wedding."

"I could ask Grams if they're hiring at the manor."

"No. You've done enough for me. And while Arianna might not want me to work with them right now, she'd worry what people would say if I was working at the manor and not for her."

"If it doesn't pan out, just let me know."

"I will. Thanks—"

He held up a finger at the distinctive ringtone coming from his phone. "Sorry." It was his boss. "Today? Yes, sir. I'll be back in Washington by twenty-one hundred hours. Thank you, sir."

"You got your job back," she said as soon as he disconnected. "I'm so relieved. You must be too."

"It's a temporary assignment. But it doesn't matter. In the end, it'll play in my favor. The princess of Merradien is coming on a state visit, and they requested that I head up the security detail for her."

"That's the princess you saved from the kidnapping attempt, isn't it?"

He nodded. "Yeah, and they're scheduled to arrive midweek. I don't have a lot of time to prepare."

"What are you waiting for? Go." She shooed him off. "I'll be fine."

"You're sure?"

"Positive."

"Okay. You've got my number. Call anytime."

"I will. Honestly, you don't have to worry about me," she said when he hesitated.

He had enough to worry about, enough people depending on him, that he didn't want to add someone else to his list of people to take care of. But whether he liked it or not, Jenna was on it now. And somehow she'd managed to land at almost the top. "Take care of yourself, and Pippa too."

"You take care of yourself, and the princess. If you'd like, I can stop by the manor for high tea and check on your mom."

He had a big family, who had no doubt banded around his mother now, but he was touched by her offer. "I appreciate that. Thanks, Jenna." He didn't know what made him do it— maybe it was her smile and the happy glow she'd gotten on her face when she thought he'd gotten his job back—but whatever the reason, he leaned in and softly brushed his lips across hers.

It was far from a passionate kiss, but he knew as soon as he pulled back that he shouldn't have done it. She'd gotten that look on her face. The same one from this morning. The one that said she wanted more than what he was willing or able to give. Especially now. But he didn't have the heart to tell her that today of all days.

Chapter Eleven

♥

Jenna blamed Logan and his kiss for putting unrealistic expectations in her head. Like the ones that started forming the moment his lips touched hers. It was like the sun had exploded inside her, leaving her with a warm, fuzzy afterglow that somehow gave her the misguided idea that everything would be right with the world.

She had a shark for a lawyer, Logan was going back to Washington to do the job that he loved, and Jenna was going home to tell her stepsisters that she was basically homeless and penniless and they were going to be just as kind and as considerate as Logan had been.

The fantasy had been nice while it lasted.

"Arianna, stop yelling," Serena said. "It's not helping. Jenna feels bad enough as it is. It's not like she intentionally left the store unlocked. How did she know Lorenzo would—"

"Left the store unlocked? She might as well have handed him the keys to the kingdom. Signed on the dotted line and given him equal rights to everything she owned. Which means your business, Jenna. Even if we can get the will overturned, Gwyneth and Lorenzo now hold more shares in Southern Belle than you do. He'll be entitled to half of everything Daddy would've left to you. Bet you didn't think about that when you set up a joint account, did you?"

"No, because I thought we'd—" She sank deeper into the leather couch when her stepsister advanced on her, stabbing the chilly air with a mocking finger. The apartment above Tie the Knot was freezing, but Jenna knew the air conditioner wasn't responsible for the shiver that ran through her.

"What? Live happily ever after? Grow up. There's no such thing as happily-ever-after. Until you can get that in your head, self-serving narcissists like Lorenzo will keep using and abusing you." Shoulders bowed, Arianna wrapped her arms around her waist and walked to the window that overlooked Main Street.

"Everything you said is true, Arianna. I should've realized that I was being played. Looking back, I can see there were small signs Lorenzo wasn't who he said he was. I just…I didn't have a lot of experience with men like him. You and Serena are used to having guys complimenting you all the time and making you feel like you're amazing and can do anything you set your mind to. Other than Daddy, no one made me feel"—she lifted a shoulder, knowing Arianna would hate what she was about to say, but it was the truth—"special, like a princess. Up until yesterday, Lorenzo did."

"Don't kid yourself. We've been played too, haven't we, Arianna?" Serena gave her sister a pointed stare, but since she had her back to them, it wasn't clear whether Arianna agreed with her or not.

Jenna eyed Arianna as she adjusted the scarf around Pippa, bringing her closer to her heart. She didn't want the baby bird to catch a chill, but she also didn't want to alert her stepsister to her presence. Arianna didn't like animals or children. Something Jenna had recently discovered. Growing up, she didn't remember her stepsister feeling that way, but what did she know? Until recently, they hadn't been close. And it was beginning to look like she should've enjoyed their improved relationship while it lasted. She had enjoyed it, and her stepfather would have been over the moon at how close they'd become.

If he'd had a dying wish, this would've been it. Not Arianna yelling at her, of course. Or Serena thinking Jenna was an idiot but not coming out and saying it. No, his fondest wish would've been them living and working together, being the loving, supportive sisters he'd always hoped they would be. They were all she had left now. Lorenzo had stolen too much. She wouldn't let him take her family from her too.

"I know I've put you in a bad position, and at the moment I can't pay back the deposits like I promised, but I will. I'm setting up an appointment with a lawyer tomorrow. He's..." Unless she wanted to be out on the street, she had to keep her lawyer's identity a secret. "Supposed to be the best. And since the will and Gwyneth are all kind of tied up in it too, I thought he could maybe take on both cases. I'm going to ask if he'd agree to take his fee from the settlement."

Arianna turned. "I'm glad you've obviously given this some thought and taken steps to address the situation."

Jenna refused to be offended by Arianna's condescending tone. She'd prove to both her stepsisters that she was as savvy as they were. Sure, she'd made a big mistake, a ginormous one, really. She'd put her trust in someone who didn't deserve it. But as of this moment, she was turning over a new leaf. She was going to reinvent herself. She no longer wanted to be the princess in the story; she wanted to be the kick-butt heroine.

Right, she was done with fairy tales and happily-ever-afters. She'd focus on proving to her stepsisters that she was worthy of a second chance. That was all she really wanted. A second chance to prove to them that they were better together than they were apart.

"Thank you," she said, choosing to take Arianna's remark as a compliment, even though, if anyone deserved to take it as a compliment, it was Logan. He'd figuratively taken Jenna by the hand and put her on the road to recovery. "I thought maybe I could work for you, free of charge, of course, until I've paid off the money you put out for the deposits, and the dress." She murmured the last because not only was the bottom of her dress in Logan's truck, but so was the top, as well as the crinoline. He'd rolled them up in the blanket and taken them with him when he'd headed to the manor first thing that morning. She'd been too panicked about the missing ring to say anything.

"It won't be a problem to reattach the bottom of the dress. I'm sure we can sell it as gently used and cover the cost of material if not the labor," Arianna said with a look that left little doubt she knew about Jenna's performance at the Salty Dog. Still, she had no idea how well used the dress had been. Reattaching the bottom to the top would be easy compared to getting the stains out and repairing the hem.

Which meant Jenna had to figure a way out of this. "Wouldn't that be bad for business though? You wouldn't want to undersell yourself or your brand. And really, I adore the dress." It was true, she did. But even more than the dress, she loved that her sisters had worked so hard to make both her day and her wedding gown special.

"All right. If that's how you feel, you can keep it."

Whew, crisis averted. And since that went so well, Jenna felt emboldened to broach the idea of the three of them going into business together. "I have a way that I might be able to pay you back sooner." At the look of interest in their eyes, she continued. "Whether the will is overturned or not, I'm not going back to Charleston. It's not the same without Daddy there, and now it feels like I was living a lie. So I thought maybe I could rent space from you. Our businesses are compatible. I match them, and you marry them." She laughed, a sudden case of nerves making it come out more like *hee-haw* than *ha-ha*. With some effort, she got her laughter under control.

As the moments dragged on without a response from either Arianna or Serena, the smile Jenna had pasted on her face grew strained and almost painful. "Or I can just work for you and get a feel for the business. We can al-

ways revisit the idea of partnering up at a later date."
She heard a small *peep* and glanced at her scarf to see
it moving. She covered the *peep* with a cough and the
movement by waving the top of her scarf as though she
were sweating and not freezing.

"I hope I'm not coming down with something.
Maybe I'll get an early night," she said, and came to her
feet.

"You and Lorenzo were supposed to be heading
home today so Serena moved back into her bedroom."
Her sisters had shared the king-size bed in Arianna's
room while Jenna and Lorenzo shared Serena's. "I
guess you can stay in my sewing room. It's a little
crowded, but there's a daybed. We can discuss what
you'll be doing at Tie the Knot in the morning."

Jenna gave her a grateful smile. "Thank you. Have a
good night."

"You too," Arianna and Serena said at almost the
same time, their half smiles as genuine as a three-dollar
bill.

It was like she was starting back at square one with
them. She reminded herself how much worse it had
been at square one, and the thought cheered her a bit.
Despite the setback, they had made progress. Huge
progress, really. After all, they'd invited her to live with
them.

However, the small blip of excitement became a
distant memory the moment she opened the bedroom
door at the end of the hall. Two sewing machines, a
steamer, and three mannequins were crammed into the
small space. Somewhere under the reams of fabric, she

imagined, was a daybed. It was like she was starring in her own special version of *Cinderella*. She had a bird. All she needed were mice and a fat cat. And a fairy godmother. There was one positive though. The sewing room felt like a tropical paradise compared to the front room.

But by the time Jenna organized the space so it wasn't as claustrophobic and cleared the fabric off the daybed, she was sort of wishing the air conditioner cooled the back of the apartment as well as the front. Only she didn't have the energy to hunt down a fan. With the scarf, she made a nest by her pillow and tucked both her and Pippa into bed. She clapped her hands to turn off the lights—an interesting discovery: Arianna was addicted to the Home Shopping Network— and then clapped again to turn them on. She set the alarm on her phone for low tide. She needed to be at the beach by one in the morning. Lucky for her, her sisters were sound sleepers.

Just as she decided on the *Jaws* theme for her alarm's ringtone, her cell phone rang. How apropos, she thought, because it was Lorenzo. She contemplated letting him go to voice mail, thought of all the reasons she didn't want to ever speak to him again, and then reminded herself about her new leaf. It was time she called him on his crap.

The phone stopped ringing. He must've gotten tired of waiting. No, she thought when the phone rang again, only this time for a FaceTime call. He must want something from her if he was bringing out his best and biggest gun—his handsome face.

"Wish me luck, Pippa." She smiled when the bird's head came up, and she gave a weak *peep*. "You're going to prove to them you're so much tougher than you look, aren't you, girl? Quit stalling," she told herself, and hit Accept.

"Oh, my sweet *bella*, look what I have done to you."

She glanced at herself on the screen and then casually moved her arm, holding out the phone at a more flattering angle. "You better be on your way back here with my car and my money or you're going to have far worse than a swollen nose, Lorenzo."

"I was in fear for my life. I had no choice. You must see this, *sì*? That Gallagher man, he is most dangerous."

"Yes, he is. So if you know what's good for you, you'll do as I asked and drop the charges against him. And you can do that when you bring my money and car back to Harmony Harbor."

He brushed her off with a wave of his hand. "I have called to warn you about Arianna. She is blackening your name, saying the most terrible of things about you."

"I don't blame her. She thinks I'm an idiot for falling for you and your lies, and she's right. Besides, she's calling you a lot worse. And that's nothing compared to what people will be calling you after Byron and Poppy Harte's tell-all about you."

"Who are these Harte people of which you speak?" In the background, she heard a woman's aggravated whisper and caught sight of blond hair. "*Sì, sì, mi amore*, I will, but first—" As though he knew the jig was up, he waved his hand behind him and gave Jenna a slick smile. She wondered how she had ever fallen for him. "I apologize. It was just the maid. Now, we must talk about your sister. She sent me the most terrible of messages from your phone."

"My sister didn't send you a text. I did."

"No, you don't understand, *bella*. She said you had relations with the craven beast who did this to me."

"I had sex on the beach with Logan Gallagher, and it was flipping amazing. Everything I wrote in that text is true. Not only does he have a magical penis, his hands are magical too. Everything about the man is—"

"You...you *puttana*!" He spat the words, spittle landing on the screen. Behind him came a frantic whisper. Jenna was impressed. Whatever Gwyneth said caused Lorenzo to do a one-eighty. Nevertheless, it took him a few seconds to smooth the anger from his face. He replaced it with a contrite smile and wiped at the screen. "I apologize. It is not easy to hear that you were with another man."

"Excuse me while I throw up at your hypocrisy."

His face tightened, and then he jerked as though someone hit him from behind. Once again, he managed to smooth the fury from his face, this time replacing it with a regretful smile. "I understand that I hurt you, *bella*. But surely we can work this out among ourselves. We settle this now, *si*? No need for this talk of lawyers. I will put half the money back in your account—"

She stared at him. How had she not seen him for who he really was? But as she asked herself the question, she had a sick feeling she knew the answer. She'd wanted the handsome husband and fairy-tale wedding so badly that she'd closed her eyes to what had been right in front of her all along. If that was true though, why hadn't her father forced her to see the light? He'd never said a negative word against Lorenzo. And Richard Bell was a smart man. Who hadn't seen through Gwyneth either.

Jenna pushed her hair from her sweaty face and blew out a breath. "You don't want me to get a lawyer involved, I won't."

A genuine smile spread across his face. "This is why I loved you, *bella*. You are so good and kind."

She got a vivid image of herself wearing a neon sign around her neck that read SUCKER. He'd seen her coming from a mile away. "Let's see if you feel that way when I give you my conditions. There's a few, so you might want Gwyneth to take notes. Are you ready, Gwynne?" She smiled. Her stepmother hated when Richard had called her that.

"Okay, so first up, you drop the charges against Logan Gallagher. Second, you return my car and all my money. Third, Gwyneth comes clean about the fake will and returns my company to me. Stop yelling, or you won't hear the rest of my proposition."

Lorenzo was red-faced and sweaty after delivering his tirade, but nodded, as did Gwyneth, who was no longer pretending she wasn't there. "If you do everything I've asked, I'll sell Southern Belle to you both at a discounted price, and, Lorenzo, I'll give you your ring back."

When they both began adamantly shaking their heads, Jenna said, "Okay, see you in court. And just FYI, my lawyer is going to make you wish you took the deal. Lorenzo, enjoy Charleston and your sugar mama as long as you can. I have a feeling you'll be headed back to Italy real soon. And not for a vacay. *Ciao.*"

Whoever said revenge was sweet was wrong. Did it feel good to look Lorenzo and Gwyneth in the eyes and stay strong and say what she had to say? Of course it did, though it might've felt better if she'd fixed her hair a little before accepting the call. Because despite his swollen nose, her ex looked like he stepped off a Paris runway, and Gwyneth, with a much sexier case of bedhead than Jenna's, looked like she'd spent the last couple of hours welcoming him home and had a gorgeous afterglow.

And there was no doubt Jenna would feel better if she could get her money and car back and knew for sure Logan's career wouldn't suffer. But Lorenzo and Gwyneth took something precious from her that no lawyer, no matter how good, could get back. They'd stolen her innocence. Her belief that people were inherently good. How would she ever be able to trust that someone was being truthful with her? If someone told her they loved her, would she ever believe them?

As though the universe decided she needed a reminder that there were still good, decent, trustworthy men out there, her phone *ping*ed with an incoming text. It was from Logan, checking in to make sure she and Pippa were okay.

Chapter Twelve

♥

Jenna's reinvention of herself from a starry-eyed romantic to her sisters' pragmatic employee at Tie the Knot was going reasonably well considering she was a reformed believer in happily-ever-afters working at a business that specialized in them. It made it somewhat easier that Arianna reinforced Jenna's newly acquired cynicism on an hourly basis and that, so far, she hadn't been dealing with the clients. Her duties consisted of coffee runs, updating Tie the Knot's woefully outdated website, and ensuring the services they outsourced were on budget and on time.

Arianna opened the door to Jenna's office, aka the storage room, and peeked her head inside. And peeking her head inside was pretty much all she could do. The quarters were too cramped to hold Jenna and a desk and her sister at the same time. Jenna had to walk sideways when she left her desk and usually ended up covered in sparkles and feathers regardless because Arianna stored the high-end fabric and embellishments in the space. The fabrics were the reason Jenna had called her stepsister back from the front of the shop.

A tiny *peep* reminded Jenna who was sitting on her desk in a cozy little bed of satin remnants. Over the past couple of days, Pippa had shown a marked improvement but wasn't quite ready to be released into the wild, sort of like Jenna, she supposed. So it wasn't exactly the best time for her stepsister to discover Jenna had a companion of the feathered variety living under her roof.

"I'll be right with you," Jenna said, all efficient CFO. She was more like girl Friday, but she'd given herself a title to aspire to. Surreptitiously, she elbowed a file folder over Pippa's bed, clearing her throat to cover the *peep*. Pippa was beginning to show signs she was a baby bird who knew her own mind, which Jenna loved but could've done without at the moment. Pippa headbutted the file off her nest. Jenna casually slid her elbow across the desk to block Arianna's view of the bird. She tapped the printer with her pen, which until then she hadn't realized was a chocolate-scented heart pen. Old habits died hard. "Sorry. I'm out of paper. I'm sure you have things to do. I'll bring the printouts up to you in a few minutes."

"How big is the discrepancy?"

"Big enough that I didn't believe it was accidental and pulled up your old invoices. You've overpaid them by thousands of dollars, Arianna."

"I've been buying my lace from them for years. I can't believe it was intentional."

"Everything jibed up until sixteen months ago, and then there'd be a small miscalculation here and there until it wasn't so small."

"I'm impressed, Jenna. I truly had no idea you were so business savvy. That sounds silly given Southern Belle's success, but I always thought it was more due to Daddy and, though I hate to admit it, Gwyneth's involvement than yours. I'm sorry for underestimating you. It makes me even more anxious to get the will overturned for your sake. I don't know what I'd do if anything happened to Tie the Knot. It's my life." She smiled. "Great job, and I mean that. If we recoup the money, and it's as much as you think, you'll have covered your deposits at the very least. It's Friday. We should go to the Salty Dog to celebrate."

The week had gone by so fast that she'd forgotten it was Friday—the night before what would've been her wedding day. She wondered if Arianna remembered that they'd planned to have the rehearsal party at the pub. Lorenzo hadn't been a fan of the idea, but Jenna had wanted something casual and fun. She'd also wanted to support her best friend's family business.

She saw the moment her sister remembered. "I wasn't thinking. Sorry, Jenna. We can do something else, or if you'd rather stay in and have—"

"Don't be silly. We'll go to the pub. You're signing the loan renewal with the bank. It's a big deal. We need to celebrate."

Clearly frustrated, Arianna tapped her forefinger and index finger on her forehead. "What is wrong with me today? My appointment is at two, and Faith Fourburger is coming in with her fiancé to sign off on her wedding dress, bridesmaids' dresses, and the tuxes." She pulled out her phone. "Did Serena tell you when she'd be back?"

"No. I thought she was still here." The muscle in her forearm was beginning to cramp, and Jenna shuffled her chair over so she didn't have to lean as far across her desk to hide Pippa from Arianna's view.

Her stepsister stabbed the keys on her iPhone. "She'd better respond, or I'll go down to HHPD and have words with Chief Benson about his officer. I bet they have a morality clause in their contracts, and it's immoral for Ryan to be chasing after Serena when he's a married man."

Serena and Ryan's situation was an unpleasant reminder of her own mother and stepfather's relationship, not only to Jenna but, based on the furious intensity with which Arianna struck the keys, to her stepsister as well. Unless Jenna wanted to deal with cutting remarks about her mother, she couldn't suggest that Serena might share some blame. She knew Ryan was a married man.

The happiness brought about by Arianna's earlier praise dissipated, leaving behind a dull and depressing weight. Jenna didn't like to think of her mother as the bad guy in the situation, the home wrecker Arianna and Serena had always made her out to be. But it was hard to fight against the evidence. It didn't mean she loved her mother any less. Nothing or no one would ever change how she felt about either her mother or her stepfather. She just wished things had played out differently. Maybe if they had she wouldn't have to work so hard to win her stepsisters' love.

"I'll see if they can change my appointment at the bank."

"No. Don't do that. I can handle your appointment with Faith Fourburger and her fiancé. I'm the one who drew up the contract and orders, so it's not like I don't know what I'm doing."

Arianna chewed on her thumbnail. "I guess."

"It really isn't a big deal, Arianna. And I'm a little surprised you're making it one." And hurt. She'd worked so hard this week to prove to them she was competent. A few moments ago, she thought she'd succeeded.

"Well, it kind of is a big deal. Or I should say Faith is. She's the reason we got the spread in *Wedding Bells* magazine, and she's the reason we've had an uptick in interest from the Boston elite. She could make our reputation, Jenna. We've never had a client as big as Faith."

"I had an extremely wealthy and socially mobile clientele at Southern Belle. You can check our reviews online. They were overwhelmingly positive, and I was the one they were dealing with, not Gwyneth."

Jenna was all about the warm and fuzzy. And no offense to her stepsister, but Arianna was hardly the one to give clients the warm and fuzzies, which she proved by pointing at the adorable little puff ball that had wobbled over to peck at Jenna's chocolate-scented pen and saying in a horrified voice, "What is that?"

Jenna considered going with *What's what?* but decided that would only tick her stepsister off. "A rescue bird. Her name's Pippa, and I promise you'll never know she's here." Pippa *peep*ed, and Jenna smiled. "She says hi, Auntie Arianna."

* * *

After the Pippa incident, Jenna thought she might've blown her chance to wow Faith Fourburger with her amazing customer service ability and have the wealthiest woman in Boston singing her praises, which would hopefully result in Jenna's sisters finally taking her seriously and allowing her to partner with them.

"One step at a time," she told herself as she arranged a lovely sterling-silver tea tray on the small table beside the chaise. She'd decided it provided the right amount of warmth, luxury, and professionalism for Faith and her fiancé to sit on the chaise with Jenna across from them on a pretty vintage chair rather than signing the papers at the antique reception desk.

She looked around the front of the shop to ensure everything looked just so. She'd left Pippa in her office. Instead of the makeshift nest, she'd created a makeshift playpen. She couldn't wait for Logan to see the pictures she'd sent him. It was the first time Pippa had stood, and Jenna felt like a proud parent. But Logan probably wouldn't be able to respond until later that evening because Princess Isabella and her entourage had arrived Wednesday.

He was playing tour guide as well as head of security. Jenna had given him some tips on protocol and suggested places the princess might be interested in seeing. Since Jenna had made it clear to him that she was over the fairy-tale thing, he teased her about her obsession with everything the princess was doing, saying, and wearing.

But come on, you didn't have to believe in fairy tales or happily-ever-afters to be interested in the comings and goings of a royal. For goodness' sake, they opened Kate Spade, Tory Burch, and Rag & Bone for the princess after hours, and she was staying at the Jefferson in a luxury suite. Jenna had begged Logan to snap a photo of what Her Royal Highness bought, but instead he sent her a *you scare me* emoji, as though she were a stalker. He'd sent the same emoji when she asked him to take a photo of the tiara.

Out of habit, Jenna checked her phone, smiling when she saw the bubble and the dot-dot-dot of him typing a response.

Cute. You missed your calling. You should be designing baby bird furniture.

Ha! And you put the secretive in Secret Service. Give me a hint what you're up to today. Pretty please. She added a praying hands emoji. She knew from following the princess's official Twitter account that they'd spent the earlier part of yesterday at George Washington's Mount Vernon estate and in the evening attended a special dinner in the princess's honor at the French embassy.

Jenna nearly dropped the phone when a photo of Logan and the princess appeared. They'd taken a selfie. They were in formal wear. Logan looked absolutely stunning in his tux, the princess equally stunning in a gown with long gloves...and her tiara!

Hey, you still there?

Yes!! I can't believe you got her to take a selfie for me...and she's wearing her tiara!

I told her you were a big fan and would also continue being a royal pain in my butt until you got your picture.

You two are looking pretty friendly, Secret Agent Man. Is there anything you'd like to share? Maybe my knight in shining armor is going to turn into a real-life prince? she teased, and then realized they really did look friendly, and happy too. Happy and beautiful. A dull ache expanded in her chest, heavyhearted at the thought. Which was crazy because she was done with men, even amazing men like Logan. It seemed her heart was harder to convince than her head.

You're slipping, Jellilicious. You're supposed to be like me, career-focused, not marriage obsessed. And marrying a princess... Yeah, I don't think so.

He was right. They'd been having conversations along those same lines practically the entire week as Logan tried to keep her on the straight and narrow and off the slippery happily-ever-after slope. Although when they first began having the *talk*, she'd felt like Logan was letting her know where he stood on love and marriage in case she might've gotten the wrong idea after their night at the beach. Which he may have picked up on her supposedly easy-to-read face.

Since he'd laughed about her gift the first time she'd told him, she wasn't about to tell him that the one-true-love feeling he might've seen on her face those two times at the beach wasn't anything to worry about. As she'd explained, the gift worked for others, not herself.

She scrolled to the photo. *I don't know, Logan. You might want to share with Princess Isabella that you're a confirmed bachelor. Because from what I can see, she's looking at you like she might think you're her one and only.*

Jenna's use of scented heart pens at work wasn't the only habit she was apparently having a difficult time shaking, she thought as she scrutinized the couple's selfie for a sign they were meant to be. But the iridescent lighting from the stage behind them stymied her efforts.

It sounds like you're in need of some face-to-face time with your reality life coach. Good thing the princess and her crew are leaving early next week. I should be able to get back to Harmony Harbor for the weekend. If I do, you and I are meeting with Connor. No more putting it off.

Wow, she thought at the feeling of joyous bliss. If her body reacted like this to the simple announcement that he was coming home for a weekend, Logan was right. She needed a reality life coach, and it most definitely couldn't be him. She cleared her throat and then rolled her eyes at herself. They were texting, not talking.

I didn't want to cancel my meeting with Connor. I had to. Arianna insisted she was coming with me.

Given how her sister had reacted to Serena's previous suggestion that they hire Connor, Jenna knew Arianna would kick up a fuss so extreme, she'd have no choice but to find herself another attorney. And from everything she'd heard and read about Connor Gallagher, Jenna didn't want anyone else but him. She'd also been told by his assistant that he was taking her case pro bono because he owed his brother. Since

Lorenzo had yet to return her car and money, Jenna accepted the generous offer without fighting too hard.

The door chimed.

I've gotta go. My opportunity to win Arianna over for life just walked in the door.

She turned to offer the couple a warm smile as she slipped the phone in the pocket of her flowy, wide-leg pants. She'd paired them with ballet flats and a short-sleeved silk top. She knew the outfit was casually elegant and well coordinated. Her favorite salesperson at Nordstrom had put the outfit together for Jenna, just like he'd put together ninety percent of her wardrobe. She didn't know what she was going to do without him. Since she had no money for clothes, she supposed it was a moot point. But their money problems, both hers and her sisters', would be a thing of the past if she wowed the couple walking her way.

The woman was tall with shiny, blond hair cut to flatter her narrow face. She wore a maxi sundress that complemented her girl-next-door good looks, her sparkling eyes, and her bright smile. Her fiancé wore Gucci from head to toe, the perfect accompaniment to his look-at-me air and arrogant smile.

"Hi. I'm Jenna Bell. You must be Faith and Steve." She offered her hand, doing her best to hide her distaste for the man. She didn't need a psychology degree to know why she disliked him on sight. He was an all-American version of Lorenzo. She took herself to task over how quickly she'd judged him. She didn't even know the man.

"It's Stephen, not Steve, and before we sign off on

my tux, I'd like to see something by Kiton. A pal of mine said it's the only brand to buy."

If you were a multimillionaire, maybe, which of course Faith was, but still. Made in Italy, a Kiton tux would come in at around fifty thousand dollars, and it wasn't a brand Tie the Knot carried. Arianna had already special ordered the Armani to ensure they'd have it on time.

"I agree, it's a beautifully made tux, Stephen. But so is the Armani you've chosen." She gestured to the divan. "Why don't you make yourselves comfortable, and we'll go over everything you've ordered to make sure you're happy with your choices."

"Didn't I just say that I'm not? I want to see the Kiton."

Faith gave her an apologetic glance and rubbed her fiancé's arm as they took a seat on the chaise. "It's a black tux, baby. They all look the same."

"That's the whole point. It's my big day. I don't want to look like everyone else."

The petulant tone in his voice was so similar to Lorenzo's that Jenna had to look away in case they read the disgust on her face. She thought about how important their business was to Arianna and pushed all thoughts of Lorenzo from her mind. She forced herself to smile and took the seat across from them. "Can I offer you some tea and lavender cookies with rosewater icing? The local bakery here in Harmony Harbor makes them, and they're to die for."

"Yeah, not really a tea and cookies man, you know. How about some Dom?"

"Pérignon?"

He looked at her like she was an idiot. She had a feeling he hadn't looked at her sister this way. "What other brand would you expect us to drink?"

"Steve." Faith shot him a look and then reached for a cookie. "They smell amazing, and tea is perfect. Don't worry about—"

"Honestly, it's no trouble. I'll be right back." Jenna had been avoiding looking directly at the couple sitting side by side on the chaise, but just then she made the mistake of doing so. Faith Fourburger wasn't marrying her one true love.

Forcing a smile, Jenna walked to the back of the shop. When she reached the small coffee bar off the fitting area, she bent to take a bottle of prosecco out of the fridge, almost positive *Stephen* wouldn't have a clue it wasn't his favorite brand of champagne. Maybe he wouldn't, but she was almost certain Faith would. Just as she had a feeling Faith wouldn't out her.

Jenna filled a champagne flute, reminding herself as she did how important it was to Arianna that Jenna win over Faith and her fiancé. But she didn't want the woman to end up like her. Then again, Faith's family had oodles of money, which meant they had lawyers on the payroll. There's no way Stephen could do to Faith what Lorenzo had done to Jenna. Faith didn't need her protection. Arianna did.

The couple looked up from an iPhone, and Faith gave a guilty start. Stephen didn't. "So that guy really took you for a ride, didn't he? No wonder you're so bitter," he said.

A hot flush worked its way up Jenna's chest to her cheeks. It felt like she'd walked into a sauna. "I'm not sure what you're talking about." She knew exactly what they were talking about. Poppy and Byron must've printed the first installment of her story. Jenna leaned across the coffee table and smiled. "I hope you enjoy your champagne."

"Wait. Now I know why your name's familiar. You're that Jenna Bell. The one who owned Southern Belle," Faith said. "Several members of my sorority live in Charleston and you found them their perfect matches. They'd given up hope before they found you. They said you're the best. I'd considered making an appointment with you last fall, but then I met Steve. We're a match made in heaven, aren't we, baby?"

Jenna's heart sank to her feet when Faith turned her smiling face to her. "My friends said you can tell within minutes of meeting a couple if they're the perfect match. We are, aren't we?"

Chapter Thirteen

♥

Jenna wanted nothing more than to tell Faith the truth. But there was too much at stake. As much as Tie the Knot couldn't afford to lose Faith's business, this was Jenna's last opportunity to win over Arianna. Her relationship with her stepsister would never recover if she blew this.

Despite knowing how much depended on her lying to Faith, Jenna's *of course you're a match* was little more than a whisper. Neither Faith nor Stephen seemed to register her verbal stamp of approval on their relationship. Stephen had turned to stare at his bride-to-be, who gazed at him lovingly.

With his features squinched up, his face didn't look quite so attractive. "Give me a break. You don't really believe that one-true-love BS, do you? The matchmaking business is a racket. They're just a bunch of con artists playing on the emotions of gullible women who have more money than brains."

"I'm neither stupid nor gullible, Steve. Neither are Libby and Scarlett, and they've been happily married for a couple years to men Jenna not only matched them with, but who she said were their soul mates."

Jenna knew the women Faith referred to. Both were successful businesswomen and as warm and wonderful as their husbands.

"Whew, soul mates, really." He shook his head and then lifted the champagne flute to his lips, patting Faith's knee as he did. "If you believe that kind of crap, I'm surprised no one has robbed you blind. But don't you worry. You've got me to take care of you now." His lips curved in a smirk just before he took a drink of prosecco.

And Jenna knew right then, deep down in her soul, that he was just like Lorenzo. He didn't love Faith. The only thing he loved about her was her fortune. Jenna forced the words past the fear of what she stood to lose and said loudly and clearly, "No, you're not a perfect match." And in case there was any doubt about her meaning, "You're not a good match at all. In fact, you're one of the worst matches I've seen in a long time."

Prosecco spewed from Stephen's mouth. He jumped to his feet, wiping the droplets from his shirt, cursing her while his fiancée's shocked gaze moved from him to Jenna. Her eyes pleaded, as though begging Jenna to take it back.

"I'm sorry. I can't," Jenna said. Faith had no idea how much she wished she could.

* * *

It was a little less than a week after Jenna had run out the doors of Tie the Knot, and here she was doing it again. Only this time it wasn't to get away from Lorenzo. It was to get away from her stepsister. Jenna was afraid Arianna was going to kill her. Her suitcase followed her out the door and onto the sidewalk.

"I'm sorry, but I don't know what you expected me to do. She asked me if they were the perfect match and—" Tucking Pippa and her bed into her open purse, Jenna bent down to retrieve her suitcase.

"Lie! Tell her of course they're the perfect match," Arianna yelled, her face flushed, her eyes glassy.

"But they're not. Why couldn't you see it? He's just like Lorenzo. He's going to make her life miserable and rob her blind."

Jenna turned her head at the sound of a car door slamming. It was Serena. She ran toward them. Officer Wilson pulled his patrol car behind her stepsister and got out.

"You don't know that. And they're adults. They'll figure it out for themselves. You have no business—"

"That was my business. And I was really, really good at it. Just ask Faith what her friends said. I . . . I have a gift. I can tell if a couple are meant to be together, and they're not."

"You actually think you're psychic? That you know if a couple is meant to be together?" Serena said.

"Oh my God, Serena, of course she doesn't have a *gift*. She was going to marry Lorenzo. And look who Daddy married—Gwyneth and her mother."

Jenna's fingers tightened around the suitcase handle.

She didn't want to do this, not on a sidewalk on Main Street, but she wouldn't let Arianna malign her mother. "My mother was his match. They were soul mates. Gwyneth wasn't."

"Of course you'd say that." Arianna lifted her hands as though she didn't have the energy to continue arguing. "You know what? I don't care anymore. Pretend you have a gift. Do whatever you want, but don't do it anywhere near my shop."

Serena tried to intervene. "Arianna, don't. You can't just kick her—"

"Did you not read the text I sent?" Arianna yelled.

Serena worried her bottom lip between her teeth and then glanced at Ryan, who came to stand beside her. "No. My meeting with the manager of the hotel took longer than I expected."

"We've lost Faith Fourburger as a client, and *Wedding Bells* magazine will no doubt be canceling the spread. Faith refuses to let us have anything to do with their wedding after stepsister dearest here told them they weren't a match." She shook her head. "I seriously can't believe this is happening. Your mother destroyed our family, and now you've destroyed our business. The apple doesn't fall too far from the tree, I guess."

"My mother didn't destroy your family, and the last thing I wanted to do was hurt you and your business. But I couldn't lie to Faith. She deserved the truth."

"Oh my God, it's not the truth. It just some...some stupid thing you've convinced yourself of. Just like you convinced yourself Lorenzo loved you and like when you were a kid and convinced yourself you were going to marry a prince. It might've been okay when you were little, but it sure as heck isn't okay now," she snapped, and then stabbed an angry finger in Serena and Ryan's direction. "You think you have special powers? Use them on these two. Are they a perfect match?"

Jenna looked at her beautiful blond stepsister standing under an old-fashioned lamppost with a basket of petunias swaying in the light summer breeze overhead, filling the air with their musky fragrance. Serena stood within inches of the burly police officer, her body leaning toward him whether she meant to or not. Jenna didn't know why she hadn't seen it before, but she did now. In the small space between the couple, a pink-tinged light danced. She wished it weren't there, wished she could lie. "Yes, they are," she said, and turned, giving her suitcase a tug to get it moving.

She didn't look over her shoulder to see what havoc her pronouncement had wreaked or to think about what pain she may have caused Ryan's wife or the untenable situation she'd just put Serena in. What had possessed her? She should've lied to her sister and to Faith.

No, not to Faith. She needed to know the truth. Serena though? She should've lied to her or at the very least told her when Ryan wasn't around. He'd been the aggressor, the pursuer. But Jenna had blurted out the truth because of Arianna. She'd wanted to prove to her that she wasn't delusional, that she didn't have a choice, that she had to tell Faith.

And once again history repeated itself and Jenna found herself drinking cocktails at the Salty Dog. Only this time she didn't have Logan Gallagher to save her from herself. Or Shay or Cherry for that matter.

"Bless your heart, aren't you a charmer," she said to the older man propositioning her from the next barstool over. He was ninety-five if he was a day. She finished licking the white chocolate sprinkles from around the edge of her glass, and it hit her why he'd asked what else she could do with her tongue.

"Floyd, get your butt off the stool and out the door before Shay gets here. She finds out you've been talking to Jenna like that and she'll show you what you can do with your own tongue," Gerry the bartender said.

"Och now, I meant no harm. The lassies these days are too sensitive. Get her another one of those on me. Along with my apologies, lass."

"Thank you, kind sir. I accept both your apology and the drink. You saved me from offering my services to Gerry here to pay for my sex on the beach." She wasn't sure she'd be able to balance a serving tray with drinks, but she was willing to give it a try.

Floyd cocked his head. "I think I've just been bamboozled by a lady of the night."

"I know you're having a tough go and you're a friend of Shay's, Jenna. But we can't have any of that going on in the bar. Prostitution is illegal, you know. I'm obligated to call the police."

"You do that, Gerry. I need somewhere to sleep tonight anyway. Do you think I can get my drink first?"

* * *

Logan sat up in the bed in his suite at the Jefferson Hotel and rubbed his hand along his stubbled jaw. "You wanna run that by me again. I think I misheard you," he said to his brother Michael.

"Yeah, I thought the same thing. But you heard me right the first time. Jenna was arrested for prostitution and—"

"Come on, you can't be serious. Who in their right mind would believe Jenna Bell was a prostitute?" Logan asked.

"Gerry, the bartender at the pub apparently. And old man Floyd. But I wasn't quite finished. She was also charged with drunk and disorderly and assaulting a police officer," Michael said.

"Okay, Wilson's gone too far this time." Logan threw back the covers and got out of bed, frustrated his nemesis was targeting Jenna and he couldn't leave DC. "We have to do something about the guy, and we have to do it now."

"Here's the thing. As much as I don't want to give Wilson credit, he's the reason Jenna ended up getting off with only a slap on the wrist, not me. He didn't arrest her. A rookie did. He tried to take her purse, which I gather had been Pippa's bed at the time, and Jenna lost it. Hence the drunk and disorderly and the assault charge. They learned the hard way not to get between Jenna and her bird. When Shay and I arrived at the station, the two of them were in lockup, keeping everyone entertained. She's a pretty cute drunk."

For a woman who supposedly didn't drink, she was making up for lost time. "So what happened? Last I heard, her opportunity to win Arianna over for life was walking through the front door of Tie the Knot. Were they out celebrating?"

"A definite no to the celebrating. Jenna was in worse shape than she was last week," Michael said.

"I'm losing patience here, baby brother. It's one in the morning, and I've had a long couple of days. What's going on with Jenna?" Logan asked.

"A better question might be, what's going on with you and Jenna? I'm asking as your lawyer," his brother said when Logan made an aggravated sound. "You're charged with assaulting her ex-fiancé, and our defense is you did so to protect her sister. If it comes out that you and Jenna are—"

Logan knew exactly what was at stake. He'd known all along, and he couldn't blame a couple of beers or the moon and the stars for why he'd been willing to take the risk. Jenna had been willing and warm, and he'd wanted her—badly. It was as simple and as complicated as that. "I'm just looking out for her. We're friends."

It was the truth if not the whole truth. Jenna was easy to talk to, and he'd enjoyed hanging out with her. His brother wouldn't be happy to learn that, for one night, they'd been friends with benefits. And Logan had found himself thinking a lot about how great those benefits had been. Though it wasn't like he had any intention of following up with a repeat. His worries that Lorenzo or Poppy might out them had faded over the past couple days. He'd been more worried about Poppy. He'd met Lorenzo's type before—the guy thought he was God's gift to women. He wouldn't want to believe that Jenna had slept with another man hours after he'd dumped her. Especially a man with a magical penis. Recalling Jenna's detailed and highly complimentary text to her ex, Logan snorted a laugh, quickly covering it by clearing his throat.

"You know, if I didn't know you as well as I do, I wouldn't be buying the *just friends* line. But I can see how she'd bring out your protective instincts."

"That's very magnanimous of you. Now, I have to get up in a couple hours, so could you get to the point... Wait a minute. Why are you up at one in the morning? You didn't just get back from the police station, did you?"

"No. We've been back for hours. As a matter of fact, up until twenty minutes ago, I was sleeping soundly. Then Shay heard someone sneaking out of the house, that someone being Jenna. Now I'm sitting at Kismet Cove ensuring my fiancée's best friend doesn't drown while she attempts to teach Pippa how to find her food. At this rate, I figure I have another half hour to kill before the tide comes back in and decided to kill it talking to you. I actually thought you'd be up. Aren't you the head of the princess's security detail?"

"Yes, but while you've always looked up to me as if I'm some sort of superhero, I actually do require sleep."

"Really? I'm disappointed, bro. I thought you were... What the hell was that?"

Logan frowned. "What's going on?"

"I'm not sure. Something just hit the rocks near... Jenna, be careful. There's a drop-off—"

Logan heard his brother swear and then a feminine shriek over the sound of splashing water.

Logan walked to the window looking onto DC's skyline and reminded himself that all the Gallaghers were strong swimmers, including his brother. Logan had just finished assuring himself Jenna would be fine when he heard her calling frantically for the baby bird. She wouldn't be all right if something happened to Pippa. His brother's voice joined hers, sounding equally panicked.

Frustrated with his inability to do anything, Logan began to pace the suite as he strained to hear what was going on at Kismet Cove, the small, sheltered bay at the base of Greystone Manor. He was just about to disconnect to call in backup for a search when he heard a low *woof* and then a happy cry from Jenna and a relieved one from Michael. From what Logan could make out, his brother's Irish wolfhound, Atticus, had saved the day, and the bird.

"Hey, Michael," he called into the phone to remind his brother he was still there. Logan wanted to talk to Jenna and had a feeling she wouldn't have her phone on hand.

"Sorry," his brother said, sounding breathless. "We had a little excitement. Jenna got caught in an undertow near the rocks, and when I went to pull her out, Pippa must have followed. Atticus spotted her and went after her. We're all good though. I'll let you get back to—"

"Really? How exactly do you expect me to go back to sleep without knowing what's going on with Jenna?"

His brother gave an unhappy grunt. "That sounds like more than concern for just a friend, big brother. Jenna, Logan wants a word." There was a pause, and then his brother muttered, "Oh, yeah, you two are so not 'just friends.'"

Obviously, Jenna's reaction was the reason behind his brother's testy remark. If the expression that came over her face was anything like the one she wore the morning after they'd hooked up, Logan could understand his brother's concern. He wondered if he should be concerned too, but none of that mattered once Jenna's voice came over the line.

"I'm just one big screwup, Logan. I ruined everything. Arianna and Serena are facing financial ruin because of me, and I nearly let Pippa drown, and I'm not sure she's getting enough to eat, and I can't afford to take her to the vet and—"

"Come on, nothing is ever as bad as it seems. Just take a couple of deep breaths and then tell me what happened."

He sat on the edge of the bed as she filled him in on what went down at Tie the Knot today. It was pretty bad and so easily avoidable that he bit back a frustrated sigh. He didn't know what was up with Jenna and this idea that she had some kind of psychic ability and could tell that Faith and her fiancé weren't meant to be together and that her stepsister and Wilson were. At least it explained why the officer was now Jenna's champion. Though Logan wondered how Serena felt about it, not to mention Wilson's wife.

But at the small break in Jenna's voice, he kept his opinions to himself. Other than to make her feel worse than she already did, it wouldn't change anything. "First off, stop worrying about Pippa. Everyone else, including the vet, wrote her off last week. The only reason she's still alive is because of you. So just keep doing what you're doing and she'll be fine."

She sniffed. "Thank you."

He smiled. She really was a sweet woman, and he didn't want to hurt her, but it had to be said. "Jenna, do you think maybe it's time you stop trying so hard to win over your sisters?"

"Arianna might take issue with that statement. All I've done this past week is embarrass them and destroy their business. I have to fix it, Logan. I couldn't live with myself if I didn't make this right. It's what my dad wanted. He wanted us to be a family. It's all I've ever wanted."

"I think I have an idea how you can do that. My cousin Finn's wife, Olivia, is having a baby any day now. She's the wedding planner at the manor, and I'm sure they're looking for a replacement. You take the job, you could send business your sisters' way."

"You've already done enough for me. I don't want your family to feel obligated to hire me."

"I'll handle it, okay? This is your chance to make things right with your sister. Take it."

"Okay. Thank you. I owe you, Logan."

"Yeah, you do. So no more drowning your sorrows at the Salty Dog. Next time I'm in town, you'll have to tell me how you ended up in jail for assault and prostitution."

She groaned. "I was hoping you didn't hear about that."

Chapter Fourteen

♥

Jenna didn't know what she'd been thinking when she'd agreed to Logan's suggestion that she take the job as Greystone Manor's wedding planner. That was the problem, wasn't it? She hadn't been thinking. But no matter her doubts about her ability to do the job, for her stepsisters' and Logan's sakes, she'd give it her best shot.

It had taken several days and part of yesterday for Logan to convince his family to give Jenna the position. They'd had several promising candidates interviewing for the job. Jenna had a lot to live up to. The other candidates' reputations and credentials were no doubt impeccable, and thanks to her last week in Harmony Harbor, Jenna's were not.

So even though Logan wasn't sure he wanted to keep the manor in the family, because of her he'd joined the Save Greystone Team. When that didn't completely win over his grandmother, he agreed to date whoever won the Bachelor of the Month auction.

Jenna had a feeling Logan didn't know that his

grandmother and his mother expected him to not only date the winner of the auction, but also marry her. She'd talked with Logan about this kind of thing enough to know that while he might agree to a date, there was no way the man would marry. At least not until sometime in the distant future. In fact, he showed every sign of being a confirmed bachelor. Jenna was thinking along those lines herself. Being a confirmed bachelorette was sounding better and better these days. All she had to do was look at Arianna, Faith, Serena, and Kimberly for evidence.

She pulled out the leather office chair and sat behind the formidable mahogany desk in the study at Greystone Manor. It was a lovely room with its ornate dark wood paneling and mullioned window that overlooked the front gardens. The window seat looked particularly inviting at the moment. She'd much rather be soaking up the morning sunshine alongside Simon than perusing the swatches of fabric laid out before her.

The manor's previous wedding planner, Olivia Gallagher, had put together boards with three wedding themes for today's bride-to-be to choose from. The first board held ideas for a garden wedding, the second board a beach wedding (always a popular choice in summer), and the third board was a rustic wedding. Olivia had exquisite taste and was well organized so there wasn't much for Jenna to do, other than pin the fabric to the boards.

For any other wedding planner, that would not be a big deal, but for Jenna it was. And after Logan had gone to so much trouble getting her the job, she couldn't let him down. She couldn't let her sisters down either. Jenna had already made notes of everything she could purchase through Tie the Knot for each wedding theme. She may not be able to replace the income they'd lost due to the Fourburger cancelation just yet, but if Jenna booked a few good-size weddings over the next few weeks, she might be able to. Unless she got fired first, she thought, chewing on a thumbnail as she stared at the swatches.

"Being a Negative Nellie isn't going to do me much good, is it, Pippa? No offense, my little friend, but at the moment, I wish you were a member of the Corvidae family instead of the Scolopacidae. You're surprised I know the difference, aren't you?" she said when Pippa wobbled across the desk on her sticklike legs to look up at her. She stroked the peep's downy head. "That's what happens when you spend hours learning everything you can about birds, even birds you're not particularly fond of. Until recently, I wasn't a fan of crows. I thought they were bad luck and scavengers. But they're actually incredibly smart. They're being trained to pick out colors on command." She sighed. "I could really use a crow right about now."

As though offended by Jenna's remark, Pippa toddled over to the fabrics, tapped one with her beak and then flung it off the desk. "Pippa." Jenna laughed as she bent to retrieve the swatch from the hardwood floor. Another piece of fabric landed on her head while she was down there, and then another.

"If you're trying to make a case for you being the smartest bird on the block, I'm sorry to tell you it's not

working. And since you're no help at all and Shay has
meetings all day, there's only one person I can call."
About a gazillion butterflies took flight in Jenna's stomach at the thought of talking to Logan. *It's just nerves*,
she assured herself.

Pippa stopped pecking at the beach wedding board
to look at her. "Fine, so I might have a small case
of hero worship. It's not a big deal. Logan's saved
me at least three times now, and we did have sex,
on the beach, under the stars, and he's an incredibly
nice man. Handsome too, and he has..." Feeling
someone's gaze upon her, she glanced at Simon, who
was no longer sunbathing but regarding her intently.
"Sorry, Simon. You can go back to sleep now. I'll
stop talking about Logan. I should probably stop
thinking about him too."

She got back to work and picked up the swatches,
studying them for several moments before placing the
ones she felt complemented each other together. Then
she attached them to the corresponding boards. Once
she'd taken a picture of each, she sent them to Logan,
asking for his opinion.

Her phone rang a few minutes later. "Hi. Sorry to
bother you. I'm sure you're busy with the princess, but
I didn't know who else—"

"Jenna, it's fine. If it weren't, I wouldn't have called
you back. So I take it you're having a problem figuring
out which fabrics go with which wedding."

"Yes, and I bet you're wishing you didn't put your
inheritance and your bachelorhood on the line for me. I
didn't think this through, Logan. Neither of us did."

"I did, and I just checked tracking. Your glasses should arrive at the manor before the end of the day."

"Glasses?"

"Yep, they look like sunglasses, only they should help you see colors more clearly and vividly. These ones are specifically made for people with tritanopia."

"I...I don't know what to say." Tears welled in her eyes, and she blinked them away. She wouldn't cry. He'd think her silly and sentimental, but he had no idea how touched she was. She couldn't seem to go a day without Logan Gallagher doing something kind for her. She didn't know how she would ever repay him.

She didn't until there was a knock on the study door just before it opened and his mother popped her head inside. "Jenna, is it? I was wondering if I could have a moment of your time?"

"Certainly, Mrs. Gallagher."

"If that's my mother, don't let her know I'm on the phone. She'll keep me on forever, and I've got to get Isabella and at least fifteen other people and two tons of luggage to the airport within the hour. I'll text you."

"All right. Thank you very much, Mr. Knight."

He laughed. "Better than 'Mr. Charming,' I guess. I'll see you Friday."

Outwardly, she didn't react to the news he was coming to Harmony Harbor, but inwardly, her butterflies did a happy dance. Which meant she forgot to remind him about the swatches—her appointment with the couple was at noon—before he disconnected. As his mother made herself comfortable in the chair across from her and Jenna returned Pippa to the decorative birdcage on the desk, there was the sound of an incoming text. Certain it was from Logan, Jenna had a difficult time not checking right away and keeping the silly grin off her face.

She inwardly berated herself for acting like an idiot and gestured to the silver tea tray and heated carafes, reminding herself to stay focused on her goal. Fate had handed her the perfect opportunity to repay Logan, and she wasn't going to waste it. "Can I offer you a coffee or tea, Mrs. Gallagher?"

"Yes, I could use a cup of tea, thanks. Black," she said when Jenna began to pour.

Jenna smiled as she stood up to bring Logan's mom her tea. Feeling uncomfortable and somewhat out of place sitting behind the formidable desk, Jenna sat in the wingback chair beside Mrs. Gallagher.

Logan's mother smiled faintly. "I can see why you earned rave reviews for customer service at Southern Belle. You're obviously a considerate person. You make people feel comfortable right away. It's a good trait to have when you're in trade." She nodded as if she'd been talking to herself.

Her years of dealing with people left Jenna with little doubt Logan's mother had something to ask or say and wasn't completely sure how to go about it just yet.

Jenna smiled. "Thank you. That's very kind of you to say."

Maura made a moue and then lifted the teacup from the saucer, liquid sloshing over the side as her hand noticeably shook. Jenna didn't want to embarrass her, but she didn't think pretending not to notice was helpful. "Sorry. I overfilled your cup," she said, and leaned across the desk to grab a napkin.

"I was right," Maura murmured, and then took the napkin from Jenna with a tight smile. "Thank you."

She appeared brittle, as if you'd place a finger on her and she'd crumble beneath its weight. Despite her impeccably applied makeup, Logan's mother looked wan, her eyes tired and dull. It was obvious she hadn't been sleeping well. Jenna's heart hurt for her, and for her son. It was because of Logan she worked up the courage to say, "Is there anything else I can get for you, Mrs. Gallagher? Are you in pain?"

Her head jerked in Jenna's direction. "Why would you ask something like that?"

"I'm sorry. I spent some time with Logan last weekend. He's worried about you, Mrs. Gallagher. He needed someone to talk to. Your confidence is safe with me. I won't say anything to anyone. Not even Logan if you don't want me to. I just thought maybe you could use someone to talk to. Someone who isn't family and can be objective."

"All my family does is talk at me and tell me what to do. I've spent my entire life doing what everyone else wanted me to. I think it's about time I did what I wanted to for a change, don't you?"

"Definitely. As women, we're not very good at putting ourselves and our needs first, are we? And you've more than earned the right to do whatever makes you happy, Mrs. Gallagher. My mom did, and her last few months were spent doing exactly what she wanted. Some of my happiest moments with her were from that time."

Maura avoided looking at Jenna, keeping her gaze firmly on the teacup. "You lost your mother to cancer?"

"Yes, when I was twelve." After she shared a little bit about her mother's diagnosis and treatment, Jenna was heartened when Logan's mother began asking questions. At least it appeared she hadn't offended the woman. She hoped it remained the case when she said, "Mrs. Gallagher—"

"Maura, please."

"Maura." Jenna smiled. "I know it's none of my business, and if you were putting off testing because you're perfectly happy to just go on living your life the way you want and on your own terms, I'd say, go you. But I don't think that's why you're not having the testing. I think you're afraid. When my mom's doctor first raised the possibility she had cancer, the worst time for us—the absolute worst—was when we didn't know what we were dealing with. Because you can't fight what you don't know, right?"

"But if I don't know, I can pretend everything's fine."

Jenna reached over and took her hand, giving it a gentle squeeze. "You might be able to pretend on the outside, but your mind never lets you forget, does it? You're living in fear, and that's no way to live. What if you're wasting all this time being afraid for nothing? You might not even have cancer."

"Given my family history and the results of the tests I've had so far, my doctor is fairly certain that I do."

"It never hurts to get a second opinion, you know."

"My son Connor has already set one up for me with

the oncologist who treated Griffin's ex-wife for breast cancer."

"I've met Lexi, and she's doing amazing. I actually wouldn't be surprised if we're planning her wedding in the near future."

"Hopefully we'll be planning both my sons' weddings before hers." She slanted Jenna a look. "You seem very fond of Logan. You're not interested in marrying him, are you?"

Knowing how difficult Maura had made Shay and Michael's life a few months back, Jenna was flattered that she actually thought her worthy of her son. "I can honestly say I've never met a man as incredible as your son. And trust me, I've met a lot of men in my years of being a matchmaker. But after what my fiancé just put me through, I have no interest in marrying or dating. I'm going to focus all my energy on my job here."

"Good. I'm happy to hear that. You're a nice young woman, and I didn't want to hurt your feelings. I should've realized given your previous profession that you already would've concluded you're not Logan's type. A dozen years before, maybe. From what he told us about his fiancée, Noreen, she was sweet and quiet, a little mousy like you. Sadly, she died only weeks after they were engaged. But I honestly doubt they would've lasted more than a year. Logan needs a strong woman. And that's actually what I wanted to talk to you about. I want to get this right, and I don't have time to waste."

If Jenna weren't stunned by the direction the conversation had taken, she would've pointed out that Maura might have more time than she knew, and this was exactly the reason why she had to see another doctor. But all she could do was stare at Logan's mother while digesting the news that she thought Jenna was quiet and mousy and totally not right for her son.

Maura leaned forward to place the teacup on the tray and then bent to pick up her bag from the floor. She opened her purse and removed two files. "I'm leaning toward Delaney Davis, the communication officer for the mayor. Physically, she's my son's ideal woman. Absolutely stunning, she's tall and blond. She's also smart and driven, a very strong woman who knows what she wants and goes after it. I really like that about her, and so will Logan. Her family isn't exactly on par with ours socially, which I feel is important, but they're politically active and have well-placed connections." She handed Jenna Delaney's file and then the one beneath it. "Victoria is my best friend Gloria's daughter. Again, beautiful and blond, though not as driven as Delaney, but socially, she's a far better match. She's a veterinarian and heiress to a dog food fortune."

And gay. Which Jenna knew because Shay had told her. Victoria had been Maura's top pick for Michael too. Jenna pretended to give each woman's file careful consideration before handing them back to Maura. "I think Delaney is a better match for Logan than Victoria, but I'm not completely sure she's the one either." *You're not sure because you think* you *are.* Jenna's eyes went wide. Where had that even come from? She told the voice in her head to be quiet.

"Really? I was so sure Delaney was perfect for him. But I trust you. I've read your reviews, and you come highly recommended. Some of the women go so far as to say you have an actual gift." She tucked the files in her purse. "There's something else I wanted to ask you, but I need your promise you won't say anything to anyone, especially my sons."

"Of course. Whatever you tell me is confidential, Maura."

"Before I met my husband, I dated his brother Daniel, and I'd like to know if he's my one."

Oh no, she couldn't be asking what Jenna thought she was. "Your husband or his brother?"

"His brother. It won't be difficult for you to observe Daniel, or the two of us together for that matter. Like you, we're staying at the manor."

Jenna had been over the moon that free room and board were part of her compensation package. Now, not so much. The last thing she wanted to do was observe Maura with Daniel Gallagher. Logan wouldn't forgive her if she ended up being the reason his mother split up with his father for good. She didn't think she could feel much worse until Maura left and Jenna retrieved her phone from the desk. Logan had once again made sure she was taken care of, giving her detailed instructions for which swatch went with which wedding theme.

* * *

Colleen took her place on the window seat next to Simon. The study had certainly been the place to be this morning. She was hoping for more of the same this afternoon. "What did I miss?" she asked Simon as

Kitty left the study. Her daughter-in-law was walking away with a sheaf of computer printouts in her hand. Colleen imagined that, like Maura, Kitty had been seeking Jenna's matchmaking advice. Lord knew she could use it.

If the cat had eyebrows, they'd reach his ears.

"All right, you don't have to get snooty about it. I haven't lost my marbles. I know you can't speak, but sometimes I get tired of talking to myself and pretend that you can. Besides, you know what I'm saying. Of that I'm certain." He was a canny cat, but she shouldn't be complimenting him. He was liable to get a swelled head, and he was difficult enough to deal with on a good day.

Colleen had been trailing Maura, prepared to do what she could to stave off an assignation between her and Daniel. She'd also been trying to gain Jasper's attention. She needed to get a peek at her book to get the full story about the Daniel, Maura, and Sean love triangle. Imagine Maura thinking Daniel was her match and not her husband of forty years. Colleen prayed there was not an ounce of truth to it.

She glanced at Jenna and blinked. "What in all that is holy has the girl got on her face?" Simon gave her the look again. Colleen waved him off. "Don't be so literal."

She was just about to walk over and see what Jenna was up to when there was a knock on the study door. Jenna looked up from the book she'd been perusing, the overlarge sunglasses with the pink lenses practically swallowing her face. "Come in."

"Hey...Ah, wow, interesting-looking shades." Connor glanced around the room. "Do you want me to lower the blinds?"

"No, it's okay." Looking embarrassed, Jenna removed her glasses. "I'm color-blind. Logan bought these for me so I could do my job without bothering him every ten minutes. This falls under lawyer-client confidentiality, doesn't it?"

"Sure, if that's what you want. But it's not really a big deal that you're color-blind, is it? If you ask me, the glasses are a bigger deal. You're lucky you can pull them off, Jenna," Connor said, flashing a brilliant smile. He was a charmer, that one. Just like his uncle Daniel.

Colleen stared at the lad. He couldn't be Daniel's, could he? No, she would've remembered something like that.

"I don't think your family would've hired me had they known I was color-blind. It's kind of important for a wedding planner. And I need the job. Thank you for agreeing to meet me here, by the way."

"No problem. I wanted to talk to my mom anyway."

Jenna looked like she wanted to ask him if Maura had agreed to get a second opinion. She wouldn't though. And the lads would have no idea they had Jenna to thank if their mother agreed to further testing.

Colleen gave Jenna a fond smile. "You did good, my girl." Maura didn't know Logan as well as she thought if she was matching him with a woman like Delaney Davis. Jenna was the one for the lad, whether he'd admit it or not. He needed someone like Jenna with her quiet strength and resilience.

"I'm sorry I had to cancel last week. Arianna wanted to..." Jenna cleared her throat. "So, can I get you a coffee or tea?"

"Don't try to protect my feelings, Jenna. I know your sister hates me," Connor said.

"Stepsister. If she were here, she'd correct you. And you're not the only one she hates; she hates me too. Probably more than she hates you."

"I doubt it," he said dryly, and leaned forward to pour himself a coffee. He held up the carafe, offering Jenna some.

"No, thank you. If I drink any more, I'll float away."

He grinned into his mug. "So tell me, what did you do to make Arianna hate you? I find it hard to believe that anyone could hate you, Jenna."

"Trust me, several people do." She filled him in on everything she'd done over the past two weeks that had earned her sister's wrath. "Why does Arianna hate you? Serena said it's because you broke her heart when you were young, but that seems an awfully long time to hold a grudge."

"It is, but as you know, Arianna is very good at holding a grudge. And I honestly never knew why we broke up, but I do know why she has a problem with me now. I represented her ex in their divorce. Initially I refused—I'm a corporate attorney—but old man Summers went to the partners at my firm and asked for me personally. The Summers own half of Boston and are one of my firm's top clients. Not exactly someone you turn down if you have ambitions to make partner one day."

Colleen sighed. "Funny, and not in a ha-ha sort of way, but I can't recall any of this. And to think all those years ago I was sure Arianna and Connor were a match made in heaven. It looks like I've got some work to do to get to the bottom of all of this, Simon. We have a long night ahead of us. Jasper has become quite adept at ignoring us when Kitty's around."

She returned her attention to Jenna and Connor when Jenna said, "You're right. She probably hates you more than she hates me."

"Thanks. And now that we've got that settled, we should talk about your ex and your stepmother. Who, by the way, I'm more than happy to wipe the court-room floor with. Lorenzo dropped the charges against Logan and insists that, in doing so, he's entitled to his ring back. If Wilson hadn't called Logan's boss or been pushing so hard to get my brother put be-hind bars, Lorenzo withdrawing the charges might've helped a bit, but as things stand, it barely moved the needle.

"So until he returns your car and the money from your savings account, I've refused to return the ring on your behalf. And that earned me an interesting call from his irate uncle, who now says he's countersuing because Lorenzo had no right to give you the ring. But don't worry. I've put my best investigator on the case and ex-pect to have something to work with soon."

"Your best investigator is Shay, isn't it?" Jenna said.

Well, that was good news, at least, Colleen decided. Shay would get to the bottom of this. "Too bad she can't see me. I could use her help," she murmured, thinking of all she had to look in to, including this Officer Wilson. Now, why did that name seem familiar?

"Yep, so you know you're in good hands. Now, I—" Connor turned when Jasper came into the room.

Colleen straightened, not liking the tense look on her old friend's face.

"I'm sorry for the interruption, but we've just received word that Master Logan has been involved in a motor vehicle accident and has been taken to the hospital."

Chapter Fifteen

♥

Jenna ducked behind the fireplace in the lobby in order to escape the notice of the members of the Widows Club as they flooded the entrance of the manor. She counted at least seven of the older women. Two of whom were carrying ominous-looking binders. They were going to pick her brain again about matches for Logan. They'd been driving her crazy for the past two days, and with no word from Logan, she was already frazzled.

She hadn't realized until then how deeply he'd woven himself into the fabric of her daily life. She missed texting with him and talking to him on the phone, which she found herself checking incessantly. It was getting a little embarrassing, but she couldn't bring herself to stop or to call.

His mother, father, and brothers had dropped everything to rush to DC as soon as they'd gotten word about the accident. Shay had been keeping Jenna up to date. Other than a concussion and some stitches, Logan was apparently all right. So were the princess and her entourage. Best as anyone could figure out, a blown tire was responsible for the SUV going off the road. But because of the previous kidnapping attempt, they weren't taken any chances, and the vehicle was undergoing testing at Quantico.

"Is everything all right, miss?" Jenna jumped at the sound of Jasper's voice behind her, bumping her nose on the fireplace.

It felt like she was bleeding. Pressing her fingertips to her nose, she turned and forced a smile. "I just wanted to get a closer look at the color of the stone for the MacGregors' Christmas Eve wedding. We're having the reception in the lobby, and I want to be sure the decorations don't clash." She cringed. She'd never been very good at lying, and Jasper seemed to be a man adept at sniffing them out.

"Quite," he said, his lips twitching as though holding back a smile.

Jenna hadn't had much to do with the older man, but she liked him. By no means did he give off the warm and fuzzies. His accent and manner were stiff and proper, but there was no doubt he loved the Gallaghers, especially the great-grandsons. If Jenna hadn't been in a state of panicked shock when he delivered the news about Logan's accident the other day, she would've gone to the older man and given him a hug. It'd been clear he was as worried as the other members of the Gallagher family. She wondered what that must be like for him, being part of the family but not really. A little like she had been with the Bells. Never quite one of them, always on the outside looking in. The thought made her feel a sense of camaraderie with the older man.

"Jasper, dar…Oh, Jenna, I didn't see you there. I see Jasper's delivered the news." Kitty gave her arm an excited squeeze. "It's incredible, isn't it? I still can't believe it myself. Oh my, they're here. Jasper, come with me. I don't want to make a fool of myself. Do you think we should have a red carpet? What about trumpets? Do we need trumpets to announce their arrival?"

"No, but we do need to clear the entrance of the Widows Club. Ladies," Jasper called out as he strode across the lobby with Kitty hurrying after him, leaving Jenna to wonder what on earth was going on.

She checked to be sure her nose wasn't bleeding and then set off after the older couple. As she got closer to the crowd gathered in the entryway, she heard the whispers. "Royalty? Here in Harmony Harbor? Staying at the manor?"

By the time Jenna reached the crowd gathered around the castle door, Kitty and Jasper had disappeared outside and the Widows Club were beside themselves with excitement. "Jenna, you're going to be planning the wedding of the century. Isn't it romantic? Meghan Markle became an American princess in May, and now we'll have our very own American prince in June."

Jenna had to stop herself from doing a happy dance in the middle of the entryway of Greystone Manor. Her prayers had been answered. The wedding of the century would more than make up for the financial loss Tie the Knot had sustained thanks to Jenna losing Faith Fourburger's business.

"I always said Logan was a prince among men," a member of the Widows Club said.

"Logan?" Jenna's voice cracked, and she cleared her throat before trying again. "What about Logan?"

Several of the women turned to look at her. "Logan's the American prince. He's marrying Princess Isabella of Merradien."

* * *

Under the steady, pale green gaze of the manor's wedding planner, Logan shifted in the wingback chair across from the desk in the study. He felt like he'd just been called to the principal's office and was about to get expelled. With her big, innocent eyes and cupid's bow mouth, the woman shouldn't be able to pull off intimidating, but she managed just fine. He didn't know what he'd done to tick her off, but obviously he'd done something because every time their paths crossed since their arrival yesterday morning, she looked like she was imagining sixty-eight ways to kill him.

He considered himself a decent, laid-back guy. People generally liked him. But he had a heavy foot, so maybe he'd cut her off at a stop sign? Or maybe she'd tried to strike up a conversation at a bar and he hadn't noticed her? She was a pretty woman, but she seemed quiet, and she was tiny, easily overlooked.

It was time to get to the bottom of this. "Have we met before?"

Oh crap. She shot him a duck-and-cover glare. He

should've kept his mouth shut. Now what was he supposed to say? "Was that a yes or a no?"

"Are you seriously going to pretend that you don't know me?"

"So we do know each other, then?"

"You're all the same," she muttered, and slid on a pair of glasses and then picked up a swatch of fabrics of varying blue hues.

Okay, so he'd apologize for whatever he'd supposedly done, and that should take care of it. After all, he had to work with her for the next couple of weeks while she planned his wedding—his wedding to a woman he was supposedly in love with but barely knew. As much as the wedding planner's attitude stumped him, so did the fact he was getting married in two weeks. He might've lost a small chunk of memory in the accident, but not enough of it to forget that a month before he'd been more than happy to remain a bachelor for the rest of his life.

"Jenna, is it?"

She lifted her head and stared at him through the pink lenses of a pair of oversized glasses that were so big they practically ate her face. His mouth twitched, and he did his best to swallow his laughter, but he lost the battle when she said in the voice of a third-grade teacher, "What exactly do you find so amusing?"

"I'm sorry, but you need to have those things sized to your face. You look like a cartoon character."

"I suppose it's not surprising I look like an idiot since you're the one who bought them for me and you seem intent on making a fool of me today."

"No, the last thing I want to do is...Wait. Are you saying I bought the glasses for you?"

"Have you lost your hearing as well as your memory?" She rolled her eyes like she didn't believe either, and then he thought he heard her say, "If I didn't need this job and this wedding, I'd be outta here. Even Charleston would be better than this." She flicked the swatch of fabric in a dismissive gesture and returned to studying it.

He got up and moved around the desk, placing his hand on the armrest to turn her to face him. He crouched in front of her chair. "I'm sorry. I shouldn't have laughed. And I'm really sorry I don't recognize you, because, clearly, I should. And it's not because you're unmemorable, Jenna. It's because I took a hit to my head in the accident and I've lost a few weeks of my memory."

"No one said anything about memory loss. They said you had a concussion and a bad cut on your hand that had to be stitched." She glanced at his hand on the armrest before she brought her gaze back to his, searching his face. Like he'd lied to her and she wasn't sure she could trust him. He didn't know why, but all of a sudden it felt important to him that she did.

"We're keeping the memory loss on the downlow, so I'd appreciate if you'd do the same." She arched a defined auburn eyebrow. "Luis and Isabella are concerned that her family would object to the marriage on the grounds I'm not of sound mind."

"They might have a point," she murmured.

He frowned. "Why would you say that?"

"I've only known you for a couple weeks, but in that time you never mentioned you were in a relationship, let alone getting married in a few weeks."

The look on her face made him question just what kind of relationship they'd been in. Things would've been a whole lot less awkward if he had his smartphone and he could track his communication over the last few weeks, but it'd been destroyed in the accident. "You and I weren't—" he began.

"No, of course not. We were...friends."

He smiled, relieved. "We must've been pretty good friends if I gave you these," he teased, thinking they must've been a gag gift.

She seemed to take offense to the teasing. "I'm color-blind, and it makes my job as a wedding planner difficult—if not almost impossible—to do." She pushed the glasses up her nose with her forefinger. "These help. They allow me to see the actual color. You bought them for me."

"Huh. I'm a pretty nice guy, then," he said, hoping once again to lighten the mood.

"I thought you were."

That said it all right there. They'd definitely been more than just friends. It was the only reason for her to be this upset with him, and she had no idea how upsetting that was for him. He was a one-woman man. He'd never cheat on someone he loved. Hell, he wouldn't even date another woman if he'd just started seeing someone.

But before he had a chance to ask her anything more, the study door opened and his bride-to-be and Luis entered the room. Isabella wore a white, sleeveless jumpsuit. She was a beautiful woman with shoulder-length brown hair and brown eyes, her demeanor similar to that of Jenna. Although with a little less attitude. Logan smiled at the thought. Luis, who was Isabella's right-hand man, reminded Logan of Jasper. The older man was also tall and thin and as adept at sharing his opinion with a singular look as Jasper. Unlike Jasper, whose hair was silver, Luis's was jet-black and slicked back from his face.

Jenna moved Logan's hand from the armrest and furtively waved him off like a dog who'd overstayed his welcome. Gracefully rising from the chair, she gave a brief bob, bending slightly at the knees. "Your Royal Highness."

Isabella offered Jenna a smile and cast a shy glance Logan's way. Knowing that she must be feeling as overwhelmed as he was, Logan gave her a reassuring smile in return. Luis said something to her in Spanish, and she nodded and took a seat in the chair Logan had previously occupied.

He introduced them. "Isabelle, Luis, this is Jenna. She'll be taking care of the arrangements for the wedding. I'll leave everything to you ladies, but for reasons of security, I will need to sign off on the plans. As much as possible, I'd like to limit the venues to inside the manor, Jenna."

"Certainly. But you should know your mother and grandmother have already been approached by the Widows Club and the town council to host luncheons for you both. There's actually a barbecue planned for this evening to welcome Her Royal Highness to Harmony Harbor as well as to celebrate your upcoming nuptials."

It amazed him how Jenna could be sweetly smiling at Isabella while still managing to convey her not-so-sweet thoughts about him. She clearly thought he was an asshat, and he planned to find out why.

Luis's eyes narrowed as though he sensed the undercurrent between them. Logan would have to ensure that the older man didn't think Jenna was a threat to his and Isabella's relationship. A former military officer, Luis wasn't to be crossed lightly. Just like the other older man who chose that exact moment to enter the study.

Let the fireworks begin, Logan thought resignedly when Jasper eyed Luis with a touch of disdain. He'd known the two men would vie for control. Logan wondered why he hadn't suggested that he and Isabella elope. Actually, he'd wondered a lot of things when Luis told him he was engaged to Isabella and they were getting married in two weeks.

At first, Logan had thought it was a joke. But it soon became apparent that, if it were, everyone was in on it except him. He hadn't wanted to hurt Isabella by questioning her, so he'd interrogated her personal bodyguard, Mateo, and her lady's maid, Pilar. All their stories jibed. Feeling like he was in an alternate universe, Logan had then spoken to the neurologist, who assured him it was possible he'd lost several weeks of memory. He hoped the neurologist's belief that Logan's memory would eventually return proved to be true.

Luis raised his hands with a look of abject horror on

his face. "What is that?" He lifted his chin in Jasper's direction.

"I introduced you earlier, Luis. Jasper's—"

"Not him, that." Luis pointed dramatically at Simon.

"He is a beloved member of the Gallagher family, sir," Jasper, who barely tolerated the cat, said in his most pretentious voice. "Your Royal Highness, may I present Simon."

"No. The animal is bad luck. I will not have him near Isabella. Shoo. *Vamoose.*" Luis went to the study door, holding it open while gesturing for Simon to leave.

The cat sniffed and lifted his nose, padding regally to the window seat, where he jumped up and made himself comfortable beside...

"What is that?" Luis said, pointing to a small bird sitting on a satin pillow.

"A baby sandpiper. Her name's Pippa, and she's very well behaved," Jenna said, casting a nervous glance from the bird to Luis. "I can put her in her cage if you're frightened, but she doesn't fly."

Unlike Jenna, Jasper's face was typically an unreadable mask no matter the circumstances. Clearly, he had an agenda today, and he turned his smirking face toward Luis, who lifted his nose and sniffed as disdainfully as Simon had. "Do not be ridiculous. I am afraid of nothing. My concern is only for my princess. A bird in the house is a bad omen. It means death shall come to someone within."

Logan thought Isabella might intercede and then remembered she always deferred to Luis, who was like a father to her. "I'm pretty sure the superstition refers to a bird flying into the house, not to a bird currently living in it, Luis," Logan said.

"I do not care. My princess and I demand the animals be removed."

"Would you also like us to fumigate the room?" Jasper asked, making no effort to keep the patronizing tone from his voice.

Jenna cleared her throat just as Luis opened his mouth to respond to Jasper and said, "If you'd prefer, we can move to one of the sitting rooms, Your Highness."

"It would be best, I think. This room is too small. My bodyguard and lady's maid will be joining us shortly," Isabella said to Jenna.

"As you wish, Your Highness," Jasper said with a small bow. "Please, follow me. Master Logan, I believe Ms. Bell could use your assistance."

"The princess requires her fiancé to escort her to the sitting room. I shall assist Ms. Bell," Luis said.

"Quite. Ms. Bell, please show Princess Isabella's manservant how to cage both Pippa and Simon."

Obviously as unhappy with the idea as Luis, Jenna said, "I can manage on my own. Thank you for the offer though. I'll be with you in a few minutes."

Logan's mother opened the door and smiled. "Oh good, you're finished. I've made an appointment at Tie the Knot to have you fitted for your wedding gown, Isabella. We need to be there in—"

"You better call and cancel, Mom. Tell them Jenna hasn't had a chance to show us—"

"No. Don't do that. Please don't do that," Jenna said,

clearly panic-stricken. "Just give me one minute. I think I have the perfect idea for your wedding." She swiped through several screens on her iPad and then turned it to his mother and Isabella, who'd moved to the desk. "It's a Cinderella theme. We'd use light blue and gold for the color scheme."

"Oh yes, it is beautiful," Isabella said, plainly happy with what she saw.

"It's absolutely perfect for a royal wedding, Jenna. I'm just concerned you won't be able to pull it together in time." His mother turned to Isabella. "Are you sure we can't push out the date by a few weeks, dear?"

Logan wondered if his mother would have better luck than him. He'd tried to push back the date in hopes his memory would return, but Luis had shot him down.

"I'm afraid that is impossible. The royal family has conceded to Logan's request that a small wedding be held here first, as it would be difficult for all of your family to get the time off to attend their wedding in Merradien."

Just one more detail Logan couldn't recall.

"Oh, I see." His mother patted Isabella's arm. "We'll just have to make it work, then, won't we?"

Even though it wasn't her nature to give in, Logan wasn't surprised his mother acquiesced without a fight. Social status and money had always been important to her. So as long as she was gaining a princess as a daughter-in-law, nothing else would matter.

"Don't worry, Maura," Jenna said. "I know exactly which vendors I'll be ordering from, and I can almost guarantee they'll have everything in stock."

"Excellent. You're a gem. I don't know what we'd do without you, darling." She smiled at Jenna and then looped Isabella's arm through hers. "All right, off we go to Tie the Knot to have you fitted for your wedding gown. Jenna," she called over her shoulder when they reached the door. "Can you e-mail them the photos so they know what we're looking for?"

"Just tell Arianna it's for a Cinderella-themed wedding and she'll know exactly what you're looking for. I wouldn't be surprised if she already has a design in mind."

Logan frowned, wondering why Jenna looked like she'd just given away a prized possession.

Chapter Sixteen

♥

Jenna had no idea why, but it felt worse losing Logan and the wedding of her dreams to Princess Isabella than it had losing Lorenzo and her business to Gwyneth. It made no sense. Jenna had thought she was in love with Lorenzo and she knew she wasn't in love with Logan. How could she be? They'd known each other for only a few weeks and in that time had maybe spent a total of twenty hours together. Were some of those hours the best she'd ever spent with a man?

She thought it might be safer to plead the Fifth than to answer. The question must have come straight from her heart and not her head. Her head knew better than to trust in the fairy tale. It knew better than to put a man on a pedestal just because he seemed to be honorable, heroic, and kind. There was no such thing as the perfect man.

Through the open window in Jenna's guest room at the manor, a light breeze ushered in the sound of laughter, music, and the scent of wild roses. The window looked onto the patio, where Logan and his beautiful princess greeted family, friends, and the citizens of Harmony Harbor.

Fairy lights were strung among the trees and shrubs while spotlights lit up the meandering flagstone paths and extensive gardens. Tables and chairs were set up on the grounds to accommodate the large number of guests. Only the Gallagher family and the princess's entourage would remain on the patio to dine once everyone had a chance to speak to the couple and offer their best wishes.

Jenna hadn't planned on attending and had her excuse at the ready should anyone ask. She had a royal wedding to plan in less than ten days and needed every minute of every day if she was expected to pull it off. But no one had asked her to come.

Still, after learning that Serena and Arianna were going to be there tonight, Jenna had no choice. She had to attend. They were the reason she was here, after all, planning the wedding of a man she'd begun to fantasize about, a man who for a few brief minutes on the beach had felt like her one and only.

She made a gagging noise, and Pippa looked up from digging in the miniature sandbox Jenna had bought and snuck into her room a few days before. She hadn't been able to refuse maid service, so she left a generous tip on her pillow each morning in order to keep the staff quiet. They refused to take her money but kept her secret anyway. Pippa was popular with the staff, and a couple of the girls had offered to take her to the beach when Jenna couldn't leave. She had a feeling she'd be taking them up on their offers over the next week.

"It's all right, Pippa. I'm not gagging on anything but my foolish romantic notions. Ironic, isn't it, that I'll be the one planning a wedding between a royal princess and a commoner? It's what I dreamed about every night for two years as I sat at my window, looking up at Greystone Manor. I used to pretend my real father was a king and he'd sent my mother and me away to protect us, and that one day he'd come to get us. Instead, Richard rode to our rescue like a knight in shining armor. I wouldn't have traded him for a king who could give me a crown and a title and all the riches in the world." A wave of loneliness and longing hit her, and she picked up Pippa, cuddling her to her chest. "I really miss him, Pippa. I miss him an awful lot."

As though she could empathize, Pippa softly *peep*ed and rubbed her downy head against Jenna's chest. She lifted Pippa away from her to look into her eyes. "I'm being selfish, aren't I? You probably have brothers and sisters and a father and mother out there somewhere looking for you. You don't want to hang out in the manor or in the study just because I want to keep you around, do you?" She brought her close again, rubbing her cheek against Pippa's head. "You have my word. I'll get you back to your family if it's the last thing I do.

"And speaking of family, I should probably get out there and see if my sacrifice has been worth it. Surely Arianna will forgive me now that I was able to recoup the deposits from all the vendors," she said as she returned Pippa to her sandbox.

Jenna had called every one of the suppliers they'd contracted for her wedding and given them dibs at a real royal wedding if they refunded her nonrefundable deposit first. They happily did so, and lucky for her, they still had everything she'd ordered in stock. The calls that made her most happy though were the ones to In Bloom, the local flower shop, Truly Scrumptious, the local bakery, and A Spoonful of Sugar, the local candy shop. Like Poppy, the women who owned the shops had been beyond nice and had felt worse for Jenna than for losing the business, so it'd felt great to place another order for at least ten times the dollar value of hers. She'd actually gotten a little weak in the knees at the budget she'd been given, hoping it was the princess footing the bill and not Logan.

She got another case of weak knees when she walked onto the patio and spotted the man of the hour. Logan stood under a tree wearing a dark suit, the glow from the fairy lights creating a halo over his head. As though he sensed someone staring at him, he looked over to where she leaned against the stone wall for support. It was still warm from the sun that was just now sinking below the ocean. She mustn't have looked crazy or stalkerish, because he smiled at her as if genuinely glad to see her. As much as she felt betrayed by him, she couldn't help but give him a genuine smile in return. Like the ones she'd given him during the best twenty hours of her life.

His smile slowly faded, and his eyes narrowed as though he was putting the pieces of a puzzle together. Maybe he was telling the truth and had amnesia. It still didn't explain why he hadn't told her about his relationship with the princess. But what hurt most was that he didn't remember Jenna and the time they'd spent together.

She couldn't hear him but read his lips as he told the person waiting in line he'd be back in a minute. He started to walk across the patio to her but was way-laid by Luis and ushered back to the princess's side to pose for Poppy, who was there to take their engagement photo. It was the first time Jenna had seen the couple together in person, side by side. She turned away. She didn't want to see. She didn't want to know. It was because of her *gift* that she was in this predicament.

"Jenna, over here."

She turned to see Arianna and Serena waving her over, both of them smiling. She blinked back the moisture that threatened to fill her eyes at the knowledge she'd been forgiven, and suddenly Logan and Princess Isabella came into focus. It was too late. The damage was done. She couldn't unsee what she had seen. They weren't the perfect match. They weren't soul mates. They weren't each other's one and only.

* * *

Logan scanned the perimeter of the patio from where he stood with his brothers and cousin Aidan in a secluded corner having a beer.

"Relax and enjoy yourself, Logan," Aidan said. "We have off-duty officers working the party."

"Thanks. I appreciate it." He lifted his beer to his mouth and once again found himself searching out the wedding planner in her yellow dress and red shoes.

There was something about the woman that called to him. It bothered him. He was a soon-to-be married man, and he couldn't shake the feeling he'd been in a relationship with Jenna. One that was important to him.

"You're on edge. What's going on?" his brother Michael asked.

Connor gave Michael a look. "You have to ask? Mr. Never Getting Married is getting married, and not to just anyone. He's marrying into royalty. Royalty who lives half a world away. Just when we finally got you back Stateside, you'll be gone again."

His brother's comment about Logan never wanting to marry bothered him. They mirrored Jenna's and his own memory of his stance on the subject. He couldn't remember it changing or why. He could alleviate Connor's concerns on one count though. "We're not moving to Merradien. Isabella wants to live in the States."

From the short time he'd spent as the royal family's guest after the kidnapping attempt against Isabella, she'd peppered him with questions about his home. So he wasn't entirely surprised when, two days ago, she'd told him she didn't want to go back. What did surprise him was that the royal family would leave the decision up to her. When he expressed his concerns to Luis, the older man had assured him all the family wanted was for Isabella to be happy. Logan wondered if it was because they thought her safer here than there.

"Good to hear, but there's something more going on with you. What is it?" Michael asked.

"Okay, I haven't told you the whole truth about the accident. Before you give me grief, Luis insisted I keep quiet about it. But I trust you guys to keep it to yourselves, and that means you don't breathe a word to anyone, including fiancées and girlfriends. Got it?"

"Don't look at me. I don't do relationships that last longer than a week," Connor said.

Logan couldn't criticize his brother since he'd basically been the same way. "Okay, so the concussion was severe enough that I've lost a chunk of memory. From what I can tell, the month of June. The neurologist is optimistic I'll get it back, but it could take some time."

"No chance it caused a personality change too? Because, big brother, I'm serious. You were as confirmed a bachelor as me," Connor said.

Logan blew out a frustrated breath. It was good to finally open up about it because his gut said something wasn't right.

"Speaking as someone who thought he was as confirmed a bachelor as the two of you, when you find the one, you're done. And yeah, I didn't believe in soul mates or perfect matches, but now I kinda do. What are you grinning about?" Michael asked Aidan.

Their cousin laughed. "You thought you were Shay's perfect match before she did."

"What can I say? I'm the romantic in the Gallagher family. So, is that what happened? You fell head over heels in love with Isabella?" Michael asked him, but Logan could hear the doubt in his voice.

"That's the thing; I don't remember. Five minutes after I regained consciousness, Luis told me Isabella and I were engaged. I questioned her personal bodyguard and lady's maid, and they all had the same story. I'd bought a ring for her too. I used my credit card and signed for it four days before the accident."

"I don't know, Logan. It sounds a little fishy to me. What about your phone?" Aidan said.

"It was destroyed in the accident. But I think I know someone I might've been communicating with."

"Who?" his brothers and Aidan asked at almost the same time.

"The wedding planner, Jenna Bell."

"Why didn't I think of that? Of course you'd keep in touch with her." Michael looked around and then waved someone over. "Jenna, can you come here for a minute?"

Logan looked to where Jenna was standing on the garden path with her stepsisters and Poppy Harte. As he turned back to his brother, Logan caught Luis's eye. The older man didn't look particularly happy with him. Luis said something to Mateo, and Isabella's personal bodyguard began walking their way. Obviously, Luis wanted Logan at Isabella's side and was sending Mateo to retrieve him, but he wasn't leaving until he got to the bottom of this. "Why aren't you surprised I'd be talking to Jenna?"

"Right. You wouldn't remember what happened." Michael pulled his phone from his pocket.

While he searched for something on it, Connor said, "For the past few weeks, all you've been focused on is protecting Jenna Bell. Her fiancé dumped her a week before their wedding, and her stepmother stole her matchmaking company from her. You hired me to represent her."

"And he hired Shay to dig up the dirt on both of them. Good call, by the way," Michael said to Connor, and then handed his phone to Logan. It was an article in the *Harmony Harbor Gazette*.

"Okay, you guys need to keep me in the loop. I had a visit from Lorenzo and his uncle. Lorenzo dropped the charges against you, Logan, not that it does you much good from what I can tell, but the only reason he did was to get the ring back from Jenna. They were expecting me to hand it over, and when I didn't, they weren't happy. I'm sure you heard about it because they were calling you next," Aidan said to Connor.

"I did, but I've been threatened by far more dangerous men than them."

"Lorenzo's not dangerous, but I wouldn't be so sure that his uncle isn't. I heard them asking about Jenna and let Jasper know to keep an eye out."

Logan looked up from the screen. "Jasper?"

"Oh yeah, Jasper. Our mild-mannered butler isn't who he seems," Michael said. "Ask Shay if you don't believe me."

"Do either of you know if Lorenzo and his uncle returned to Italy or went back to Charleston?" Aidan asked.

"No. You?" Connor asked Michael, who shook his head in the negative.

"Okay, as a precaution, I'll pass around their photographs to security. Now, I better get back to Julia before she tells Jenna to order me a tail for the wedding. I'm okay with a mermaid-themed wedding, as long as I'm not dressed as a merman," Aidan said, nodding to where Jenna had been waylaid by his future wife.

Logan laughed. "You're having a mermaid-themed wedding?"

"Yeah, and you know what they say about people living in glass houses? You're having a Cinderella-themed wedding, big guy," Aidan said as he walked away.

"What's going on?" Logan asked when his brothers shared a glance.

"It's not your fault—you obviously didn't know—but Jenna was having a Cinderella-themed wedding here at the manor. Shay said she'd been dreaming about it since she was a little girl and saving for it about that long."

"And her fiancé didn't only dump her, he took the money she'd been saving for her wedding, and her car," Connor muttered. "I can't wait to get that guy in court."

"I wished I'd done more than give him a bloody nose," Logan said, handing back his brother's phone after reading about his actions in the local newspaper. "I'll talk to Isabella about the wedding. Explain—"

"No. Don't do that. As hard as it is on Jenna, it probably saved her a lot of time. Mom said she's already got everything ordered. She pretty much thinks the sun rises and sets on Jenna now."

"Really? That doesn't sound like Mom. Unless you're keeping something from me and Jenna's an heiress."

"No, she's not," Michael said, sharing another glance with Connor, who lifted a shoulder in return. "I feel bad breaking this to you again, but we think Mom is sick." His brother shared what the amnesia had stolen from Logan. "Anyway, Mom refused to have further testing until Jenna talked to her. Shay thinks you're the reason Jenna approached Mom about the diagnosis in the first place. I think she's right. You must've told Jenna about it. There's no other way she could've known."

"That doesn't sound like something I'd do." He was private about his personal life and didn't share easily.

"Jenna lost her mom to cancer when she was twelve. Maybe she talked to you about it and you shared. I don't know, but however it came about, we owe Jenna. Connor got Mom an appointment with a world-renowned oncologist, and she's agreed to see him."

"Well, that's good news at least. So, is that why she left Dad?" he asked, searching for his parents on the patio. He hadn't talked to his father, who had just arrived a few minutes ago and was talking to Kitty and Jasper. His mother was talking to Isabella and Luis, with her brother-in-law Daniel at her side. Just then she waved over Jenna, who'd been slowly making her way toward Logan and his brothers.

"That's what we thought, but now we think there might be more to it. Or, to be more specific, that there's another man involved," Connor said.

Logan frowned. "You can't be serious."

"I wish I wasn't. But apparently Mom and Uncle Daniel were an item before she and Dad were. I guess you didn't get that far in the article, but they had a fistfight the day Mom told us about her diagnosis and the day Uncle Daniel came home. We still haven't found out if it was a coincidence he showed up the same day we staged our intervention or not. And none of them are sharing."

"Are you forgetting Uncle Daniel is married to Aunt Tara?" Logan asked.

"Are you forgetting we're talking about Uncle Daniel? Aunt Tara is wife number three—or it might be four, no one really knows. With his track record, he's probably left her."

"It might be something we want to find out. But right now, I need to find out if I've been texting Jenna, and if I have, what I've been saying." He felt someone's eyes on him, and he turned.

Mateo was standing a few feet behind him. He was several inches shorter than Logan, about thirty pounds lighter, and at least a decade younger, but he was sharp, fast, and had killer instincts. "I am sorry to disturb you, but Luis asks that you return to the princess."

"Tell Luis I'll be right there, Mateo. I just need to ask the wedding planner a question," he said as Jenna approached.

Poppy caught up with her, and the two women appeared to be having a heated discussion.

"I thought Poppy and Jenna were friends. I wonder why Jenna's trying so hard to get rid of her," Michael said.

"I think we're about to find out," Connor said when Jenna couldn't shake the other woman and they both walked over.

"Hi." Jenna gave them a forced smile. "You wanted to speak to me, Michael?"

"Actually, I did. I'm really sorry about earlier, Jenna.

Why didn't you tell me...?" Logan trailed off because he couldn't say anything about the amnesia in front of Poppy. The woman was a reporter.

"That you had sex on—" Poppy began.

Jenna gave a panicked squeak and covered the other woman's mouth. "Don't listen to her. She's been drinking."

"Is she saying that you and I—" Logan managed to get out before Poppy pulled Jenna's hand away.

"Had sex on the beach?" she whispered angrily. "Yes, that's what I'm saying. And she might think you're Prince Charming with a magic penis, but I think you're a real tool...toad, pretending that you don't know her just because you hooked up with a princess."

Chapter Seventeen

♥

"What is that about the princess, Ms. Harte?" a man asked from behind them, the rolling *r*'s giving him away. Luis's *r*'s were like the Energizer Bunny; they kept going and going. Unfortunately, the man didn't resemble a cuddly bunny in the least. He actually made Jasper seem soft and fuzzy in comparison.

Poppy whispered a pained, "Oh crap."

Which no doubt summed up how every member of their chummy little group was feeling about now. Though Jenna would have opted for something stronger. *Oh crap* didn't exactly cover her extreme embarrassment or her panic that she would be the cause of an international incident and the Gallaghers would fire her.

She needed this job. Arianna and Serena were actually speaking to her again and planning a night out at the Salty Dog to celebrate their collaboration on the wedding of a lifetime. The Bell sisters, wedding planners to royalty. That's what they'd said.

Now, would someone else please say something? she pleaded in her head, because she was too afraid

if she opened her mouth the truth would come out
or Luis would see it on her face. She was so accustomed to Logan stepping in to fill the breach that she
was surprised to hear Michael's voice instead. Without thinking, she lifted her gaze to Logan. He wasn't
looking at Luis or his brother. His gaze was focused
on her. The last thing she wanted to do was look at
him after Poppy had hit him with the truth. And what
was with her telling him Jenna thought he was Prince
Charming and had a magic...It wasn't only his penis
that was magic.

If he could read everything on her face, she could
read it in his eyes. He'd truly had no idea they'd made
love on the beach that night. He had no idea she'd let
the moon and the stars mess with her head and her heart.
It wasn't his fault their conversations over the past couple weeks had made her feel like there was something
more than that one night between them.

Like the amnesia, maybe Logan and Isabella had to
keep their relationship a secret. Celebrities did it all
the time. And while it was no excuse, the couple had
been in a long-distance relationship, with the added
strain of Isabella being a royal and Logan a commoner. And maybe Jenna had caught him on a night
when the pressure had gotten to be too much and he'd
needed her as much as she'd needed him. Just for that
one night. He'd never promised her more, but in a
way, he'd given her more. Like her job and a second
chance with her sisters.

She tilted her head to the side and offered him an
apologetic smile both for Poppy's comments and for the

shabby way Jenna had treated him earlier. He shoved his hands in the pockets of his pants, bowed his head, and gave it a slight shake. She may have forgiven him, but it didn't appear that he'd forgiven himself. She knew why. Whatever the reason he'd kept his relationship with Isabella secret, he'd cheated on her with Jenna, who'd been ignorant of it all, becoming the other woman through no fault of her own.

She felt movement beside her. Luis had edged closer to listen to whatever Michael was saying. Since Luis wasn't calling for her head on a platter, Michael must've figured a way out of the mess. Thank goodness for secluded corners, angry whispers, and lawyers.

"Sorry we kept him from Princess Isabella, Luis. Like I said, there was a legal matter that needed to be taken care of. And Poppy and Jenna have just brought another urgent matter to our attention."

"And this matter, it involves Her Royal Highness?"

Michael got an *oh crap* look on his face, because clearly he'd thought whatever baloney he'd been feeding Luis was enough.

Connor stepped in to fill the breach. "It does. You see, Luis, Poppy's writing an article about Logan and Isabella's love story for her paper. The citizens of Harmony Harbor are all about the romance, you know. And, well, Poppy's upset that Logan doesn't have any photos of him and Isabella together. I know it probably sounds crazy to you, but she's concerned people will start questioning their relationship."

Crazy to Luis? It would sound crazy to anyone. Connor had taken it too far, and for the first time, Jenna second-guessed leaving the fate of her inheritance and business in his hands.

She glanced at Luis, who seemed distressed by the charge. A charge Jenna could sort of address on the princess and Logan's behalf. It might even put her in Luis's good graces. The man had made it pretty obvious he wasn't a fan.

"I have a great photo of Logan and Her Royal Highness." Oh crap. She hadn't thought this through.

"And where, may I ask, did you get this photograph?" Luis asked.

Jenna cleared her throat. "Uh, well, Logan sent it to me." Heat traveled up her neck to her face as everyone's eyes narrowed on her, Logan's included. "He knows I'm a huge fan of Princess Isabella. I stalk her on social—" She raised her hand. "That came out wrong. It's just that I might be a little royalty obsessed. Stalkerish and obsessive. I'm probably scaring you, aren't I? But I promise, it's not like that. It's the fairy-tale effect. American girls are brought up on them. The whole Prince Charming riding to the princess's rescue, so damaging. Horribly damaging. Anyway, I'm so over them now I can't even tell you. So you don't have to worry about me. Not that you had to worry about me before." *Sweet baby Jesus, be quiet, Jenna, before they take you away in a straitjacket*, she told herself.

Beside her, she could feel Poppy's shoulder's shaking as she kept her laughter inside. Connor and Michael didn't even bother trying and laughed out loud.

"Trust me, no one in their right mind would ever question your motives, Jenna," Logan said. "If you can get me the photo, I'd appreciate it. Actually, why don't you just bring me your phone, and I'll hook it up to the printer." He didn't seem to be having any trouble keeping a straight face. There was something in his eyes, but it wasn't amusement.

Wait? Did he just say...? "You want my entire phone, not just the picture?" She couldn't give him her phone. She hadn't deleted her text to Lorenzo. And hooking it up to the printer? That didn't make sense...Unless he was just placating her, lulling her into submission so he could check her history and see if she really was a stalker. She liked the old Logan much better than this one.

"Yeah, if you don't mind."

His mother saved her from answering. "Darling, poor Isabella is wondering what's happened to you," she said as she approached on Daniel Gallagher's arm. "Is everything all right?"

"Everything's fine. Where's Dad?" Logan said, obviously unhappy to see his mother with his uncle and not his father. The longer he was at the manor, the unhappier he would be because his uncle was clearly looking to replace his brother in Maura's affections. Jenna wouldn't be handing over her phone to him, but noting the lack of pink light dancing between the couple, she might be able to nip Maura's affair with her brother-in-law in the bud.

"Now, don't get testy with your mother, son. Her fancy heels are getting stuck between the flagstone, and she needed someone to lean on. If anyone deserves your—"

Connor intervened, "Uncle Daniel, we haven't finished our conversation about your last dig. Let's grab a
drink at the bar. Poppy, you should join us. Interview
my uncle the famous archaeologist for the paper. Your
readers will be begging for more."

As they moved away, Logan said, "Mom and Luis,
do me a favor and keep Isabella company while I go
with Jenna to grab the photo off her phone. I'll be ten
minutes at the most. The photo is for an article Poppy
is doing on me and Isabella," Logan responded to his
mother's questioning frown.

Jenna prayed Maura or Luis would object, but they
didn't. In fact, no sooner were the words out of Logan's
mouth than Luis hurried off to Isabella's side, leaving
Maura standing there.

"You walk your mom back, Logan. I'll get my phone
and bring it to you." That would give her the opportunity to delete anything incriminating, including her text
to Lorenzo.

"It's fine. Mike will walk her back. Get Dad while
you're at it, baby brother. He hasn't spent nearly
enough time with Isabella."

Michael nodded and held out his arm to his mother.

"Maura," Jenna called out as they began to walk
away, "remember the question you asked me the other
morning?"

Logan's mother tilted her head to the side with a
frown. "No, I...Oh, yes, the perfect match."

"Yes. I've had a chance to look into it, and he's not."

"You're sure?" she asked, looking disappointed.

"Ninety-nine percent positive."

"All right. Thank you for looking into it for me, darling."

"Interesting. My mom doesn't take to a lot of women, but she's obviously taken with you," Logan said, guiding her toward the French doors with a hand at the small of her back.

She swallowed a small sigh of regret. She'd missed the feel of his hands on her, the feel of him standing so close. And maybe because she'd missed him, she picked up on the resentment in her voice when she said, "We have some things in common, and it helps that I'm not the type of woman her sons would be interested in. And before you say I don't know what I'm talking about, I'm best friends with Michael's fiancée, Shay."

He moved his hand to let her walk ahead of him through the dining room, where some of the older guests had congregated to chat in the relative quiet and bug-free environment. "That's not true, though, is it? I was obviously interested in you or we wouldn't have—"

"Are you crazy? Don't say that, especially around them. They may be getting on in years, but it doesn't mean they're deaf." She lifted her chin at the Widows Club. "Follow my lead," she said out of the side of her mouth. Then, to the women gathered around the brass easel at the top of the stairs, she said, "Hello, ladies. I hope you're enjoying the evening. Logan and I are just going up to my room to get a special little something for Princess Isabella."

"You're not so hot at subterfuge, are you?" Logan murmured, a touch of amusement in his voice. Then he turned on the charm for the older women, who gathered around him to pet and flatter. They were obviously proud to know the man of the hour.

While he was occupied, Jenna took a step back and slowly eased her way out of the crush and across the lobby to the grand staircase. She raced up the stairs, taking two at a time, desperate to get to her phone without Logan looking over her shoulder. She sighed, relieved when her foot hit the landing. At least she'd have the opportunity to delete...

The elevator door opened to reveal Logan, leaning casually against the glass wall with his arms crossed. Maybe it was the lighting in the elevator or the amusement in his eyes, but the man looked more gorgeous than he had a right to. *Delectable* and *devastating* were just two of the words that came to mind.

She resisted the urge to make a run for her room and said, "You didn't have to leave your fan club, you know. I'm perfectly capable of getting my phone on my own."

"I know, but then I wouldn't have the opportunity to talk to you alone. There are some things you need to understand, Jenna."

"No. I don't need to understand anything. We weren't in a relationship, Logan. We had sex within hours of meeting each other." She wondered what was wrong with her, saying things like that out loud. She looked around, relieved that they seemed to be alone in the hall.

"So we had sex and then that was it. No further contact?"

"You know we did. It's why you want to see my phone, which, by the way, feels a little stalkerish. And if you think I'm going to let you go through all my texts and my search history, you'll be sadly disappointed." She stopped at her door and took the passkey from the pocket of her dress.

She felt him move in behind her, close enough that his body brushed against her back as he bent to whisper in her ear, "Afraid I'm going to find out all your dirty little secrets?"

"You're my dirty little secret," she said, closing her eyes when the words came out of her mouth. What kind of hold did this man have on her? He made her say things she'd never think of saying. He also made her want things she'd never thought of wanting, like a man who was engaged to another woman. "Logan, I—" she began as she went to open the door.

"Jenna, move aside. Now," he said, gently pushing her out of the way as he reached inside his jacket and pulled out a gun.

"What...? Oh my...Pippa," she cried out at the sight of her room torn apart. The dresser drawers were pulled out, the bedding had been ripped from her bed, and hangers and clothing were scattered over the floor. She tried to push past Logan, but he held her back with his arm.

"Pippa's okay. Just give me a minute," he said, closing the door in her face.

"Please don't be lying to me. Please don't be lying," she half-whispered, half-sobbed, pressing her ear to the door. She heard Logan comforting Pippa as he walked around her room, the sound of the closet door opening and closing. It dawned on her then that there was the possibility the person who'd broken into her room was still there.

"Jenna, you can come in now."

She sagged against the door and then opened it. With his back to her, Logan was crouched on the floor talking to Pippa in a soothing tone of voice. Pippa was beside herself, pacing from the window to the bed and back while frantically cheeping.

"That's a good girl. You're okay. Come here, now," Logan said, and Pippa stopped to blink up at him and then practically flew to him. He gently scooped her up and came to his feet, cuddling her to his chest. He turned and used that bird-whisperer voice on Jenna. "No one hurt her. Come here." He held out his arm, and she walked to him. He held her close, and she rested her cheek against his broad chest, placing her hand on Pippa while fighting back tears.

They weren't because she'd been scared witless for both Logan and Pippa or because someone had torn her room apart. They were because he was here for her again, making her feel like everything was all right, making her feel like she wasn't alone anymore. She allowed herself to indulge in the fantasy for only a few seconds before moving out of his arms, time enough for her to pull herself together and blink away any evidence of tears.

"Can you tell if anything is missing?" he asked, his voice rougher than it had been moments before.

She nodded. "I left my purse on the end of the bed

with my wallet inside. My phone was on the night-stand. They're gone." And to think she'd been worried about Logan reading her texts. Now a perfect stranger would be.

"Check and see if anything is missing from the jew-elry tray in the bathroom."

"I doubt they'd be interested. It's costume—" She walked into the bathroom and then remembered one item of value. One look told her what her sinking stomach already knew. "Lorenzo's ring is missing."

"Aidan mentioned something earlier that I think you should know, Jenna. Lorenzo and his uncle were in Har-mony Harbor last week."

"You think it's—" A knock on the half-opened door interrupted her, and Michael stuck his head inside.

"Jenna, have you seen Lo—" He spotted his brother across the room, and she sensed the disap-proval in the way he raised his eyebrow at Logan. She felt ashamed for the brief time she'd spent in his arms. She may not have acted on her feelings for him, but Logan was as good as a married man. Like Richard had been. Jenna had never judged or ques-tioned her mother and stepfather's actions. Even at the tender age of ten, she'd known they were meant to be together, and to her mind, that was all that really mattered. It had taken her an awfully long time to re-alize that wasn't true. There were consequences to a forbidden love.

Logan walked to Jenna and placed a hand on her shoulder, as though delivering a message to his brother. She just wasn't sure what it was. "Jenna's room was broken into. The ring is gone, and so is her phone and purse. Tell Aidan to put out an APB on Lorenzo and his uncle."

"Jenna's room isn't the only one that was broken into. So were Isabella's and Grams's."

Chapter Eighteen

♥

Something was rotten in Denmark. Colleen had sensed it less than an hour after the royals had arrived at the manor. It was a shame, really. A royal wedding at Greystone was the coup of a lifetime. They couldn't afford to buy publicity like this in a million years. The paparazzi was camped outside the gates. Reporters from around the world were begging to get inside the manor, offering a small fortune for an exclusive interview with the bride and groom-to-be.

The Hartes had already been granted the interview though, so the other reporters had to make do with the citizens of Harmony Harbor, who were only too happy to share their stories about the Gallaghers with the press. Which made Colleen nervous. There'd been mention of her and her book, *The Secrets of Harmony Harbor*, and not always in the most flattering light.

Logan had come off well, not a bad word to be said against him to the press from anyone except Officer Ryan Wilson. And even he had tempered his remarks. No doubt thanks to the three lawyers in Logan's family and Aidan, of course. A good thing her great-grandsons were on the job because she and Simon were having a devil of a time getting Jasper's attention. And with his time taken up with the wedding and the power struggle with his nemesis Luis, Colleen didn't hold out much hope of getting him to cooperate anytime soon.

"I suppose it's high time I took another crack at the book myself," she said to Simon, who sat at her feet. Colleen had parked herself beside Jenna and across from Logan at the table in the manor's dining room. It was time for the taste testing. There were four white china plates sitting between them, each with a large slice of cake. At the end of the table were tiered wedding cakes of different designs. The only thing missing was the bride-to-be.

"Did you sleep okay?" Logan asked Jenna, obviously trying to make conversation. Other than the clatter of cutlery, pots, and pans, and the odd grumbled command from the kitchen, there was nothing to break the awkward silence that had fallen between the pair after their initial greetings.

Jenna looked up from her iPad. "Yes, thanks. You?"

To which Logan nodded.

Colleen didn't know how anyone got any sleep last night with all the excitement. Police officers had swarmed the manor and the grounds searching for clues until the wee hours of the morning. Aidan had immediately contacted the Charleston Police Department to ascertain Lorenzo's and his uncle's whereabouts. According to Aidan, Lorenzo was with Gwyneth, and his uncle had returned to Italy two days before.

Now the police were focusing on the attendees at last night's soiree. Apparently not everyone who was there had been on the guest list. Logan had spent most of the night and half of the morning tightening security. It was too bad Colleen couldn't share her thoughts on the matter. She had a fairly good idea who the thief was, and if her great-grandson weren't such a fine man, he would've twigged to what was going on right under his nose much quicker than this. But he was beginning to sense things weren't quite what they appeared to be. Now the question was how far the ones involved would go to keep their secret.

Logan picked up a fork and pulled the first plate toward him, his eyes on Jenna as he did.

Jenna's gaze jerked from her iPad to him, and she twisted at the waist to look around. "What are you doing?" She went to pull the plate from him. "We have to wait for Princess Isabella."

"She was supposed to be here twenty minutes ago. If she doesn't want to choose the cake, I will." He speared a piece of cake and held the fork out to her. "Better yet, you will. Come on, you've been eyeing this cake for the last twenty-five minutes. Don't bother denying it."

Colleen chuckled. "And you've just given yourself away, my boy. You wouldn't know that if you hadn't been watching her the entire time. She's just as bad. Both of you pretending to be working on your devices."

"It's banana and chocolate marble cake with buttercream icing," Jenna said, leaning in and opening her mouth to accept the bite he offered. She moaned.

"That's amazing. Here, you have to try too." She picked up a fork and scooped up a piece for him.

He leaned in in much the same way Jenna had, only he watched her while he took the bite and then closed his eyes on a groan. "Okay, we don't have to try any more. That's the one."

"No, we have to try the red velvet," she said, and Logan agreed, picking up his fork.

But instead of feeding themselves, they kept feeding each other like it was the most natural thing in the world, having a lot of fun while they were at it, as evidenced by their exaggerated moans and laughter.

"I've been around for almost a hundred and six years—" Simon looked up at Colleen and meowed. "Don't be so literal. I'm here, am I not? Anyway, for all the years I've walked this earth, this is the first time I've seen a couple use a cake tasting as a form of foreplay." Thinking she'd offended Simon's sensibilities when he got up and padded away, she chuckled.

But she soon learned his sensibilities had nothing to do with it. The princess and her entourage had arrived, and their sensibilities had clearly been offended by the sight that awaited them.

"No way. You've got more on your face than I do." Jenna laughed, leaning across to dab at Logan's mouth with a napkin.

"I'm telling you, you have more." He picked up a piece of chocolate cake and shoved it in her mouth, grinning. "See, what did I tell you?"

"Oh no, you did not just do that." She laughed, wiping away cake crumbs as she picked up a piece and tried to do the same to him, but Logan grabbed her wrist and held it away from him.

"You can't..." As though finally registering someone's attention upon them, Logan looked over. Releasing Jenna's hand, he picked up a napkin to wipe his mouth.

"What is the meaning of this? Her Royal Highness has arrived to taste the cakes for her wedding, and this is what awaits her? Really, Ms. Bell, if this is how you handle something as simple—"

Jenna looked stricken, rising awkwardly to her feet. "I'm sorry. I'll have fresh pieces cut and brought—"

"Jenna, sit down. It won't be necessary. We've been waiting more than forty minutes for you to arrive, Isabella. We have to be at Tie the Knot in half an hour, so I'll pick the flavor, and you can pick whichever cake design you want. Sound fair?"

Mateo looked sharply at Logan and then pulled out a chair for the princess, guiding her solicitously into it as though she were a hundred and six.

Isabella nodded her thanks to her bodyguard as she looked under her lashes at Logan. "I apologize for being late. I had difficulty sleeping last night."

"We all did. Yet we were here. On time."

Luis's gaze narrowed on Logan. "A word, if you please."

"No, Luis, I don't please. Apparently, we do things a little differently in Harmony Harbor than you do in Merradien. Politeness, consideration, and respect for other people and their time matter. I suggest you all get used to it."

"Logan," Jenna said, clearly aghast.

Colleen had to admit to being surprised herself. This was not the great-grandson she knew and adored, but, she admitted, she had seen this side of him before. He had a long fuse, but he didn't like games, and he didn't like people who were disrespectful or inconsiderate.

"Now, I'm sure Jenna has things to do, so why don't you decide on which cake you want, Isabella. Is there anything else you need us to taste?" he asked Jenna.

She avoided looking at him and focused on the princess instead. "The cakes can wait until after you've had your fitting, or I can incorporate them into the family dinner this evening if that will make it easier for you, Your Highness?"

"Yes, thank you, Jenna." The smile Isabella offered the other woman was genuine, so much so that Colleen wondered if she'd misread the situation. She glanced at Luis, Mateo, and Pilar, who all stood protectively behind the princess with their arms crossed, none of them pleased with Logan.

If they thought their pointed stares would make a whit of difference to the lad, they didn't know him very well. He was as protective as they were, only he'd offered his protection to Jenna on the day her fiancé jilted her. Colleen wondered when he would finally realize he'd offered her his love too. Oh yes, she'd heard all about their romantic night on the beach. It was hard not to since she'd followed them to Jenna's room last night.

And while she might have lost touch with Jenna growing up, she knew the girl as well as she knew the boy. Neither was the type to have meaningless sex. She believed there'd been a touch of magic in the air that day that brought them together, or maybe it was an old lady's prayer, an old lady who was living betwixt and between. She smiled, liking the sound of that, wondering if it could be so easy for the rest of her great-grandchildren.

From out in the lobby a woman shrieked, "Jenna Bell, you get out here and face me!" There was the sound of a scuffle. "Get your hands off me or I'll call the cops. I'll say what I've come here to say! She told my husband he was meant to be with another woman!"

Colleen groaned. "Sorry, my girl, it's my fault. I tempted fate by talking about how easy it all had been."

"Excuse me. I need to take care of this," Jenna said, red splotches appearing on her neck and face.

"Jenna, what's going on?" Logan called after her, pushing back from the table.

Luis reached out as if to stop Logan. "There is no time for this. You and the princess must choose the wedding cake. Your appointments at Tie the Knot are in—"

"I told you I don't care. Pick whichever one you want. I'm good as long as we go with the banana and marble cake with buttercream icing," Logan said as he went after Jenna.

Colleen noted the way Luis stabbed the cake Logan had indicated with a fork and then caught the secret smile Mateo and Isabella exchanged. She'd been right; there was definitely something rotten in Denmark.

* * *

For the past few weeks, Jenna's ratio of happy days
to crappy ones had overwhelmingly been in the crappy
column, but this one was beginning to feel like it would
win the prize for crappiest day of all. Even though the
taste testing had been kind of amazing...until it wasn't.
Apropos, she supposed. It seemed to be hers and Logan's thing. She gets dumped; she and Logan make
love. She gets robbed; Logan holds her in his arms. She
finds out Logan is marrying another woman, a princess
no less...Okay, so she had no positive counterpoint to
that. Which was probably a good thing because, if there
were, she might do something really, really stupid like
tell him she had feelings for him and that they were
meant to be and he and Isabella were not. And that
would probably turn out as well as it had in the Ryan
Wilson love triangle.

Logan called out to her, and she fought the urge to
turn around and say, *Stop it. Stop being such a nice
guy and looking out for me. Stop making me smile. Stop
making me laugh. Stop making me want you. Stop making Luis think there's something going on between us,
or you'll cost me my job.*

"Is that her? That's her, isn't it?" a dark-haired
woman said, trying to duck around Jasper, who was doing his best to keep her corralled in the entryway of the
manor.

Jenna had known as soon as she'd said the words that
day on the sidewalk outside Tie the Knot that they'd
come back to bite her, and here they were, doing just
that. Luis trying to get her fired might be the least of her
worries. The Gallaghers wouldn't be happy that she was

the reason for the drama unfolding in front of at least a dozen guests.

She hurried up the steps to the entryway. "It's okay, Jasper. I'll talk to Mrs. Wilson. I'm so sorry for—" Jasper stepped aside, and the words backed up in her throat when she got a full-on look at Ryan's wife. She was pregnant. Serena was having an affair with a married man who was expecting a child. "Mrs. Wilson, I had no idea. I'm so sorry. We can talk in—"

"Oh, so it would've been all right to tell my husband he was meant to be with another woman had I not been pregnant? Is that what you're trying to tell me? Spouting that soul-mate rubbish like you're some kind of seer. Come on, get out your crystal ball. Show me how it works. I'd like to know why my husband of eight years thinks a woman he's known for months is his perfect match and not me. Me, the woman he begged to marry. The one he promised to love and honor—" She sounded like she was on the verge of breaking down, her hands rising and falling, closing into fists as though resisting the urge to grab Jenna and shake her.

Jenna didn't blame her. She wanted to shake herself. "Please, come with me, Mrs. Wilson. I promise, I'll make it right." How she planned to do that, she had no idea.

The other woman opened her mouth, her face twisted to no doubt deliver a more damning assessment of Jenna's character. But she didn't get a chance. Logan's large, warm hands came down on Jenna's shoulders to give her a comforting squeeze before he moved her aside.

"Give me a minute," he said to her, and then turned to the woman. "I understand you're upset, Mrs. Wilson. You have every right to be. But it's not good for either you or the baby. Jasper, can you bring some tea to the study, please?" he asked, using his bird-whisperer voice as he gently guided the woman out of the entryway and down the hall.

"Why don't you fetch the tea and biscuits, miss? It'll give you a few minutes to decompress while Logan calms Mrs. Wilson down," Jasper suggested to Jenna.

"Thank you, Jasper. I'm really sorry about this. I'll—" She turned as Ryan Wilson walked into the manor in uniform.

"Officer Wilson, I suggest you give your wife a moment before speaking to her. I'll see to the tea and biscuits, Jenna. You can see to him." The censorious tone in Jasper's voice made it clear what he thought of the officer.

Jenna nodded and then took Ryan by the arm, pulling him out of the entryway and down the hall. "What were you thinking? Why would you tell your wife that I said Serena was your one and only?"

He dragged his hand through his hair. "I don't know. She'd just found out about me and Serena, and she was upset, and she's pregnant. So I thought it would help her understand. I didn't want to hurt her. I did love her. Maybe I still do, and now with the baby...I wanted her to understand that I couldn't help it. You can't fight destiny, right?"

"You're blaming the fact you cheated on your wife

on destiny? Give me a break. You were having an affair with Serena long before I said the two of you were a perfect match."

"No, that's not true. I was trying to get in her—"

Jenna gasped and shoved him with both hands. "You're a pig, and match or no match, Serena is better off without you, and so is your wife."

He grabbed her wrists and snarled, "I'm warning you. Don't try to get between me and your sister or my wife."

She wrenched her hands away, rubbing her wrists. "You're unbelievable. You really think now that this is out in the open you can have your cake and eat it too?"

"I don't think it. I know it." He straightened his uniform shirt and adjusted his holster. "Just remember what I said and you won't get hurt. Now, where's my wife?"

Jenna closed her eyes at the sound of the study door banging open. In her need for privacy, she'd dragged him within a foot of the study. Whatever magic Logan had worked ended the moment Mrs. Wilson spotted her husband in the hall. Logan didn't look any happier to see Ryan than Ryan was to see him. This could go downhill fast, and she didn't want Logan to get into any more trouble on her account.

She was trying to figure out how to get rid of him when Jasper's voice came from behind them. "Master Logan, the security officers manning the front gates need a word."

"Tell them I'll be with them in—"

"No, it's fine, Logan. Please, I've got this. You need to do your job."

He looked from her to Ryan, who was trying to placate his now-crying wife, and then back to Jenna. "You're sure?"

"Positive."

He nodded, gave Ryan a hard stare as he walked by, and then said something to Jasper before heading out the door.

"You're all right, miss?"

"I'm good, Jasper. Thank you," she said as the couple continued their quiet conversation. Ryan stroked his wife's hair, kissing her on the forehead as he begged her forgiveness. Jenna felt like throwing up, and that feeling only intensified when she saw the pink light dancing between the couple and murmured without thinking, "You're a match."

Mrs. Wilson's head lifted from her husband's shoulder. "What did you just say?"

"Nothing. I didn't say anything." She wanted to save the woman from her husband, not deliver her into his greedy, adulterous hands.

Ryan's wife stepped away from him to advance on Jenna. "Yes, you did. I heard you. You said we're a match, didn't you? Tell me. Tell me the truth."

"Yes, you are. You two are the perfect match."

"Did you hear that, Ryan? We're a match, not you and that other woman. We are, you and me."

"What did I tell you this morning, babe? There's only you for me. You and the baby. Now you got confirmation, we're good, eh?"

"Yes, of course." She rose onto her toes to kiss his cheek and then looked at Jenna. "You should be more careful what you tell people. You nearly wrecked our family."

"She made it right, babe. We're all good now. No hard feelings." As he walked his wife toward the entryway, he looked back at Jenna as if she were lucky she'd seen it his way.

As soon as they left, she went in search of Jasper. She found him dusting the shelves in the library. She wasn't surprised he'd stayed close by. "I can't get through to Tie the Knot, and I need to check on one of the orders," she told the older man, who'd proved to be as wonderful an ally as Logan. Logan, she had to stop thinking about him.

"You're certain you've recovered from your altercation with the Wilsons, miss? I don't mind going to Tie the Knot and checking on the order for you."

"Thank you. That's very kind of you, Jasper, but I'm fine. I thought I'd pick up mini cakes for Princess Isabella to taste while I'm downtown. She can sample them while they're at Tie the Knot for their fittings. She didn't get the opportunity to earlier."

"Ah, yes, I seem to recall hearing Luis complaining about it. Don't you worry, miss. Master Logan shut him down rather adroitly. And while I appreciate your conscientiousness, I believe you should take his side in this. He was making a point that I believe the princess would do well to heed. If she is truly planning to live her life with him as a commoner, it's best she learns what that entails. Master Logan wouldn't be happy that the woman he's chosen to wed isn't considerate or kind to others." He raised both eyebrows and dipped his chin. "Perhaps you should spend more time with the princess, miss. You're exactly the type of woman he'd wish Isabella to emulate."

"If you give her a chance, I think you'll quite like her, Jasper."

"I'm impressed. I pride myself on keeping my feelings from others. You're not only highly sensitive though, are you? From what Mrs. Wilson said, I deduced you see auras. Is that correct?"

"Yes. It's why my matchmaking company did so well."

"Ah, and Master Logan and Princess Isabella, are they a match?"

"Until half an hour ago, I would've said no. But I'm beginning to think that maybe people can become a perfect match after they've been together for a while." Either that or people can have more than one soul mate, as she'd seen with her own eyes.

"Let's pray that is so. Master Logan is one of the best men I know. I wouldn't like to think of him in a loveless marriage."

Her hand automatically went to her chest. Her heart hurt thinking of Logan trapped in a loveless marriage. He struck her as the type of man who would continue trying to make a marriage work rather than get out of it. "We won't let that happen, Jasper."

His lips twitched. "No, we most definitely will not, miss."

"I'll be back in time to organize tonight's dinner,"

she said with a wave, and headed for the door, looking back as she pulled it open. "Jasper, in case you're wondering, you and Kitty are the perfect match."

He beamed. "Thank you, miss."

Jenna smiled. When love was meant to be, it was a beautiful thing.

Chapter Nineteen

♥

The manor's front door had just closed behind Jenna when she realized she had no way to get to Tie the Knot. Hitching a ride with the royals and Logan was out. The less time they spent together at this point the better. She wanted to beat both them and Ryan to her sisters' shop. It looked like calling a cab was her only shot until she spotted her best friend striding up the front walkway.

Shay did everything with purpose and style. It might be seventy-eight degrees in the shade, but the woman still managed to look cool in her motorcycle boots, jeans, and a tank top. "Hey, just the person I was looking for. Where are you off to?" Shay asked.

"You don't want to know." She gave her friend a hug. "We missed you at the party last night."

"Yeah, I heard I missed some excitement. Logan's got the place locked up tight," she said, turning to look at the guards manning the gate.

"Tighter after last night. There's two checkpoints to get on the grounds," Jenna said.

"Tell me about it. It took me ten minutes to get through security."

"You should've just flashed your I'm-almost-a-Gallagher badge. Which, by the way, we need to discuss."

"Don't you have enough on your plate with the royal wedding?" An older couple walked toward them along the path, and Shay nudged her head toward the other side of the manor.

Jenna followed her to a bench. "It hasn't been as difficult as you might think."

"No, because you basically handed them the wedding you've been planning since you were ten. I couldn't believe it when Michael told me. Why would you do something like that?"

"It made it easier to plan, for one. And it's not as if I'll ever be getting married. At least this way I'll get to see my ideas come to fruition. You have to admit it's perfect for a royal wedding."

"Are you sure it's been easier? I would've thought it'd be tough to plan a wedding for a man you slept with, especially a man like Logan Gallagher."

"I should've known Michael would out me."

"He's worried about you. He's afraid you have feelings for Logan."

"Why would he think that?"

She gave her a look. "You're an open book, Jenna. Besides that, I know you, and I saw you and Logan together that night. Still, it would've been obvious to anyone at the bar that you guys had that indefinable *it*. You clicked. Michael saw it, and so did Cherry."

"It's all Cherry's fault. She's the one who put the idea in my head."

"So you do have feelings for him?"

"Yes, but it's one-sided. I clicked, and he didn't. If he did, he wouldn't be marrying Isabella."

"Things may not be as they seem. Logan..." She gave her head a slight shake. "Never mind."

"You can't just say something like that and not follow through."

"Yeah, I can, and I just did."

She took Shay's hand and rubbed it on her arm.

"What are you doing?"

"Rubbing some of your cool and kiss-my-butt attitude onto me. Do you think it'll stick? I need it to last at least an hour."

Shay shook her head with a laugh. "You're nuts. What are you doing that requires attitude?"

"Telling Serena that she has to dump Ryan Wilson even if he is her one and only. I think the guy is sleazier than Lorenzo."

"Lorenzo might be worse than you know," Shay said.

She shifted on the bench to face her friend. "That's why you couldn't make it last night. You were in Charleston investigating Lorenzo for Connor, weren't you?"

"I would've been investigating him even if Connor hadn't hired me."

"Aww, I love you, Shaybae." She hugged her best friend.

"I love you too. But call me Shaybae again and

you're not allowed to hang out with Cherry anymore."

"Okay. But feel free to call me Jellilicious anytime."

Shay laughed. "A bunch of old-timers asked Charlie the other day when Jellilicious was making another appearance. He had no idea what they were talking about. It's a good thing Cherry didn't hear about it or she'd be booking you on weekends."

"I'll keep that in mind." Jenna looked over to see Mateo waving at the limo driver, who was having a cigarette near the front gates. "I have to get to Tie the Knot. Hey, would you mind giving me a ride?"

"Sure. If you can give me at least an hour," Shay said as she stood up. "Aidan rounded up everyone who was working the party last night for me to interview. It's actually what I wanted to talk to you about. Your engagement ring, it was a family heirloom, an incredibly valuable family heirloom, but it wasn't Lorenzo's or his family's."

"Whose was it?"

"It belongs to the Bianchis. A powerful family in Florence, Italy. Lorenzo was engaged to one of the daughters until her family had him investigated. He escaped with the ring and little else. I guess he decided he'd be out of their reach in the States," Shay said.

"Let me guess, he's not a count."

"No, but she's a countess. And while I know there's no love lost between you and Gwyneth these days, I think Lorenzo's behind everything, including forging the will and stealing Southern Belle from you. He'll be desperate now that he knows the ring is missing. My gut is he'll be showing up in Harmony Harbor any day now.

"The guy who was here with him last week isn't his uncle, Jenna. He's a PI hired by the Bianchis. Lorenzo paid him off and bought himself some time."

"With the money I saved for our wedding."

"'Fraid so. Connor's trying to get a court order to freeze all of Gwyneth's assets. It's a long shot, but at this point, it's about all we can do. My advice would be to try to talk to Gwyneth."

"I can try, but I guarantee she's as stupid about him as I was. I just wish I'd seen through him before it was too late. You did."

"It's my job. And I should've warned you, but I was afraid I might be wrong. I'm not exactly the most trusting of people. Michael says I think everyone's guilty of something. Don't beat yourself up though. You're one of at least twenty women the man used and took to the cleaners. He's had lots of practice."

"Misery loves company. And speaking of misery, I have to go and impart some on my sister." Jenna glanced at the Harley in the parking lot. "Exactly how guilty do you feel about not sharing your concerns about Lorenzo and saving me from a broken heart and—"

"No, you're not taking my bike. Last time you tried riding it, you drove it into the dumpster at the back of the pub."

"Nope, that was the second-to-last time. The last time, I rode it up and down Main Street—"

Shay crossed her arms. "Is that right? And when exactly was this?"

Busted. "The long weekend in May. You were away with Michael. Cherry dared me. Please, I need some of your attitude to get me through the day, and there's nothing like a hog between your legs—"

"Promise never to say that again and you can take it." Shay dug her keys from her jeans and tossed them at Jenna. "You might want to change before you go."

"I don't have time. I'll be fine. I'll wear your leather jacket, and my pants are just a tiny bit above my ankle."

"Yeah, that's not why I suggested you change. You're wearing red sandals with light purple pants and an orange blouse with bright yellow and green flowers. I thought your stuff is coordinated for you."

"It was, but whoever broke into my room tossed my closet. I'll just leave your leather jacket on. I'll look like a badass babe."

"You better get going if you want to beat the royals 'cause it sounds like they're coming this way, badass."

Five minutes later, Jenna wasn't feeling so badass when she found herself boxed in at the stoplight by two real-life biker dudes on their Harleys. As evidenced by the tattoos on their bulging biceps and the patches on their black leather vests, they were the real deal.

The ginormous man on her left grinned at her. "Hey, foxy, your daddy let you take his bike out for a spin?"

The man with a braided white beard on her right said, "Nah. The way little ginger here rides, I'd say PMS."

"I don't have PMS, and this isn't my—"

Both of them threw back their heads and roared. "PMS means you haven't been out on your bike for a while, foxy," ginormous guy informed her while wiping tears of laughter from his eyes.

Despite that she clearly amused them, they made her a little nervous, which might explain why she said, "I'm new to the life. This is my best friend's hog."

"You don't say. Would've thought you were born to the life, ginger," braided beard man said. At her frown, he explained, "Ginger on account of your hair." He touched the long white locks trailing down his back. "It's why Cueball called you 'foxy.'"

"Oh, so you're Whitey?"

He revved his engine and winked. "Shotgun."

She revved her engine. "Nice to meet you, Shotgun and Cueball. Bottom light. Bye." She waved, cringing upon realizing what she'd said. Old habits died hard. Because she was color-blind, Richard had taught her that the top light meant stop, the middle light slow down, and the bottom light meant go.

In the rearview mirror, she could see them laughing as they turned off Main Street. She totally just lost her cool factor by saying *bottom light* and giving them a cutesy wave. Long live the dorks. At the next stoplight, she revved the engine again, the sound giving her confidence a boost. She did it again, smiling as she felt the power of the bike rumble through her.

Then a truck pulled up beside her, and she felt the driver's eyes on her.

She'd channel Shay. Her best friend would own the bike, rev the engine, and then give the driver a kick-butt stare, as in *I'll kick yours if you keep looking at me*. Jenna tried one on for size and then twisted in the seat to give the driver a full-on glare that immediately turned into a full-on smile.

Logan laughed. "Quit revving the engine and flirting with bikers."

Butterflies took flight in her stomach at the thought that he'd been watching her with Cueball and Shotgun. "I wasn't flirting...Bottom light. I've gotta go."

She took off like a shot and had to zig around one car and then zag around another to avoid hitting it. In the rearview mirror, she caught a glimpse of Logan. He was no longer laughing. She wondered if he'd believe she was practicing her defensive driving. But when she spotted the police cruiser parked outside Tie the Knot, she no longer cared what Logan thought. All she cared about was getting to her sister. She made it the rest of the way in record time, pulling in behind the cruiser, but it took her a minute to get the bike balanced properly. Once she did, she took off at a run, bursting through the door of Tie the Knot.

Arianna looked up from the computer on the reception desk. "Jenna, what—"

"No time. Where's Serena? I have to talk to her."

"In my office. But wait. She's with—"

"Wait until what? He impregnates her along with his wife?" she yelled over her shoulder as she raced through the empty (thank God) fitting area to the office. She didn't knock. She just flung open the door. "Stop, Serena. You have no idea what...Sorry, I thought you were someone else."

"Chief Benson, this is my sister Jenna. At least I'm assuming it's my sister under the helmet."

She took it off her head. "Yes, it's me. Hello, Chief Benson. I'm really sorry to interrupt you."

"No problem. We were just wrapping up. All I need is your signature on the complaint, Serena, and then I'll take appropriate action."

"You're filing a complaint against Ryan?"

Her sister worried her bottom lip between her teeth and nodded.

Jenna went to stand beside her. "Good, I'm glad. Chief Benson, I'd like to file a complaint against Officer Wilson too. He threatened me this afternoon. I never should've told him that he and my sister were meant to be, and I realize that I made a difficult situation worse, but it doesn't justify him threatening me." She repeated what he said to her, showing Chief Benson how he'd handled his gun.

"Did anyone hear him threaten you?"

"No. I'm pretty sure they didn't."

"It'd be better if we had a witness, but I'll file your complaint as well." He moved to the door, gave them a nod, and said, "I'll be in touch."

She turned to her sister. "I'm so sorry, Serena. I never should've said anything."

"What are you sorry about? I'm the one who got involved with a married man."

Jenna sat on the edge of the desk. "How involved were you?"

"Flirting, kissing, talking on the phone, meeting for a walk or lunch. He told me his marriage had been in name only for years. According to him, they stayed together because it made sense financially, but he was going to leave her. And then I found out she's pregnant."

"He's not a nice man. I feel sorry for his wife. It was obvious today that she believed him."

"So do I. I think we should talk to her, Jenna. He's going to do this again. I'd be surprised if I was his first."

"I know, but you didn't see them together, Serena. And you didn't hear or see him when he threatened me."

"I just think it's important she knows everything. You wished we'd been more forceful sharing our concerns about Lorenzo with you."

"Arianna kind of was."

Serena grinned. "She's forceful about everything, and that's the problem. But if Shay had shared her concerns, you would've listened."

"I like to think I would have."

Voices filtered back from the front of the shop. "Sounds like royalty has arrived." Serena stood up and leaned over to hug Jenna.

"What's that for?"

"I know we told you last night, but I'm not sure you realized how much we both appreciate what you did. Especially after how Arianna treated you. It couldn't be easy letting Princess Isabella appropriate every last detail of your dream wedding. Arianna was up until three this morning making a sample of the dress for the princess to try. It's almost identical to yours, Jenna."

"At least she didn't appropriate the groom," she quipped, ignoring the tiny, telling crack in her voice.

Jenna might have feelings for Logan, but it's not like she thought in a million years she'd ever marry the man.

"No, but everything else. I can't tell you how relieved Arianna was when all the deposits we'd paid out showed up in the business account." She hooked her arm companionably through Jenna's, who looked up as Arianna hurried down the hall, a panicked look on her beautiful face.

Jenna wondered if Connor had arrived for his fitting. "I'm sending Logan back. You have to keep him"— Arianna ran to the last fitting room and flung open the curtain; there was a tux hanging from the hook—"in here."

"You want me to keep him in the fitting room? How? Why?"

"Because Lorenzo and Gwyneth just parked up the street, and they're coming this way. We can't have any drama, Jenna. Not here. Not with the press gathering outside on the sidewalk. It'll ruin us. Please, keep him back—"

Serena cleared her throat and smiled. "Perfect timing, Logan. Jenna's all set to fit your tux."

Jenna noted that his surprise matched her own. But she also saw the near panic on Arianna's face at the thought of anything going wrong with the royal's fitting, and that won out over Jenna's desire to walk straight to the front of Tie the Knot and greet Lorenzo with a punch in the nose right before she called the cops and then hauled her stepmother to the back of the shop for a heart-to-heart.

"Don't look so nervous," Jenna said, doing her best

to keep her own nerves under control. "You're in good hands, I promise. Go and put on your tux while I talk over the wedding plans with Arianna and Serena." She shooed him off, waiting until he was in the fitting room with the curtain closed.

"What is it?" Arianna asked, leaning back to look down the hall toward the front of the shop.

Lowering her voice to a whisper, Jenna said, "I understand why you don't want a scene—"

"No, it's not that I don't want a scene, Jenna. I can't *afford* one. So just get in there with Logan and keep him there," Arianna said, steering Jenna toward the changing room.

Jenna dug in her heels. "Wait. You don't understand." She quickly filled them in on what Shay had learned about Lorenzo.

"Okay, so as soon as we get rid of them, I'll call the police. And then, once Lorenzo is locked up, we'll talk to Stepmother Dearest—" Arianna's eyes went wide at the sound of a familiar accented voice coming their way, and she pushed Jenna toward the fitting room. "Don't let Logan out until we tell you the coast is clear. He'll cause a scene for sure."

Of course he would, because Logan and his cousin Aidan believed Lorenzo was responsible for the break-in at the manor. Still... "He's changing," Jenna hissed at her sisters.

Serena whipped open the curtain, and Arianna shoved her inside.

Jenna fell into Logan, her hands landing flat on his bare chest. "Hi." She looked down and quickly looked

up again. "Sorry. I'm just really anxious to see you in
your tux." At least he had boxers on. She lifted her
hands and took two steps back...into the wall. "Well,
this is a little tight, but we'll have to make do. We don't
want Isabella to get a look at you in your wedding finery
before the big day." And from the continuous chiming
from the front of the shop, the rest of the royal entourage had arrived.

"Are you okay?"

"Yes, although it is a little warm. I'll just take this
off," she said, attempting to get out of Shay's leather
jacket without hitting him.

"Turn around," he said, helping her out of the jacket
when she did as he said.

"Thank you." She faced him with a bright smile and
put the jacket on the chair in the corner. "Now it's your
turn." He gave her a look, and her eyes went wide. "No,
that's not what I meant. It's your turn to put on your tux.
It looks lovely, doesn't it?" She leaned in. "What color
is it?"

He raised an eyebrow. "Powder blue."

"Powder blue." She pressed her lips together to keep
from laughing, but it didn't work.

"Yeah, powder blue." He stepped into her, his hard
body brushing against hers. She could smell his cologne
and feel his heat. "So, do you want to tell me why your
sisters want you to keep me in here?"

"I can't."

"You sure about that?" he said, his fingers trailing
over her cheek as he tucked her hair behind her ear. He
leaned closer and bent his head, his lips lightly brushing

her ear as he whispered, "Don't lie to me, Jenna. Tell me what you're hiding."

She fought the urge to turn her face so that his lips would be on hers, to wrap her arms around him. "Maybe they thought it was a good time for us to talk about... your song. You know, the song you'll sing to Isabella. I've heard it's a Gallagher tradition."

And it worked, just like she knew it would. She'd reminded him of the woman he was about to marry, a woman he was supposed to be so in love with that he had a song just for her. A song that would tell the world how much he loved her.

He stepped away, and she felt cast adrift without an anchor.

She heard footsteps, and then his mother's voice came through the closed curtain. "Logan, darling, what was the name of the man whose photograph you were passing around to the security guards this morning?"

He held Jenna's gaze. "Lorenzo Romano."

"Lorenzo. I thought it sounded familiar. I'm almost positive it was the man who was just in Tie the—"

Logan whipped back the curtain.

Chapter Twenty

♥

Logan sat on the beach with the rocks at his back, a guitar on his lap. The full moon's path shimmered across the water as the waves rolled lazily onto shore. It was a beautiful night, warm with the smell of woodsmoke on the air from a bonfire he could see flickering on a distant shore. It was a night that should be spent with the woman he was going to marry in his arms. Only Isabella had no interest in spending the night on the beach, and Logan wanted the wrong woman in his arms.

He strummed his guitar, waiting, hoping for inspiration to strike. Jenna had been right. So far, each of his cousins had serenaded his bride on their wedding day. It was expected now, the ultimate expression of the groom's love for the woman walking down the aisle toward him. And the last thing Logan had wanted to be reminded of when he'd been pressed up against Jenna earlier. He wondered what would've happened had she not brought it up. He knew what he wanted to happen.

Kissing her had been pretty much all he'd thought about since last night in her room—kissing the icing from her lips at the cake tasting, kissing the scowl from her face when she looked over from the Harley to give him attitude, and kissing her when they were together in the fitting room.

With her body pressed tight to his, he'd come really close to giving in to his desire. He might have had his mother not interrupted them, alerting him to the reason Jenna had decided to join him in the changing room in the first place—Lorenzo Romano. A man Logan couldn't remember but had heard and read enough about to want to go a few rounds with him. Supposedly that's what Jenna had been protecting him from. He neither bought the excuse nor liked it.

He plucked at the guitar strings, feeling more than just pressure to come up with a song. Jenna wasn't the only one who was lying to him, and it was becoming more obvious as each day went by. He'd been down there half the night, racking his brain for the lyrics that would fit with how he felt about Isabella. There was a reason he couldn't think of any. He didn't love her. He barely knew her, a woman he was going to marry in a week. He was torn between confronting her or keeping up the charade for a few more days to get a better idea of what was going on in case Isabella's life was in danger.

After all, he'd been hired and paid well to protect her, and there'd been the kidnapping attempt months before. Was this just a deeper layer of protection made possible because of his amnesia? Or was he putting off confronting Isabella because this was his dying mother's dream come true?

A bouncing beam of light caught his attention, and he slowly put down his guitar, careful not to make a sound. There were guards posted around the grounds, but this wasn't a member of the security detail. He'd put himself on the rotation tonight. He had a two-way radio and turned off the volume so as not to alert whoever was coming onto the beach. For a second, he thought it might be Isabella taking him up on his earlier offer. The woman was slight and about her height. His reaction to the thought was telling. As was his reaction seconds later when he realized who the woman was.

Jenna bent down, her profile captured in the lantern's light for a second before her auburn hair fell forward. She murmured something, set Pippa on the sand, and then turned with her back to him, looking out at the ocean. She wore a simple white cotton nightgown that fell to her calves. The light from the lantern gave subtle hints of the body beneath. His breath hitched when she reached down to gather the hem of the nightgown in her hands, a whisper of sound as the fabric slowly moved its way up, revealing an inch of smooth, silky skin and then another. There was nothing he'd rather do than sit back and watch her strip in the moonlight, but...

"Jenna, you're not alone."

She screamed, pressing a hand to her chest. "Sweet baby Jesus, you nearly gave me a heart attack."

"And everyone else in a mile radius." He turned on his radio and let the security team know everything was all right. Pippa raced across the sand toward him. "She scared you too, did she?" he asked as he picked up the peep and brought her to his chest. "She's awfully cuddly for a bird, isn't she?"

Jenna walked over and sat down beside him, leaning in to rub her cheek against Pippa's head. He looked down at her hair spread across his chest, the temptation to stroke the shiny red mane difficult to resist. His stomach muscles tensed in response to her hand resting on his abs. She went perfectly still and then slowly withdrew her hand and sat up. "She's only a few weeks old. I've had her almost since she was born." She glanced at him. "You were with me when I found her. You and Poppy."

Given how she looked at him and the reluctant way in which she made the admission, he figured it had something to do with the night they'd spent together at the beach. "I wish I remembered." She had no idea how much. "How did we find her?" His voice came out rough, thick with emotions that he shouldn't be feeling, especially on a warm, sultry night drenched in moonlight. He cleared his throat.

"Poppy had heard that a nest had been found on the beach and had come to take pictures. Baby sandpipers have always been a big deal in Harmony Harbor. Anyway, she kind of found us at an awkward time—"

"We weren't—"

"No! We were on a public beach, and it was morning."

He grinned at her outraged expression. "Good to know we were at least a little circumspect."

"I wouldn't go that far. You had clothes on, but I didn't."

"Really? That doesn't sound very considerate of me. I should've done a better job protecting you."

"You did a very good job protecting me that night. At least two times, and then—"

"I don't know if I'd classify practicing safe sex as doing a very good job protecting you, Jenna."

She placed a hand over her face. "I wasn't talking about sex and condoms."

"We did use one though?"

"Yes, we did. But I was talking about everything else you did to protect me that night, not only from Lorenzo but from falling off the pole at the bar and breaking my neck." She made a face. "And for the record, I'm sorry I didn't tell you Lorenzo and Gwyneth were at Tie the Knot. I don't exactly agree with how Arianna and Serena chose to handle it, but I wasn't about to argue with them."

"We'll get back to Lorenzo, because there's something you need to hear, but I want to know what's with your relationship with your sisters. I get that you're younger than them, but I don't get why you let them dictate to you. Your opinion is as valid as theirs. From what I've seen, you're not a pushover."

"No, I'm not. But I'm also not their real sister. I'm their stepsister, and for a long time, they wished I wasn't. It's only in the last few months that we've become close. Maybe because it was just me and my mom for so long, family's really important to me. Harmony Harbor used to seem like this perfect little microorganism of what life was like back in the day with Mom and Dad and two-point-five kids. I wanted that. I didn't want to be different. All I've ever wanted is to fit in."

Because he'd had what she wanted, he couldn't totally empathize with her, but he could see how it impacted her life even to this day. "Is that why you were going to marry Lorenzo?"

She hugged her knees to her chest. "I can't believe I was actually going to marry him. It's embarrassing to think about now. I was so stupid."

"Don't. Don't say that about yourself. My brother filled me in on Shay's investigation. The guy is a sociopathic con man with a long list of victims."

"Yeah, women like me who were lonely. Women he could convince would never have a chance at happily-ever-after without him. I didn't realize until about a week ago that while for the most part he was all flattery, compliments, and praise, he was also undermining me and working on my fears."

"And that's why you needed to come clean with me that the guy was at Tie the Knot instead of going along with your sisters. Because now he and Gwyneth are on the wind and that's not good."

"I'm sorry. It's kind of my default playbook with them. They get mad, and I do everything I can to make them happy, including letting them shove me in the fitting room. I still can't believe they did that or that I let them. You were half-naked. If the situation had been reversed…"

"I didn't mind, Jenna. The only thing I minded was that my mother interrupted us." He reached over and tucked a strand of hair behind her ear.

"I—" she began, stopping when he absently caressed her face with his fingers.

A man's voice came over the radio as he checked in with each station. Logan moved his hand away from Jenna's face and responded to the security guard.

Jenna cleared her throat, the moment clearly over. "Maybe Lorenzo and Gwyneth are in Bridgeport?"

Bridgeport was the town adjacent to Harmony Harbor. "We checked there and practically every small town across three counties, and it's not like we can tie up HHPD's resources any more than we already have. They're stretched to the max with adding extra security here and managing the press and tourists."

"The town's tripled in size. Business on Main Street is booming, especially the ones cashing in on the wedding. The hardware store is making a killing. Yours and Isabella's faces are plastered on half the products in the store."

Great, one more reason why he had to go through with the wedding. People in town were counting on it. More to the point, Jenna and her sisters were.

He didn't want to think of that now and changed the subject. "So, what are you doing down here? Couldn't sleep?"

"No. I come down around this time every night. Sandpipers hunt for food at low tide. Pippa's gotten really good at it. Now I have to start thinking of next steps."

"Like?"

"I have to find her family. I'll have to go back to where we found her. She doesn't really get along with the sandpipers at Kismet Cove."

"Is that right?" he said, holding back a smile. The

woman got to him. She was the type of woman you hold on to and don't let go. Jenna Bell was a forever girl.

"No, they treat her like...well, you'll see." She pointed to the sandpipers coming out from the surrounding rocks to feed along the shore. Jenna stood up and peeled off her nightgown to reveal a black racerback bathing suit. There was nothing sexy about the suit—it was basic and plain—but he couldn't look at her without wanting to strip it off her. He needed a distraction and decided giving Pippa a pep talk would work.

"Don't you worry about them. You've got this, Pippa. Go out there like you own the beach. Don't suck up to them. Just go and have fun." He put her down and gave her a little push with his finger in the direction of the other birds.

"She's doing it. Wow. You really are a bird whisperer," Jenna said as Pippa walked through the sand on her spindly legs, straight for the other birds.

He sighed when Pippa veered off at the last minute. "You spoke too soon. And it's not the other birds; it's her."

"How can you say that? Look at her. She's a baby and all by herself. You'd think they'd come over and introduce themselves, welcome her to the pack."

When he started to laugh, she gave him an offended look and walked off.

"Babe, that's not the way of the animal or bird kingdom. She's gotta make a place for herself and earn their respect. Stop babying her."

"Typical male response," she muttered.

And as he watched her lay that lithe body of hers down in the sand to encourage Pippa to join the other sandpipers at the water's edge, the lyrics of a song came to mind. He reached for his guitar and began to play Brett Young's "In Case You Didn't Know." He'd found the perfect song for his wedding, only Isabella wasn't the woman who'd inspired the choice or the feelings.

Jenna turned her head, and he held her gaze as he softly sang part of the chorus, the part that told her he was crazy about her. He didn't know how or why, but what he did know was it was true. He got that feeling deep inside that you get when you know something is right.

Now what was he supposed to do?

* * *

Free of her corporeal form, Colleen enjoyed the ability to travel through doors and in and out of rooms at her pleasure. However, along with the advantages of the ability, there were also disadvantages. Like seeing Jasper in bed with Kitty, and they weren't sleeping. Colleen shuddered as she walked straight out the door of her daughter-in-law's suite and into the upper hall.

That'll teach her to go into Kitty's room at this time of night. It couldn't be helped though. After hearing Ryan Wilson threatening Jenna outside the study, Colleen needed to get a look at her book, and she'd spent the entire afternoon and evening trying to pick up the key to fit it into the desk drawer's lock. She'd try again tomorrow. Only this time, she'd insist Simon help.

There had to be something they could hold over the lad's head to get him to leave Jenna alone. Colleen had recorded enough secrets to blackmail the entire town of Harmony Harbor, yet this one eluded her. Even if she remembered, she'd still need the pages from the book and Jasper's help to see that they fell into the right hands and not the wrong ones.

And speaking of wrong hands, she thought, looking at the princess's lady's maid. Pilar stood under the gold-framed portrait of William Gallagher, talking on her phone. She didn't trust the woman.

Colleen glanced down to see Simon staring at the portrait of the family's patriarch and gentleman pirate with what looked to be a smile on his face. "He's a fine-looking man, I'll give you that," she said to the cat.

She could've sworn Simon preened at the remark.

"I don't know what you have to be proud of. It's not like you had anything to do with the man's looks..." She trailed off, glancing from Simon to the portrait and back to Simon again. "Are you trying to tell me you're him? He's you?"

Simon gave her another catlike smile and then sauntered off like he was lord of the manor, and well he might be. Though Colleen didn't have time to think long and hard on the matter because just then Pilar whispered into her cell phone, "Yes, sir, I will. And please tell His Royal Highness that I am doing everything in my power to ensure the princess returns home unmarried and without incident...Yes, I can handle it on my own...Thank you. My family would be most honored and humbled to accept whatever you feel my

service to the crown deserves. I must go," she murmured as the door to Colleen's old suite opened.

Luis stuck his head into the hall. "Do they believe
you're still loyal to the king?"

"Yes, but their patience wears thin and their concern
grows. We will not be able to stay their hand much
longer. Word of the wedding has reached them, and
they are planning to send three members of the king's
guard to retrieve the princess on July sixth, the night before the wedding. The only way to protect the princess
and to ensure that she does not have to return to Merradien is for her marriage to Logan to be moved ahead and
the details kept from the press so no one at the palace
learns of the change in plans."

Luis nodded. "Do not fret, Pilar. I will have the date
changed first thing in the morning. I should not have
given in to Logan, but he would've become more suspicious if I asked that they be married right away as we
had initially planned. And speaking of Logan, we have
a bigger worry. Mateo managed to break into Jenna
Bell's phone. The couple has had relations. They're
down at the beach together as we speak."

He looked around the upper hall, caught sight of Simon, and scowled before turning his attention back to
Pilar. "Perhaps we can use this information to our advantage. Without Ms. Bell's help, we will not be able to
pull this off. We must find a way to make her comply
with our wishes."

Chapter Twenty-One

♥

Jenna had just sat down at her desk when Luis walked into the study without knocking. *Just how I wanted to start my morning*, she thought, and then remembered how easy her face supposedly was to read.

Up until a few weeks ago, Jenna would've classified herself as an early-morning person, but Pippa's one a.m. feedings had taken a toll and turned her into a late-morning, preferably noon, type of person. However, since she wasn't a royal princess, she was at her desk at nine a.m. like the rest of the working stiffs. Which meant she better keep her head down or Luis would know just how unhappy she was to see him.

Pretending she was checking her e-mail, she held up a finger and said in an overly cheerful, *happy morning to you* voice, "I'll be right with you."

As her irritability factor this morning seemed to have ratcheted up a notch, or five, she wasn't entirely sure she could lay the blame on being sleep deprived or on Luis's visit. Her level of testiness probably had more to do with Logan sharing his wedding song in the wee hours of the morning on a secluded, moonlit beach after she'd just experienced another *he's my one* feeling.

She should have Poppy on speed-dial. The thirty-something woman could act as Jenna's sponsor. Every time Jenna had a *he's my one* feeling, she'd call Poppy, who'd then remind her the man was marrying a princess in one week's time. As their wedding planner, Jenna shouldn't need to be constantly reminding herself of that fact. Not to mention it wasn't that long ago she was supposed to be marrying her own Prince Charming.

She shuddered at the thought, shocked at how quickly she'd gotten over Lorenzo. Her picture should go under the word *fickle* in the dictionary. No sooner had the idea crossed her mind than she thought of Logan and a new page of the dictionary appeared with his photo under *forever*.

At the sound of a throat clearing, Jenna looked up.

"I have a matter of some urgency to discuss with you, Ms. Bell," Luis said, his lips curving into a smile as he took the seat across from her.

She'd never seen the man smile before and looked behind her. No one was there, so obviously it had been intended for her. She wondered why that made her nervous.

"I apologize for keeping you waiting..." She trailed off, making it sound like an aborted sentence instead of saying his name as she'd initially intended. She didn't like calling him Luis. It sounded too informal for a man who looked like he commanded respect with a whip. She'd been tempted to ask how he'd like her to address him but was afraid he'd say *Master*. "I was expecting to hear back from one of the suppliers."

"Nothing has gone awry, I trust?"

"No. Everything's right on schedule."

"Splendid. I was afraid the change in dates would create a problem for you. I should've trusted that someone as capable as yourself would have it handled."

"Sorry, I'm a little lost. What change of date are you referring to?"

"Why, the only date that matters, my dear. The date our beloved princess will marry the Gallagher prince."

If Jenna weren't gripping the armrests on the chair to keep from sliding onto the floor in a faint, she might've wondered at his use of *Gallagher prince*. As far as she knew, she was the only one who'd referred to him that way. In her head, of course, and on the diary in her phone. She gave a laugh that sounded like she'd been sucking on helium for a week. "Okay, so we're postponing the wedding to allow the royal family to attend? I did wonder. I thought perhaps they hadn't approved of the match."

"The royal family is not attending due to prior commitments. They're thrilled our princess is marrying a man who is considered a hero in my country. And although it is not for public fodder, and I must warn you, you would be sued if word leaked about the baby, His Royal—"

"B-b-aby?"

"Why, yes, and the royal family is beside themselves with joy at the news. It's why we moved the date from July seventh to July fourth. And while I may not have shared the true reason at the time, I did tell you we needed to return to Merradien by the sixth for a royal announcement."

She didn't need Poppy after all. Jenna had her own happily-ever-after bubble buster sitting right in front of her. "I was never informed about a royal announcement or a date change, Luis. If I had been, I would've told you it was impossible. It was hard enough to pull everything—" She was barely able to keep the panic from her voice.

"I must say I'm shocked by your level of incompetence, Ms. Bell."

"Incompetence? I don't know where any of this is coming from. Surely the royal family can wait a couple of days to make the—"

"No, they do not adjust their schedules to suit you, Ms. Bell. The wedding has to be held on July fourth as you were informed and agreed to four days ago. If you don't believe me, check your day planner."

"My phone's missing. I—"

"You didn't put it on your phone." He stood up and leaned across the desk to point at the computer. "You entered it onto the computer, as well as in the leather day planner in the top drawer of the desk."

"I don't have—" She opened the drawer, and sure enough there was a leather planner inside. Jenna held it up. "This isn't mine, Luis. It must be Sophie Gallagher's, the manager of the manor. She's away, and I'm using her office temporarily until construction on Olivia's is complete." Kitty had decided to renovate Olivia's office and create two work spaces while Sophie and her family were in California for her friend's wedding. They weren't due back for another week.

"If this is how you do business on the manor's behalf, I highly doubt they'll keep you on. I'm afraid I have to speak to—"

"No, just give me a moment, please." Her hand shook as she opened the day planner to July, and there beside Wednesday the 4th, written in ink, was *Princess Isabella and Logan Gallagher Wedding*. The names blurred on the page. "I don't understand. I don't remember writing this." She looked up. "You have to believe me, Luis."

"I was standing right here when you wrote it."

She turned to the computer and brought up the schedule for the upcoming month. And there it was again beside Wednesday, July 4th. "I don't understand how this happened." She felt like she was losing her mind.

"You were somewhat overwhelmed at the time. If it helps, I came to speak to you right after we returned from our first visit to Tie the Knot. I had just heard from His Royal Highness about the scheduling conflict. I also spoke to you about the menu for the soiree in the garden that evening."

"I remember you coming to talk to me about Princess Isabella's allergy to pine nuts. I double-checked the menu and spoke to the kitchen."

"And before you went to speak to the chef, I asked that the change be made. The request clearly upset you, but I felt that was more about your obvious feelings for Logan than for the timeline, as we'd made the arrangements only hours before."

"Obvious feelings for Logan? I don't know what you're talking about." It was the best she could come up with. Her head was spinning with details and dates, trying to figure out how she could pull this off. If she said she couldn't do it, she was almost certain he would demand that she be fired.

He wouldn't fire her sisters out of spite, would he? They had a substantial amount of money invested in the wedding. No, they'd be okay. They couldn't get anyone to outfit the bridal party on such short notice. That wasn't necessarily true though. It was amazing what people could accomplish with the right incentive.

"Come, come. It is obvious to everyone, even to Her Royal Highness, how you feel about Logan. Your behavior these past two days has only proved our concerns. I imagine that learning Logan is to be a father with another woman is most painful for you, so it is probably for the best that you have made this egregious error and now must resign your position as wedding planner."

"No, please, I need this job. I still don't understand how I could've made the mistake, but I'll make it right. Logan and I are friends. All I want is for him to be happy." It was true, she did. And it reminded her of the promise she'd made to Jasper. With a baby on the way, it was more important than ever that Logan and Isabella find their way to being each other's one and only. She needed to believe that they could, for their sake and the baby's. She wanted more for Logan than an unhappy life and unhappy wife.

"Good. On that, at least, we can agree. And now I imagine it is clearer to you why Logan and Isabella are in such a rush to wed even though their relationship is somewhat new. Anyone can get swept away on passion. None of us are immune."

He had no idea how close to home his words hit. "Well, there's nothing more romantic than Harmony Harbor in the summer, and once I've worked out the logistics with the suppliers for the fourth, I'll arrange for Logan and Princess Isabella to have some one-on-one time together. Away from the manor and the wedding plans. Some fun and romantic dates is just what they need."

"Perhaps I've misjudged you, Ms. Bell. And as that appears to be the case, I am willing to give you a second chance. But there is one small detail that needs to be taken care of so no one learns of your egregious error."

That sounded good to her. "What's that?"

"Other than the suppliers, whom you have my permission to offer a monetary incentive to meet the new deadline and to keep quiet, no one except you and I will know that the wedding will be on the fourth instead of the seventh."

"Not even Logan and Princess Isabella?"

"No, not until the morning of the fourth. The majority of the guests are family and friends who live close by and who were no doubt planning to attend the Fourth of July festivities anyway. We'll just move the ceremony back so that the fireworks go off moments after they are pronounced man and wife."

Jenna couldn't have envisioned a more perfect ending to the ceremony herself. But she could've thought of a better ending for her morning. "Excuse me a moment," she said to Luis, and answered the ringing phone on her desk. "Greystone Manor, Jenna Bell speaking. How may I help you?"

"You may help me by returning my ring, *bella*."

"Lorenzo, there was a break-in at the manor and the ring was stolen. But you already know this."

"I'll leave you to your call. We'll speak more of the arrangements later," Luis said, and quietly left the study.

"I don't believe you. If it was stolen, someone would have tried to sell it or pawn it by now. There has been no word of the ring on the streets, and I have checked every pawnshop from Boston to New York. Return my ring, and I will speak to Gwyneth about returning your shares in Southern Belle."

"I can't return something I don't have, Lorenzo."

* * *

If Logan and Isabella were sitting in her office at Southern Belle, Jenna would've told the couple ever so gently that not only were they not a perfect match, they didn't have enough in common to be friends, let alone lovers. Well, clearly they'd been lovers since Isabella was carrying Logan's baby.

Once again, Jenna's gaze found its way to the other woman's stomach. It was hard to tell she was pregnant. Isabella wore a floaty floral sundress and wide-brimmed hat. Jenna knew she was in trouble as soon as she saw what the woman had on. She'd told them both to dress for a fun and adventurous day. Logan had listened; he had on a pair of board shorts and a T-shirt that hugged his impressive pecs and six-pack. Jenna had on a cute pair of stretchy pink shorts and a tank top that matched perfectly because she'd worn her glasses to check herself out. Mateo, who the princess had insisted come along, had on sweat shorts and a T-shirt that kept riding up to show his incredibly ripped physique. The guy was almost as well built as Logan.

Jenna looked away and found herself captured by Logan's intent gaze. He raised an eyebrow. Busted. She grinned and lifted a shoulder. "All right, I have a fantastic day planned for the four of us."

She didn't add that she'd had a fantastic day planned for them yesterday too. Isabella had blown her off for breakfast at the mayor's and a luncheon at the yacht club, while Logan had spent the day organizing security for the Fourth of July. It had been Jenna's idea that they mention there would be a party in their honor on Independence Day so Logan had a plan in place when they sprang the surprise wedding on them. The more Jenna thought about it, the more she didn't like it. The only element of the surprise she did like was that the press would be surprised too. If no one blabbed. Poppy and her sisters knew, of course, but they'd been sworn to secrecy.

Jenna glanced at the questionnaires in her hand. She'd practically had to beg Logan and Isabella to fill them out, which was how she'd discovered just how completely incompatible the couple were. She hoped by pushing them out of their comfort zones they'd bond and build trust in each other. She wondered why she'd never thought to do this with Lorenzo. Probably because the man had made her believe they were the perfect match.

She hadn't heard from him again. She glanced at
Logan. Until that moment, she'd forgotten to tell him
about the call. Her only excuse was that she'd started
calling suppliers as soon as she'd hung up with
Lorenzo. It wasn't like it made any difference though.
He and Gwyneth were still MIA.

"Jenna?"

She looked up, and Logan tapped his watch.

"Uh-oh, someone didn't read my list of no-no's,"
Jenna said. "Hand it over. And your cell phone." She
held out the waterproof bag. "You too, Princess Isabella
and Mateo. All right, now we're ready to start the day,"
she said once they'd done as she asked. "The first thing
we're going to do is go whale and dolphin watching."

"Cool. I haven't done that in years. We used to go
out with Captain Bill."

Maybe this was going to work after all, she thought,
gratified by Logan's enthusiasm. And she had a special
surprise for him. "Well, guess who just happens to be
taking us out on the water today? Captain Bill! Yay!
Isn't that the...?" She caught the look on Isabella's
face. "You don't want to go whale and dolphin watching, Princess Isabella?"

"Please, call me Isabella. And no, I'm sorry, I don't
like the water. But you and Logan can go. I'll join you
for the next activity."

"Sounds good. Come on—" Logan began.

Apparently, the day was going to go as badly as
she'd initially suspected. "No, no, I'm sure I can find
an activity we'll all be excited about." She looked at
her list. "I guess that means wakeboarding is out?"

she asked Isabella, trying to hide her own disappointment.

Logan didn't do as good a job hiding his disappointment when Isabella agreed wakeboarding wasn't for her.

"I've got an idea. How about fishing? We don't have to go out in a boat," Jenna suggested.

"Great idea. I know the perfect spot. I haven't been—" He glanced at Isabella. "So that's a *no* too?"

"Please, you and Jenna go. I have a book I've been wanting to read."

Logan blew out a breath and crossed his arms.

"We'll go for a hike instead," Jenna said with determined cheerfulness. "There's some lovely trails…" She glanced at Isabella and knew she'd struck out again. As though sensing his princess was getting upset, Mateo said something to her in Spanish. She gave him a wan smile.

"Okay, follow me, everyone. And this time I'm not taking no for an answer," Jenna said.

"Where are we going?" Logan asked, as Jenna walked toward the pond and the wooden bridge. He held up the radio. "I need to let security know."

"We're going to the spa for a couples massage, and then we're going to have a picnic on the beach." When her plans were greeted with put-upon sighs, she said, "Please try to curb your enthusiasm."

Chapter Twenty-Two

♥

If Jenna's plan was to show how ill suited he and Isabella were, she'd be happy to know it was working. They were in one of the cottages on the estate that had been used mostly by the extended Gallagher family during holidays and summer vacations. His brother and Shay were living in one just up from here that had been kept for his family's use. This one had been converted into a spa.

The manager, Tina, was a nice enough woman, but a little extreme. "All right, relax on your pillows; feel the tension leaving your body and melting into the floor. Close your eyes and breathe in, pushing out your tummy and opening up your rib cage. Hold it for five and then release for five. Lovely. Again."

He heard the quiet padding of her bare feet on the cedar-planked floor, and then she was behind him. "So tight," she murmured, digging her fingers into his shoulders. He opened his eyes to see Jenna watching him while trying to keep a straight face. To the other side of her, Mateo and Isabella sat cross-legged on their pillows, both of them breathing deeply and rhythmically.

"Let's get this tension out of you," Tina said, leaning her whole body into his back as she worked her elbow into his shoulder blade. She was going to get more than tension out of him—he was going to cry out in pain if she didn't let up.

"Um, Tina, maybe you should use your hands instead of your elbow. It looks like you're really hurting him," Jenna suggested.

"You know what they say—no pain, no gain. Wink, wink. Now, Jenna, close your eyes and breathe."

"I'd love to, but we're scheduled for a picnic on the beach in forty-five minutes. So maybe we can start the couples massage?"

"I suppose so, although I really hate to interrupt these two. Just look at how in sync their breathing is. Beautiful." She stood behind Isabella and Mateo with her hands on their heads. "Came back to us now...That's it. Very nice. All right, now turn and face each other. Mateo, you take Isabella's hand in—"

"No, they're not a couple. Logan and Isabella are," Jenna said.

"Are you sure?"

"Ah, positive. Haven't you read the news?" Jenna asked as she went to stand beside Tina.

"And pollute my mind with all the negativity? I don't think so. I've been on a news fast for more than a year."

"Oh, okay, well, these two"—Jenna waved her hand between Logan and Isabella—"are getting married in two— Oh gosh, what am I saying? Five days. They're getting married in five days."

Any of the tension Tina had managed to release in

Logan came flooding back. Today had proven what he already knew; he couldn't marry Isabella. And from what he could tell, Isabella wouldn't be heartbroken. The only ones who would be were his mother, Jenna and her sisters, and pretty much all the business owners in town. If there were more time, he'd ride things out until his memory returned and he knew what was really going on. But there wasn't time.

Tina rubbed Jenna's arm. "Let me guess, you're the wedding planner. No wonder you're so, ah—" She put up her hands, palms out, and silently screamed.

"Really? I thought I was calm. Argh," she cried out when Tina jammed her fingers in Jenna's shoulders.

"I told you. Your muscles are as badly bunched up as Logan's." Tina let go of Jenna to help Isabella to her feet. "Take your pillow and sit in front of your fiancé. Jenna, you sit in front of Mateo."

"No, that's fine. I'll just go sit on the deck until they're finished, thanks. Enjoy the...argh. Stop doing that," she said when once again the older woman jammed her fingers in Jenna's shoulders, nearly bringing her to her knees in front of Mateo.

Logan bowed his head at the thought that he wanted to trade places with the younger man. He glanced at Isabella, who was watching Jenna and Mateo with a look of longing on her face. She caught him looking at her and gave her head a tiny shake as if it wasn't what he suspected, but he knew it was exactly what he thought. He'd witnessed the stolen glances between the pair, the brush of hands, the touch of fingers, the way Mateo watched Isabella when she wasn't aware of him doing so, and Logan hadn't felt one iota of jealousy.

He hadn't really felt anything except a desperate need to get to the bottom of what was going on. When he'd learned no one from Merradien was attending the wedding, he'd had his first stab of insight. He was Isabella's ticket to citizenship in the States, nothing more and nothing less. He was sure of it. The attempted kidnapping had probably been the catalyst. There'd been talk of an arranged marriage, and she'd balked. Only he hadn't been able to get her alone to talk because Luis, Pilar, or Mateo was always around, and he couldn't be sure whose side they were on.

Once they were at the beach having the romantic picnic Jenna had planned, he'd ask for some privacy and talk to Isabella then. Knowing he was finally going to take control of the situation, he felt the tension in his body begin to release.

"I want you to take the lady's right hand in yours and lightly stroke from the top of her shoulder down to her fingertips." Tina sighed when Jenna started to laugh. "Press a little harder, Mateo."

At least Jenna looked like she was having a good time. Isabella looked like his touch pained her.

Tina glanced at them and came over to take Logan's hand in hers, stroking it down Isabella's arm. "All right, gentlemen, take your partner's hand and gently knead. Mateo, maybe not so gentle."

Logan lightly kneaded Isabella's hand as Tina suggested and, in return, got another grimace from his bride-to-be. He couldn't take it anymore and said,

"Okay, time to trade partners." He didn't miss the relief on Isabella's face or the panic on Jenna's.

"No. The whole point of this exercise is for you and Isabella to—" Jenna began before Tina interjected.

"Whatever you were hoping for obviously isn't happening. At least this way you'll all get rid of some tension."

Logan wasn't so sure about that as Jenna sat in front of him and Tina had her turn around and lie back in his arms.

"Isabella and Mateo, take the same position, please. Now, gentlemen, stroke your hands up and down your partner's arms from the shoulders to the fingertips. Wonderful. Much better, much, much better." She walked to the far end of the cedar-paneled room and turned a switch, filling the space with the sound of rain on a tin roof and rolling thunder in the background.

Tina returned with two small vials, handing one to Logan and then one to Mateo. "Pour a small amount in your hand and then rub your palms together to heat the lavender oil. Once it's warm, gently massage the oil into your partner's arms, starting at the shoulders and working your way down to the tips of their fingers. When you hear the bell, you'll switch positions and, ladies, you will massage your partners. And then we'll move to the full-body massage."

"No time for bodies. Arms and hands are good. Oh gosh, so good. Really, really good," Jenna moaned, and Logan had to agree with her. He was not giving her a full-body massage in front of Isabella, Tina, and Mateo, but he definitely planned to bring her back to the spa once he ended his engagement to Isabella.

Fifteen minutes later, they said their goodbyes to Tina. "I hope you'll come again and bring your friends. Logan, you make sure Jenna gives those gorgeous muscles of yours some time and attention." She gave Jenna a playful swat. "You greedy little thing. I thought you were going to start purring any minute. We certainly know whose hands you prefer. Wink. Wink."

By the look on Jenna's face, this wasn't how she'd imagined the day going either. He leaned toward her as he held open the door. "You and I need to talk. But first I need to talk to Isabella. Alone."

"Of course." She nodded, trying to smile but failing miserably.

He went to take her arm to try to explain, but she moved out of his reach. "Jenna, it's not what you think."

"I don't know what you mean." She hurried to catch up to Mateo and Isabella while Logan retrieved his gun from the lockbox behind the door.

"You're a smart man, so I'm sure I don't have to tell you you're marrying the wrong woman, do I?" Tina said.

He didn't think it would be appropriate to say *I know, and I'll be back with the right woman in a few weeks for a couples massage*, so he just smiled and tucked the gun in the waistband of his shorts. "Thanks again, Tina."

Logan caught up with Jenna and Isabella at the start of the trail into the woods. "Where's Mateo?"

"He's gone to pick up the basket and blanket at the manor. Jasper was having everything prepared."

"Mateo should've waited till he spoke to me." Logan tensed, an uneasy feeling coming over him as he scanned the woods. Something or someone was watching them.

"I'm sorry. I thought you wanted..." Jenna glanced from him to Isabella. "I'll catch up to him and send him back."

At the snap of a branch, Logan shook his head and pulled her back. He got his gun in his hand and then reached for the radio to call for backup. It was too late. He registered movement fifteen yards away and quickly pushed the women back. "Behind that tree," he yelled. He got off a shot, but so did the shooter. Logan lunged for Jenna and Isabella, bringing them both to the ground seconds before a bullet slammed into a tree a foot in front of them. Covering them with his body, he scanned the woods. A door just up from the path slammed.

"It's Shay," Jenna said, a slight hitch to her voice, but otherwise she was holding it together. "Everything's going to be okay, Isabella. Nothing's going to happen to you," she comforted the crying woman.

Shay ran to them, bent low, gun in hand. Logan tossed her the radio. "Call for backup. I'm going after them. I'll cover you until you get Jenna and Isabella out of sight."

"No. Don't go in there by yourself. The security guards will be here—" Jenna began.

"Trust me. I've got this, Jenna. Go with Shay."

Crouched by a tree, he slowly swept his gun from left to right as he focused on the woods. He could hear Shay calling for backup on the radio as she got the women to safety. As soon as he heard the sound of their feet on the wooden deck and the door to his brother's cottage closing, he moved out. He stayed off the path, stepping carefully through the brush, not wanting to give away his location, using the trees for cover, looking for broken branches that would give the shooter's position away.

In the distance, he heard at least three, maybe four, men coming his way. It had to be members of the security team. If the shooter was still in the woods, he'd hear them too and would make a break for it now. In a matter of seconds, he proved Logan right by laying down fire.

The bullets ripped through the tree Logan was crouched behind. He needed better cover and dove behind a boulder. His foot snagged on a root, jerking him back. He fell hard, hitting his chin, his teeth slamming together, rattling his brain and shaking his memory free. It took only a moment for the memories of the last month to return in full and for him to regain his bearings, but it was long enough for the gunman to get away.

At the sound of the security team entering the woods, Logan identified himself and slowly pushed to his feet. When they reached him, he took one of the officers' radios and let Shay know his status and that of the shooter.

Despite the situation, the corner of his mouth lifted when he heard Jenna in the background demanding to know if he was okay. At least he now understood where his feelings for her were coming from and no longer had to feel guilty about them. He was just about to ask

Shay to put her on but decided against it. He might give
himself away, and they had an audience. For now, it
was best no one knew his memory had returned. Which
was why he sent four members of the security team
to the cottage to escort Jenna and Isabella back to the
manor instead of doing it himself. He needed time to
sort through his memories for clues as to why Luis, Pilar, Mateo, and Isabella had lied to him.

He and Isabella hadn't had a whirlwind romance in
DC like they'd professed, and they weren't engaged. Isabella had asked him to go back to Tiffany's and pick
up the ring he'd supposedly given her the day of the accident. She didn't want anyone to know and promised to
wire Logan the funds once she'd returned to Merradien.
Only she had no intention of returning to her homeland.
He was sure of that now. And just as sure of the identity
of the man who would've placed that ring on Isabella's
finger if he had the means. Now Logan had to figure
out if Mateo had been trying to take him out. Or was Isabella in as much danger here as she was in Merradien?

* * *

Colleen stood at the French doors that opened onto the
balcony of her suite in the tower. Logan and Aidan
were there along with the head of security and Isabella
and her entourage. Luis was holding court, standing in
front of Colleen's old canopied bed, laying out a case to
prove Jenna was behind the assassination attempt.

"It's plain for anyone to see that the woman is in
love with you. She wants Isabella out of the way. She

planned the day. Chose the spa, a place where you'd have to walk through the woods, and sent Mateo back to the manor."

"Don't let him make you doubt Jenna, my boy. That girl wouldn't harm the hair on a flea," Colleen murmured.

Logan rubbed his hand along his jaw. "You're saying she hired a hit man?"

"I don't understand why you find it inconceivable. Just the other day we saw her on Main Street riding with two bikers. Clearly, she has connections to the underbelly of society. I've read all about her ex-fiancé, and she's still in contact with him." Colleen's great-grandsons shared a glance at the news.

"How do you know that?" Logan asked.

"I was in the study when she took the call. They were discussing the missing ring. From what I heard, he didn't believe it had been stolen. Perhaps she offered to give him his ring back in exchange for assassinating Isabella."

"Her ring was stolen, and your theory has about ten other holes in it," Logan scoffed.

Luis was an accomplished liar. It was too bad Colleen didn't know where they'd hidden Jenna's phone or the ring so she could implicate the lot of them in the thefts at the manor. Things would begin clicking into place for Logan anytime. He'd know he was being played then. He needed to figure it out soon or he'd find himself married to the wrong woman.

"Is there a reason you don't wish to implicate Ms. Bell? Both Isabella and Mateo tell me that you were partnered with her instead of your fiancée for the massage."

Logan gave the couple a hard look.

"No, my boy. It's Luis and Pilar you have to watch. They're the ringleaders. They've set all this in motion. We just need to find out their motivation."

"My cousin will be questioning you in the next room, Mateo," Logan said. There was a knock on the door, and he went to answer it. "Thanks for coming. Pilar, Shay will be questioning you here. Luis, you come with me. Isabella, you're free to get something to eat in the dining room." He nodded at the head of security, who accompanied Isabella out of the room.

"What of Ms. Bell? Will you not question her?" Luis asked.

"My cousin will, once he's finished questioning Mateo."

Colleen went to follow Logan and Luis down the spiral staircase to the lower level, but a demanding *meow* brought her up short. "What is it? Can't you see I'm busy?"

Simon *meow*ed again, lifting his chin toward Kitty's tower room across the way.

"Is Jasper there, then?" At what looked like a nod, Colleen hurried to her daughter-in-law's door and walked through it. "Thank the good Lord and the Holy Ghost," she murmured at the sight that greeted her. Jasper sat on the edge of the wingback chair, frantically flipping through her memoir.

As she rushed to his side, he glanced her way. "It feels like the air conditioner is working overtime, so I imagine Simon let you know I was here, madam, and with no time to lose, I'm afraid. I apologize for ignoring your attempts to take out the book. I'd begun to wonder if it shouldn't be locked away for good. But I don't know what else to do to help the young miss. I'm hoping you have something about Jenna's family that will allow her to deal with her stepsisters and stepmother." He flipped through the pages, clearly upset.

"You have a soft spot for the girl, haven't you, my boy? I can't say I'm surprised. I had a soft spot for her too. And much to make up for."

If it weren't for Colleen's interference, Jenna wouldn't have been deprived of her father for ten years. Colleen had been good friends with Arianna and Serena's great-grandmother and had taken a special interest in the family. When it had come to Colleen's attention that Richard was having an affair with a waitress in town, she'd confronted him on the street. He wasn't a local boy, so she didn't know him well. Perhaps if she'd known him better, she might have believed him when he said he and his wife were separating. It was only for his young daughters' sake that he returned to Harmony Harbor on weekends from his job in the city.

But she didn't trust the handsome charmer and laid down the law. If he didn't quit seeing the waitress, Colleen threatened to have Richard fired from his fancy job in Boston. She was a Gallagher, after all, and the Gallaghers knew people. It helped when your grandson was governor of the state. There was nary a whisper about the affair again.

Oh, there was talk when the young waitress found

herself with child, but Colleen threw suspicion another man's way and soon the talk died down. And when her own guilt got the best of her, Colleen would have a coffee at the café and leave the mother-to-be an overlarge tip. One day it got to be too much for Colleen, and she offered the waitress a job at the manor. The pay and tips were far better than at the café.

Still, every time she saw the young mother and daughter, the guilt ate at Colleen. It got worse when she'd overheard Richard's wife with a group of her friends at a baby shower. Two wrongs don't make a right, but it became clear Richard's wife no longer loved him. She did like his money though. So many years had passed by then, but Colleen still felt the need to do something, and she sent Richard an anonymous note letting him know he was Jenna's father and that her mother had never stopped loving him.

"I couldn't protect Jenna from Ryan Wilson's threats, but I'll protect her from her stepfamily and Luis," Jasper muttered as he drew his finger down the page. "He thinks I don't know what he's up to, trying to point suspicion at Jenna when he's the one they should be focused on. He'll learn his folly soon enough. He's underestimated me."

Other than *Ryan Wilson*, the rest came to her as mumbo jumbo. She couldn't focus on anything but that name. She knew there was something about the lad. It was important. Her mind had been poking at her since...Her eyes went wide. She remembered. Ryan's grandfather had been chief of the Harmony Harbor Police Department. Colleen had him fired before he uncovered the truth about that long-ago summer night. She crouched low, pushing at the pages, flipping them with her finger. Jasper needed to know how dangerous Ryan Wilson could be to them all.

"I don't have time for this, madam." He briskly flipped the pages back to her notes about Jenna's family. He stabbed the page. "Ah, there it is. Right in front of...Oh, madam, what have you done?"

"I was protecting one family at the expense of another as it turned out. But as best I could, I made amends." A lot of good it did trying to explain when Jasper couldn't hear her.

"Difficult as it may be for Jenna to learn she lost ten years with her father because of you, she'll at least have proof she's as much a Bell as Serena and Arianna."

Colleen looked from Jasper to the book. Surely he'd know this was not a revelation that would work in Jenna's favor. All the child had ever wanted was her sisters' love. She'd not get it if Jasper was to reveal that Richard Bell had an affair with Jenna's mother more than a decade before he'd taken her as his wife, and Jenna was the result.

"Are you mad? Think it through, my boy. You want to help Jenna, not harm her," she cried as he began tearing out the relevant pages. Colleen dove on top of the leather-bound book to stop him. Instead, her body went through both the book and coffee table to land on the floor beneath. She tried again, but it was no use. She couldn't stop him.

Chapter Twenty-Three

♥

Jenna stared at the detective sitting across from her in the study. It was slightly disconcerting because Aidan looked a lot like his cousin Logan and even more disconcerting because it was becoming clearer by the minute that he believed her capable of murder. "I thought you wanted to question me to see if I'd witnessed something that would help in your investigation, but that's not it at all, is it? You think I had something to do with this, don't you?"

"No one is accusing you of anything, Jenna. We're questioning everyone who has—"

"Are you questioning Shay?"

"Well, no, but she—"

"Are you questioning Isabella?"

"No, but she's the—"

"Then why are you questioning me?"

He looked up at the ceiling before returning his gaze to her. "Because it was suggested that you had means and motive."

She pressed a hand to her throat. It was worse than

she suspected. Somebody had actually accused her of the crime. "Who would say something like that? I have no means. I have nothing, thanks to my ex-fiancé and my stepmother. If I didn't have this job and free room and board, I'd be out on the street. And what possible motive could I have? If something happened to Princess Isabella, there'd be no wedding, and I need there to be a wedding. I'm the wedding planner. The town needs there to be a wedding, and that includes my sisters."

"Those are all excellent points," Aidan admitted.

"Then why aren't you writing them down?" she asked.

The study door opened before Aidan could answer, although he might've released a relieved breath when Logan walked into the study. Jenna hadn't seen Logan since he charged four members of the security team with delivering her and Isabella back to the manor while he and the others combed through the woods. Jenna had taken the time to change into a work-appropriate sleeveless sundress, but Logan remained in the board shorts and T-shirt he'd worn earlier.

Except now they looked like he'd been in a battle. His shorts were ripped and covered with dirt and grass stains, and there was what appeared to be a bloodstain on the front of his T-shirt. His chin had been cut, and there were two light scratches on his right cheek. She might've felt sorry for him if he hadn't sent his cousin to question her as a suspect in an assassination attempt.

"Is everything okay in here? Did you get Jenna's statement?"

"Statement? Are you sure you don't mean my signed

confession? I can't believe you think I'm guilty of this, Logan. You have no idea what I've had to do to pull this wedding off. You have no idea the hours I've put in or the time I've spent racking my brain for ways to turn a woman who's not your one and only into your perfect match." What was wrong with her? Just because it was the truth didn't mean she had to blurt it out. What if they asked...?

"Did it bother you that Logan was marrying a woman he didn't love, Jenna?" his cousin asked. At least he didn't ask if she thought she was Logan's one and only.

The man in question leaned against the wall with his arms crossed. Unlike her, his face was a closed book. It bothered her that Logan stood there watching instead of coming to her defense. Which meant she wasn't about to admit her feelings with him in the room. "You're his cousin. Wouldn't it bother you if you thought he was marrying someone he didn't love?"

"Of course it would, but I'm his cousin, not someone who's *in* love with him."

"Aidan," Logan said, a warning in his voice.

Jenna bowed her head, her face growing hot. Logan thought she was in love with him. Aidan did too. After today, she could no longer deny it, even to herself. When he was going back into the woods to hunt for the shooter, she'd felt a terror like she'd never known. She'd been afraid she was going to lose him, and not just to another woman. She actually could handle that. He and Isabella were having a baby together, and he'd made the choice to marry her. Getting killed doing what heroes do, putting someone else's life above your own, never seeing him again . . . She would've had a hard time living with that.

"This is why I'm conducting the interview, not you," his cousin said before returning his attention to Jenna. "Would it bother you enough to have someone try to scare off Isabella?"

So she really was a suspect. She reached for the phone.

That at least got a reaction out of Logan. He pushed off the wall. "Who are you calling?"

By the wary edge in his voice, he knew exactly who she planned to phone. "Your brother and my attorney. So if you have any further questions for me, you can direct them to Connor."

Aidan groaned, while Logan exhaled a frustrated sigh before saying, "You can hang up, Jenna. You don't need an attorney."

"Really? Maybe you should share that with your cousin," she said, refusing to look at him. She was hurt that he felt it necessary to allow Aidan to question her and didn't want him to read the emotion on her face.

"Jenna, the accusation was made in front of Aidan and the head of security. I didn't have a choice but to have you questioned."

Maybe, but he could've done it himself. She couldn't help but feel he was avoiding being alone with her. She supposed she didn't blame him after the massage session. Not for the first time, she wished she'd never suggested it. If Logan had figured out she was falling for him, he probably thought she'd maneuvered it so she'd end up his partner. Her gaze shot to the two men.

"You think I orchestrated the couples massage session to draw you into the woods and then got rid of Mateo by asking him to get the picnic and blanket at the manor."

The men shared a look. "Did you ask him to go back to the manor or did he offer to, Jenna?" Logan asked.

"I remember mentioning the picnic, but I'm not sure if I asked him to go or he offered. I'm sorry. I honestly can't remember," she said, sensing Logan's frustration. Now that she looked at the situation from their point of view, she could see why someone might think she had played a part in the shooting. If she didn't want to find herself in jail, she needed to come clean. "I wouldn't break your confidence if I didn't have to, Logan, but I really don't want to go to prison for something I didn't do. Aidan's your cousin, so he probably already knows about the baby, right?"

Logan stared at her and reached for the back of the chair. "You're pregnant?"

"Me? No, you and Isabella are. Because of the amnesia you don't remember, do you? I'm sorry." She frowned. "Wait a minute. How could you forget something like that? Surely you and Isabella talk about the baby when you're together. Actually, from what I've seen, you probably don't."

She looked up at Logan. "You and Isabella aren't a perfect match. As far as I can tell, you aren't a match at all. But I want you to be happy, Logan. I don't want you to spend your life in a loveless marriage, and you're the type of man who would. You wouldn't ask Isabella for a divorce. You'd just keep trying to make... Why are you both looking at me like that?"

"You just made a case for motive, Jenna," Aidan said.

"I know. That's what I'm trying to tell you. Logan, you were there. Isabella vetoed all my other ideas, and I was desperate to find a way to help you bond and develop trust in each other. You might not be each other's true loves, but that doesn't mean you couldn't have a wonderful marriage with some work. That's why I suggested the couples massage. It's supposed to supercharge a couple's trust and intimacy."

They didn't look like they believed her, which obviously meant Logan hadn't felt a tenth of what she had during the session. "Trust me, it does." Okay, so maybe that was the wrong thing to say, she thought when Aidan raised an eyebrow at his cousin. "Watch the pottery scene with Patrick Swayze and Demi Moore in the movie *Ghost* and you'll see what I mean."

Afraid Aidan might ask how their massage session had worked out for her and Logan, Jenna decided it was a good time to continue her attack on their theory. "So, as you can see, my motive for going to the spa was pure. I have no reason to want either Isabella or Logan hurt. And since it wasn't me out there shooting at us—as in Logan, Isabella, and *me*—you obviously think I paid someone to do it. As I told Aidan, I have no money. I also don't know people who would do something like that or where you even find them."

"The person who implicated you suggested you used your ex-fiancé's engagement ring, which we all now know is very valuable, to pay for the services of your biker friends," Aidan said.

"Shotgun and Cueball? But I just met them at the stoplight. And the ring was stolen from my room. You know that."

"We only have your word that it was, Jenna. Is there a reason why you didn't contact HHPD, or at least tell Logan, when you heard from your ex-fiancé? A man you know we're all looking for. A man you kept Logan from going after the other day at Tie the Knot."

"I—" Saved by a knock on the door, she thought when Aidan got up and opened it, revealing her sisters.

"Sorry. Are we interrupting something?" Arianna asked, looking from the Gallagher men to Jenna.

Just an attempted murder investigation, Jenna quipped in her head, and then prayed neither of the men would mention why they were there.

"No, we're good. Thanks. Jenna, I'll talk to you later about the last item on our agenda that Aidan mentioned." She should've known Logan wouldn't let her off the hook for long. "Wedding stuff," he explained to her sisters. And she could've kissed him for protecting her butt. A few minutes later, she wished he had stayed.

"We were so worried when we heard about the shooting, Jenna. Do they have any idea who did it?" Serena asked as she and Arianna lowered themselves onto the chairs in front of the desk.

Me, she thought. "No, but it's possible it was nothing. Maybe someone was hunting crows or squirrels." Both were out of season, but it had been known to happen before.

"That's not the rumor going around town. They say it was an assassination attempt on the princess. They're lauding Logan as a hero," Arianna said, glancing at Serena. "You might want to talk to him about Ryan. See if he has any suggestions as to how to protect yourself. You too, Jenna."

"Why? What's going on?"

"Based on our complaints, Chief Benson didn't just put Ryan on desk duty; he fired him," Serena said.

"Have you seen him since he was let go, Serena? Did he threaten you?" Jenna asked. She didn't want to make her sister nervous, but from Jenna's interaction with Ryan the other day, she thought Serena had reason to be. The man didn't seem like the type to forgive and forget.

"Oh, she saw him all right," Arianna said, giving Serena a tight-lipped look.

"What was I supposed to do? He wouldn't stop calling me and trying to get back together. He bragged about how his wife would never suspect a thing. She's pregnant, Arianna." Serena looked at Jenna. "I taped his phone calls and then went to his wife and played them for her. He came home just as I was leaving. She left him the next day, and then he was let go from HHPD."

"Oh, wow, you definitely have to talk to someone, Serena," Jenna said, proud of her sister yet terribly concerned for her safety.

Serena shrugged. "I don't think killing glares count as a threat. The police can't do anything."

"I know someone who can. We'll talk to Shay about it."

"That's a good idea, Jenna." Arianna smiled and then glanced at Serena, who didn't seem happy about what was coming next. And there was definitely something coming, as evidenced by the way Arianna moved to the edge of the chair and leaned in. "Gwyneth called with a proposal, and Serena and I think we should accept."

"Wait a minute. When did you hear from her? You know the police are looking for Gwyneth and Lorenzo. I hope you let them know she's been in contact." The last thing Jenna needed was the police thinking she'd kept this from them too.

"We will, okay? We just heard from her an hour ago," Arianna snapped, and then held up her hands. "Sorry, I don't mean to be defensive. It's just that this isn't easy. I want you to know that. But both Serena and I think this might be the only way to end the stalemate with Gwyneth."

"So what exactly is she proposing?"

Arianna shared a glance with Serena before saying, "She wants you to waive your rights to Daddy's estate. If you don't, she's going to try to have you legally removed."

"On what grounds?"

"That technically you have no legal right to the estate. You aren't a Bell. I mean, we know you feel like one, Jenna. But really, you aren't. Daddy married your mother, but he didn't adopt you."

"I see," Jenna managed to say despite the thick ball of hurt that was stuck in her throat. As much as she'd wanted Serena and Arianna to love her, she'd wanted to be Richard Bell's daughter. She'd even brought it up one day. There'd been a father-and-daughter dance at school, and she asked Richard if maybe he could adopt her. He'd said they didn't need a piece of paper to prove they were father and daughter.

"Arianna," Serena said in the voice she used when her older sister had gone too far. "Jenna, you know Daddy loved you like a daughter. Trust me, so do we. And this is nothing more than us going along with Gwyneth so we can all move forward. The estate will be split three ways."

"Just a moment please," she said when someone knocked on the study door, barely able to keep the anger and hurt from her voice. "So the three of you get the house and all the contents, and my business too? Well, of course, then. Give me a pen and I'll happily sign away my rights to what used to be my life."

"Don't be so dramatic. It's just on paper. We'll split everything with you and then sign over our shares of Southern Belle to—" Arianna turned when the door to the study banged open and Jasper strode inside.

"Don't sign anything, miss. You have as much right to your father's estate as your sisters. Richard Bell was your biological father."

Chapter Twenty-Four

♥

The revelation of Jenna's parenthood had gone as badly as Colleen had anticipated. Jasper stepped back from the three women yelling at one another with a shell-shocked expression on his face. Apparently, he didn't have the good sense God gave him and had actually expected this to go well.

Jenna waved the papers in Arianna's face. "How does this become all about you? You're not the one who lost out. I did. For ten years, I didn't have a father, and then for the rest of the time I had someone I adored who I wished more than anything was my father, and he was. Only he couldn't tell me because he knew exactly how you and Serena would react. Just like you are now."

"How do you expect us to react, Jenna? We've just found out that not only was your mother the reason our father walked out of a twenty-year marriage, but he cheated on our mother with yours years before. All our memories, everything we believed about our parents' relationship was a lie. The only reason he stayed with us was because Colleen Gallagher black-mailed him."

"If you expect me to feel sorry for you, try again. You got everything I wanted. You always did. We had next to nothing, Arianna. My mother struggled to put food on the table. You think people here didn't judge her, judge me, well, think again."

"Maybe she should've thought about that before she went after a married man. She deserved what she got. She—"

Colleen was afraid the fight was about to get physical and focused all her energy on the book sitting on the corner of the desk, cheering when she managed to push it off and it landed on the floor with a heavy *thud*. Too bad her prowess didn't extend to manipulating locks and turning keys. However, her attempt to draw their attention away from the fight was all for naught. They were so caught up in the drama, Jasper and the three girls didn't even notice, but they did notice when Logan strode into the study.

"What the hell is going on in here? I heard you all the way to the lobby." His gaze moved over the three women. "Jenna honey, are you okay?"

Arianna looked from Logan to Jenna, her eyes narrowed. "My God, have you no shame? The man is getting married in two days." She shook her head with a bitter laugh. "I can't believe I even asked you that. You're just like your mother. A homewrecker. You don't care who you hurt as long as you get what you want."

"That's enough, Arianna. Jenna hasn't done anything wrong," Logan said, reaching for Jenna.

Jenna's shoulders sagged as the fight visibly went out of her. Her feelings for Logan meant Arianna's accusations weren't far off the mark. Or maybe Jenna was just trying to come to terms with all she had learned. Whatever it was, she didn't want Logan's comfort and shrugged his hand from her shoulder. Colleen hoped the girl didn't blame her great-grandson for what she had done.

Jenna walked toward the door and then turned. "Tell Gwyneth that I'll see her in court. You might want to share with her that my lawyer, Connor Gallagher, tells me there's a very good chance she'll end up in a cell alongside her boyfriend. At least until he's extradited back to Italy."

* * *

Jenna had just been granted her fondest desire—Richard was her father. Only instead of joy, it brought heartache along with more questions.

She glanced at the papers on the nightstand beside her bed. She'd read them at least ten times. They were splotched with tears now. Some of the ink had faded after all the years that had gone by. But it didn't change the facts of her parents' affair. The lies told, the secrets kept.

Still, she knew her mother. She was a good, decent woman no matter what Arianna believed. And her father was a good and decent man. They weren't perfect. They made mistakes just like everyone else. No one got through this life without making them. But they'd tried their best to do the right thing. Her mother didn't try to win Richard back after he returned to his wife. She didn't track him down upon learning she was pregnant with Jenna, his child. But she had no doubt that her mother would've told him the truth if he had asked. Only Colleen had beaten her to it.

Jenna understood now why he'd lavished her with love, attention, and gifts. He'd been making up for lost time. He'd done the same with her mother. Only they didn't have a lot of time together, not as much as they deserved. For their own sakes, she wished her parents had been more selfish. Life was short; love was a gift.

But her father had loved Arianna and Serena too. He hadn't known about Jenna back then. He wouldn't have been the man she loved and admired if he didn't put his daughters' feelings above his own. And Colleen Gallagher had threatened his livelihood, his ability to provide for his family. He wouldn't have risked that, not in a million years.

Jenna couldn't work up the energy to be mad at the manipulative, nosy older woman who'd changed the course of their lives. Colleen Gallagher had gotten involved in a situation that she knew nothing about, but she'd gotten involved for what she believed were the right reasons. And when she realized her mistake, she'd tried to make amends. Jenna had always wondered why Logan's great-grandmother had taken such an interest in her, and now she knew.

She cuddled Pippa to her chest. She owed Logan an apology. He'd followed her from the study and tried to get her to talk to him, but she'd pushed him away, and

not very nicely, she was afraid. It had been too soon
after Arianna had tried and convicted her of being a
homewrecker. Her sister was right though. Jenna had
no business seeking comfort from a man who would
be married in less than two days. Still, Logan had been
offering friendship and didn't deserve Jenna's anger because she wanted more.

"Take it from me, Pippa. The best thing that happened
to you was the sandpipers at the beach rebuffing you.
Family and lovers are overrated. You've got me, and
I've got you." She looked up at the knock on the guest
room door, standing to put Pippa in her sandbox. "I'll get
rid of whoever it is, and we'll go for a walk." Part of her
hoped it was Logan, while another part of her hoped it
wasn't. No matter what she'd told Pippa, Jenna was still
afraid she was at the comfort-seeking stage.

She opened the door, surprised to see Princess Isabella and Mateo. Before she even got *hi* out of her
mouth, they'd pushed their way inside. "I'm sorry,
Jenna. We didn't know who else to turn to," Isabella
said.

After Mateo shut the door, he reached for the
princess's hand, and Jenna saw what she hadn't allowed
herself to see at the spa. A pink light danced between
the couple, and she felt their love down to her toes.
Until that moment, she hadn't realized that the warm,
fuzzy feelings, the deep sense of contentment she'd always felt when faced with soul mates, was the love
they felt for each other. Isabella and Mateo had found
their one and onlys. And while that usually made Jenna
happy, in this instance, it made her mad.

"How could you do this to Logan, Isabella? He loves you. You're expecting his baby."

"Please, may we come in and explain? The day has been difficult for Isabella. I want her to sit."

"Yes, of course." Jenna gestured to the bed. "Can I get you something to eat or drink?"

"No. We don't have time. Pilar will be looking for Isabella," Mateo said as they sat side by side on the edge of her bed. They looked young, scared, and hopelessly in love.

"The baby isn't Logan's, is it?"

Isabella shook her head. "No. The baby is Mateo's. We love each other, Jenna. We wished to be married, but my family refused."

"They think I'm not good enough for her. My family is not rich or powerful or of royal blood. But Isabella is my other half. I cannot live without her."

"Mateo, I can't help you unless you tell me the truth. Were you the one who shot at Logan today? Did you try to scare him off?"

"No. I would not do that. He is a good man."

"Jenna, trust me. Neither Mateo nor I want Logan hurt on our account. Logan does not love me. We were never engaged. He is an honorable, heroic man. And those very attributes are the reason why, when Logan lost his memory, Luis used them to his advantage," Isabella said.

"Luis is forcing you to marry Logan?" Jenna asked.

"It's not what you think. Luis is like a father to me. He's trying to protect me. Both he and Pilar have risked much to help me. My family wish me to marry a man who is twenty years my senior and a distant cousin. I had just discovered I was expecting Mateo's baby when they announced the match. I panicked. I didn't know what to do. Neither Mateo nor I did. We can't fight my family, you see. They're too powerful. I have always wished to live in America, so I told Mateo we would run away and we would come here. But we didn't know how to do so on our own."

She looked helplessly at Mateo, who took over for her. "We aren't proud of what we did, but we didn't know of any other way, Jenna. Isabella told Luis she was in love with Logan, that they had an affair. Luis, he likes and admires Logan, and he didn't wish Isabella to be forced to marry by her family. He and Pilar came up with the plan and helped us get to America."

"And that is when things began to unravel," Isabella said. "Luis and Pilar could tell Logan had no interest in me. We had to tell them the truth. They were not happy to learn I was in love with Mateo and having his baby. But we couldn't go back to Merradien. Luis took matters into his own hands the day of the accident. He said it was God's will that Logan lost his memory."

"We went along with Luis's plan because we thought Logan's memory would return, but it hasn't."

"Pilar, she's buying us time. She pretends to be on my family's side, but soon they'll come looking for me."

"You need to tell Logan the truth."

They shook their heads. "We can't. For Logan's sake, it's best that he knows nothing of this. I will make a video recording absolving him of all knowledge and involvement. Otherwise, he would be at the heart of an international incident and would most likely lose his job with the Secret Service."

Suddenly it hit Jenna what they wanted from her. "You want me to help you get away, don't you?"

They nodded. "We know it will put you in a difficult position, Jenna. But you are the only one we trust. Will you help us, please?" Isabella begged.

They were star-crossed lovers. If she didn't step in, what would become of them? They had everything standing against them and nothing but each other and a baby on the way. "Of course. Of course I'll help you."

"Thank you, Jenna. We will be forever in your debt." Isabella stood and took Jenna's hands in hers, kissing her on each cheek. "I must go, but Mateo will stay, and you can come up with a plan. We must be gone before the wedding."

"Then we better think fast. Luis has a surprise for you and Logan. The wedding is Wednesday, not Saturday."

"We know. That is why we came to you today. It was not a surprise to us. Pilar can put the family off for only so long. They will be sending someone for us by Friday at the latest. We must be long gone by then."

"What about Luis and Pilar?"

"They both come from wealthy and powerful families, and that will afford them some protection. But they cannot know of ours plans, Jenna. They will put a stop to it. They do not wish me to marry Mateo. They believe only Logan and his family can offer me the protection I need."

* * *

Logan figured he'd given Jenna enough time on her own. She needed to hear the truth, or as much of the truth as he knew about his relationship with Isabella. All that mattered to him was that she knew Arianna was wrong. Jenna had nothing to feel guilty or ashamed about.

Although Logan felt guilty about the part his great-grandmother had played in tearing Jenna's family apart. And because she had, it was possible Jenna would want nothing to do with him. The thought bothered him a lot. If his memory hadn't returned, he might wonder why that was, or maybe he wouldn't given the past few days. It was becoming apparent that Jenna Bell had a way of working herself into Logan's heart.

He gave his head a slight shake at the romantic notion. The woman was rubbing off on him, he thought as he picked up the bakery bag and left his room on the third floor. He took the stairs to Jenna's room on the second floor. He was just about to lift his hand to knock when the door opened. It was Mateo, the man he suspected of shooting at him today. And he was speaking privately with Jenna, who his cousin suspected was somehow involved. He'd had words with Aidan about those suspicions, but now it looked like he might owe his cousin an apology. At the very least, Logan wouldn't be telling Jenna he'd regained his memory.

He caught the panicked look Jenna and Mateo exchanged and forced a smile. "Hey, Mateo. How's it going?"

"Very good, sir. Her Royal Highness asked that I convey her gratitude to Jenna for her kindness today."

"Yeah, Jenna was incredible today. She handled the situation like a real pro. You'd almost think she'd been expecting it."

A hint of surprise flickered in Jenna's eyes, and then her lips flattened before she said to Mateo, "Tell Her Royal Highness that I was happy to be of service, but I did what anyone else would have done."

He nodded. "Good evening to you both."

"Thanks, Mateo. You too." He looked down at Jenna. "Aren't you going to invite me in?"

"No."

He leaned against the doorjamb. "Why's that?"

"Your comment about me expecting the assassination attempt, for one. You're not very subtle, Logan. If you really think I had something to do with today, I told you, call my lawyer. I'm tired. I've had a really crappy day, and I want to go to bed."

He'd let Aidan and his suspicions get to him, and he'd overreacted to seeing Mateo in her room. "Yeah, you have, and I'm sorry if I just made it worse. Let me in, Jenna. I won't ask any more questions about the shooting."

She hesitated, and he held up the bag from Truly Scrumptious. "I brought you cupcakes. Banana and chocolate marble with buttercream icing." *Peep.* "See, Pippa wants me to come in."

The bird dropped something at his feet that made Jenna gasp. Logan crouched down, brushed off the wet sand from Jenna's engagement ring, and held it up. "Something you want to tell me?"

Chapter Twenty-Five

♥

Afraid she was about to hyperventilate, Jenna put her head between her legs. "I can't do it. I can't pull it off."

The wedding was in two hours. They were in a sitting room off the ballroom. A sitting room in which Shay had discovered a secret door that led to a labyrinth of passageways under the manor. The first call Jenna had made after being grilled by Logan about Lorenzo's ring was to Shay. Her best friend had taken some convincing, but eventually she'd given in and agreed to help Isabella and Mateo escape. Their other best friend had come along for the ride.

"Jellilicious, you can pull anything off if you just believe," Cherry said.

"You've been on my Pinterest boards, haven't you?"

"Yes, and they're all positive and sparkly and sweet just like you usually are, but the past couple days you've been negative, glum, and grumpy. What's up?" Cherry asked.

"Oh, I don't know," Jenna said. "How about the fact Logan and Aidan think I'm behind the shooting in the woods? My stepsisters are actually my half sisters and, if possible, hate me even more. Logan thinks I lied about the ring being stolen, and I'm helping the woman he's sworn to protect and who he might possibly be in love with, but who doesn't love him, escape. How did I let you all talk me into this?"

"Suck it up, buttercup. You're the one who talked us into it," Cherry reminded her.

"And I am the one who is responsible for all of you getting involved. I'm sorry, Jenna," Princess Isabella said from where she sat on the couch. "Perhaps you don't have to pretend you're me for the wedding ceremony. Could we not just sneak out now, Shay?"

Jenna felt bad for saying anything. The other woman looked exhausted and scared, but better than Pilar, who at that moment slumped in the chair next to the couch. The cup of coffee Shay had drugged fell onto the floor.

As she walked over to retrieve the cup, Shay said, "No. The best chance to pull this off is if we leave just before the wedding starts. At the very least, we'll have an hour head start. The caterer's truck we're *borrowing* will be empty by then. Security will have its hands full with everyone coming for the Fourth of July celebrations, and it'll be dark out. Not to mention that Logan has doubled up on security in the ballroom, so there will be less on the grounds."

At the reminder, Jenna sort of forgot that, for Isabella's sake, she had to watch what she said. "Yes, because if another attempt is going to be made on Isabella's life, they believe it'll be then." Only it wouldn't be Isabella; it would be Jenna.

Shay nodded. "Makes sense."

"Bless your heart. I'm glad you're so calm about the likelihood of me getting shot at."

"Logan's prepared for it. He's not going to let anything happen to you."

"To Isabella," Jenna corrected.

"Right." Shay fitted her hands under the arms of the unconscious woman. "I'm going to get rid of Pilar now." Jenna gasped, and Shay rolled her eyes. "I'm tying her up, taping her mouth shut, and putting her in the closet."

"Isn't that dangerous? What if she gets sick?"

"She'll be fine, but we'll check on her. And once you're found out, you can let her out."

"I really wish you hadn't mentioned the found-out part." She looked at Cherry. "Don't tell me to suck it up again."

"Logan will understand why you helped us once he watches the tape, Jenna," Isabella said.

"You're sure about this, Isabella? You and Mateo haven't had second thoughts?" Jenna asked.

"We are nervous, yes, but happy, and very grateful for all of your help. We are excited for our new life in America. Shay has found us a place to live, and we have new identities. And, of course, the money you gave us, Jenna. It was very generous. One day, we hope to be able to repay you."

Shay had pawned Lorenzo's ring with a reputable dealer. She told him to keep it in his safe and a buyer—the family to whom the ring belonged—would be calling him within twenty-four hours. Shay made an anonymous call to Italy to tell them where the ring could be found and the amount to offer the dealer. It was the same amount as the finder's fee the family had offered to pay.

Jenna didn't want to think about money. If she did, she'd have to think about who was going to cover the cost of the fake wedding to the fake princess. If Logan and Aidan didn't throw her in jail for orchestrating the disappearance of said princess, even if the princess wanted to disappear, the Gallaghers would fire her.

"Um, I think we have a problem," Cherry said from where she stood in front of the long mirror. She was holding up a wedding gown that looked a lot like Jenna's original dress, only shorter.

Shay came out of the closet and looked from Jenna to the dress. "Okay, that's not going to work. If you walk out in this dress, they'll know it's not Isabella. Call your sisters."

"I can't. They hate me. Besides that, they won't help with this. And you said yourself, the more people who know, the more likely we are to get caught."

"We have to risk it. And now that I think about it, tell them to bring a second wedding veil. We'll layer them one on top of the other so it's less likely they can see through it."

"Don't worry, Shaybae. Once I do her makeup and hair, they'll think Jenna's Isabella. They have similar bone structure."

"There, so we're good," Jenna said.

Shay crossed her arms. "Call your sisters."

Jenna took out her phone. Mateo had returned it yesterday along with everything else he'd stolen the week before. Luis had ordered Mateo to break into Jenna's room. It had also been his idea to break into the other rooms to avoid suspicion falling on them should anyone recall Mateo being close by when Logan had talked about looking at Jenna's phone. Mateo had also stolen her ring to make the robbery more realistic, only he'd tripped over Pippa's sandbox and hadn't realized it had fallen out of his pocket until he'd gotten back to the tower room.

The bag of stolen goods was currently residing in her room. She hoped no one did a random search or she'd be in bigger trouble than she already was.

She took a deep breath and then scrolled through her contacts and pressed the call button. Her sister picked up. "Serena, I'm in trouble. I need your help. Yours and Arianna's."

* * *

Jenna looked down at the bowed blond heads of her sisters as they knelt at her feet, checking the length of the layer of tulle they'd added. "I really appreciate you coming when I called. Thank you."

She noticed something was missing when the words came out of her mouth. There was no hesitation, no worry as to how they'd be taken, no desperate eagerness to please. She truly appreciated her sisters dropping everything to come when she called, but she would no longer bend over backward to make them happy or appease them.

In a way, the pages of the Gallagher matriarch's journal had set Jenna free. Logan's great-grandmother had poked her nose in Jenna's family's business and stirred the pot, but in the end, it was the actions and choices of her mother and father that decided the paths their lives would take. She realized she didn't need a piece of paper to know her father had loved her. And love was all that mattered.

Serena lifted a shoulder. "We're your sisters. You said you were in trouble."

"You've always come when I was in trouble, haven't you?" she murmured, wondering why she'd never seen it before. When she'd fallen off the slide at school and the teacher couldn't reach her parents, Arianna had come. When her mother died, they were there. They'd taken turns staying with Jenna and her father for two weeks until they were on their feet. When she was away at boarding school and desperately lonely, Arianna's buying trip somehow took her to Switzerland. They were the ones who talked to her about her period, boys, kissing, and sex. They may not have been the sisters she dreamed of, but they'd always been there when it truly mattered. "But I haven't been there for either of you, have I?"

"You're the baby." Arianna said.

"If you still want me to sign off on Daddy's estate, I will. We need to move on, and the only way to do that is to get this settled."

"No. You were right. Arianna called Gwyneth as soon as we left and told her it wasn't going to happen."

"How did she handle the news?"

"Exactly how you'd expect, tantrums and threats," Arianna said, but then she tilted her head as though thinking more on the matter. "Maybe a little desperate and scared too. I have a feeling they've bankrupted Southern Belle, Jenna."

"I'm sure they have. It doesn't matter. My reputation as a matchmaker is shot. And shortly, my reputation as a wedding planner will be too. I'm sorry. I'd hoped to be able to send more business your way, but now—"

"It's fine," Arianna said in a very un-Arianna-like manner.

Serena sighed. "Tell her why it's fine, Arianna."

"No. She'll start believing she really does have a gift, and people will look at her like she's a Froot Loop."

And there was more proof of Arianna trying to protect her, and the way she went about it was exactly why Jenna had taken so long to realize it.

Serena rolled her eyes at their sister before saying to Jenna, "Three of Faith Fourburger's friends have booked their weddings with us because you told Faith the truth and didn't care about losing business."

"Our business," Arianna said, and then gave Jenna the side-eye. "You've got a job with us if you want it."

"It's Arianna, so you can't tell, but she really wants you to take the job. We both do. Faith has booked an appointment next week to see you. She's bringing her new boyfriend to meet you."

"Wow. I didn't expect this." Jenna didn't get to enjoy the moment with her sisters for long. Cherry slipped back into the room with Isabella. Desperate to find Pilar, Luis had requested an audience with Her Royal

Highness. And the Gallagher women, like the rest of the family and friends, had been in a tizzy since learning the wedding was today. Luis put their complaints to bed with one word—*baby*. Now they couldn't wait to get the couple married so they could start planning baby showers.

Cherry's presence hadn't been questioned, as they'd introduced her yesterday as a hairstylist and makeup artist.

"It's almost showtime. Shay and Mateo are waiting for us in the tunnels." Cherry gave her an up-and-down look and nodded. "Once you put on the veil, you're golden."

"Cherry is right, Jenna. And I told Luis that Pilar thinks she spotted one of the palace guards on the grounds and will remain outside to ensure the ceremony take places without interference so he will not question her absence, and he will also be anxious and distracted and less likely to pick up that you are you and not me. But don't speak to him when he escorts you to the ballroom. Just nod and sniff as though you are crying. He will expect me—you—to be upset."

There were guards outside the door, and Shay had been hired as Isabella's personal bodyguard for today. To cover for her absence, Shay would approach one of the guards who were stationed outside the manor within the next five minutes. She'd tell him Mateo had burst in on the princess and upset her, and that he'd last been seen heading for the woods.

"Don't worry. We'll divert Luis's attention and anyone else who gets too close," Arianna said.

"You'll stay with me?"

"Of course. We're your official ladies-in-waiting," Serena said.

"You're getting your fairy-tale wedding after all, and this time you're actually marrying a man worthy of being called Prince Charming." Arianna wasn't big on apologies, but this felt like one.

Cherry's phone chimed, and she glanced at it. "Okay, Shay's just alerted the guard, and she and Mateo are headed for the van. Good luck, Cinderella," she said, and gave Jenna a hug. "See you on the flip side. Come on, Isabella."

The princess thanked them profusely and then hugged Jenna goodbye.

As the secret panel closed behind them, someone knocked on the door. "We need to check on the princess and confirm she's all right," a guard called in.

"One moment, please," Serena said as they quickly put on Jenna's veil.

While Serena went to open the door, Arianna attached the second veil to the first. "Stop shaking. You'll give yourself away."

"I'm getting into character. Isabella would be shaking."

Arianna snorted a laugh. "Sure you are."

Her sister was right. The shaking hadn't been an act, and now the bouquet of pale yellow roses and light blue hydrangeas trembled in her hands.

As the guards gave a cursory look around the sitting room, Luis entered. He wore a military uniform and a gentle smile on his face. "You will see it's for the best, my princess. Logan is a good man. He will keep you safe. Mateo is just a boy," he whispered as he guided her toward the ballroom.

Jenna nodded and sniffed, nearly letting out a panicked shriek when they reached the entrance to the ballroom and he went to lift her veil.

Arianna leaned in and slapped his hand away, whispering, "Leave it. You'll ruin the effect. The groom will lift the veil when he kisses the bride."

Mesmerized by the man standing at the front of the ballroom beneath gauzy fabric lit up with tiny lights resembling twinkling stars, Jenna didn't hear Luis's response. White upholstered chairs with yellow and blue sashes tied at the back lined either side of the gold runner. Pots dripping with flowers circled the dais and lined the stairs to resemble an enchanted garden.

Logan stood alone on a raised dais wearing a black tux. He looked more regal and powerful than any prince and more ruggedly handsome than any man she had ever seen. And for one moment as she walked up the aisle toward him, she let herself believe it was real. The tremors stopped, and she glided gracefully toward him as if she were truly a princess. She heard the murmurs to her left and right, but her focus remined on the man who stepped down to offer her his hand.

"Your Highness," he murmured, snapping her out of the fantasy.

She put her gloved hand in his and ascended the dais. Turning to face him, she saw his mother and father, his grandmother, his brothers, uncles, cousins, and their wives and children. His mother glowed with happiness.

The woman Jenna had grown fond of would hate her after this. They all would. She moved her gaze back to Logan and started when she noticed his brows drawing inward as he scrutinized her face. There was no way he could see her well enough through the veil to know it wasn't her. Yet somehow he knew something wasn't right. She lowered her gaze, looking to where her sisters told her they'd be sitting. They weren't there. Her heart began beating like a caged canary, drowning out the priest's words.

Logan gently squeezed her fingers. She looked up, and he nudged his head at the priest. *I do.* It was her turn to say *I do.* She whispered the words. Again Logan's eyes narrowed, but it was his turn to speak, and in his deep voice, he said the words she now knew she wished he'd say to her someday. But he never would, not after he learned of her betrayal.

The frantic pounding of her heart caused a rushing sound in her head and the voices were odd and muffled. She looked over so she wouldn't miss the next part of their vows. The longer she could keep them from discovering who she was, the more time Shay had to get Mateo and Isabella to safety. But as she went to turn her head, she noticed something wasn't right. The fabric that created the backdrop wasn't lying flat. It was...

From outside came the sound of fireworks exploding, and the priest smiled and raised his voice to say, "I now pronounce you—"

"Logan," Jenna yelled when she spotted a gun poking out through the backdrop. She threw herself at him, bringing him down just as a bullet whizzed past.

Logan rolled her under him. "Jenna?"

"Shooter! Everyone down!" a man yelled. There was the sound of running feet as security swarmed the dais.

"Behind the curtain. To the right," Jenna said.

Logan told security where to go as he lifted the veil from her face. He looked like he was struggling with the urge to either kiss her or put her in handcuffs. Instead, he rolled agilely to his feet as he pulled out a gun. "Aidan, get Jenna out of here."

His cousin ran over and looked down at her. "What the hell?"

"We'll find out soon enough. For now, keep her safe." And without a backward glance, he ran to the back of the dais with his gun drawn.

"Yeah, safe in a jail cell," Aidan muttered, offering her his hand. She would've refused, but the wedding gown made it awkward to get up on her own unaided.

By the time she came down off the dais, security had cleared the ballroom of all but the Gallagher family. "I don't understand. Where's Princess Isabella? Jenna, what's going on?"

"I'm so sorry, Maura. I know how much you wanted Logan to marry a princess. But it truly wasn't meant to be."

She gave a small nod. "He wasn't her one true love, was he?"

Undeterred at the sighs and disbelieving sounds that met Maura's words, Jenna said, "No, he wasn't."

Logan's father stepped up to put his arm around his wife, and Jenna saw the dancing pink light. Despite everything, she smiled and leaned in to whisper in Maura's ear, "But your husband is yours."

At least she could give Maura that. She hoped she'd bring him to her appointment with the oncologist next week. So far, she'd refused.

"Okay, so you don't believe they're meant to be. We got that. But what we need to know is where you've stashed Princess Isabella, Jenna," Aidan said.

Behind Logan's parents, she saw Michael look around, and then he gave his head a slight shake as if he'd just figured out his fiancée, who was nowhere to be seen, must somehow be involved. He stepped forward at the same time as Connor, and they both said, "Jenna, don't say a word."

"You have got to be kidding me. You're both representing her?" Aidan groused.

They looked at each other, shrugged, and then nodded at Aidan. "Yeah."

"Thank you," Jenna said. "And I promise I won't say anything after this, but Pilar is in the closet and someone should probably let her out."

It didn't seem to matter to Aidan that Jenna held true to her promise to Michael and Connor and wouldn't say another word. And it didn't seem to bother Aidan that Connor and Michael said they'd have him charged with harassment if he kept it up. It actually got worse when Luis broke free of the security guards, grabbed one of their guns, and raced up the aisle threatening to shoot Jenna if she didn't spill her guts. She was actually a little surprised when Aidan stopped him.

The Gallagher women finally stepped in on her behalf, suggesting that she at least be allowed to change. As she was escorted from the ballroom to the sitting room, she searched the crowd for her sisters. She needed them now more than ever. But they weren't among the groups of people scattered throughout the lobby. They weren't in the sitting room either. It was empty.

A phone *ping*ed from under her pile of clothes. Praying it was her sisters or Shay, she ran over and shoved the clothes out of the way.

Come to Tie the Knot. Come alone or your sisters die.

Chapter Twenty-Six

♥

Other than a shell casing, there'd been no sign of the shooter. Which meant he was still at large, possibly somewhere on the grounds, and most likely still in Harmony Harbor. And Jenna was out there on her own and running scared. "What do you mean she's gone?" Logan said as he walked through the ballroom.

"The women in the family had a problem with me trying to get to the truth. It doesn't seem to bother them that a woman is missing, a royal princess, no less," Aidan said.

"Are you the reason she took off?" Logan asked, fighting the urge to punch his cousin or punch a wall. He was as angry at Jenna for not coming to him for help as he was at Aidan for her disappearance.

"Look, I get that you have feelings for the woman, but right now you have to look at the evidence, and it's pointing directly at Jenna as Mateo's co-conspirator. We have to find her and get her to confess before we have an international incident on our hands."

Her room had been searched, and they'd found the

items that had been stolen last week. Still, it didn't jibe with the woman he knew. She wasn't a thief; she wouldn't hurt anyone. Would she try to save him and Isabella from a loveless marriage? Yes, that he could believe. Would she put herself in harm's way for him? Yes, and she had. And that's what scared him the most.

His brothers were in the sitting room. Michael looked over, unable to hide a guilty grimace. Now things began to make more sense.

"Please tell me your fiancée isn't involved in this," Logan said to his brother. That just put a whole other spin on things. He called in the head of security. "Has Mateo been found?"

"No, sir." The guard confirmed his suspicion.

"Have Luis go with you and check to see if any of Mateo and Isabella's personal belongings are missing." He looked around the room. "Someone had to have seen Jenna leave. She can't have just disappeared."

Connor cleared his throat. "My brother, who is also my client, has no personal involvement in the princess's or Jenna's disappearance whatsoever, but in a view toward expediency, he suggests you look behind hidden panel number one."

"The tunnels," he and Aidan said at almost the same time. Michael knew every hidey-hole and passageway in the manor. He'd been charting them since they were kids playing pirate. It explained why Jenna suggested the princess get ready in this room. Shay must've known about the hidden panel.

They found Jenna's glass shoe at the bottom of the first flight of stairs. Logan held it in his hand. It wasn't that long ago that he'd picked up her shoe on the street. She'd been a stranger then, but now she wasn't. Despite his best efforts, he'd fallen in love with her. Twice, and each time in a matter of days. And he couldn't shake the feeling she was in serious trouble.

"Search the—"

"Sir," one of the guards called down to them, "we have a man who says he knows what happened to both the princess and Ms. Bell."

The man was Ryan Wilson. He looked like he hadn't slept or washed in a week, and he smelled like stale whiskey. His stance was belligerent and arrogant. "Interesting turn of events, isn't it, Gallagher? You need me now or your pretty little princess is gonna die."

His brothers held Logan back, but they'd forgotten about Aidan. Wilson put up his hand. "I wouldn't if I were you. I'm the best lead you've got."

"What do you want, Wilson?" Logan gritted out.

"Money, and lots of it. You owe me. You got me kicked off the force, and I lost my wife."

"Take responsibility for your actions. You threatened Serena and Jenna Bell. That's why you were fired," Aidan said.

"Why don't you Gallaghers take responsibility for your actions? I've got a pile of dirt on your family dating back decades. If you don't want the truth to come out, I suggest you pony up. You agree now, and I'll tell you what I know about Jenna. If you don't..." He shrugged.

"If anything happens to her, you'll be culpable. I'll make sure you're charged with obstruction. Everyone in this room will testify that you lied to my cousin." Logan jerked his thumb at Aidan. "You have five seconds to tell me what the hell you know about Jenna and Isabella's disappearance."

A security guard pushed his way into the room. He took Wilson by the arm and gave him a shake. "Tell him what you know. If you don't, I'll tell my sister to cut you out of the baby's life for good."

Wilson wrenched his arm away from his brother-in-law's grip. "Fine. But I expect something in return."

"Tell us what you know," Logan said.

"Your shooter is Jenna's ex-fiancé. He was gunning for her, not you or the princess. He got to her sisters. Last I saw of him, he was dragging Arianna and Serena through the tunnels with a blond woman. My guess is he somehow got in touch with Jenna and told her he had her sisters."

Logan went over and fisted his hands in Wilson's sweat-stained T-shirt, holding him up against the wall. "And the reason you saw all this is because you were stalking Serena and Jenna. You were planning a way to get back at them, and then Lorenzo came on the scene and it looked like he was going to take care of it for you so you wouldn't get your hands dirty." He shoved him at the security guard. "Cuff him and take him to HHPD."

They all turned at an insistent *meow*. Simon sat at the open panel. Jasper, who had just entered the room, said, "I would suggest we follow the cat."

* * *

By the time Jenna found her way to Main Street, the wedding dress was in tatters and her hands, legs, and feet were scratched and bloody. If she got out of this alive, she'd let the Gallaghers know just how far those tunnels go. If it hadn't been for Simon, the Gallaghers' black cat, she wouldn't have known where to go. He'd led her along the tunnels as though he'd built them himself. She'd used the flashlight on her phone to follow him.

At one point, she could've sworn she heard the sea churning above them, crashing against the rocks. The walls were rough-hewn stone and dripping with water. She'd almost turned back, but then she thought about her sisters and took Cherry's advice and sucked it up. Not long afterward the tunnel widened, and she spotted some stairs and a small wooden door. She had to bump against it a few times with her shoulder to get it to open. She'd ended up in a wooded area near the docks. Now here she was in the alley behind Tie the Knot. Alone. Simon had left her.

She crept along the back of the shop, looking for some kind of weapon as she did. She spotted a garden trowel in one of the flower pots that sat on the back step. Arianna had recently taken up gardening as a means of alleviating her stress. Jenna was glad she hadn't told her it wasn't working. Picking up the trowel, she stuffed it down the front of her bodice. She pulled off what was left of the veil and stuffed it down her top to conceal the outline of the trowel. She turned to try the door, but it was already open.

"*Bella*, so nice of you to finally join us," Lorenzo said, and hauled her inside. He let her go, gesturing with a gun to move ahead of him. "It's time for a family re-union," he said.

She walked up the steps, past Arianna's office, and then into the fitting area. Her sisters were gagged and tied up on the floor. Behind them, Gwyneth paced.

She turned on Jenna as soon as she saw her. "If you had signed off on the will, none of this would've happened, you selfish little girl."

"I'll sign it as soon as you let my sisters go."

"Too late, *bella*. We have a much better plan. Did you know your stepmama inherits your portion if you should die?" Lorenzo gave her a chilling smile. "On one hand, it was too bad I missed my shot. While on the other, failure is so often opportunity in disguise. As such, we have decided to kill all three of you, so my Gwyneth will inherit everything. Watch them while I get the gasoline," he said to Jenna's stepmother, and walked to the front of the shop. But not before Jenna had seen the look in his eyes. He was lying. She knew it deep down to her bones.

"I should've had everything right from the start," Gwyneth said, and for the first time, Jenna noticed her words were slurred. "I had to share his love all those years. The least he could've done is reward me for putting up with the three of you and for listening to him bemoan the loss of his true love. I hope he's happy with her now."

Jenna heard the splash of liquid hitting the floor and then smelled gasoline. He was going to torch the place with them in it. She caught her sisters' panic-stricken gazes. She needed to turn Gwyneth against Lorenzo, or she needed to take her down. "No doubt you'll soon find out," she said.

"What are you talking about?" her stepmother snapped.

"If he's willing to kill us for money, what's to say he won't kill you? He robs, cheats, and lies. There's nothing he won't do for money. Even marry you."

"What do you mean, even marry me?"

"He used to laugh at how you dressed, how you spoke, how needy you were for love and attention," Jenna said, goading the woman to come after her.

Gwyneth took the bait. Snarling, she ran at Jenna, who struggled to get the trowel out of her bodice. It was caught in the lining. The fabric tore just as her stepmother reached her, and Jenna brought the trowel down on her head. Gwyneth crumpled to the ground.

At the sound of clapping, Jenna looked up. Lorenzo laughed. "I know you so well, *bella*." He picked up the trowel and then tossed her some rope. "Tie her up." When she didn't move, he withdrew a gun from his pocket and motioned for her to do as he ordered. "Don't try anything," he said, and went to retrieve the gasoline tank he'd dropped down the hall.

Jenna did as he asked, keeping an eye on him while she searched her stepmother's pocket for her key chain, where she always carried a mini corkscrew. Jenna would be ready when he came to tie her up. Tightening her hand around the keys so they wouldn't jingle, she dragged Gwyneth closer to her sisters. Propping her stepmother on her side, Jenna pretended to be tying the rope while she untied Arianna.

The rope fell away from her sister's wrists just as she heard Lorenzo return. He set down the empty gas can and a briefcase near the back door. Jenna recognized the briefcase as Arianna's. It had been their father's. Lorenzo must've cleaned out whatever cash and jewelry they had on hand. "Come here, *bella*."

Jenna glanced at her sister. She had to do as he asked or risk him noticing Arianna's hands were untied. As Jenna pushed to her feet, her stepmother moaned, and Lorenzo shot Gwyneth.

Jenna gasped and went to go to her stepmother's aid. Lorenzo grabbed Jenna by the arm and yanked her upright. "How could you? How could you shoot her? I thought—"

"You thought I was in love with her? Come, now. Your investigator friend has learned enough about me that you know I was just using Gwyneth. As you can see, she's no longer any use to me. But your stepmother is devious in her own right and would've found a way to track me down. Now that will not be a problem. And neither will the three of you."

"No, we won't. We won't say anything. Take whatever you want, but just leave us alone."

"You no longer have anything to offer me that would change my mind."

"Wait. That's not true. The ring was found. If you let us go, I'll get it for you."

"It is too late. The Bianchis were made aware the ring was missing. Their hired hand had an informant within the HHPD. Thanks to you and your sisters, I am a dead man walking." He took her by the shoulders and turned her to face her sisters. "You have a job to do. I'm giving you the opportunity to seek your revenge against your evil stepmother and sisters before you die. But first I will have my revenge against you, Arianna Bell. You will watch your precious Tie the Knot go up in flames around you." He pulled a box of matches from his pocket.

"No," Jenna cried out, making a grab for the matches. Serena's and Arianna's screams were muffled under the duct tape as he aimed the gun at Jenna.

"Don't move, or your sisters will die a slow and extremely painful death," he said as he pocketed the gun to light the match. Running toward the hall, he threw the lit match, igniting the gas.

Before Jenna could make a move, he turned with a gun in each hand.

She shook her head, backing away from him with her hands raised. "Go ahead and shoot me. I won't shoot my sisters."

He aimed the gun and fired. The bullet hit Serena in the leg, and the three of them cried out. "The next one is for Arianna. I can either make it fast, or I will make them suffer."

"No, no, don't. I'll do it," she said, her mind racing for a way out of this. She would have a second at most to act when he handed her the gun. She needed a moment to prepare. "I love you, both of you. I'm only doing this so that you won't suffer." Her sisters' faces blurred, and she brushed the tears away so she could see Lorenzo and the gun. At least this way, she'd die trying to save her sisters.

"The kind and good sister. It didn't get you very far, did it?" Just like she expected him to, he pressed the muzzle of the gun to her temple as he handed her the other one. She closed her fingers around the butt and then immediately jerked to the right at the same time she ducked and aimed the gun at his stomach, pulling the trigger. As soon as the bullet left the barrel, she dove for his legs, tackling him to the ground. His shot went wide as he fell backward and hit the floor hard. The bullet from his gun must've hit the gas can near the back door because, all of a sudden, there was a loud explosion, and the curtains over the door burst into flames and the window shattered.

Jenna pushed her gun across the floor to her sister and then crawled around Lorenzo—who was moaning and clutching his stomach—to get the gun that had fallen from his hand and skittered across the floor. She thought she was safe, but she wasn't. He rolled, grabbing her by the hair to jerk her backward. She held back a cry, pushing forward despite feeling like her hair was being ripped from her scalp. She stretched out her fingers to reach the butt of the gun.

With a roar, Lorenzo flung himself on top of her, reaching past her. Her chin hit the floor, her teeth slamming together. His fingers closed around hers. And then a gun went off and he became deadweight, his fingers convulsing before going limp. Jenna turned her head to see Arianna standing, holding the gun in both hands. Her sister had saved her. She'd shot Lorenzo.

A cry of horror and relief built up inside Jenna, but she pushed the emotions down. There wasn't time

to focus on anything but escaping. Suffocating black
smoke had filled the room. The walls glowed eerily, and
the air was filled with a *hiss* and *whoosh* as something
else went up in flames. Swallowing her panic, Jenna
moved out from under Lorenzo and scrambled across
the room to help Arianna untie Serena, whose sobs were
muffled. "You're going to have to help her get out,"
Arianna said as she made a tourniquet for Serena's leg.

"Of course." Jenna put her arm around Serena's
waist to help her to her feet. "Wait. Where are you going?" she called to Arianna, who was headed in the
opposite direction.

"My office. I have to get—" There was a crash
from the front of the shop and then the voices of men
calling out.

"Arianna, leave it!" At the same time Jenna realized
her sister was gone, a man charged through the smoke
toward her. Logan. He took Serena from her, passing
her back to his cousin, and then he lifted Jenna into
his arms.

"Two more back here," he called out.

"Three. Arianna went to her office. Put me down and
go find her, Logan. I can make it."

"Jenna Bell, I'm never leaving you on your own
again." A firefighter ran down the hall. It was Logan's
cousin Liam. "Arianna went back to her office."

Chapter Twenty-Seven

♥

There was a smattering of applause when Logan carried Jenna out of Tie the Knot. Several people in the crowd across the street yelled out her name, while the majority cheered. Cameras flashed as people, including Poppy Harte, took photos of them leaving the burning building. The two businesses on either side had also caught fire. They'd be lucky if they didn't lose the entire block.

Crowded with emergency vehicles, Main Street was lit up with red and blue lights. Logan crossed to the waiting ambulance where Aidan had just placed Serena. It wasn't until he'd set Jenna beside her sister that he got a good look at her, and nearly passed out.

"What are you doing?" she asked when he quickly scooped her into his arms, searching for a vehicle he could take. He was surprised she was still conscious with the amount of blood she'd obviously lost.

"Getting you to the hospital right away. Aidan, tell one of your deputies to give me the keys—"

"I don't need to go to the hospital. I need to know Arianna is okay." She tried to get out of his arms.

He tightened his hold. "Stop fighting me. You're not all right. You've…" He couldn't tell her she was covered in blood. "You're in shock right now, so you probably can't feel your injuries—"

"Trust me, I can feel them. My head and chin hurt, and so do my feet from walking miles without shoes, but other than that, I'm honestly fine, Logan. Please, I can't leave until I've seen with my own eyes that Arianna—" She broke off as firefighters came out of the building carrying Lorenzo and Gwyneth on stretchers. "They aren't dead?"

"Apparently not." A muscle jumped in his clenched jaw. What he wouldn't give to have a few minutes alone in a room with Lorenzo Romano. Logan wanted to know what happened in that back room tonight, what Lorenzo had done or said to her, how badly he'd hurt her or made her suffer. Jenna didn't appear to be traumatized or in shock. Obviously, she and her sisters had fought back and taken the control from their captors, which would go a long way in aiding their recovery from whatever had happened here tonight.

"Jenna," Serena said from where she sat in the back of the ambulance. She nodded at the burning building.

People were cheering and clapping as Logan's cousin Liam came through the doors with Arianna in his arms wearing an oxygen mask. From the grim expression on Liam's face and the way he jogged to the waiting ambulance behind theirs, Arianna hadn't escaped without injury.

"Logan, please let me down. I need to see her."

He had a hard time letting Jenna go. He felt better

with her in his arms. Still, he reluctantly did as she asked. She put her arm around Serena, and together they walked back to the ambulance behind theirs.

Aidan clapped him on the shoulder. "Relax. She's fine, big guy. It's obviously not her blood she's wearing." He handed him a set of keys. "Julia parked my pickup outside Books and Beans. You can take it. I'll catch up with you at the hospital later. It's going to be a long night."

When Logan reached the ambulance, his cousin was doing his best to answer Jenna's and Serena's questions. "No, I'm sorry. Whatever it was Arianna was trying to save is gone. No, she didn't tell me," Liam said.

"Is she going to be okay?"

Logan turned to see his brother Connor coming up behind him. He was the one who asked the question.

"She's suffering from smoke inhalation and has burns on her hand and arm. It'll take some time, but I'm sure she'll be fine." He nodded at the paramedic. "We should let them get her to the hospital."

Before the paramedic got the door closed, Connor climbed inside. Serena and Jenna looked surprised, but Logan wasn't. Once the ambulance had pulled away with the lights flashing and siren wailing, Aidan helped Serena back to the waiting paramedic, and Logan carried a protesting Jenna to his cousin's pickup.

"This is embarrassing. You can't keep carrying me around like I'm some helpless woman."

"I don't think you're helpless, far from it. But we're in the middle of Main Street and your feet are bare."

Logan beeped the lock button on the keys and carefully lowered her to her feet beside the door. "Although that's not the only reason I wanted you in my arms." He raised his hand to her face, and the words came out rough. "I almost lost you tonight."

Jenna wrapped her arms around his waist and rested her cheek against his chest. "I was afraid I'd never see you again. It was hard enough thinking my sisters and I were going to die, but at least I had the chance to tell them I loved them." She lifted her face to look up at him. "My biggest regret would've been not telling you how I feel. I love you, Logan. And it's not because you keep playing my knight in shining armor or because I know you and I are meant to be. Okay, so maybe it's a little of that, but it's more because of the way you make me feel whenever I'm with you. And loving you is my only excuse for doing what I did. I'm so sorry I didn't tell you everything. I was trying to protect you."

"Yeah, and I'm beginning to understand how my brother Michael feels."

Her face lit up. "You think I'm like Shay?"

"I think you're courageous and kind."

"You remember what I said that night at the Salty Dog." She frowned. "You got your memory back?"

He nodded. "Yeah, and I remember every minute of every day with you, Jenna."

"Of course you do, because I'm your one true love." Her eyes went wide. "I'm not just your one true love, am I? We got married today."

"When I got my memory back, I figured out Mateo was the father of Isabella's baby, so I wasn't about to marry a woman I didn't love and who didn't love me. We're not married, honey. Our priest was an actor."

"Umm, Logan, you didn't grow up in Harmony. I did. And that priest wasn't an actor. It was Father O'Malley."

"It can't be. Jasper knew I was using the wedding as an opportunity to draw out the shooter. I told him to hire an actor to replace the priest." He opened the door and helped Jenna into the truck as he pulled out his phone. "Hey, Jeeves, the guy that married me and Jenna was an actor, wasn't he? Really? Is that right? I see. Okay, but we didn't have a marriage license. We did? You did? So you're telling me you knew Jenna was going to trade places with Isabella? Yes, Jeeves, I realize you know everything that goes on in the manor. What I'd like to know is why you chose not to explain it to me. Yeah, well, you have some explaining to do when I get back to the manor." Logan looked at her as he disconnected. "So, apparently, you've rubbed off on Jasper, and he decided we were meant to be and pulled some strings to get us a valid marriage license. We're married."

She laughed. "Does that mean we get the bridal suite tonight?"

"Seriously, that's all you have to say?"

"No, it's not." She framed his face with her hands and kissed him deeply, and then broke the kiss to smile up at him. "It seems silly to ruin a perfectly good wedding night."

He pulled her to him and kissed her like he'd wanted to when he'd lifted her veil and saw the face that he'd never tire of, and for a minute, he forgot he was stand-

ing on Main Street and the cab light provided a clear
view of what they were doing to the crowd on the street.

At the sounds of laughter and clapping, he reluctantly pulled back. "I love you too. Maybe we'll wait
and get divorced next week."

* * *

Three weeks later, Jenna and Logan were still man and
wife. They wouldn't be for long. They'd both agreed
that while it made a great story, it wasn't the way they
wanted to start off their married life. Not that they
planned to get married anytime soon. Unlike his cousin
Aidan, who was getting married in two days.

To Jenna's mind, the best thing about Aidan and Julia's wedding was that Logan had gotten time off work
to come home. Thanks to the video Princess Isabella
had made, Logan had been cleared of all charges and
reinstated to the president's security detail. He'd been
back in Washington for more than two weeks.

For Isabella and Mateo's sake, it was a good thing
Logan had contacts in high places. Because he did, the
couple no longer had to live in fear that they'd be made
to return to Merradien. However, they chose to remain
in the small town where Shay had relocated them, and
they also chose to keep their new identities. Pilar and
Luis were making arrangements to join them soon.

Pippa sat in the sand beside Jenna, waiting for low
tide. Well, Pippa was waiting for low tide. Jenna was
waiting for Logan. He was stopping by the hospital to
see his mother before coming to the manor. Ten days

ago, Maura's test results had come back. She had a benign ovarian tumor, not ovarian cancer. She'd had the tumor removed yesterday, and her prognosis was excellent.

Cheep, cheep. Pippa got up and hurried off. "You're going the wrong way..." Jenna trailed off, smiling when she discovered the reason for Pippa's excitement.

"At least someone's happy to see me," Logan teased as he bent to pick up Pippa and give her a cuddle.

"I'm beyond happy. I'm over the moon," she said as he sat beside her in the sand, barely able to keep her hands off him. She wrapped her arms around his waist, and he slid his unoccupied arm around her, holding her close. She tipped her face up. "I missed you like crazy."

"I missed you like crazy too, honey." He kissed her, and she released a happy sigh at the feel of his mouth on hers.

At the sounds of sandpipers flocking to the mud flats, Pippa *cheep*ed to be put down.

Logan seemed as reluctant to break the kiss as Jenna was, but he gave in to the little tyrant's demands. Releasing Jenna, he bent down to set Pippa free. They laughed as she rushed headlong for her peeps. No veering off in the opposite direction, she joined the sandpipers along the shore.

"How was your mom tonight?"

"In a bit of pain, but otherwise doing really well. I hear you dropped in to see her yesterday."

"I did. We had a nice visit."

"Yeah, and I can tell by your voice she told you what she told me. I don't get it. I thought she'd be going home once she left the hospital and not moving back here."

She rubbed his arm. "I know. Maybe she just needs some time."

"What she needs is Uncle Daniel to leave her alone." He glanced at her. "You heard? I don't know why I even asked. Of course you'd know he's not leaving town."

"He's actually running for mayor. I think your mom's agreed to be his campaign manager."

"Things are starting to make sense now. There's nothing she loves more than a political race."

"She'll find her way back to your dad eventually. They're meant to be."

He smiled and took her hand in his, bringing it to his lips. "Like us."

"Yes, like us. And I've been thinking about what you said, about opening a matchmaking business in DC."

"I didn't mean to put pressure on you, Jenna. I'm fine with the long-distance thing. I mean, I'm not totally fine with it—I'd rather be with you—but if that's what we have to do, we will."

"You didn't pressure me, Logan. I want to be with you as much as you want to be with me. So I hope I'm not rushing you, because instead of next summer like you suggested, I was thinking more like November."

"Really? That's the best news I've had all week," he said when she nodded.

"We'll have received the money from the estate by then. It's not a lot, but it's enough to get my business up and running. And Arianna should be back on her feet in a few weeks, and I've finally got Shay to agree to a date." She grinned. "They're having a wedding at Halloween, and the guests are expected to come in costume."

Logan laughed. "Let me guess, the bride and groom are going as Wonder Woman and Steve Trevor, and we're going as Cinderella and Prince Charming."

"Very good guess, and I found you a pair of powder-blue tights."

"Like that's going to happen. Now, come on." He lay back in the sand and pulled her down with him. "We haven't stargazed in a while."

"We haven't done quite a few things in a while," she murmured suggestively.

"You're right. Why don't we leave the stargazing till later?"

It wasn't until they were hunting for their clothes in the sand much later that she realized Pippa wasn't with them. "Where did she go?"

Logan sat up and looked around. "Over there." He pointed to the rocks. "Your baby's flown the nest, Mommy. She's made a new family." Jenna sniffed back tears, and Logan smiled and wrapped her in his arms. "You've got a new family too, honey."

FBI agent Michael Gallagher never dreamed that his job would bring him back to his hometown of Harmony Harbor. Or that one of his best leads would be the woman he once loved.

Please turn the page for an excerpt from *Driftwood Cove*.

Chapter One

♥

There'd been no foreboding signs to alert Shay Angel to the danger, no warning that this was the day her past caught up with her and her life might be on the line.

Her morning had started off the same as usual. The alarm on her bedside table went off at seven, and she hit the snooze button three times at ten-minute intervals just like she always did. She didn't fall out of bed or trip over her boots on the way to the shower. Her one-bedroom apartment was sparsely furnished, and her boots were right where she'd left them—directly at the end of her bed, toes pointed toward the door in case she needed to make a quick exit.

Even the unreliable showerhead had cooperated today. Her five-minute shower had been exactly the way she liked it, hot and strong. Just like her coffee, which she drank from an oversized travel mug that read *Do I look like I "Rise & Shine"?* Her assistant at the security company she worked for had a sense of humor. Shay didn't.

Nor, for the most part, did she do friends, which

her assistant was desperately trying to change. Lately—okay, so in the past ten years—Shay didn't do boyfriends either. Something else her assistant was desperately trying to change by signing Shay up on every matchmaking app known to mankind. Without Shay's permission, of course.

Just one more reason Shay had been lulled into thinking the day, for the most part, would be pretty good. She'd had forty-five minutes of peace and quiet before she'd left for work. No pings or beeps and bells and whistles from texts or emails from the apps she was signed up for alerting her to a new and perfect match.

She'd met her match a long time ago. Only he turned out to be perfectly imperfect. And he was calling her at a perfectly imperfect time. She reached for the vibrating cell phone on her desk and hit Decline. She'd stopped taking his calls ten months before but couldn't quite make it official by blocking him completely. He was one of the reasons she'd accepted the job in Vegas. The move put twenty-three hundred miles between her and her past, in which Michael Gallagher had played a starring role.

But she didn't have time to think about him now, or ever, really. She had bigger worries to contend with. Like the cop who sat on the other side of Shay's desk with a familiar, suspicious look in her eyes.

"In less than three months, four of the homes your company installed security for have been robbed of more than a million dollars in diamonds. I don't believe it's a coincidence that your clients are the ones being targeted, Ms. Angel." Detective Sims slapped a file onto Shay's desk.

Working to keep any sign of worry from showing on her face, Shay drew the manila folder toward her. There was no way she'd give Detective Sims the satisfaction of seeing her sweat. Shay's petty-criminal parents had imprinted her DNA with a deep dislike and distrust of law enforcement, but she didn't have to like or trust Sims to know the woman wasn't making up the evidence in the file.

Over the past five days, Shay had been trying to convince herself that no one at Sterling Security was involved in the break-ins. Then yesterday she'd overheard a conversation between her boss and an installer and could no longer deny the likelihood that they were in this up to their ears.

Which totally blew, because her suspicions put her bright and shiny dream for her future at risk. She'd left her job in New York to work for Ray Sterling, a man who was renowned in the security business. She'd planned to learn all that she could from him and then branch out on her own. Now...

Without saying a word, she closed the file and held the gaze of the woman sitting on the other side of her desk.

Shay's uncle Charlie had taken up where her parents left off. He'd taught her how to not only run a con and make a cop with a single glance, but also how to elude and confuse them. Other than the summer she'd turned nineteen, his lessons had served her well.

Sims's dark eyes narrowed beneath her frosted blond fringe.

Leaning back in the chair, Shay crossed her arms as she waited for the detective to show her hand. It didn't take long.

"Do not try to intimidate me. I've heard all about your Superwoman act. How you saved your assistant and got Ace Rodriguez and his gang of thugs out of your neighborhood. But you don't scare or impress me like you do the beat cops. I know who and what you really are." Sims leaned forward and tapped the file with a hot-pink fingernail. "You were put away for grand theft auto at nineteen. Not much of a leap between stealing cars and stealing diamonds, now, is there? So tell me, Angel, where were you on the nights in question?"

Charlie and her parents had been good teachers, but it was prison that taught Shay the most valuable lessons of all. Number one, how to stay alive. And number two, that she'd do whatever it took to ensure she was never put away again. Even if it meant turning on the man who held the key to making her dreams come true.

First, though, she needed more proof to support her suspicions that her boss's son was behind the break-ins. If he was, it meant Ray had found the perfect fall guy, or girl in this case. He'd correctly predicted that Detective Sims would focus on Shay. It wasn't like he had to be especially smart or a mind reader to guess that she'd draw the detective's interest. Everyone and their mother knew that in law enforcement's eyes, once a con, always a con.

In the five years since she'd walked out of the prison's gates, Shay had been on the receiving end of the expression. If it wasn't said to her face, it was whispered behind her back or delivered with raised eyebrows and knowing smirks.

Another cliché she knew to be true: It takes a thief to catch one. And that's exactly what she planned to do. Once she got rid of Sims.

Given her own concerns over the robberies, Shay had been prepared for a visit from the Las Vegas Metro Police Department. Still, it ticked her off that she was on the top of Sims's suspect list, the emotion evident in her voice when she said, "I was working the crisis hotline the night of the first robbery, and I had a one-on-one MMA session that clears me of the third break-in."

"You don't expect me to take your word for it, do you? And what the hell is a private MMA session anyway? Do I even want to know?"

"Mixed martial arts. I'm an instructor at Elite Gym," Shay responded through clenched teeth, reaching for the kitschy holder on her otherwise empty desk. Her assistant, Cherry, a former stripper who was into all things crafty, had made the card holder for Shay as an early Valentine's Day gift. Which meant it was pink and sparkly and covered in hearts. And smelled like Love's Baby Soft perfume. Cherry must have given it a fresh spritz that morning.

According to her assistant, the fragrance was imbued with the power to bring out Shay's inner girly girl and break her dating dry spell before the most romantic day of the year. Despite wanting to hurl at the task before her, Shay felt a smile tugging on her lips as she withdrew a business card from the holder. The reluctant smile faded as she turned the card over to write the names and numbers of the people who would provide her alibis.

She'd have to talk to them. Let them know the police would be calling to verify her whereabouts for the nights in question. Instead of throwing the card at Sims like she wanted to, Shay flicked it across the desk with the end of her pen.

After glancing at the names, Sims raised an eyebrow. "Judge Watkins. I'm surprised he didn't ask for another instructor when he found out you were an ex-con. He's a hardass. You would've served ten years instead of five if he'd presided over your case."

Other than Ray, and obviously Sims, no one in Vegas knew that Shay had done time. Any chances of keeping her record private were gone now. Sims would see to that. Shay had met her type before.

"I have an appointment in twenty minutes, Detective. If there's nothing else…"

"You're not off the hook yet, Angel. You're missing alibis for two of the break-ins."

"You know as well as I do that one person is responsible for all four robberies, and it's not me."

"And how exactly did you come to that conclusion?"

"How do you think? I've spoken to my clients and read the reports." There was something off about Sims's reaction, her tone of voice, and it gave Shay pause. What if there was more to this than she knew? She came up with a question that might immediately rid her of the worrisome suspicion now niggling at her brain. "If you're planning on questioning Ray and his son, you might want to get on that. They're leaving to-day for the security conference in New York."

"Why would I want to question the Sterlings? They're one of the richest families in the state. It's not like they need the money nor would they benefit from the negative publicity. Ray's well respected and—"

"Let me guess, a generous benefactor to the mayor's last campaign." It was as if history were repeating itself. If it came down to her word against the Sterlings', Shay didn't trust the law to be on her side. She'd learned the hard way that the same rules didn't apply to the rich and connected.

It's why she'd accepted Ray's offer last March—to earn the respect and power that went with having a fortune. She wanted to learn from the best, and once she had, she planned to develop a concept she could franchise. The security industry was a 350-billion-dollar business, and she wanted a big piece of it. But she had a long way to go before she earned the kind of coin that guaranteed her a get-out-of-jail-free card.

"Watch your step, Angel," Sims said as she came to her feet. "And don't leave town."

"I'm curious, just how well do you know Ray?" Shay said to the woman's back.

Her hand on the knob of the office door, the detective hesitated before turning to face her.

A faint, knowing smile lifted Shay's lips. She'd been bluffing, but from the slight flush of color on Sims's cheeks and her initial hesitation, Shay had obviously hit a nerve. It shouldn't come as a surprise. The detective was Ray's type...a man who'd been divorced four times.

It also explained why Sims had ended up here today, targeting her. Shay nosing into the investigation had made Ray nervous, and he knew the perfect way to shut her down and protect his son. She'd made the mistake of confiding in him a few months back, sharing her greatest fear.

"What are you insinuating?"

A younger version of herself would have told Sims exactly what she was suggesting, but Shay liked to think she'd become smarter, more strategic. Self-preservation won out over righteous indignation and revenge every single time. "Nothing, but now that you mention it, you're awfully defensive. Can't say I blame you, though. Connected as he is, Ray probably has your boss on speed dial, doesn't he? Don't worry. I won't tell him you're harassing me. I know you're just doing your job."

Sims looked like she was trying to decide whether she'd just been threatened or whether Shay was clueless.

"I am just doing my job. It has nothing to do with office politics or my relationship with the Sterlings."

So, clueless it was. Except Sims's mention of her *relationship* with the Sterlings was either a Freudian slip or strategic. If it was strategic, the woman had correctly surmised that Shay wouldn't let up on the investigation and somewhere there was evidence of her relationship with Ray. Which would also mean Sims knew Shay was playing her.

"Relax, I believe you. Now I really do need to head out for my appointment or I'll be late, and that would make my boss an unhappy man." Shay had every intention of making Ray Sterling a very unhappy man before he left for NYC. She refused to have the threat of prison hanging over her any longer than she had to.

* * *

Sitting in a black Challenger outside Ray Junior's apartment building, Shay hacked into the security system and remotely took control. She kept an eye on the front of the building while angling the exterior cameras so that one captured the entrance to the casino across the road and the other one focused on the parking garage.

There was no time for her to celebrate successfully overriding the security system. She might get in the building undetected, but she still had to deal with the cameras in the elevators and on Junior's floor. And then there was the matter of searching his apartment in under an hour in order to confront her boss before he left town.

As she leaned over to grab her knapsack off the floor, the passenger door opened and a blond bombshell slipped in. A decade older than Shay, her thirty-nine-year-old assistant wore a hot-pink leather jacket, matching miniskirt, and thigh-high white shiny boots.

"What are you doing here, Cherry? I need you back at the office." If things went south, Shay didn't want the Sterlings looking at her assistant. Cherry needed this job even more than Shay did. "Wait a minute, how did you even know where I was?"

Cherry made a limp wrist hand drop, the stacks of

rings on each finger no doubt weighing down her hand. "How many times do I have to tell you? If you don't want anyone to know where you are, stop driving Hell Baby."

A powerful muscle car, the sleek black Hellcat with its yellow rims was Shay's pride and joy. "Okay, you found me; so what do you want?"

Glancing from the building back to Shay, Cherry blinked eyes framed with long blue lashes that sort of matched her eyes. "I know you're desperate for a man, but Ray J, Shaybae? Do you seriously not look in a mirror?" She tugged on Shay's ponytail that stuck through the hole at the back of her ball cap. "You have this lush black mane that you never let down to play, stunning gray eyes, and pillow lips. Like it or not, girlfriend, you're a ten even sans makeup and with the Goth uniform. And poor Ray J, he's a two on a fab hair day, and that's me being kind."

About a fifth of what Cherry said actually registered with Shay. The part where her assistant thought she was desperate and, worse, the part where she knew this was Junior's apartment building. That was the thing about Cherry—with her blond-bombshell looks, people underestimated her.

Including Shay, it seemed. "I'm not desperate. What I am is busy. I have to drop off an estimate for Junior. He messed up his numbers again, and I fixed the quote as a favor. Don't let him or his father know I said—"

Cherry's cell phone rang, and she held up a finger. "I routed the office calls to my phone. Sterling Security, how may I be of service?" She made a face and then smiled like the person on the other end of the line was standing in front of her. "An adorable pink heart that was attached to your purse? Umm, right, you didn't say adorable. But you have such a fashionable flair, Detective Sims, that I just knew it must be."

"Seriously?" Shay muttered, flicking the *adorable* pink heart hanging from Cherry's bag.

Cherry pointedly ignored her and continued. "Don't you worry, I'll find it if it's here. All right, you have yourself a good day." She disconnected and held up her hands, her rings catching the sunlight and making a rainbow in the car. "What? She made me nervous, and you know what happens when I'm nervous or upset."

"Yeah, you steal things, and one day it's going to get you in trouble that even I can't get you out of. You need to see a shrink."

"We both might need one when I tell you why she makes me nervous."

"She's a cop. Of course she makes you nervous." It's something they had in common.

"No, it's more than that. So much more. But I don't want to tell you. I can't. If I do, it's going to—"

"Just spit it out."

"All right, but don't say I didn't warn you. It's about the robberies. It's Ray J. He got mixed up with some bad dudes, and he's feeding them the inside scoop on our clients."

"Are you sure? Does Ray Senior know?"

"I'm not sure if he knows. I saw Ray J at the Purple Peacock with the scary dudes. I know, I know. It was just that one time. But, hey, it's a good thing I went.

Harry, the bartender, he's an old friend of mine. He gave me the scoop." She wrung her hands. "I know how much you admire Ray Senior, and I'd rather remove my implants than hurt you, Shaybae, but you need to know. He's setting you up to take the fall."

"I figured that out when Sims was questioning me. Last night I overheard Ray talking to one of the installers. Junior is no longer allowed on the jobs."

"Okay, so what are we going to do?"

"I need hard evidence against Junior. Evidence that I can blackmail his father with. Either he calls off Sims or I take what we know to the…DA," she said, thinking about Michael's earlier call.

He was an assistant district attorney in Boston. If worse came to worst, she'd ask for his help. He, out of anyone, would know someone here that she could trust. Her hands got sweaty at the thought. She didn't like depending on anyone. They always let her down. It's why she fought her battles alone. This time, though, she couldn't afford to take the risk. She'd do whatever it took to protect herself. And Cherry.

"You need to go back to the office and forget everything you just told me. That way, when this is over, you'll still have a job."

Cherry sniffed and flicked her overprocessed hair. It might have made for a dramatic performance if her rings hadn't gotten caught in her teased blond locks. Her words made up for it, though. "I meant what I told you the night you saved me in the alley. I'm your slave for life. You got me the job at Sterling, and I'm not staying there without you. I won't work for a man who rewards all the overtime you put in by throwing you under the bus. Where you go, I go." She tilted her head. "Just for curiosity's sake, do you know where we're going? Don't worry if you haven't thought that far ahead; I'll do a tea reading. That way we can be assured of ending up in the perfect place. How does Greece sound? I hear Greek men like blondes." She twisted a lock of hair around her finger and then glanced at Shay. "Not on your bucket list?"

"Let's deal with one thing at a time, okay?" she said, feeling a little panicked and slightly claustrophobic at the idea of not only being jobless but being responsible for Cherry too. Right now, though, she had more important things to worry about. She glanced at her phone. "We have half an hour to get in and out of Junior's apartment without getting caught."

Cherry fluffed her hair and stuck out her impressive triple Ds. "Don't you worry, I haven't met a man I couldn't distract."

Her assistant was nothing if not confident, Shay thought as they walked to the front doors of the building. Stepping behind the potted palm at the entrance, she remotely changed the angles of the cameras in the lobby and outside the elevator doors. Once Cherry began singing Shania Twain's "Man! I Feel Like a Woman" off-key and strutting her stuff, Shay took one last look around before heading for the door to the left of the elevators. Cherry would hang out in the lobby to distract security and keep an eye on who came into the building.

Shay hip-checked the door to the stairs open while

digging in her knapsack for her lock kit. If she'd had more time, she would've lifted Junior's keys and made a copy for herself. She reached the twelfth floor in record time and eased open the door to look down the deserted hallway, noting the locations of the cameras as she did.

Once she shut down the security feed, she'd have just under seven minutes to break into Junior's apartment before they rebooted the system and got the cameras back online. Shay leaned against the door, doing a trial run in her head. Confident she had everything planned out to the last second, she set the alarm on her phone for four minutes and then raced down the blue paisley carpeted hall to the door at the far end.

It took her twenty seconds. Less than four minutes later, she opened the door to Junior's apartment and disabled his alarm. She was just about to close the door when the bell on the elevator dinged and the doors slid open to reveal a frazzled Cherry on the phone.

"Yes, yes, I see her. She's okay. She picked the lock, and she's inside his apartment to get the evidence."

Shay had to practically lift her jaw off the floor to speak. "Have you lost your mind? Who are you talking to?"

"The Sterlings are on their way up," Cherry said in a frantic whisper, shoving the phone at Shay. "Talk to him."

Like she had time to talk to anyone with the Sterlings headed their way. She glanced at the second elevator; it was on the third floor. Jerking Junior's apartment door closed, she grabbed Cherry by the arm and raced back down the hall to the stairway.

"Slow down; I'm in heels, and you're in motorcycle boots," Cherry complained, as if that were the only reason she couldn't keep up. The woman considered shopping an exercise.

Shay put a finger to her lips, dragging her assistant behind the door just as the elevator dinged. Shay peeked around the edge of the blue steel door to see the Sterlings step off the elevator. Someone calling her name drew her up short. She glanced at the phone. *It couldn't be*. She let the door close and leaned against it. Holding up the phone, she stared at Cherry.

"It's Special Agent Gallagher. He called to speak to you, and I thought we could use the help when I saw the Sterlings getting out of their car. He says he's a friend of yours. Talk to him. Let him help."

The voice sounded like Michael's, but it couldn't be. He was an assistant district attorney, not a special agent. Maybe it was his cousin Aidan, who was a DEA agent. Shay had done some undercover work for him two years before. The reasoning made sense, and her racing heart slowed.

Hefting her knapsack over her shoulder, she nudged Cherry to get her moving down the stairs and put the phone to her ear. "Aidan?"

"Aidan? No, it's Michael. What's going on, Shay? Are you okay? Are you safe?"

It *was* Michael. She'd recognize his deep, sexy-as-sin voice anywhere. Even with a note of concern giving it a rougher edge, it affected her the same as it always had. Like he'd reached through the line and stroked her with his strong and elegant fingers. A door slamming on the floor they'd just left drew her attention. She cocked her head, waiting for the Sterlings to start yelling, to come running their way. There was nothing but the crinkle of leather and the click of Cherry's heels on the concrete stairs.

"Shay?"

"Sorry. Yeah, I'm good. We're okay."

"Sure you are. You just have someone trying to frame you. For once can you be straight with me and admit you need help?" She heard the worry and frustration in his voice, and it reminded her of the night she'd ended up in his arms, and eventually in his bed. The night she'd tangled her fingers in hair as black as a starless winter's night, gazed into eyes as blue and as warm as the Atlantic Ocean on a summer's day, and trailed kisses along a jaw as chiseled as the rocks that lined the harbor.

There'd been a time when she'd loved him beyond reason. Sometimes she was afraid that she still did. It's why she'd stopped taking his calls. She gave her assistant the evil eye. It didn't do her much good. Sprawled over the handrail trying to catch her breath, Cherry sounded like she needed oxygen.

Shay nudged her to keep her moving while defending herself to Michael. "I didn't do anything wrong. I didn't break any laws."

"So you're telling me that you didn't enter the apartment after picking the lock?"

She heard a hint of amusement in his voice. "They're setting me up, Michael. I won't go down for something I didn't do. I won't."

"Trust me, they won't get away with it. I won't let them. Just...Hang on a minute."

She wanted to believe him, but she'd lost her innocence a long time ago. There'd been a time when she'd trusted him, though. When she'd believed it didn't matter that they came from two different worlds. She'd thought a love like theirs could survive anything and anyone.

She frowned at the thought, unable to believe that she'd ever been that naïve. She supposed it was possible. But the sentiment seemed more like something Michael would have believed. He'd been an idealist and an optimist. He'd also been incredibly persuasive. So different from her in so many ways.

All things considered, it wasn't really surprising that she'd been the one who'd paid the price the summer their worlds collided. Her life had ended up in tatters. Michael's, as far as she knew, had remained as privileged as ever.

There were muffled voices in the background and then Michael came back on the line. "All right, in the next couple of minutes an agent will call you on this number. He'll arrange a meet. His name is Tom Bryant. You can trust him, Shay. I promise, everything will be okay."

A lump formed in her throat, surprising her. She would have expected relief, not this odd sense of longing for what might have been. "Thanks. I appreciate your help."

"Yet if it was up to you, I wouldn't have had the chance to give it to you, would I? The only reason you're talking to me right now is because your friend—"

"Wait. Why did you call? And why did you lie to Cherry and say you're with the FBI? Did you think I—"

"I didn't lie to your friend. I am with the FBI, and you would've known that if you hadn't cut me out of your life, Shay. As to why I was calling, it'll keep. We'll talk after you've met with Tom and gotten the situation there under control."

A door slammed several flights below, immediately followed by the sound of booted feet running up the stairs. *Crap.* She yanked Cherry upright and practically carried her back to the floor they'd just passed. "Your friend Bryant? You better send him here, like, now, Michael. Our situation has…" A bullet shattered the concrete an inch from her head.

About the Author

Debbie Mason is the *USA Today* bestselling author of the Christmas, Colorado, and Harmony Harbor series. Her books have been praised for their "likable characters, clever dialogue, and juicy plots" (*RT Book Reviews*). When she isn't writing or reading, Debbie enjoys spending time with her very own real-life hero, their three wonderful children and son-in-law, and two adorable grandbabies, in Ottawa, Canada.

You can learn more at:

AuthorDebbieMason.com

Twitter @AuthorDebMason

Facebook.com/DebbieMasonBooks/

USA TODAY BESTSELLING AUTHOR

DEBBIE MASON

Sandpiper Shore

"Heartfelt and delightful!" —RAEANNE THAYNE,
New York Times bestselling author, on *Mistletoe Cottage*

SANDPIPER SHORE
By Debbie Mason

USA Today bestselling author Debbie Mason's latest novel in the feel-good and charming Harmony Harbor series. Jenna Bell loves her job as a wedding planner...until she meets with her newest clients and discovers that the groom is the man she's loved for years. For Secret Service Agent Logan Gallagher, seeing Jenna after all these years brings back feelings that he's fought hard to forget...and makes him wonder if getting married to someone else would be the biggest mistake of his life.

Fall in Love with Forever Romance

IT TAKES TWO
By Jenny Holiday

In this hilarious romantic comedy, *USA Today* bestselling author Jenny Holiday proves that what happens in Vegas *doesn't* always stay in Vegas. Wendy Liu *should* be delighted to be her best friend's maid of honor. But it means spending time with the bride's brother, aka the boy who once broke her heart. Noah Denning is always up for a challenge. So when Wendy proposes that they compete to see who can throw the best bachelor or bachelorette party in Sin City, Noah takes the bait—and ups the stakes. Because this time around, he wants Wendy for keeps.

Fall in Love with Forever Romance

New York Times
Bestselling Author
LORI WILDE

"A dynamite novel
that readers will treasure
for years to come."
—*RT Book Reviews*

Valentine,
TEXAS

Previously published as *Addicted to Love*

VALENTINE, TEXAS
By Lori Wilde

From *New York Times* bestselling author Lori Wilde comes a heartwarming story about love, second chances, and cowboys...Rachael Henderson has sworn off love, but when she finds herself hauled up against the taut, rippling body of her first cowboy crush, she wonders if taking a chance on love is worth the risk. Can a girl have her cake and her cowboy, too?

* Formerly published as *Addicted to Love*.